Fallen Angels

P W Reed

Fallen Angels
(The Prophet Factory Book3)

Also by this Author

The Prophet Factory
The Lost Children

Available in paperback from Amazon.com and other book stores
Available on Kindle and other devices

My thanks go to Ian (my editor and cover designer)
Tricia (wife, sounding board and critic) and Jane
(proofreader) for their encouragement, support and help.

CHAPTER ONE

Laslo Ginthem ran for his life. The simple fact he was suddenly attacked was terrifying enough but it had been unprovoked and it was obvious his assailant did not respond to reason. The fear induced adrenalin rush was enough to enable him to beat off the initial attack and flee back down the tunnel. Then the emergency lights went out and plunged him into darkness and a hopeless panic. He stumbled along in the dark using his hands to feel his way along the tunnel. The rough rock cut his hands and he smeared himself with blood every time he attempted to wipe the sweat from his eyes. The pounding of his heart grew faster and louder with every stumbled step he took. Eventually he collapsed exhausted onto the floor of the tunnel. He lay there desperately trying to control his breathing lest the sound attract his pursuer. Slowly his laboured breathing eased and he licked his dry lips. He was on his hands and knees but was too afraid to move. Every muscle was tense and his right arm began to tremble with the strain. The trip to the drill head which had led up to his attack was played back over and over again as he attempted to make sense of the sudden violence which had erupted. No matter how many times he went through it he struggled to come up with any reason for it.

"I was just doing my job!" The words came out as a forlorn whisper. He bit his lip in frustration for being stupid enough to make a sound. His arms and legs all now shook with the effort of holding up his body. Beads of sweat ran down his face, collected briefly on his lips and nose before dripping onto the tunnel floor. He imagined he could hear the drops as they hit the floor and echo back down the tunnel. His ears strained for any sound coming from the blackness behind him. All was quiet and he dared hope. Slowly he moved his body round until he sat, back against the tunnel wall, knees pulled up under his chin. He wrapped his arms around his legs and rocked gently back and forth. The movement somehow reassured him.

The thing to do was review his position, he told himself. He had to think calmly and logically if he was to escape this nightmare. Concentrating hard he attempted to reconstruct his wild flight. The drill head was in a side tunnel from the main one. He had turned left from the main tunnel to get there. The moments after the attack were lost, all he could remember was the fear and the look on his attacker's face. The eyes were expressionless, a dull dead stare. He closed his eyes tight to rid himself of the image. Remain calm and think logically. He must have come back the same way as there was no other exit from the drill head. That means he must have come back to the main tunnel but did he turn left or right? He felt nauseous now and he could feel tears welling up in his eyes as he thought of his partner Delna and their daughter Sophie. He let out a sob but immediately clapped one hand over his mouth. *'Can't make a noise!'* Those eyes closed tight again to reluctantly dispel the image. '*Right, I would have turned right! I would have followed the gradient back towards the surface. Yes, right!*' He could clearly remember now running up a slope. '*Then there was the fork. Did I take the left or the right?*' He hit the side of his head with his fist as if that would jolt the memory back into place. He struggled to remember the path he took on the way in. '*The fork, did I come from the left or right?*' His heart sunk as he suddenly remembered. '*I remember the tunnel joining from the right. We came round a bend and there it was. Oh God I took the left fork on the way back. I forgot about that tunnel, I thought I was at the bend!'* He looked back down the tunnel from where he had come even though he could see nothing in the darkness. *'If I'd taken the right fork I only had the bend to go before I would have seen light from the mouth of the tunnel.'* He could feel the tears running down his face as a depressing hopelessness descended upon him. He rested his head back against the side of the tunnel and stared up at yet more endless darkness.

'It's dark!' It was so obvious it had never occurred to him before. His attacker had turned off the emergency lighting after the initial attack had failed and he had struggled free of his grip. The darkness had hindered his escape so it was something to fear. It hid his pursuer but it also hid him. *'No lights!'* The emergency lights which gave the tunnels a pale, insipid glow had been turned off to hamper his escape but no sign of lights now to indicate the whereabouts of his pursuer! Had the flare of temper and cold eyed stare which provoked the attack died down just as quickly? Perhaps the other one had restrained him, calmed him down. The point was, with no lights he was invisible to them and that gave him hope. The idea of returning the way he had come, to actually move back towards his attacker filled him with dread but it was the only chance he had. He lay there staring back along the tunnel, building up his courage to make that move.

***

The figure sitting on the floor was hunched up and staring away from him, back down the tunnel from where they had just come. Although he only viewed him in multiple variations of the colour green the detail was amazing. The cuts on the hands, the face streaked where the tears had washed a path through the grime and blood, the stains on the trouser knees. He had never used the night vision visor before. It hung in the drill cabinet

3

alongside the first aid kit and the emergency rations. It had been a stroke of genius to remember them. He had followed Ginthem every step of the way, his footsteps hidden by the other man's stumbling gait and laboured breathing. At any time he could have ended the chase but Ginthem kept heading in exactly the right direction. Why struggle and drag the man along when he was going there by his own free will. They were almost there and if Ginthem had carried on just a few more metres he would have finished the job by himself. However it looked like he had decided to halt his headlong flight and was now considering his options. It made no difference because he was within easy reach. Now was the time to act, just in case he had worked out he had taken a wrong turn, before Ginthem decided to creep back the way he had come. A green outstretched arm came into view through the visor and the hand edged closer to Ginthem's ankle.

The shock of something suddenly grabbing his ankle made Ginthem scream out but it also froze him to inaction. By the time he started to struggle it was too late. He lost his balance as his leg was pulled away from under him. Kicking and screaming he was dragged along and attempting to gain hand holes in the tunnel floor just resulted in broken finger nails and scratched hands. The more he struggled the firmer the grip on his ankle became. After being dragged along for a few seconds they suddenly came to an abrupt halt. Ginthem swung his leg round in an attempt to kick the hand which held him but it only resulted in him receiving a vicious kick in the groin. Resistance crumpled as the pain surged up through his body. His ankle was released but only for a second to enable the assailant to use both hands to grab him by the shirt front, pull him to his feet and hurl him to one side. He braced himself for a heavy landing on the tunnel floor but instead found himself in free-fall. With arms and legs flailing wildly in some pathetic hope that this would

4

stop his descent. Laslo Ginthem came to the realisation he was going to die. Mercifully he had little time to dwell on the thought. Hitting the first outcrop of rock on his descent killed him outright. The broken rag-doll of a body continued to tumble into the darkness.

The murderer watched the green image fade from sight and then turned away. The chasm was too deep for any sound to reach up to the ledge. On the floor he spotted Ginthem's CommsLink which must have fallen from his pocket during the struggle. With a swift kick it was sent over the edge to eventually be reunited with its owner. Quickly returning to the main tunnel he uncoupled the water pipe and dragged the end back down the side tunnel. Spending as much time as he could afford he washed down the walls and floor, hoping that he was thorough enough to remove any trace of blood. With the task complete he returned to his normal duties.

***

The nine members of the drilling crew stood around the plastic tables and benches in the part of the accommodation block used for dining and recreation. They were all in their work clothes except Gurd and Rolm who were standing there in their underwear having just been dragged out of bed. Mol Gurd was wearing a stained sleep suit and his thinning, dyed hair, was a tangled mess. He stood yawning and scratching his testicles. Sara Rolm stood with her arms wrapped across her chest as if protecting herself from nonexistent cold weather. She stared at the floor with her auburn hair, usually tied back, hanging over her eyes and swayed slightly from side to side. The voice of the crew manager, Petre Ull, rang out loud and clear and quietened the mumbling. Despite his slight frame he had a deep bass voice.

"So who saw him last?" The group of miners just exchanged glances with each other and shuffled their feet. No one spoke. Ull sighed. "Okay, Chang did you see him at breakfast?"

Boniface Chang looked nervous and confused but Ull did not read anything into that, Chang always looked nervous and confused. He was short and had the coffee coloured complexion typical of most of humanity. His features were plain as if the skin on his face had been stretched into position, giving no hint of the ancestry his surname suggested, and his hair was cropped so short it was difficult to discern its colour. His appearance was so unremarkable he almost went unnoticed. Chang desperately looked round in the hope one of the others would speak up. His silent wish was granted.

"Yes, me and the boy were here at the same time." Milton Dang jerked a thumb towards young Will LeBon who was his shift partner. There were three two man shifts, one first class driller and one second class driller. Dang was the senior man. He was a good looking young man with the physical build of a typical miner. His hair was unfashionably long, reaching his jacket collar. The unusual haircut he sported caused his left eye to be half hidden by a sloping fringe. It was probably the height of fashion over six months ago back in the Federal part of New Eden. "He was finished before us and left."

Ull glanced at LeBon for confirmation and the youngster nodded. "Did you see him again?" Ull returned his attention to Dang.

"No." Dang shook his head. "Half hour later we were at the drill head for the start of our shift." He rubbed his chin as if he had just remembered something. "Mind you, we had trouble with the power coupling and had to close the head down to make some adjustments. I thought I heard somebody moving about in one of the other tunnels just as the head powered down. I listened but didn't hear anything else so thought it was just my imagination."

Ull turned to LeBon for confirmation. The youngster shrugged his shoulders. "Milton said he heard something but I didn't. I listened but.." His voice trailed off.

"When was this?"

Milton Dang sighed as if bored with the effort of remembering. "Just before the shift ended."

Ull returned his attention to Chang. "Right Boni, so we've established you saw him at breakfast. Did you see him again after that?"

"No." Chang sounded far from sure. Ull decided it was pointless questioning him further. Chang was not the sharpest drill bit in the crew.

"Willard, you were here all the time. Did you see him at all?"

The technician nervously fiddled with the jack connection implanted behind his right ear. "I saw him looking into the storage bins about mid morning. Later on, I can't recall the time, I saw him head down the track towards the mine. Didn't see him again."

"Can you roughly estimate the time?"

"Well I saw him at the bins after I'd done the maintenance checks, couldn't have been more than an hour doing that so it must have been about 1100. I was going into the Rec. I got a bite to eat and then watched a holo-tab. When it finished I got up to get myself a cup of coffee and noticed him walk pass the window towards the mine. It could have been around 1400 but it could have been a little later or a little earlier."

"Sligo, Dirk, you were on the late shift. Did you see him?"

Sligo Edmuson was a huge man who stood head and shoulders above the other drillers, themselves each over two metres tall. A hand the size of a dinner plate stroked his bushy salt and pepper coloured beard. "Saw him last night and he arranged to meet us here and come to the drill head but he never

7

turned up. I reported it to you." A man of few words, he had nothing further to add.

"Dirk?" Ull stared at Albright and waited.

"Why ask me? I was with Sligo the whole time." Albright glared back at Ull. The crew manager did not push him any further. Albright had a short fuse and a violent temper.

"Anybody else see him?" They all remained silent. He wondered if their reticence was more to do with a reluctance to get involved. "Then we better organise a search for him. Right, pair up in your shift teams. Willard you're with me. We'll take the mine tunnels with Sligo and Dirk. Milton, Will, you take the valley from the road West to the river. Mol, you and Sara take the valley East as far as the Perrin Gap."

"We're off duty!" Gurd's response was to be expected so Ull ignored it.

"You can start with searching all the buildings here and then move on to the Gap." A little extra task just for being uncooperative, an action which would not go unnoticed by the rest of the crew. "I want everybody back here in two hours time unless we find him. Keep your CommsLinks on and report back if you do. Pity we haven't got a scanner, it'd make the job a damn sight easier!" They all stared at him. "Move! If we don't find him the shit's really going to fly." They jumped at his command, but some with more enthusiasm than others.

***

Petre Ull handed out the assignments before they entered the mine. Edmurson and Albright were allocated the tunnels at the far end of the mine to cover the last two active tunnels and the current active one. This would enable them to resume their shift as soon as the search was completed. Ull and Willard would search the rest of the tunnels before returning to the camp to help the search there. Most of the old tunnels had been back-filled with waste from the newer ones so there was fewer places where Ginthem could have wandered. Willard was far from convinced there was any point in this search but he waited to voice his opinion until Edmurson and Albright were out of earshot.

"We're not going to find him in here are we?"

"We don't know that so we have to be thorough in our search." Ull gave Willard a smile and led the way into the mine.

"Like the others are going to be thorough! They were hardly enthusiastic about it. And what would an experienced mine inspector be doing wandering about in here unaccompanied? It's against all corporation rules!"

"The others will be thorough, don't you worry. We're a team and they all know the importance of finding him, whether it be alive or dead. If we don't the chances are the police will stop the drilling while they conduct a search. I take your point about the rule book but we don't know what his state of mind was. He certainly appeared fine when he arrived but cancelling appointments and not turning up for Sligo and Dirk's shift without any explanation was odd to say the least. Perhaps I should have said something at the time."

"Why would somebody just go off their head without any warning?"

"Trouble at home, trouble at work or some medical problem, who can say!" Ull stopped at the first side tunnel and peered down it. The dim emergency lighting added nothing to the clarity of vision, just created a mosaic of shadows.

"You did warn Ginthem about this didn't you?"

"I told him this tunnel was out of bounds."

"But not why?"

From his body language the question obviously hit a nerve. "He never asked." Ull bit his lip. That sounded like he was shifting any future blame onto the missing inspector. "He wouldn't have entered a restricted area on his own and the lighting's not good but it's still good enough to see the edge of the ravine."

"Of course we don't know what his state of mind was like and if the idea of suicide was in his head? Ideal place for a jumper!"

"Don't say that Zon. If he's thrown himself down that ravine they're bound to stop the drilling." There was real concern in his voice now.

"Nah! Don't suicides leave notes? That's what I've always heard anyway." Willard attempted to reassure Ull, his mild baiting of the site manager had pricked his conscience. "You can't blame yourself if his brain overloaded or, like Dirk, his medication didn't work. Nothing you could do about it."

"We'll look anyway, must be thorough!" Ull still sounded worried as he moved into the side tunnel. Willard reluctantly followed him.

"It's more likely he wandered off to take in the scenery, not many people get to visit the Great Arkins!" Willard made another attempt to reassure Ull for despite everything he was still very fond of the man. "It might look picturesque but it's still a jungle out there. If he was unlucky enough to run into one of those poisonous spiders or those wild dog like things."

Ull turned and smiled at the younger man. "Too far north for the spiders and when was the last time we saw any wild animals? They're more frightened of us but I appreciate what you're trying to do Zon." Ull placed a hand on Willard's shoulder and then caressed the back of his neck. "You're probably right anyway, more chance of a freak accident out there and it's not beyond belief he might have just dropped dead of something they can't screen for." Ull glanced round and could now see the edge of the ravine. "And if I can see it from here so must he have if he came this way. I'm blowing all this out of proportion." He let out a sigh. "That bloody bonus has put us all under pressure and Ginthem going missing..." He shook his head. It was no good going over the bad timing of Ginthem's disappearance again and again. "Come on let's check the other tunnels and hope the others have better luck."

Ull made a thorough search of the tunnels and even called out Ginthem's name at regular intervals but to no avail. There were few places for a body to lie which were not in plain view. Willard dutifully followed Ull's lead but with little expectation and even less enthusiasm.

***

Sligo Edmurson and Dirk Albright's search had been the quickest in for order them to get some drilling in before they reconvened in the accommodation block. The tunnel being used to back-fill waste from the current drill head was the longest and the most dangerous due to the loose waste which had not yet been compacted. If Laslo Ginthem had met with an accident in the mine this was the most likely place. The loose rubble made it easy to lose your footing and fall. However it would need to be a freak accident if it resulted in a life threatening injury. It was no surprise to either man when the tunnel proved to be empty. Even so Edmurson spent some time shifting some of the rubble in case Ginthem had fallen while the waste pipe had been in operation and had been covered by the waste. His methodical approach was watched by Albright who grew more irritable as the minutes passed.

"Come Sligo, we're wasting drilling time."

Edmurson paused only long enough to give his partner a disapproving look before continuing his rummaging of the waste. "He was a human being Dirk, not some stray animal! He deserves some consideration even if it's just finding his body so the family can have closure. He might have been somebody's husband or father, he was definitely somebody's son." Albright briefly thought about arguing the point that Ginthem meant nothing to them so they owed him nothing. However, he had attempted to use that particular line of argument before in other situations and knew it did not work with Edmurson and besides, his partner had gone beyond any tie of friendship, at least as far as Albright was concerned, when his medication had failed and his old behavioural problems had resurfaced. The others had all been for reporting his condition to the corporation but Edmurson had spoken up in his defence. The big man shared the same idealistic concept as Petre Ull; they were one big family. It was only Albright's respect for, and the feeling he owed Edmurson, which prevented him from shattering the naive view. However it was not in Albright's nature to give anybody the benefit of the doubt and his irritability was rapidly feeding his temper so he had to malign somebody and if it could not be Edmurson he would settle for Ginthem.

"If you ask me he's hiding!"

Edmurson paused again, this time with a confused expression on his face. "Hiding! Why, for Corp's sake, would he do that?"

Albright hesitated. As with most things he had not really thought this through before he opened his mouth. "To pretend he'd gone missing."

Edmurson gave Albright some time to elaborate on his last statement but as no further explanation appeared to be forthcoming, he prompted him. "And why exactly would he want to do that?"

Albright bit his lip. 'Why all the bloody questions!' he thought. 'They all did this, pushing him, querying every fucking thing he said and did.' He could feel himself getting agitated and needed to say something, anything to relieve the pressure. "To make us think something has happened to him. We do this search, don't find him and so have to report it to Central. They call the police in and the drill head gets closed down." The words now came in a torrent as the safety value was released. "A fucking corporation trick to get us moved out of here. Scheming bastards get us out and move in a low-grade team and save on the bonus. Fucking hiding somewhere to cheat us out of the bonus and you're worrying about him! Typical corporation ploy and Ginthem went along with it. Nice fat bonus for him no doubt!" Albright was rigorously nodding his head in agreement with himself. "Fucking corporation plot to cheat us out of our bonus. Bastards! And we're playing along with it! Believe very word of it and go searching for the bastard as if something had really happened to him." Albright was clenching his fists in rage and did not even notice Edmurson approach until he felt a hand upon his shoulder. He looked up and saw the calm features of Edmurson's face.

"Take deep breaths Dirk, like we practised." Albright instinctively obeyed. "Well done Dirk! Now keep the breathing going and try and clear your mind of these thoughts."

"But..."

Edmurson did not give Albright time to continue. "But how would they explain Ginthem's reappearance?" Edmurson kept his voice slow and calm.

"What?" The question confused Albright but distracted him and helped him concentrate on his breathing.

"If the man is hiding then at some point he will have to come out of hiding. How does he and the corporation explain that? I doubt if the corporation could pay enough to make somebody want to disappear for ever!" Edmurson could see Albright was far from convinced with that argument and had to admit one or two of this crew would probably give up their identity, family and friends if the price was right. "Cheaper to pay the difference in bonus than pay for a new life." Edmurson was not convinced about this argument either. He would never consider it, no matter what the they offered, but some men's lives would come cheap. However Albright appeared to be weakening in the face of the cheaper option point.

"They might have killed him?" He was clutching at straws now and his uncertainty was undermining his agitation.

"How did they do that? He was alive this morning and the only other people here are us?" Suddenly aware that this remark could add to Albright's paranoia Edmurson quickly added, "and how could they avoid the body being found? It doesn't make sense Dirk, does it?" There was an unreasonably long delay before Albright nodded his agreement. 'Come on let's get back to the drill head. Think about how you're going to spend that bonus." The final distraction did the trick and Albright smiled and nodded his head. Edmurson gently led him back down the tunnel and then on to drill head to begin their delayed shift. Although Albright appeared to be calm now Edmurson was concerned about the man's mental stability and wondered for the first time if he had been wrong to talk the rest of the crew into concealing Albright's problem.

***

Mol Gurd did not like anyone but, then again, nobody much liked Mol Gurd! He was a product of his upbringing. His mother was a 'medhead' and spent most of her time in a self-induced haze, but with a social partner like Mol Gurd Senior anybody would have made the same choice. At least the mental stupor took the edge off the regular beatings. At some time Mol Gurd's father had crossed the line between irresponsible hedonist and sociopath. Enforced medication had eventually curbed his worse excesses but not before he had planted the seed of corruption in

14

his son. The centre of Mol Gurd's universe was himself but, unlike his father, he had learnt to limit or hide his worst traits. He was cunning, manipulative and a dangerous man to cross. He was also a bully and like most bullies targeted the weak and vulnerable.

"What you doing retard?"

Boniface Chang jumped at the sound of Gurd's voice and quickly closed the external storage box he had been investigating as if he had been caught doing something wrong. "I look for man." He backed off as Gurd approached. "I do like Petre ask!"

"In a storage box full of tools? You idiot! What you think Ginthem did, cut himself up into manageable chunks so he could fit in there?"

"I don't know." Chang looked bewildered. Petre Ull had told him to search the camp and that was what he was doing. He never thought any further than that. Limiting his search to areas big enough to conceal a body never entered his head.

"I don't know." Gurd snarled. "What a fucking waste of space you are. I don't know why Ull puts up with you."

"Leave him alone Mol." Sara Rolm spoke without thinking and she took a step back when she saw the look on Gurd's face. "You know why Petre keeps him on, he's a fucking good cook! I've never seen you turn down one of his specials." Rolm got the words out as quickly as she could, hoping they would mollify Gurd. It appeared to work as Gurd grunted and turned away from Chang. Rolm gave Chang a small reassuring smile before following Gurd to search the main storage unit. The smile soon faded from her lips for she knew Gurd would not forget her mild admonishment and she did not have to wait long. As soon as the storage unit door closed behind them he rounded on her.

"Don't you ever talk out of turn to me, especially in front of that half-wit.' Gurd accompanied the remark with a quick punch to Rolm's ribs. She winced from the pain and staggered back a pace but then quickly stepped back to face him, showing Mol Gurd any weakness was a mistake she only made once. "You remember who's boss here. You don't cross me, you don't talk out of turn and you do as you're told." Gurd smiled and gripped her head with one hand and with his other hand ran his finger across her lips. "You be a good girl and you'll do fine. You keep your mouth shut about my business and nobody gets hurt." He smiled again but this time it was unpleasant, mocking one. "Remember what happened to the last person you spent too much time talking to." He gave her head a squeeze and then released her. Rolm stepped back and hoped her heart would not burst as it pounded away in her chest. Mol Gurd could certainly install fear in you.

***

The search had proved fruitless. It had been obvious he had not wandered off into the jungle. To easily move through the thick undergrowth would have required him to cut his way through. No laser trimmers were missing from the stores and there was no evidence anyone had either cut or forced their way through. The two crews were satisfied he had not taken that route as they had struggled to make any headway and never reached their targets. The tunnels were empty and with drilling suspended he would have responded to their shouts anyway if he was still alive. The compound had been searched twice and they inspected any area large enough to conceal a body. The crew were now back in the dining area waiting for Ull to address them.

"I can only think he wandered into the side tunnel which leads to the cavern and fell into the ravine." Ull's words failed to convince him, let alone the rest of the crew.

16

"How did he manage to do that with the emergency lighting on? It was Mol Gurd who asked the question which everybody else was thinking.

"Perhaps he threw himself down there!" Dang smiled but he was only half joking with the remark. He didn't know Ginthem and what had happened to him was of little concern to him.

"He was a bit odd!" offered Willard.

"Fucking weird!" confirmed Albright.

"Either way we have to inform the authorities." Ull was resigned to the fact, he had no other course of action but did not relish the consequences.

"If we say we think he chucked himself down the ravine they'll shut down the mine and try and recover the body. Bang goes our bonus! I didn't volunteer for an extra tour in this shit hole because I enjoy your company."

"Dang's right! They'll send somebody to investigate and then close down the drilling while they call in specialist equipment to search the ravine. When we first found it we knew the bloody thing was deep. Chuck anything in it and you never hear it hit the bottom. No thud, no splash, nothing! Our tour could end before they found him, if they found him at all!"

"So what do you suggest Dirk?" Ull did not seriously expect an answer but Albright gave him one.

"Say nothing or tell them he just walked off. By the time they realise his chip went dead we could have finished the tour."

"And when they ask us why we didn't report the fact he had just walked off into the jungle what do we say? We thought he intended to walk home rather than wait for the next transport? They'll try and contact him anyway if he doesn't report back in the next day or two." Ull shook his head in admonishment and Albright lowered his head and stared at his feet in embarrassment. He now wished he had thought through the idea before opening his mouth.

"Then report him missing but don't mention the ravine. Willard said he saw him heading down the track towards the mine but it also leads to the jungle. Nobody actually saw him in the mine so he could have wandered off into the jungle." Dang could see some of the others warming to his idea so he quickly pressed on. "There's evidence that somebody went into the jungle because we went in to search, so who's to say he didn't go in first?"

"You're seriously suggesting we lie to the authorities?" Ull was amazed that the others appeared to be eager to support this idea.

"I'm suggesting we offer an alternative opinion. Hey, we don't know he chucked himself down the ravine, it's just our opinion. We could have missed his trail, fucking big jungle Ull! Even if they eventually do close the drilling down we might have extracted enough ore while they waste time searching the jungle to still give us a reasonable bonus. Shit Ull, the man's dead what difference is it going to make to him if they take a little longer to find the corpse?" Some of the others nodded their heads in agreement.

Ull had grave doubts about that course of action but his hesitation encouraged the idea. Willard took advantage of the pause to shed more doubt. "Come on Petre, Dang's right! The poor sod is dead so what's a little delay? Why should we lose out on a big bonus because some lunatic loses it and commits suicide? We all agreed to sign on for another tour for one big pay day. For Corp sake Petre we've all worked hard and just when it's going to pay off we throw it all away? We backed you up on the new tunnel, the least you can do is back us up now!" There was a murmur of agreement from the other members of the crew.

Petre Ull looked round at the expectant faces. They were right in saying they had backed him up over the new tunnel. On the thin evidence that they had discovered a Zelman crystal deposit they had started the new tunnel and then all agreed to sign up for another tour in the hope they had stumbled upon the mother load. When at first they failed to find more crystals their support never wavered. They had faith in his experience and judgement, so how could he now let them down? How could he take the bonus away from them, see them idly sit around while the authorities mounted what could turn out to be a fruitless search, and watch the next crew get the bonus? The Corporation would never allow them to sign on for a third tour.

It was still against his better judgement when he finally pulled out his CommsLink. He glared at each member in turn. "We don't lie, mislead or attempt to embellish the story. Is that clear?" The rest of the crew nodded in agreement. He waved on the device and reported the situation to the Mining Corporation control centre. The rest of the crew watched and listened intently, attempting to work out what control was saying from the one sided conversation they could hear. Ull waved off his CommsLink and addressed them.

"Control are going to advise the authorities on what's happened. We can continue drilling until the police arrive but then we have to comply with their instructions." Sighs of relief and the odd smile accompanied that news. "We are to e-tape off the tunnel leading to the cavern and the path to the jungle. Nobody should cross those lines again before instructed to do so by the police. If that's clear then let's get on with it. We can get at least one more shift in before anybody arrives."

"I'll sort out taping the path if Albright sorts out the tunnel." It was Dang who volunteered and Albright nodded his agreement. Ull gestured with his hands for them to get on with it and returned to his office to prepare for the arrival of their unwanted visitors. Dang grabbed Albright and Mol by the elbows and steered them to one side.

"I'm going to extend a couple of the search paths we made so they reach the river and the Gap It gives them a choice of that lunatic either throwing himself into the river or wandering off across the Gap. I'll hack about a bit more to give the impression that we searched and found existing paths."

"Ull said not to embellish our story." Mol sounded unsure.

"Ull told us to search as far as the river and the Gap. You, you lazy bastard, stopped short the same as me but I don't remember you telling Ull that!" Mol still looked unsure.

"You can tell Ull now that you didn't do a proper job Mol. Milton is just offering to finish your job for you. It's not embellishing, it's doing the job in retro...something."

"Retrospect." Dang patronisingly patted Albright on the back for making the effort.

"Yeah, retrospect! Don't want the police to think you didn't do the job right because you had something to hide."

"What do you mean?" Mol now sounded defensive.

"If Ginthem didn't throw himself into the ravine them one of us did!"

"I didn't touch him!" Mol now sounded aggressively defensive. "I was in bed when it happened."

"And you have the benefit of a witness?" smirked Dang.

"You shut your mouth Dang."

"Doesn't mean the police won't ask questions if they know you didn't bother to search properly. Why not? Did you know there was no need looking for Githem at the Gap?"

"They could ask you the same thing!"

"Exactly my point Mol! Why cause ourselves problems and shut down the drill head when we can put it right by finishing the search?"

"Come on Mol, you know Milton's talking sense." Albright put a hand on Mol's shoulder. Mol shrugged it off and took a step back from the other two.

"Alright, you do whatever you like and I'll go a long with it." Mol narrowed his eyes and gave Dang a threatening glare. "But you shut your mouth Dang about my business or you'll regret it!" Mol backed off, keeping his eyes on Dang until the last moment.

"What got into him?" asked Albright. "You don't think he did chuck Ginthem into the ravine do you?" Dang said nothing but raised one quizzical eyebrow.

**

Will LeBon had approached his task with the minimum of enthusiasm. Where the path from the camp to the mine met the edge of the jungle he had given a few half-hearted sweeps with the laser cutter. A sharp word from Milton Dang prompted him to cut a swath into the undergrowth but only a few metres deep. He then repeated the action a few times as he followed Dang towards the river. The lead driller led the way, trimming the edge of the existing path in an attempt to make it look as if it was freshly cut.

"Do you actually think the police will fall for this?" LeBon was hoping his question would cause a change in heart and Dang would abandon the idea and let him return to his holo games, something he regarded as a much better use of his time and effort.

Dang paused his cutting to look back. "Firstly, do you think your average police officer is any brighter than a second class driller?" Dang did not wait for a reply to his rhetorical question. "Secondly, we don't know Ginthem didn't come this way! Do we? It sounds more reasonable that he wandered off into the jungle and got into trouble than an experienced mine inspector would wander off in a mine on his own."

"But he could have!"

"Yes Will, he could have. That's the point! He could have wandered into the mine and over the edge of the ravine, he could have wandered off the ridge at the end of this path and into the river, he could have wandered off and got lost in the Gap or he could be lying dead ten metres away from us. All possible options and all would need to be explored by the police. All we're doing is helping them select the first option to examine."

"What if this isn't the right option?"

Dang gave an exasperated sigh. "Then they'll try another one. The more time they spend exploring our preferred options the better. Our hope is that they leave the ravine in the mine as the last option which gives us a better chance of keeping the drill head going and salvaging some of our bonus." Dang returned to his task and increased his pace to make up for the time he had wasted.

"But what if we end up leading them away from where he is and he's still alive?" Dang increased his pace once again, annoyed at LeBon's containing interruptions but the younger man would not be put off so easily. "If he dies because of the delay in searching the right place we'd be partly responsible!"

"For Corp sake Will! If, if, if! Let's face the facts, if he was still alive we would have found him or at least heard him during our search." Dang then added, to fend off further interruptions,"Even if our search wasn't that thorough. The man's dead, and that's regrettable, but us losing our bonus isn't going to alter the fact. It'll not bring him back!" Dang continued to clear the edge of the path with wild slashes of the laser cutter fuelled by his growing irritation. This time it was not directed at LeBon but towards the missing Ginthem. The rising resentment finally spilled over. "And another thing." Dang spun around and pointed the laser cutter at LeBon, who took a step back thinking he had pushed his line manager too far. "Suicide is a fucking selfish thing to do. Fucking up our bonus just because he couldn't cope with what shit screwed his head up." Dang paused when he saw the look on LeBon's face."And what sort of bastard does something like that to his family?" The last remark appeared to appease whatever sensibility of LeBon's he had offended so Dang continued with his chore and LeBon sullenly followed, still doing as little as possible when Dang was not watching. The journey to the end of the path was completed in silence.

Dang looked back with satisfaction to the path they had cleared. "Let's hope Gurd and Albright do as good a job!" He turned and took the last few paces to the ridge, shuffling forward until the tips of his work boots hung over the edge. Leaning forward slightly he stared down the twenty metre drop into the swirling waters of the river. It was still swollen by the rains and while it was not the torrent it had been, it was still enough to sweep away anyone who accidentally fell into it. In a couple of weeks it would be reduced to a mere trickle as the dry season took hold.

"Why do you do that?" It was a question LeBon had asked before but the added danger of the edge of the ridge giving way under Dang's weight had prompted the repetition. "Doing that at the mine ravine was bad enough but there's more chance of that edge giving way than rock." Dang glanced round and smiled at LeBon before shuffling forward a few more centimetres and peering once again down to the river. The smile remained. "Petre Ull said it was dangerous to go near the ravine."

"Dang gave a little laugh. "Petre Ull said it was dangerous!" He mimicked the words of LeBon, adding a childish whine. "Petre Ull is an old woman! Health and fucking safety! It bores the hell out of me." Dang turned his head to face LeBon. "Living on the edge, if you'll pardon the pun, is what humans are all about. Risk everything, risk death and life becomes so much more real. Nothing makes you appreciate life more than the experience of almost losing it." Dang gave another little grin. "Did you know a near death experience is a great aphrodisiac? Almost choking to death just before sex is standard foreplay for some. You get the urge to fuck everything and anything! That's a primeval urge which has survived this sterile world."

"And if you lose your balance what's the difference between that and a selfish suicide?"

The grin died on Dang's lips. "Think you're clever eh? You carry on thinking that way and you'll come to a sticky end my friend. I take calculated risks to enhance my life. I don't fucking hide behind medication and I deal with problems head on, not take the ultimate way of avoiding them."

"If you're so sure he committed suicide why not tell them?"

"Trying to prove my point about being clever?" Dang tapped the side of his head with a finger. "Think about it! Think about what Ginthem said to us. You think that sounded like the thoughts of a rational man?"

"If we explained that."

Dang cut him short. "What? We admit we saw him this morning and that we saw him in the mine? Are you stupid boy? That would possibly make us the last people to see him alive and you know what they say about that! The last person to see anyone alive is their killer?"

"But if it was suicide!"

"And how do they prove that? What's their incentive in proving suicide when it's easier and more career enhancing to catch a murderer, or murderers." Dang hoped LeBon would grasp the significance of that last word. "Even if they don't take the easy route what we say would put him in the mine at the right time and make the mine the centre of the search." Dang paused for a comment from LeBon but none was forthcoming. "Kiss goodbye to keeping the drill head running and kiss goodbye to the bonus!" Dang pointed a finger at LeBon to stress the importance of what he was going to say next. "We don't get involved, we don't say anything and we get our stories straight before the police arrive and we stick to them. That understood?"

LeBon nodded his head. He had learned the hard way to always end up agreeing with Milton Dang.

CHAPTER TWO

The sound of the office door sliding open made Vitch Tolman look up from his CommsLink. He smiled on seeing the familiar figure of Kanah Gantz framed in the doorway. She had been on sick leave recovering from her wounds received during their last case. Tolman himself had luckily just been on the fringe of the action and had avoided the gun battle. Despite drawing his weapon he had never come near to firing it in anger.

"Hi Kanah, welcome back. How you feeling? You look good!"

Gantz returned the smile and gave a nod in the direction of their boss, Inspector Goodridge. She took her customary seat next to Tolman.

"I'm fine now Vitch." She turned to face Goodridge. "Thanks for letting me tack on a vacation to the sick leave. It did me the world of good."

Goodridge waved a hand in a gesture to indicate it was no big deal, although he had argued long and hard with his superiors before they allowed it. "You deserved it Kanah, after what you went through. Just glad you're alright now."

"Yes, I'm fine," she repeated although the truth was she still had nightmares over the ordeal. Not only had she narrowly escaped death herself but at one time she thought she would have to watch a terrorist kill her close friend Ja Nemi. She smiled at her last thought. She still referred to him as a close friend, even to herself. He was a lot more than that. She

27

returned her attention to Tolman. "And how are Carla and Tolman junior?"

"Aaron!" said Tolman with a broad smile. "We finally got round to agreeing a name for him. Carla is permanently tired and Aaron is permanently hungry but other than that mother and son are doing great. She told me to be sure to invite you round for a meal. We would have done it sooner but once you were fit enough we'll busy with the move."

"Ah yes! You moved into the Gelmar Park area didn't you?"

"Two weeks ago and we've only just got rid of the last of the moving crates. I couldn't believe how much rubbish we had accumulated in that tiny apartment."

"How does it feel to be Friend Tolman?" The term was a New Brethren one conferred on people who were not members but were considered to have similar principles and morals. They were life-style members rather than full religious ones. Usually they lived and behaved like a full 'brother' or 'sister' but were unable to fully commit to the idea of the New Brethren vision of God. Although that vision did not take the form of some supernatural being but rather a name to encompass total knowledge. When the New Brethren learnt the meaning of life, the Universe and everything, they will finally understand God. This gave them a burning desire for knowledge and made the New Brethren education system the envy of the Federation. It must be said many 'converts' had done so to enable them to enrol their offspring into New Brethren schools. This worked to the benefit of the New Brethren for it made a fertile breeding ground for future committed members; give me a child until the age of seven and I'll return you the man. It was her children's education which had fired Tolman's partner, Carla, to move into a New Brethren commune. Tolman's elevation to 'Friend' because of his involvement in the Midwich case had made that move possible. A fact which had always embarrassed Tolman, a lifelong atheist.

"I'm getting used to it, slowly. Carla has thrown herself into it though. Always got her nose in a copy of the White Book her friend gave her when we first moved in." The White Book contained the teachings of the New Brethren and laid down the rules which governed their lives. It was their moral compass. His tone was jocular but in truth he was uncomfortable with his partner's increased interest in the New Brethren religion. Deep down Tolman was still a non-believer and far from convinced he was their friend. "Oh and I almost forgot, the dinner invitation is also extended to Nemi." That remark was accompanied by a mischievous little smile, hinting at the relationship which everybody thought they were having. Everybody except Gantz and Nemi.

"Thank you, I'm sure he'd love to come." Gantz no longer protested at any suggestion she and Nemi were a couple. Although not everyone was happy with the idea of a Gnostic and a pure human as a couple. She smiled to herself. Their relationship was not what everyone else thought it was. They spent as much time with each other as work demands would allow but the relationship appeared to have stalled at the friendship stage. She decided to change the subject as it was beginning to make her feel uncomfortable. "Any news from New Earth about Stern or Ester?" Her question referred to two people involved in their last case. One, Ester, an escaped terrorist, the other a private investigator working for the Corporations. Both were considered a risk to the New Brethren.

"Both still in stasis on the trip back. Another couple of months before Stern arrives and at least that until the transporter gets back, assuming she's on it!" Replied Tolman.

"Still on tenderhooks then!"

Tolman hesitated before asking the question which had been playing on his mind for some time. "The New Brethren still going ahead with the..." He paused, not sure of which words to use next. "The breeding program?" As soon as he had said it he decided he had used the wrong phase.

"You mean the genetic engineering programme?" If Gantz had been embarrassed by the question she gave no indication of it.

"Not the term to really bandy about." Tolman had deliberately avoided the exact same term. It was the last taboo for mankind and the programme the New Brethren had embarked on would be considered illegal. As a police officer this fact still made Tolman very uncomfortable.

"It may be illegal at the moment but we're not producing super humans Vitch! We're producing a hybrid from two species. I'm a product of a natural process and do I scare you?"

Tolman smiled. "You certainly do, but not for that reason."

"When the time is right the Federation will see that we're no danger. Besides, it's our future, our destiny, a fulfilment of the New Brethren existence." She checked herself at that point. "Well at least a major step in the journey."

"Always the long term view with the New Brethren! I hope the Federation is as understanding as you think."

"They will be!"

"Well I've never doubted you before but I'll still keep my fingers crossed."

"Thank you Vitch. I'm sure the New Brethren will sleep easy when they get to know about that."

Goodridge watched this scene unfold with a degree of satisfaction. Before the Midwich incident there had been an element of competition between his two deputies, a little tension, but now the shared experience of the last case had brought them together. From a professional point of view he regarded it as a positive feature. They were now more of a team. It was a pity that operational demands would temporarily split the team up. That thought brought him back to the present and he realised, regrettably, he would have to interrupt the reunion and get on with the morning briefing.

"Right that's enough idle chat, let's get on with the job in hand." Tolman and Gantz shifted their attention to Goodridge. "I'm afraid our reunion isn't going to last long. I've been given the job of getting the main police command post in Port Nilmon set up. At the moment we have a small force of officers on temporary secondment but so far it's been mainly night-watchman duties. However, the population is increasing at a rapid rate so we need a permanent presence there. Ideally I would have picked you Kanah for this one but it came up while you were still hospitalised so Vitch, much to his displeasure, got the short straw. As he's already started I can't see the point of changing now. I had intended to put you in to help with the selection process for new recruits to be assigned there." The two deputies nodded their agreement. Tolman was not really the administrative type so was not in the least offended by the suggestion Gantz would have been first choice for this particular job. They both also realised Gantz's special gift made her the ideal choice for vetting new recruits. "That's what I had intended but now I'm afraid you'll have to take on the manning issue as well Tolman. A new case has come up and Kanah is the only spare body I have."

"If it's a juicy one boss I'm not going to be happy!" Tolman was only half joking.

"It's a strange one!" Goodridge waved on his CommsLink to refer to his notes. "There's a small, remote, mining camp buried in the Great Arkin Mountain range. It was one of the test drilling sites the Council had to agree to when we started the Midwich site. The Corporation wanted some concessions if the

New Brethren planned to build a settlement in an area where future development had been banned. The Great Arkin range was so far away from Midwich the Council agreed. Five test sites were agreed but only one proved to be worthwhile for further development. It's called MCGA3 and is over a hundred kilometres into the range."

"You can always rely on the Corporations to come up with either a catchy or romantic name for one of their settlements!"

"It's not really a settlement Vitch." Goodridge rarely spotted a Tolman quip or sarcastic remark. "Small scale mine so a minimum workforce. No families, support industries or recreational facilities. The crew do a six month tour. Three two man shifts, one tech support, one admin who doubles up as part-time cook and a manager. Nine people with nothing to do but work, eat and sleep. How they cope with a six month tour is a wonder!"

"Good pay and a three month rest period, again on full pay." Tolman stated the obvious reason but pulled a face to show it was not a deal which would appeal to him. "But I agree with you boss, I couldn't do it." He glanced at Gantz. "Enjoy my home comforts too much!"

"The first strange part of the story," continued Goodridge. "Two weeks ago their tour was due to end but every one of the crew volunteered to do a further six months. Despite the fact that production levels had fallen in the last few weeks and the Corporation were thinking of closing down the site. It was no longer worthwhile sending a daily transport to pick up the ore. When contacted the crew manager explained that the current seam of ore had run out but they had opened a new shaft and expected production to improve so the Corporation agreed and signed them up for another tour."

"I would have signed them up for a psyche evaluation!"

Goodridge did spot that one. "Perhaps not such a joke Vitch in view of what follows. However, it no doubt saved the Corporation a lot of credits not having to supply a relief crew."

"Must never forget the bottom line!"

"The what?" It was the first time Gantz had spoken. It was in her nature not to interrupt with comments, fatuous remarks or jokey asides. She left that to Tolman.

"How much profit they're making," explained Tolman. Gantz nodded her understanding.

"Which is why the next strange thing to happen did get the Corporation's attention. Production figures plummeted. Repeated calls to the site manager just produced the same story. The new shaft was progressing and they expected production figures to increase significantly. The Corporation usually allow a few days to access the worth of a new find but this had been going on for almost two weeks. Something had to be done so three days ago they sent out a mining Inspector on the next available transport." Goodridge paused and waved his hand over his CommsLink to display an image on the office wall behind him. It was a thin faced man in his mid thirties. "Laslo Ginthem, thirty six years of age. He had a social partner and one twelve year old daughter. Had worked for the Mining Corporation since graduating from University and had been living on New Eden for the past six years."

"You keep using the past tense boss."

"Can't get anything past you Vitch!" It was unclear if Goodridge was making a joke or a serious comment. "Yesterday his ID chip went dead and within three hours of that happening the site manager had reported him missing."

"If they can be that precise they must have been monitoring his chip."

"Yes, good point Vitch, which means they know something which they're not telling us, or an entire crew volunteering for a double tour of duty was so unusual it set alarm bells off. We weren't contacted until late yesterday with an almost plausible excuse for their actions. However, the delay would suggest to me that they contacted their lawyers to help them come up with a story to cover their arses." Tolman stifled a smile. It was out of character for Goodridge to be so crude. "If they sent Ginthem alone into a situation where they had doubts about the mental stability of the crew they have left themselves wide open to a compensation claim by his widow." Goodridge hesitated, unsure if the term widow would apply to social partners. On reflection he decided he was just being pedantic and continued. "Either way this one is now our responsibility."

"If it took three hours to report the death and even longer for the Corporation to contact us surely that points to the crew, or at least one of them being responsible for Ginthem's death!"

"Not quite as clear cut as that." Goodridge stepped in to explain. "The site manager organised a search before he reported in so that could explain the time delay. And of course Ginthem's death could have been accidental. Also, as far as I'm aware, the corporation didn't tell the crew they were monitoring his chip or that the chip had ceased functioning. In that case organising a search was a reasonable thing to undertake." Goodridge injected the comment to put an end to speculation. "However, I don't intend to take any chances by sending you into a situation where we have so little intelligence. I've got a patrol craft on standby at the space port. An Officer, Sonia Delgardo, will met you there. She's an experienced officer so should provide a good back up. I want you to leave as soon as possible. There is a time limit as I want you there before any possible crime scene has degraded to the extent it's worthless. You investigate what's gone on and you report back to me as soon as possible. I suggest you leave the pilot on board ready for a quick exit should the need arise. I don't like the idea of my officers being in an unknown situation with back-up so far away."

"Kanah can look after herself boss, you're being far too cautious!" Tolman winked at Gantz.

"I've only just got her back Vitch so I'm going to be cautious." Goodridge returned his attention to Gantz. "I'll download information about the crew to your CommsLink. I suggest you familiarise yourself with their details on the flight. Any questions contact me."

"Right! I'll get prepared. I'll see you all in a couple of days." She rose and left the room.

"She'll be fine boss! Sending a Gnostic is hardly sending somebody in blind. It will probably turn out to be some accident caused by Corporation piss-poor maintenance."

"Yes I'm sure you're right Vitch." Goodridge attempted to sound convinced but he looked pensive.

"But boss!" Tolman could usually see the 'but' coming from the tone of Goodridge's voice.

Goodridge hesitated. "Psychological evaluations are a bit pointless for Gnostics. The fact Kanah passed is fairly meaningless. If she wanted to return to work she could easily sidestep the examiner."

"Not really Kanah's style boss!"

"I know but that leaves me with a contrasting concern. Her childhood conditioning will limit her abilities and she'll be alone up there."

"She'll have back-up from the officer you're sending with her."

"She's a Gnostic Vitch! She's never alone but up there distance will break her mental link with the other Gnostics. She'll be alone in a sense we could never really appreciate." Goodridge paused to reflect on his own words. "I'm worried about what effect that will have on her so soon after her traumatic experience during the last case."

Tolman would have liked to reassure Goodridge, having experienced that mental link, but it had been a fleeting moment which he had struggled to comprehend at the time. He could not begin to imagine what it was like for Kanah to have a permanent link or even begin to guess the effect of suddenly losing it. His earlier confidence in her ability to cope had become seriously undermined.

***

Kanah Gantz went straight back to her apartment to pack an overnight bag. It was a single bedroomed apartment on the edge of the New Brethren quarter. Chosen for its proximity to work, the area appealed to singles working in the Federal or Corporation parts of the city. Although of simple design with New Brethren style furnishings, the area it was in was considered a little down market because of its position. The more devout or well to do New Brethren frowned at being this close to the 'Fedups'; a New Brethren nickname for the secular part of the population. Of course nobody would dream of saying as much to Gantz, who as a Gnostic was regarded as a prophet and therefore far too holy not to pick them up on such bigotry. They were widely known to have a special gift; extreme intuition, remarkable perception, sixth sense, clairvoyance, second sight! All vague and spiritual as you would expect with a religious sect, but few knew the truth. The wider New Brethren community were not yet ready for uncomfortable truth, which was that Kanah Gantz was a half breed. The existence of aliens was the big secret but the more dangerous one was that the settlement of Midwich was the home of a project to produce the next generation of genetically engineered Gnostics. Genetic engineering was the last taboo of the Federation. Cosmetic genetic engineering was of course acceptable; who would not prefer to select a blue eyed blond or sultry eyed brunette than rely of the vagaries of natural selection? Why let your child run the risk of some hereditary disease or buck teeth or hair lip or cleft palette? But enhancements to intellect or strength could produce a race of super humans and who could predict their attitude towards lesser mortals? The New Brethren project to take the next step to be nearer to their God could be interpreted by some as playing God, even if the Federation failed to acknowledge the existence of a supreme being.

She had a couple of hours to spare before she had to be back at police headquarters to pick up the patrol craft so she made herself breakfast. Her original intention was to to have breakfast with Tolman after the morning briefing so they could catch up on their respective gossip, or rather allow her to interrogate Tolman to extract all the detail on Tolman junior which he had forgotten to tell her. The urgency of this case had wrecked that particular idea. Armed with a cup of synthetic coffee and a bowl of 'Morange', a local dish of wild grain and Culberries, akin to a fruit porridge, she made herself comfortable on the small terrace and enjoyed the view over the nearby park. Between spoonfuls of her breakfast she attempted to call Nemi on her CommsLink. She knew he would be working but wanted to speak to him to explain that she would be away for a few days and to let him know Tolman would be in Port Nilmon. Nemi was also there to set up a Colonial barracks and she knew he would want to take the opportunity to meet up. Unfortunately there was no reply from Nemi so she had to settle for leaving a message. She felt a little disappointed in not being able to hear his voice once more before she left. It was an unusual feeling for Gantz but she put it down to her growing affection for him. They had first met when Goodridge had taken her with him to the maternity hospital to intercept Nemi. He had guessed the New Brethren secret; that they were genetically altering foetuses to produce a new generation of Gnostics like her. It had been her job to introduce him to the Collective and convince him to keep the secret. Their minds had touched and the moment had a profound affect on both of them. She had experienced something similar with other Gnostics and the Collective but never with a pure-bred human. She had found a term in human literature, soul-mate, which came close to describing her feeling but it was always related to a romantic attachment, an idea she baulked at. Nemi had, therefore, become her friend but emotions raised by their recent close call with death had undermined her position. She smiled at the thought of him and then pushed him to the back of her mind and got on with preparing for her trip.

She arrived back at the office well before the agreed time and made her way to the roof where the patrol craft was already waiting on the pad. Officer Sonia Delgardo had also arrived early and was sitting in what little shade the roof top provided. She had the typical coffee coloured complexion of a Federation citizen and wore her hair cropped short. Her muscular build and flat chest gave the impression of a male at first glance and her delicate facial features appeared at odds with the rest of her. Gantz approached her and introduced herself.

"Can't believe I'm getting to meet Kanah Gantz, let alone work with you!" Delgardo's enthusiasm was as surprising as her appearance.

"I didn't realise I was that famous." Gantz shook hands with Delgardo, a little taken back at her own apparent fame and that the officer engaged in such a tactile New Brethren greeting.

"Everybody knows how you took out the terrorist leader when you were badly wounded and saved your lover from being his next victim."

Gantz thought about protesting at Nemi being described as her lover but decided their relationship would be far too complicated to explain to a complete stranger so let the comment pass. "That makes it sound rather more dramatic than it actually was. I was scared most of the time and reacted instinctively. In the end I was just very lucky." Delgardo nodded in agreement but her expression indicated she understood Gantz's modesty. Heroes would behave like that. Gantz, like the lover comment, let the unspoken inference pass without response.

"Have you been briefed?" Gantz thought it best to move onto the business in hand.

"I studied the download while I was waiting for you." Delgardo glanced at the patrol craft. "The pilot shouldn't be long, he's just gone off for a shit." She hesitated. Perhaps she should have tempered her language, but then decided anyone who had gone through what Gantz had would not be shocked by anything! "Said we could take off as soon as you arrived."

"What are your first thoughts on the case?" Gantz asked the question to help form an opinion of her temporary partner.

"I thought you could tell! The rumour is you're a Gnostic." The response took Gantz by surprise. The existence of the Gnostics was common knowledge amongst the New Brethren, or at least the rumours were. It was the worse kept secret she had ever come across. However Delgardo did not come across as a member of the New Brethren. The hesitation to respond was picked up by Delgardo. "I have friends who are New Brethren," said Delgardo by way of explanation. "I'm okay with it, like, being able to get inside somebody's head, wow!" Delgardo accompanied the remark with a disarming smile.

"It's not that simple, in practice it's more like picking up feelings."

"So you can't actually read my mind? You know, get in there and find out my darkest thoughts?"

For the second time in as many minutes Delgardo had taken Gantz by surprise. Her, for want of a better word, bluntness and her casual acceptance of Gantz's ability was a refreshing change. Even the New Brethren who knew Gantz fell into one of two camps; those who revered her gift and regarded her as a prophet and those who were wary, if not a little afraid of her. Most people, even New Brethren, had things they would rather keep private. "I would never try! Bad idea for both parties."

"Wow!" Delgardo nodded. She did not really understand and would never come close to grasping the concept. Only people like Nemi and Tolman who had experienced the link could, perhaps, get some vague idea of what it was like. Even then, their experience only scratched the surface.

"So let's play safe and you tell me what your thoughts are." Gantz again steered the conversation back to the current case.

"Could be any number of things happened out there. I don't like making assumptions, assumptions are little more than guesses. Admittedly Ginthem's death sounds suspicious and the fact the Corporation was monitoring his chip is a bit odd. Not the normal thing to do and suggests they were worried for his safety. I mean, we monitor chips on missing person cases and to track suspects so the Corporation must have pulled some strings to get permission to monitor a private individual." Gantz nodded but more in approval of the fact Delgardo was wary of jumping to conclusions. "But the Corporations work in mysterious ways. Not even sure they know why they do some things. Of course being isolated like that for six months would send me crazy so this could be a case of one of the crew going berserk!"

"Crews tend to have regular psychological evaluations," pointed out Gantz.

"Yeah, and they have regular maintenance checks but that doesn't stop accidents due to equipment failures. I'm been on a few callouts like that. Mining crews might be relatively well paid compared to most unskilled jobs but they're cheaper than techs, and a drilling rig costs more to repair if it breaks down than death benefit! Psyche evaluations are in place to reassure people if you ask me. I wouldn't trust a corporation evaluation, not if my life depended upon it!"

Gantz nodded again. She remembered Tolman's comment about the bottom line. "I agree, an accident can't be dismissed. My boss thinks the Corporation is keeping something from us but that could just be to avoid any suggestion of negligence. Still we'll play it carefully until we know exactly what's happening out there. Have you read up the profiles of the crew yet?"

"Not yet, I was saving that pleasure to stave off the boredom of the trip. No hyper-drive and no onboard entertainment on a patrol craft and it's likely to be cramped on that thing." She nodded towards the waiting ship. "It's been stripped down to accommodate the extra pulse cells required for the journey. Also the pilot, well, let's just say he appears to be a bit of a character!"

Gantz smiled, she was beginning to like Delgardo. "Same here! We'll have plenty of time to read them up and compare notes before we reach..." Her voice trailed away as she spotted the pilot approaching them.

"Morning ladies, Al 'Wildman' Singh at your service. Well I feel a lot better for that! I hope you ladies have been, toilet facilities are a bit limited in a patrol ship. Not really built for long haul trips." The pilot was a short man in his late fifties. He sported a full beard and longer than regulation greying hair tied up in a pony tail. Police pilots were hard to come by, some actual flying skill was required rather than the ability to program a drone, so they were allowed some latitude in appearance and attitude. Some took full advantage of that latitude and Pilot Officer Al 'Wildman' Singh appeared to be one of them, highlighted by the 'ladies' remark which ignored their rank. His coffee coloured complexion was sunburnt a darker hue and exaggerated the sparkle in his eyes. He stood there with a broad smile on his face. Wildman, by his nickname and demeanour was one of life's characters. "Are we ready for a trip into the unknown?" His smile widened and Gantz indicated they were ready. "Then climb aboard my lovelies, buckle up and if you must be air sick make sure you pull open the door before you throw up. An eight hour flight smelling of vomit is something we all want to avoid, believe me!"

***

Gantz made herself as comfortable as possible. The seats in the patrol craft were cramped for leg room and the padding was at a minimum. She glanced across at Delgardo and wondered how she managed to get into the seat at all. She was almost a foot taller than Gantz so her knees looked uncomfortably close to the back of the seat in front of her. The ship looked more roomy from the outside. The additional cell packs filled the limited space in the back of the cabin and had forced the two rear seats to be pushed forward. The seat next to Wildman Singh had more leg room but to Gantz's surprise, or perhaps it was not that much of a surprise even with her limited introduction to him, that particular position was taken by a large mongrel dog called Keith. Again this was against all the regulations. Gantz did point this out to Singh but he just winked and gave a chuckle. Keith wagged his tail, put his head on the back of his seat and stared at Gantz with sad black eyes. It was obvious

Keith had practised this appealing look before and it worked again. Gantz stroked him behind the ear and made no further protest.

"I hope he's had a shit before boarding!" Remarked Delgardo.

"Of course," shouted Singh as he fired up the engines. "And he's a bitch by the way!" Delgardo opened her mouth to ask the obvious question and then thought better of it. She doubted that she would believe the answer even if she got a straight one.

The ship settled down into the familiar rhythmic hum of the pulse engine. There was a hiss and a slight jolt as the ship slowly rose from the roof top. It stirred up a cloud of fine sand which the wind had blown in from the desert at the edge of the city. It momentarily clouded her view before they rose higher and she could see the city stretched out before her. It was a sight which never failed to bring a smile to Gantz's face and this time it was bathed in bright sunlight. Row upon row of low-level white buildings emphasising the highly coloured tiles used as decoration around walls and windows, broken by ribbons of green parkland. The sunlight reflected off the running water of the parkland fountains to make the city sparkle as if it was inset with diamonds. It was beautiful and it was her city and she was proud of the fact it was her job to protect it. She gazed lovingly at the view, taking in every last detail as they sped across the New Brethren quarter and headed for the river. Once across they were over the jungle and all that could be seen was a seemingly endless canopy of tree tops. An undulating patchwork of green formed by the huge common native trees, referred to by the locals as 'broccoli on steroids'. Gantz opened up her CommsLink and waved it on. She found the download and selected the mining crew profiles. It would be some time before this view changed so she began reading.

Petre Ull, Site manager. Thirty-two years of age, born on New Earth and transferred to New Eden twelve years ago. No social partner registered. Started career in administration and promoted through the grades to current position two years ago. Worked in desert based rigs South of the capital city until test drilling was allowed in the Great Arkin Mountain range. Worked on two of those test sites with his present crew. Appointed to MCGA3 when the first crew to work there had finished its tour of duty. Last psychological evaluation prior to secondment to test drilling program. Last full medical evaluation prior to tour of duty at MCGA3. Both evaluations passed, no comments or observations noted. Corporation records show that despite a limited education Ull is intelligent and competent at his job. Socially has few friends outside the work environment but that was common amongst the mining industry. No recorded interests or hobbies. Medication and alcohol for recreational purposes only. Religion, none recorded.

'A fairly typical Federation citizen,' thought Gantz. She flicked to the next pen portrait.

Zon Willard, technical support. Thirty-one years of age, born Solar 1 and emigrated with his family to New Eden twenty-two years ago. No social partner registered. Started career as a computer technician after connection insert procedure. '*A plug head!*' thought Gantz. Prior to that, worked in several casual jobs. Spent three years in a software factory before joining the Mining Corporation as computer technician and drilling software engineer. Moved to drilling crew when test site program initiated. This was considered a step down in career as his role now is purely maintenance and not development work. Last psychological evaluation prior to secondment to test drilling program. Last full medical evaluation prior to tour of duty at MCGA3. Both evaluations passed, no comments or observations noted. Corporation records show a number of minor disciplinary actions against him all resulting in fines, most related to poor timekeeping. No recorded interests or hobbies. Medication for recreational purposes only. Does not consume alcohol. Religion, none recorded.

Boniface Chang, administration support. Thirty-nine years of age, born on New Earth and emigrated to New Eden with his parents under the second chance law. No current social partner registered but two previous cancelled social contracts. Two dependent children, one by each of former social partners. Various low grade jobs before joining the Mining Corporation four years ago. General administration duties, odd jobs and part-time cook for the crew. Last psychological evaluation prior to secondment to test drilling program. Last full medical evaluation prior to tour of duty at MCGA3. Both evaluations passed but with comments. Low IQ and a timid, almost subservient personality. Has trouble forming relationships. Requires constant supervision. No disciplinary record. No recorded interests or hobbies. Medication for recreational purposes only. Does not consume alcohol. Religion, Corporation. Gantz paused, it never ceased to amaze her how anyone could put down 'Corporation' as their religion, but a frightening number of citizens did. She flicked to the next.

Dirk Albright, driller. Forty-seven years of age, born on Solar 2. Transferred to New Eden by the Mining Corporation ten years ago. Second generation miner from the Solar 2 asteroid belt. Sparkle Venner registered social partner, third contract. Two dependents, Dirk junior and a younger daughter, Bless. Driller second class who worked on desert sites before joining his current crew. Last psychological evaluation prior to secondment to test drilling program. Last full medical evaluation prior to tour of duty at MCGA3. Both evaluations passed but with comments. Low IQ with behavioural and anger management problems. Requires constant supervision. Poor disciplinary record and one period in the Isolation Facility during his youth. Most incidents involved disagreements with co-workers and the ISO-cube time was the result of a violent bar fight. Improved record since joining his current crew. Medication for recreational purposes and anger management. Does not consume alcohol. Religion, none recorded. Gantz made a mental note of Albright's violent streak.

Milton Dang, driller. Twenty-seven years of age, born on New Eden. His parents emigrated to New Eden under the second chance law. No current social partner registered but one previous cancelled social contract. No dependants. Spent most of his working life in various maintenance jobs after connection insert procedure. Joined the Mining Corporation three years ago. Driller first class who briefly worked on desert sites before joining current crew. Last psychological evaluation prior to secondment to test drilling program. Last full medical evaluation prior to tour of duty at MCGA3. Both evaluations passed but with comments. Narcissistic personality, problems with authority figures. Corporation records show a number of minor disciplinary actions over attitude to superiors, all resulting in fines. No recorded interests or hobbies. Medication for recreational purposes only. Does not consume alcohol. Religion, none recorded.

Sligo Edmurson, driller. Fifty-two years of age, born on New Earth. Transferred to New Eden by the Mining Corporation twenty-three years ago. Lowe Florence registered social partner, second contract. One previous social partner cancelled after second contract. Five dependants, Sven (m), Lull (m) and Miriam (f) from previous social partner and Carl (m) and Elm (f) from current social partner. Driller first class who worked on desert sites before joining his current crew. Last psychological evaluation prior to secondment to test drilling program. Last full medical evaluation prior to tour of duty at

MCGA3. Both evaluations passed, no comments or observations noted. Has an interest in wood carving. Medication and alcohol for recreational purposes only. Religion, none recorded.

Gantz was getting bored with the repetition and so she decided to speed read the last three. It revealed more of the same. A sixty-one year old first class driller called Mol Gurd, and two second class drillers, both youngsters, Will LeBon, aged eighteen and Sara Rolm, aged nineteen. Gurd had a similar record to Albright but had avoided any ISO-cube time. LeBon passed all evaluations but was described as an introvert with an interest in holo-games and the remarkable thing about Rolm was the fact that she was a girl. Although there were many women in the Mining industry very few were drillers. Gantz wondered if any sexual tensions had arisen with one woman in a crew isolated by its remote location? The chances were Sara Rolm was more than capable of handling herself but Gantz refused to dismiss the idea entirely. She turned her attention to a map of the site. The camp was situated half way up one of the foothills rather than one of the main mountains. A wide plateau provided a natural base for the buildings which comprised the uniform prefabricated oblongs which were used for temporary accommodation. At the widest end of the plateau was the transport landing area. If it was big enough to land an ore transporter there would be plenty of room for their patrol craft. Next to this were four storage bins for the ore awaiting transport. About twenty metres further away from these, where the plateau narrowed, and close to the hill side were three buildings which were marked as the main office, accommodation block and storage hanger. At the far end of the plateau a road led down the hillside to the bottom of the valley. There in a small clearing stood two more buildings, one marked machine store and the other power generator. On the other side of this clearing the entrance to the mine was marked.

She studied the layout for a few minutes before opening up each marked building in turn to expose the internal features. The main office was split into three sections, the smallest being the manager's office. Next to that was a small storage room and the largest section, which had a separate entrance, contained the water purification plant. The accommodation block contained twelve sleeping compartments, a dining area which doubled up as a recreational area and a kitchen. Six sets of tables and chairs were positioned nearest the kitchen and more comfortable armchairs and sofas were between those and the sleeping compartments, accessed via an internal corridor. Each sleeping compartment had its own shower and toilet facilities. The storage hanger contained a general storage area, a large cold room and a walk-in freezer. From the plans the accommodation appeared sparse and cramped. Gantz imagined the addition of equipment and personal possessions would only exacerbate the situation. Living in those conditions for six months must put a strain on relationships so tempers could flare up. Perhaps the introduction of an outsider like Ginthem acted as a spark to already smouldering tinder. 'But why sign on for another tour if the isolation was getting to them?' Gantz decided it was no use speculating. The reading had made her feel nauseous so she closed her CommsLink and focused on the horizon until the feeling subsided.

Gantz glanced around at Delgardo and saw she had also finished reading the notes and was now stroking Keith the dog, who was lapping up the attention. "Decided to make friends with that smelly old mongrel?"

"No, I thought the dog would be better company."

"I heard that!" From the tone of his voice Singh had taken the remark as the joke Delgardo had intended.

"Any further thoughts on the case?" Again the question was aimed at getting an opinion of Delgardo rather than an opinion from her.

"Nothing in the brief to suggest anything other than an accident. Ginthem was sent out to investigate the drop in productivity but that could be as simple as this new drilling not producing the expected results. If it wasn't an accident then we're left with two possibilities; one, somebody at the site killed him or two, he killed himself."

"How likely are those options, considering the information we have at the moment?"

Delgardo gave that question more consideration. "Ginthem had his last psychological evaluation over two years ago but he passed without any problems and he had a social partner and they had just renewed their contract for a third time, and he had a twelve year old daughter. If life suddenly became so unbearable he had an urge to end it I can't see an obvious reason. Not that that means there wasn't one, just I can't see what it could have been. Perhaps we need somebody to talk to the social partner." Delgardo paused and Gantz nodded her agreement. "If we disregard suicide then that leaves us with murder. However why would any of the crew want to kill a mine inspector none of them had met before? Unless they have, perhaps something else to check out. There's a couple who might be a bit odd and one has a temper and a history of violence but what motive would any of them have? All the options appear as unlikely as they are likely. We need to know a lot more about what went on down there when Ginthem arrived."

"Agreed." Gantz smiled. Delgardo was so far proving to be a level headed, thoughtful police officer. She guessed Goodridge had hand picked her rather than just grabbed the first body available. Prompted by Delgardo's comments Gantz sent a message to Goodridge to provide more background on Laslo Ginthem, specifically his home life, any problems at work and whether he had previous dealings with any of the crew members. She then stared out of the window until the monotony of a seemingly endless view of treetops drove her back to the briefing notes.

CHAPTER THREE

Delgardo stretched up in her seat to look through the windscreen of the craft. She could just make out a blurred line on the horizon which marked the start of the Great Arkin Mountain range. The broccoli-trees were now beginning to thin out, to be replaced by slightly smaller trees with thin trunks. Some of the trunks had purple coloured creepers spiralling up them from the dense undergrowth which covered the jungle floor. Their uppermost branches spread out wide and touched the branches of the surrounding trees. They appeared to be supporting each other, as if without support those thin trunks would collapse under the weight of their own canopies. "How much longer Officer Singh?"

The pilot spun round in his seat and Delgardo could see he had his CommsLink in his lap. He had been playing games and watching holo-films since take-off. "Less than an hour girlie." He noticed her eyes staring at his CommsLink. "Hey girlie, you didn't think I've actually been flying this thing for the last seven hours did you?' He winked at her. "I'm only here to press the right buttons, that's if there were any buttons to press." He stared off into the distance as if he had slipped into a trance. "Haven't pressed a button since I was in training." He closed his CommsLink and slipped it into his jacket pocket. "And call me Wildman girlie, not this formal shit."

"I'll call you Wildman when you stop referring to me as girlie or lady."

"Sounds a deal! What do you want me to call you?"

"Officer Delgardo."

"I didn't think you'd want to get that intimate this early in our relationship." The irrepressible smile never left his lips.

Delgardo smiled and shook her head in response to the remark. "Okay Wildman, its Sonia."

"What about your boss?" Wildman cocked his head towards Gantz.

"Boss will be fine Singh." The reply came from Gantz. She narrowed her eyes at Wildman. "I assume this craft has it's own in-built navigation system?" Her tone betrayed the doubt she had in her own assumption.

"On a piece of junk like this?" Wildman laughed. "No way boss! These old things are used for short search and rescue flights. Need somebody to steer on those type of jobs, can't program in stuff like that really." He paused again to consider his last statement. "Well I suppose you could now on the latest models." He shrugged his shoulders and returned to his main point. "I'm only really here to keep an eye on the scanner during a search or to ferry officers about. If we had the up-to-date drones they have back on New Earth, what do they call them?" He answered his own question. "SkyScan, that's it! I wonder how much the Corporation paid the creative genius to come up with that startlingly original name? Anyway if we had those unmanned flying scanners I'd just be a glorified taxi driver." He shook his head sadly. "If there were any taxi drivers left that is! I'm a dying breed, that's me! No use for pilots now except on remote planets like this where the locals have obsolete equipment until they can afford something better. Another couple of years and I'll have to move on to the next colonised planet, if they find another one before I'm put out to grass."

Gantz ignored Wildman's stroll down memory lane. "Then if we've no auto-navigation I presume we've also no auto-pilot."

"That's right boss!"

"Then who's flying this, as you call it, piece of junk?"

Wildman's smile broadened. "Keith!" Gantz glanced at the dog. It was curled up in the co-pilot seat with one leg resting across its head, its paw hovering in the centre of the holo-controls. Gantz stared at Singh and he was quick to respond. "Don't worry boss she's got hundreds of flying hours under her collar." He winked at Gantz. "Bet you've guessed why my name is Wildman."

"Not the first thing which came to mind Singh."

"Come on boss, you think these things are difficult to fly? Just point them in the right direction!" He saw the look Gantz gave him and he swallowed the smile. "I studied the schematics for this area before we left boss." He paused, half turned and pulled forward his right ear to show Gantz that he did not have an implant. "I'm not a plughead!" He glanced at Delgardo. "No offence Sonia." Delgardo self-consciously raised a hand to touch her own implant.

"Point taken, Wildman, but perhaps it's time to relieve Keith?"

Wildman's smile returned, she hadn't referred to him as Singh, he swung round and took command of the controls, tapping Keith's head to wake the sleeping dog. It sat up, stretched and yawned.

Gantz turned to Delgardo. "What's your speciality?" It was a kinder reference to her implant than the derogatory 'plughead' term commonly used.

"Forensics."

"That could prove useful!" Gantz smiled. Goodridge had indeed selected well. "Even if we find it was an accident." Delgardo nodded. The comment from Wildman had touched a nerve. Implants were common enough, in fact it was rare to find anyone without one, but it still made her feel inferior to her two companions and she was desperate to impress Gantz. For her part Gantz sensed Delgardo's unease and dropped the subject.

The smudge on the horizon was beginning to come into focus. Some of the higher peaks in the mountain range could be detected. Greys and a hint of white were added to the palette of greens and browns of the jungle. Gantz was fascinated. For all her life she had lived under clear blue skies which only changed with the coming of the rainy season. She had never seen snow. Of course she had seen holo-tabs of snow on the Great Arkins taken during the early planet survey, but actually seeing it for real on the higher peaks she found strangely exciting. She regretted the fact the mining camp was situated in what was considered merely the foothills of the range closest to them. No chance of flying over the higher peaks and getting a closer look at the snow. The patrol ship started a slow descent and the tree tops could now be seen in detail. After a few minutes they began to thin out, giving way to a tangled mass of smaller trees and areas of dense undergrowth. All the while the mountains loomed larger. The sheer size and extent of the range took her breath away. If these were regarded as foothills she could hardly imagine what the biggest mountains looked like. She realised how small her own personal world on New Eden was compared to the size of the planet. For the first time she noticed the temperature had dropped. It was only a few degrees but it felt much more comfortable and the damp patch in the small of her back, from sweat caused by sitting for far too long in her seat, was drying up. She wondered for how long even the New Brethren could resist moving North from the edge of the Southern deserts. Here New Eden could live up to its name.

They appeared to be descending faster now but Gantz realised it was, in fact, the ground rising. Rolling hills dotted with trees amid a sea of swaying grass were followed by valleys choked with jungle. In one valley she saw the glint of sunlight on water which indicated a river mostly hidden from sight by the vegetation. In the distance the mountains appeared to go on for ever. She never realised just how great the Great Arkin range was. They were now over some of the smaller peaks and Wildman adjusted the flightpath to follow one of the valleys that curved round the base of one of those mountains. A large expanse of jungle came into view, a gap in the row of peaks. From the briefing notes she guessed this was the Perrin Gap and knew the camp site was nearby. As they followed the curve of the valley she could see over Wildman's right shoulder an ugly scar on the hillside to their right. As they got closer she could make out the prefabricated buildings of the camp. They had arrived.

***

The dust kicked up by the patrol ship when landing had alerted the camp of their arrival. Two men had appeared from the office doorway and now stood waiting at the edge of the landing pad. Gantz recognised them from their profile holo-pics. The taller of the two was the site manager, Petre Ull and the shorter one Zon Willard, the site technician. The expression on their faces, although not hostile, was far from welcoming. Further back, standing in the doorway of the accommodation block, were two other figures whom she identified as Chang and one of the young drillers, Will LeBon. Chang stared at them with a blank expression which conveyed nothing at all. LeBon appeared to be peering around Chang as if he was attempting to hide from them. The patrol craft hovered for a moment, repositioned itself so that it was dead centre of the landing pad and then, with a hiss accompanied by a slight jolt, it settled onto the ground.

Gantz put a hand on Wildman's shoulder. "Stay put, don't leave the ship. Once we've checked out the situation you can join us. If anybody approaches the ship or you don't hear from us within half an hour then take off. Report the situation to Inspector Goodridge and follow any instructions he gives you."

"You're making me nervous boss." There was a smile on his face but Gantz sensed the remark wasn't as lighthearted as Wildman made out.

"I'm over cautious Wildman, I get it from my boss." She patted him on the shoulder and clambered out of the doorway closely followed by Delgardo.

Gantz paused to take in the surroundings. The reality was a little different from the holo-site plans she had been studying. Those didn't show the rutted ground and the rubbish strewn around the site. Piles of coiled cable, bits of broken drill heads and mounds of discarded rock and earth. The buildings were streaked with dirt from the last rainy season and the whole site had an air of decay and neglect. The thought of staying here for a couple of days was depressing enough and she wondered how these people could put up with it for months on end. Delgardo obviously felt the same way. "What a shit hole!" She had said it under her breath but Gantz heard it anyway.

They approached the two waiting men and Ull nodded a welcome and looked her up and down. Gantz guessed he regarded her as far too young to be in charge.

"Petre Ull, site manager and this," he gave a nod towards Willard, "is Zon Willard site tech."

"Deputy Gantz and this is Officer Delgardo." She nodded back to them guessing an offer to shake hands would confuse them. It was a form of welcome rarely used outside of the New Brethren, physical contact with strangers was avoided by the general Federation population.. "Flight Officer Singh is sorting out a minor problem with the extra power cells we had to bring. It was a very long trip!"

"The Corporation didn't offer you the use of an ore transport? I doubt if it would have been more comfortable but it would have been a darn sight quicker."

"No they didn't! In fact they were some time informing us of the situation here."

"Tight bastards." Ull nodded in agreement to his own observation. "I wouldn't read anything into the delay, they were probably running the situation by their lawyers. Working out the financial cost of the various options for whatever happened."

"Perhaps you can fill me in on what exactly has happened here?"

Ull looked surprised. "You don't want me to show you to your quarters first? I thought you might want to freshen up after your journey."

"I'd sooner assess the situation so I can report back as soon as possible."

Ull nodded and jerked his head towards the office. "Yeah, sure! We can talk in the office. A bit more comfortable than standing out in this heat." He turned and walked back towards the open door. Gantz and Delgardo followed him inside. Willard hovered in the background unsure of what to do and then decided he would not be needed and sloped off towards the accommodation block. Ull sat behind his desk and offered Gantz the chair opposite. There was only one chair available so Delgardo leant against the wall by the open doorway.

"Can I offer you a drink?" From the unenthusiastic tone, the question was asked out of an automatic politeness. However, Gantz found that her mouth was dry so she accepted the offer. "Coffee, fruit juice or water? The coffee's synthetic."

"Water will be fine."

Ull looked across at Delgardo but did not bother to repeat the question, just waited for her reply.

"Water will be fine for me too."

Ull manipulated the desk controls and two tumblers of water and a plastic container of steaming coffee rose from the drinks dispenser built into the desk. Ull placed the waters in front of Gantz, took a sip from the coffee and pulled a face. "Tastes like shit but gives you a good buzz." He sat back in his chair and took another sip of his coffee.

"You were going to brief me on what exactly has happened to Laslo Ginthem."

Ull sighed. He looked bored. "Well there's not much to tell. Ginthem arrived here the day before yesterday. The transport arrived about 13.00, 13.15, something like that. I showed him to his quarters and then went back to the transport to help Chang unload the supplies. Once the transport had taken off I left Chang to put the supplies away and I went back to the office." He paused to take another sip from his drink. "I expected Ginthem to take a shower and then get some sleep. Corporation transports aren't the most comfortable forms of transport."

"He didn't do that?"

"Couldn't have been more than a couple of hours and he appeared in here. Like you, he was eager to get started." His tone suggested the last comment was not meant as a compliment. "I repeated everything I'd already told Central. He then outlined what he wanted to do and what he wanted to see."

As Ull showed no intention of volunteering any more information Gantz prompted him. "And exactly what was that?"

"The usual stuff these people do! He wanted access to the production figures, analysis reports and check the samples."

"Surely most of those would be available to him without travelling here in person."

"Yeah of course. The only things he would need to come here for were the samples which are held on site."

"Unless he wanted to compare the records." The comment from Delgardo drew an unfriendly glance from Ull. He shifted in this chair to avoid having to look at her.

"You were saying," prompted Gantz.

"Samples are kept on site but the analysis reports and production figures are downloaded to Central." There was a hesitation. He glanced nervously at Delgardo. She was staring intently at him. He took a sip of coffee before continuing. "Look, there have been cases where records have been..." He hesitated again. "Nothing like that has happened here but there have been cases of fake records being sent to Central. Part of Ginthem's job would have been to review computer security and check nothing like that has occurred."

"Not unheard of boss. The site manager skims a little off the figures and sells the extra." Delgardo had done her homework for this case.

"There's nothing like that going on here. I'd be a complete idiot to report falling production rates like we've had while selling off the ore. It would guarantee that Central would send somebody like Ginthem."

"The jury's out on your idiocy level, we don't know enough about you yet." Ull shot Delgardo a black look for that remark.

"That's enough Delgardo." Gantz decided to rein in the enthusiasm of her assistant for the moment. "Please go on Ull."

"I'm trying to be helpful here and I get unfounded accusations directed at me as soon as you people land."

"Nobody's accused you of anything Petre. Officer Delgardo was just confirming your explanation was correct. We're here to ascertain what happened to Laslo Ginthem. Your help and cooperation is appreciated. Please do continue."

Ull wasn't fooled by that explanation and took an instant dislike to Delgardo. However, for some reason he felt the Gantz woman was more reasonable and he knew being obstructive or antagonising either of them would not work to his advantage. He needed to be helpful and not raise any suspicions that Ginthem's disappearance had anything to do with him or his crew.

"We worked on a schedule together. He would start off in the office checking the samples and records. That would have kept him busy for the rest of the day. Yesterday he was supposed to interview the support staff. That's me, Willard and Chang and then meet up with one of the drilling crews, Edmurson and Albright, to inspect the current shaft and drill head operation."

"You said he was supposed to?"

"Look, when he arrived he seemed like your standard mine inspector, dull and routine fixated. Spent time in here on his own, ate by himself and went to bed early that night. As far as I know he never spoke to anyone other than me and did nothing but work, eat and sleep."

"I sense a 'but' coming Petre."

Ull gave an audible sigh. "The next morning he starts to behave strangely. He cancels the support staff meetings and refuses to tell me why, or what he intends to do instead. I can't explain it but he was just odd! He avoided the other members of the crew and they claimed he was giving them strange looks."

"Are you claiming he had some mental aberration during the night?"

Ull sighed again and fidgeted in his chair. "I don't know it could be..." Ull fell silent.

"It could be?" prompted Gantz.

"I've seen something like it before but it doesn't make sense." Ull appeared reluctant to elaborate further.

"Just tell me." Gantz's voice was calm but firm.

"It was years ago. I was deputy manager on a big desert site. Production started to drop so they sent in an inspector who went through all the routine stuff. A nice guy and he got on really well with all the drill teams. He joined in the social activities and joined us in trips to New Eden to hit a few of the clubs and bars. A couple of days before he was due to make his final report he withdrew into his room after work. He avoided people he had been laughing and drinking with a few days earlier. It was really weird!" Ull paused to take another sip of his coffee. "The crew had been together for four years on that site and..." He struggled with attempting to explain it to Gantz. "Have you ever worked with a group of people and it all just gels? It seemed so right and it was more like one big family?" Gantz nodded her understanding. She had never really experienced it with work colleagues but it struck a cord with her. It was how she would have described her relationship with Nemi. She waited patiently for Ull to continue. "He suddenly realised what would happen when he submitted his report. Production levels were not going to improve so his recommendation was to close the site. The crew would be split up and reassigned. The family would be broken up and dispersed and he would be partly responsible. He felt like shit and couldn't look them in the face. Wasn't his fault but he still felt bad about it."

"And you think Laslo Ginthem was going through the same thing?" Delgardo had interjected and her scepticism was plain to hear from the tone of her voice.

Ull gave her another nasty look and addressed his reply to Gantz. "I just said it reminded me of the situation but, as I said!" He raised his voice and cast another black look at Delgardo before returning his attention to Gantz. "It doesn't make sense! Ginthem didn't know anybody here and he hadn't really even started the review so couldn't have made any decision yet."

"Production figures were down and had been for some time."

"We explained all that to control. It was a blip, that's all!"

"Perhaps Ginthem didn't see it that way."

Ull took a large gulp of coffee and wiped his mouth on the back of his hand. He appeared agitated and the faint darkening of his shirt at the armpits gave away the fact he was starting to sweat.

"Something you're not telling us?" Delgardo was stopped from further comment by the raised hand of Gantz.

"Why don't you think Ginthem would close the site?" Gantz's voice conveyed sympathy and concern with Ull's predicament.

"Look..." Ull shifted uncomfortably in his chair. He should have been straight with them right from the beginning like he had been with Ginthem. It was a stupid move because it now looked bad. "Look, production was low because the ore deposit is played out. We knew that as the tour was coming to an end. Then we found traces of Zelman crystal." Ull paused and stared at Gantz as if to push the point home. "You've heard of Zelman crystal?"

"Something used in hyper-drives?"

"An integral part! If it wasn't for Zelman crystals we'd still be travelling at light speeds. If there is one thing that has made it possible for us to spread across the galaxy it's Zelman crystal!"

"So it's valuable!"

"Unbelievably so! We only found trace but there had to be more of if. We had a crew meeting and decided to sign on for another tour in the hope we found it before they closed down the site." He paused to considered his next words. "We claimed that we'd opened up a new shaft because we found another seam of ore. We thought that would give us time to find the crystals."

He glanced up at Gantz and then to Delgardo. "We weren't attempting to hide the crystal find, just buy us some time. We're a grade A crew and are on a high percentage for bonuses. If we had informed control of the possible crystal deposit there was every chance the bastards would have refused to agree to another tour and replaced us with a junior crew who would be on a lower percentage bonus. You live for a find like this! Just a small deposit would set us up for life."

"And did you find this deposit?"

"The early shift did the day before Ginthem arrived."

"Convenient!"

Ull flashed Delgardo another unfriendly scowl. "Does she have to be here?"

"Yes she does, and she makes a valid point."

"I logged in the original trace when we first found it, way before Ginthem arrived and my report was sent in as soon as we confirmed the main deposit. The evening before he arrived."

"Still very convenient timing." Delgardo kept up the pressure on Ull.

"I don't care what you think Delgardo!" Ull then addressed Gantz. "I've told you all this because the sample and report were recorded and Ginthem inspected the records so he knew the potential of the site. So why act as if he was going to close it down. That's what I meant by saying his behaviour made no sense." Ull sighed and ran a hand through his close cropped hair.

"We'll check the records."

"You do that, we've nothing to hide. You can see whatever you like and question whoever you want. Look if the corporation knew what I've just told you without getting clearance from them I'd lose my job. It's commercial in confidence but I've told you and the crew and I will cooperate fully with your investigation." He paused. He baulked at asking these people for a favour but it had to be done. "My only request is that you allow us to continue drilling. We'll stop if it's absolutely vital to your investigation but please understand what the bonus means to my crew."

Gantz considered the request for a few moments. "At the moment I have no objections to that."

"Thank you Deputy Gantz." Ull sounded relieved. It was not exactly routine but Gantz reasoned the crew would be more cooperative in answering her questions. The fate of their bonus was in her hands. She also reasoned the Corporation would be a lot more cooperative.

"Can you run through what happened yesterday for me?"

"Not much more to tell. Just before he retired for the night Ginthem informed me the interviews with the support workers were cancelled. I asked if anything was wrong or if I could arrange anything else for the morning and he said no. Claimed he wanted to just have a look round the site. I didn't argue, it was up to him how he ran the inspection. I didn't see him again. Boni Chang, Milton Dang and Will LeBon saw him at breakfast yesterday morning. That was about 04.30, 04.45. He eat on his own and left the accommodation block before Milton and Will. They were on the early shift which starts at 05.00." Ull finished off the dregs of his coffee and ordered another. "You want another drink?" Gantz and Delgardo both declined. "Zon Willard saw him about 11.00 hanging around the storage bins and again later, he couldn't recall the time but guesses it was about 14.00. Could have been a bit earlier, could have been a bit later. He was passing the accommodation block heading towards the path which leads down to the mine. That was the last time anyone saw him. The schedule we had arranged had him meeting Sligo Edmurson and Dirk Albright for the start of the late shift at 16.00. He hadn't turned up by 16.30 so Sligo reported the fact to me. I got the whole crew together, found out what I've just told you and organised a search. Sligo, Dirk, Zon and I searched the mine tunnels, Milton and Will searched where the jungle starts at the bottom of the path which leads to the mine. They started there and moved West until they reached the river. Mol and Sara, after helping Chang search the camp, searched the jungle East until they reached the Perrin Gap. No sign of him, he'd just disappeared!"

"What's the shift pattern like?"

Ull thought it was a strange question for Gantz to ask but did not not query her reason. "This planet has a thirty hour day. We work three shifts, early from 5.00 to 13.00, late from 16.00 to 24.00 and the night shift from 26.00 to 3.00. At the moment Milton and Will are on early, Sligo and Dirk on late and Mol and Sara are on nights. The gaps in between are used for any drill head maintenance which is the responsibility of Zon, or me as backup."

"Where were you when you spoke on the first evening?"

"In the Rec, the part of the accommodation block used for dining and recreational purposes."

"Who else was there?"

"I can't really remember. I was just passing through on the way to my room." He paused and scratched his head. "Boni must have been there to serve the night shift breakfast. Mol and Sara were up waiting for their shift to start. Sligo and Dirk were still on shift I think. Milton was there but I can't remember seeing Will or Zon. To be honest I didn't pay that much attention, Ginthem waved me over as soon as I came in so I went straight across to him."

"Thank you Petre you've been most helpful. I need to report in and then get our gear from the ship. If you could then show us to our quarters and perhaps let us have access to the site database and samples store?'

"Anything to help sort out this. I'll get Chang to rustle up some food for you?"

"That would be appreciated. Thank you." Gantz rose from her chair and indicated to Delgardo that she should follow her. Once outside she spoke freely.

"I want you to research any cases of theft from mining sites. The Corporation might not be too eager to help so if you run into any delaying tactics or downright refusal suggest we might have to close down the operation here. If Ull has reported a deposit of Zelman crystals to them a loss of production might encourage them to be cooperative."

"You think these crystal things might have something to do with Ginthem's disappearance and the delay in reporting it to us?"

"A friend once told me about a remark he made during another investigation. He's a fan of crime fiction and said the most common motives for murder were sex and credits. I think we would be foolish to dismiss the crystals!"

"Do you think the crystals are the reason the corporation were tracking Ginthem's chip so closely?"

"If this is a big deposit then they stand to make big profits and experience tells me that is the time the Corporations get paranoid."

"Puts a big question mark over the murder option though. If this bonus they could earn is worth so much why would any of them risk having the mine closed down?"

"Good point Sonia. I get the feeling we might be here some time before we get to the bottom of this."

CHAPTER FOUR

After they had unpacked the overnight bags from the ship
Wildman secured the ship by switching on the scanning
monitor. Anyone who came within ten metres of the craft would
set off alarms on the ship and on the CommsLink of all three
police officers. Ull was waiting by the accommodation block
door to show them to their quarters, which were the three at the
far end of the corridor from the recreational and dining areas.
As suspected they were basic and cramped. A single bed with a
cabinet at the foot of it made up one side of the room. On the
other side was a desk and chair and a door that led to showering
and toilet facilities. The decor was light grey and dark grey, a
favourite colour-coordinated scheme for the Corporations. At
the end of the room, opposite the entrance door, and again in the
shower room was a plasiglass window set high in the wall
which let some natural light in. Gantz suspected the
accommodation in an Isolation Facility was of a better standard.
She unpacked her bag and shared her clothing between the
hangers and drawers in the cabinet. Sitting on the edge of the
bed she studied her temporary home and decided it was
depressing. No doubt the other rooms were brightened up by
personal items and holo-pics of their nearest and dearest. It then
struck Gantz that she had no personal items to adorn the room.
Her apartment was just as bare and impersonal as this
makeshift accommodation. She had no holo-pics, she found them
rather tacky anyway, and even if she did possess them whose

69

images would they hold? She had no family, they were all dead! The other Gnostics were in constant touch, except now where distance had robbed her of the link. She gave an involuntary shiver at the thought. So far she had been distracted by the case and her interaction with Delgardo and Wildman but now, trapped in this room, cut off from them she realised how terribly alone she felt. For the first time in her life she understood the loneliness which pure humans lived with their whole lives. How could they bare it? Her only pure human friends were her colleagues, Goodridge and Tolman and she now pitied them for their sad condition. Of course there was Nemi. Gantz sighed as she realised how much she missed Nemi. It prompted her to open her CommsLink but even then she first reported in to Goodridge. It gave her spirits a boost when the hologram image of his head appeared.

"Good to see you Kanah, I've been worried. What's the situation there?"

"Strange sir, but I don't consider we're in any danger. I've only spoken to the site manager so far but get the impression I'm not getting the whole story from him, although he has provided some additional information which the Corporation neglected to tell us. It appears they have found a deposit of Zelman crystals. Highly valuable so I would suspect their reticence is down to the usual 'commercial confidentiality' line."

"Wouldn't be the first time a Corporation has kept the Federation in the dark! Well if vast amounts of credits are involved I assume you have your first possible motive."

"Except it brought us in and could actually close the mine down. I think their might be more to this so I'll keep digging. Could you run background checks on all the crew plus Ginthem? I'd like to know if there has been any previous contact between any of them."

"Anything else?"

"Not at the moment, I need to interview everyone first and get a better feel of what's been going on."

"Okay, but don't hesitate to call me. How are you finding Officer Delgardo?"

"So far she appears to be very capable if a little abrasive. She adopts an aggressive interviewing technique. I assume you did your own research on her and didn't just pick the first available body!"

"I admit I took a passing interest in her record. I'm not sending one of my best officers off without the best back-up I can find. I thought you might compliment each other. I think there used to be a term 'an iron fist inside a velvet glove' which I thought very appropriate."

There was a muffled voice in the background and it appeared to say 'carrot and stick'. "Is that Tolman I can hear?"

"Yes he popped in for some last minute tasks before he sets off for Port Nilmon, or so he claims. I'm sure it's sheer coincidence he appeared about the time we expected to hear from you."

Tolman's familiar voice came in clear and loud. "I came in to reassure the boss. I told him you'd be fine but he worries about you. He even referred to you as his finest officer when we all know you're his second finest officer."

Gantz smiled. "You being his finest!"

"How perceptive of you! Glad to see you've still got that special ability of yours even if you're thousands of kilometres away. I'd better be getting off or I'll miss my connection. Good luck up there and we'll arrange a date for that meal when you get back."

"We'll compare case notes then. I'm sure your admin work will be riveting!"

There was a muffled reply which sounded like 'that hurt Kanah Gantz' as Tolman presumably left the office.

"Kanah." There was a long and deliberate pause before Goodridge continued. "How are you feeling?"

Gantz mirrored the hesitation. She knew Goodridge had picked up on Tolman's remark about her abilities and he knew enough about Gnostics to be aware of their limitations. "I'm fine sir."

"Kanah this is me you're talking to. How are you coping?"

There was an even longer silence as she remembered the depressive emptiness she felt the first time she entered her bedroom. "I'm not really on my own sir. There's Delgardo and the pilot we have is an entertainment in his own right. Nine crew members and lots to keep me occupied. I'll be fine, honestly." Goodridge said nothing and studied her face but found no clue there as to her true feelings. Gnostics had no use for reading body language so never developed any themselves beyond learning the basics of smiling and frowning. When they wanted to, like now, they could present a blank canvas devoid of emotion. Goodridge was forced to accept her words at face value, he would never presume to second guess a Gnostic, especially one he considered to be a friend. Gantz guessed as much so attempted to reassure him. "I'll not pretend it's easy sir but I can cope with it."

Her honesty eased his worries and he forced a smile. "You've been through a lot Kanah and I didn't get a psychological evaluation after the trauma you suffered at Midwich."

"There was..."

"I know there was no point in a psychological evaluation for you but it would have reassured me! I have no point of reference with you and I'm concerned that losing your mental link is just adding extra pressure onto you."

"I can cope sir."

"Keep me in the loop and do not hesitate to contact me if this all proves too much for you."

"I promise you'll be the first to know if I suffer any form of stress."

Goodridge nodded. "Fair enough Kanah. Good luck and I'll get straight on to that research."

"Thank you sir, good night." Gantz closed down the CommsLink.

The conversation had taken longer than she anticipated. She glanced at the time and saw it was almost 22.00. The call to Nemi would have to wait. She needed to eat and get to work on the site records before she could relax for the night. She also needed to get out of the room and back in the company of other people.

Delgardo and Wildman were already seated at a table by the time she entered the dining area. All the other tables were empty and she realised by this time Edmurson and Albright would be on shift and the others were probably sleeping or relaxing in their rooms. The latter, no doubt, to avoid the three police officers. She nodded a hello and sat down. Almost immediately the squat figure of Boniface Chang appeared from the kitchen area carrying three plates on a tray. He kept his head down and his gaze fixed on the floor to avoid eye contact. He almost threw the plates onto the table, such was his eagerness to retreat back into the safety of his kitchen.

"He did it!" said a grinning Wildman.

"You know this for a fact?" asked Delgardo.

"I was attempting to engage him in polite conversation before you came in. The man almost shit himself. Guilt written all over his face. If I'd asked him there and then he would have given me a full confession."

"To what?" enquired Gantz.

"Anything you like! Some people are so stupid they fail to even qualify for a plug, no offence Sonia, but our mister Boniface Chang would fail a test if it only comprised writing down his own name." Wildman paused to look down and inspect his plate. "Mind you it looks like he can cook a bit, unless this is a decanted tray meal." He took a forkful of food from his plate, sniffed it and then tasted it. "That's too good to be tray food. At least we won't starve to death. I'd even give this to Keith!" he scraped up another forkful. "So what are your first impressions Boss? Accident, suicide or murder?" He gave a dramatic emphasis on the last word.

"Too early to say."

"Any prime suspects?"

"Too early to say."

"Any motive?" That question was accompanied by a smile. "Don't tell me, too early to say! Don't think it might have anything to do with the Zelman crystals?"

"How do you know about that?"

"I talk to people Boss. Mostly rubbish but they tend to talk back. I have a knack of getting people to tell me things they wouldn't tell their own mothers. I could have been a barman except they're rarer than pilots nowadays."

Gantz studied Wildman. He appeared intelligent but displayed a personality which bordered on the professional idiot. She couldn't work out if this was his natural personality or a carefully projected persona. She could usually tell but Wildman sent out a lot of conflicting messages and there was no way she was going to take a peep inside that particular head. Her training since childhood deterred her from going down that path. It was too risky and she knew the price paid by Gnostics and members of the Collective who took that risk

"You're only the transport pilot Wildman so not part of this investigation. You understand that?" Wildman nodded. "Of

74

course you'll have a lot of spare time on your hands and I can't order you not to talk to people."

"Yes Boss." Wildman looked suitably chastised. Delgardo's eyes flashed from Gantz to Wildman and back again and wondered if she actually correctly understood the exchange.

***

Delgardo was tired. She had been up early for her normal shift and had been patrolling in the Federal quarter for over three hours before she got the call and the secondment with Gantz. It was then a rushed trip home to pack an over-night bag before catching a ground transport back to police headquarters. That was followed by almost a seven hour flight in a cramped police patrol craft. The only break she had was a quick shower and a hurried meal. The first thing she had done when they entered the privacy of Ull's office was to put in a call to the Mining Corporation control centre and requested any information on any thefts or criminal action at any mining camp. As Gantz had predicted, there was some prevarication at first but they did download some information in the end. She also double checked police records for confirmation. Now she was checking the site database records. Gantz had been inspecting the sample store and was now working on her CommsLink.

When she finished with the site records Delgardo gave a sigh of relief and checked the time. It was 24.30 and she had been awake for over nineteen hours. She stood up and stretched her body. There was a small cubicle at the back of the office with a toilet and wash basin and she half stumbled into there to fill the basin so she could splash cold water onto her face. It helped, but not much. She returned to the office.

Gantz glanced up and saw the exhaustion etched into her partners face. "Sorry Sonia I lost track of the time. A quick briefing and we'll call it a day. What did you come up with?"

Delgardo checked her notes on her CommsLink. "Theft from mining sites isn't as common as you would have thought, at least not by the crews. The most common loss is through piracy, either gangs hi-jacking transport ships or attacking the mine and making off with the storage bins, but even those cases are rare. Big rewards but big risks as well! Usually limited to asteroid belt mining though. No recorded incidents of that happening to a planet based operation. Skimming used to be a problem but now there are so many security measures in place it's a rare occurrence nowadays. No drill head can be started up unless it's coupled properly with the ore sledge." She slowed down as she read the technical detail. Even if she did not understand it she wanted to ensure she had read it properly. "That's a sealed pipe which goes directly to the storage bins. I guess it's that huge half buried pipe which runs round the edge of the camp. You can't uncouple the pipe at the storage end unless you've closed down the drill head."

"What about when you uncouple to fill up the next storage bin? Can you get access to the contents of the full bin?"

Delgardo referred back to her notes. "The access opening automatically closes when you uncouple the pipe. All the bins come with an inspection tube for taking samples but from the schematics they sent me it hardly looks big enough to get your arm in. I suppose they could be stealing the crystals a handful at a time, if they're that valuable! Still seems unlikely as you couldn't empty a bin that way. I did ask the question but they said the bins are sealed at a fixed weight. Any discrepancies when the transport arrives to pick up the bin would be noticed. The crew would lose their bonus, which in the case of Zelman crystals would be more valuable than what they could steal."

"I guess they could substitute what they had removed."

"Bins are inspected when they are emptied so that would be noticed. It has been done and the members of the crew responsible had arranged for a private transport to pick them up just after the adulterated shipment had left. Nobody ever got away with it scot free though. The Corporation usually tracks them down. I checked that fact with our records."

"Well I doubt if the Corporation would admit to the ones that got away but even so, as a motive for Ginthem's disappearance it looks unlikely."

"But not impossible! I should imagine everyone who attempts to rob the Corporation thinks they've come up with a foolproof method. If these crystals are as valuable as they say then it would be a spur to some very creative thinking."

As a New Brethren, Gantz could have queried that particular assertion but she knew enough about 'Fedups' and their obsession with credits to realise what Delgardo said made sense. "We keep that particular option open then! Any luck with the site records?"

"Ull was telling the truth! The report went in just when he said it did and reported the crystal deposit. I ran a diagnostic check on the system and there's no evidence of the records being tampered with but Central confirmed his story, albeit reluctantly. I thought that was odd but then again Corporations can be paranoid at times. Just in case they have an accomplice at Central I asked for more in-depth records on the crew just in case we had a hidden computer genius but the only one who might be capable of it is Willard. It's a big might though!"

"Well the samples check out as well. A trace sample of Zelman crystal logged when Ull said it was. The only thing missing is a sample from the main deposit but as they've only been mining it for two days and they've had the Ginthem problem to deal with, that fact on it's own is hardly significant. Ull was evasive at the interview but I think he knew keeping quiet about the crystal find until the crew had signed on for a new term would make us suspicious. I got the impression he was avoiding the truth rather than attempting to lie to us."

"Good enough for me boss!"

Gantz smiled at the remark. "Then you have more faith in my abilities than I have! I said I got the impression he was avoiding the truth, not that I was sure what the truth actually was. I think he was telling the truth about the crystals but..."

"There's something he's not telling us?"

"We'll see what develops. I also got a more detailed profile of Laslo Ginthem from my boss, Goodridge. He'd already set that in motion before we left. Steady job, good marriage sorry, social partnership, not on medication, took the occasional drink of alcohol but not to excess, no gambling addition, no sex addition and his psychological evaluations have been passed without comment, and before you say anything I know with Corporation tests that's not something you can rely on. Goodridge interviewed his boss, his work colleagues, his family and friends. We get a picture of mister average or as Petre Ull said, dull and routine fixated. Nothing to suggest suicide."

"Unless he suddenly realised he was dull and routine fixated!"

Gantz gave a wry smile at Delgardo's droll remark. "On that note I think we'll call it a day. Tomorrow we'll interview the crew. I've created a time line from what Ull told us, I'll download it to you. I want to place everybody on it. Who was where and when."

"I wondered why you asked Ull about the shift pattens."

"Well, what I didn't tell Ull, or you for that matter, is that the Corporation was monitoring Ginthem's chip. It ceased to function at 14.18 precisely, which places his death in-between shifts, so if he was murdered we have nine suspects!"

"Why would the Corporation begin monitoring his chip?"

"Good question and the obvious answer would that it's something to do with the Zelman crystals given their delay in reporting his disappearance and their reluctance to even confirm the find."

"Would that mean while Ginthem was sent out here originally because of the falling production figures the crystal find upped the importance of his visit. They might even have been monitoring the entire crew but whether they were also tracking their movements we'll never know. That sort of monitoring requires a court order which the Corporation wouldn't get so if they were doing it they'll never admit it."

"So the crystals are looking like a possible motive?"

"If I was a betting woman, which I'm not, that's where my credits would be at the moment. But we still don't know if any of the crew has had previous dealings with Ginthem. Goodridge will chase up that for us.""

"Should we..."

Gantz cut Delgardo short. "We should get some sleep. We start again in the morning and follow procedures. I want to confirm we have a crime first, any motive can wait."

✦✦✦

Gantz and Delgardo paused as they stepped out of the office. There was a light breeze blowing from the East, coming in from the Perrin Gap, and it had a cooling effect on their bodies. Delgardo had found the small office stifling, it had begun to give her a headache so she said goodnight to Gantz explaining she would take advantage of the fresh air to clear her head. Gantz nodded but also lingered, looking up and marvelling at the star filled night sky. With hardly any light pollution it was an even more magnificent spectacle than the view back in the city. She would have stayed longer but fatigue had set in and she realised that physically she still had not fully recovered from the ordeal of her last case. There was no way she was fit enough to cope with such long working days. She left Delgardo and dragged her weary body to the depressing little bedroom. She was too tired to call Nemi now so she stripped off her clothes and flopped down on the bed. Luckily she had no time to dwell on her loneliness for within minutes she was fast asleep.

The site was almost in total darkness. One dim emergency light over the door to the office and another over the door to the accommodation block. The edge of the plateau on which the site stood merged into the gloom. It would have been easy for Laslo Ginthem to wander over the edge if he had taken a late night stroll but he had vanished in broad daylight. Delgardo guessed that late night strolls to take the air did not feature in the daily routine of a mining crew. She checked the time. It was 25.40. If she had not been so tired she would have stayed longer. After one last glance at the night sky she headed for the accommodation block. As she entered she could hear Chang clattering about in the kitchen, no doubt preparing breakfast for the night shift. She wondered when he ever got to sleep. The sound of muffled voices drifted in from the corridor leading to the bedrooms and she realised it must be the night shift coming out of their rooms. As she turned the corner the voices abruptly stopped. Mol Gurd and Sara Rolm stood in the doorway of one of the bedrooms. They looked surprised to see Delgardo and she noticed Mol had quickly pulled his arm back, releasing the grip he had on Sara's arm. The girl quickly squeezed past Mol and headed towards the dining room.

"Always have to wake her up!" He flashed Delgardo an unpleasant smile. "She can't get used to these night shifts." He wiped his nose on the back of his shirt cuff. "Better get a bite of breakfast." He lowered his eyes and shuffled off down the corridor. Delgardo watched him go. She took an instant dislike to Mol and made a mental note to mention the incident to Gantz in the morning. Whatever was going on between the two miners it was going to make them late for their shift.

CHAPTER FIVE

Wildman had spent the previous evening, after eating with Gantz and Delgardo, reading in the recreational area. He was alone, except for Keith who lay at his feet with her head resting on her front paws. Chang had disappeared as soon as he had served their meal, no doubt to get some sleep before the late shift ended and came in for dinner and the night shift rose for breakfast. Wildman spent no more than an hour reading and thinking before he retired for the night. He slept well and was up again at 03.00. He hung his uniform in the wash closet and dressed in civilian clothing; a baggy pair of fading red trousers, a multi-coloured shirt, which was as baggy as the trousers were, a black waistcoat and a beaded pill-box hat he had picked up in a New Brethren market. His attire was not at all fashionable by Federation or even New Brethren standards but it was very Wildman. He had then taken Keith out for exercise.

They did a tour of the site, or rather Keith did a tour of the site smells. She ran from one part of the camp to another and from object to object sniffing at anything she found. Wildman wondered just who or what she could scent. She was a cross between two Old Earth breeds which had migrated with man from their original home and although she came across other dogs in the city there were unlikely to be have been any out this far North. There was a small dog-like creature native to New Eden but they tended to inhabit the open scrubland to the South. Wildman had scant knowledge of the local flora and fauna so had no idea what would venture into the camp at night from the jungle. One thing for sure from Keith's behaviour, it was nothing that frightened her! Wildman wandered down the path towards the mine entrance and the jungle but stopped short and gave Keith a good workout getting her to run up and down the sloping path, creating a small dust storm as she did so. When she was breathing heavily he judged she had had enough exercise and walked her back to the accommodation block for breakfast.

He glanced around as he made his way to the kitchen serving area. Milton Dang and Will LeBon were seated at one of the dining tables half way through their breakfast. In the recreational area Mol Gurd, a hairy beast of a man with greasy, straggly hair, which had obviously been dyed, and salt and pepper beard stubble, sat nursing a drink and watching a holo-tab on his CommsLink. Even from this distance Wildman could identify it as a pornographic one. He briefly looked up for long enough to give Wildman an unfriendly stare and then returned his attention to the holo-tab. On the other side of the recreational area, about as far away as she could be from Mol, sat Sara Rolm. Not a pretty girl by any stretch of the imagination but her strong features were not unattractive. At first glance, with her muscular build, short hair and work clothes, she could pass for a man. She was studying something on her CommsLink. She looked up when Wildman entered and gave him a brief, forced, smile before returning to her CommsLink. Wildman thought he detected a sadness in her eyes.

Wildman paused and studied the wall in the recreational area. A large area was given over to a display of wood carvings. Not an unusual form of decoration for New Brethren areas but not the sort of art work he would normally associate with a mining camp. Then he remembered reading that Sligo

Edmurson's hobby was wood carving. He smiled as he wondered if Gantz and Delgardo would be surprised to learn he had actually read the briefing and the crew profiles. No doubt they would have said it was out of character for him. People always judged his character from his appearance and he encouraged such lazy assertions; it worked to his advantage.

He peered at each carving in turn. Most were life studies of the other crew members but a few landscape scenes were also included. They were crude in their execution but had a primitive charm and displayed a surprising level of skill. The one depicting Mol Gurd was particularly eye-catching. Edmurson had captured the man's, almost feral, look remarkably well. Wildman took a step back, compared all the portraits and concluded he had been rather unfair in his initial assessment of Edmurson's talent. He could now see they were quite subtle caricatures. The one of Boniface Chang had a surprised and almost childlike expression, there was an air of superiority about the Milton Dang portrait and a confused and angry look to Dirk Albright. There was a sadness conveyed in the Sara Rolm image and was it shyness depicted in the Will LeBon one or perhaps something else he could not quite grasp? 'These give a better feel of the crew than the profile notes' thought Wildman. The Zon Willard and Petre Ull ones defeated him for they looked like ordinary studies. Noticeable by its crudeness compared to the others was the one of the artist.

The landscapes were of less interest. One Wildman guessed to be a view of the Perrin Gap, one appeared to be of a small jungle settlement, one seemed familiar but he could not recall where it was and the last one depicting a waterfall he did not recognise at all. No doubt places Edmurson had seen during his various tours of duty. The rumble from his stomach reminded Wildman he had come in for breakfast so he moved on to the kitchen counter and studied the selections displayed on the food dispenser. It was the standard limited selection of tray meals. He knew by experience the breakfast choices were by far the worse.

"You want me to cook you breakfast?"

Wildman looked up and saw that Chang had quietly appeared from the kitchen. His stance was almost stooped, the head slightly bowed and his shoulders rounded. It gave the impression he was deliberately attempting to make himself smaller so as not to be noticed. The tone of his question was almost apologetic.

"Will it be as good as last nights meal?" The flicker of a nervous smile was all Wildman got in reply. Chang could not bring himself to actually say yes. "Then one Boniface Chang special it is!" The request was accompanied by a big smile but Chang could not summon up the courage to return it and scampered back into the kitchen as if the friendly gesture had actually frightened him. Wildman sauntered over to the table occupied by Dang and LeBon.

"Mind if I join you?" Dang gave a disinterested shrug of the shoulders but then gestured with his hand towards the empty chair opposite him. LeBon looked up and nodded but his eyes told a different story. "I'm Al Wildman Singh by the way and this is Keith. You can call me Wildman and you can call the dog Keith." He gestured towards the dog and then sat down and leaned forward to inspect Dang's plate. He took a sniff to take in the aroma. "Is that the Chang special by any chance?"

Dang grunted. "The man's an idiot but he can cook. It's why Ull keeps him on. Not a bloody lot of use for anything else but saves us from living on tray meals from a bloody vending machine for six months. Believe me after even two months of that we'd be hungrily eyeing up your dog." Dang nodded towards Keith as if Wildman might be confused about which dog he was referring to. Keith had clambered up on the chair next to Wildman and appeared to be waiting patiently for her breakfast. "He normally eat up the table?"

"He's a she and she has impeccable table manners."

Dang looked him up and down while using his tongue to dislodge a sliver of meat from his teeth. "You've got a bitch called Keith! I guess I can see where the nickname came from."

"It's actually my middle name, not a nickname. My father led a very boring existence and wanted his son to be more adventurous, more of a free spirit. He thought the name might encourage me!"

"Crazy runs in the family then!"

"I see it more as unorthodox."

"So how did you end up in the police?" The tone of Dang's voice implied he did not think much of Wildman's career choice.

"Always had the urge to fly and travel. They sort of naturally went together so I trained to be a pilot. Started on shuttles. Man was that boring! Space port to orbiting station or ship and then back again." He looked wishfully off into the middle distance. "At least I got to press buttons in whose days!" He suddenly returned from is private reverie. "Moved on to internal flights. On a good day it was from A to B and back again. At least with that job I took in some scenery but not really what I had in mind to satisfy my wander lust. I moved on to transporters. Planet to planet and back again. Didn't think that one out properly, I hadn't really moved on from shuttles had I?" Dang's nod was accompanied by the hint of a smile. "Tried the Colonial Corps and for a while that was great but they didn't like my, let's say individualistic approach to flying. They said I had a problem with authority. Total bullshit; authority had a problem with me! We parted company, I wish I could say amicably but I'd be misleading you, so I headed here to a frontier planet and a New Brethren one at that! The police had a terrible shortage of pilots and very old equipment where I could press buttons again and I was a pilot so we came to a compromise. They agreed to employ me and I agreed to fly for them."

"Despite your less than amicable split with the Colonials?"

"As I said the police were desperately short of pilots."

Dang smiled and looked Wildman up and down. "I must admit you don't look much like the police!"

Wildman glanced down at his attire. "No I don't suppose I do! Well I consider myself off duty now and I will be until they want me to fly back. I don't think they intended to include me in the policey bit."

Dang chuckled at that remark. "What are the other two like? Both woman aren't they?"

"Not so sure about Delagrdo." Wildman gave Dang a wink. "But she seems okay. The other one, Gantz, is in charge. Doesn't come over as one of life's fun people. New Brethren and you know what they're like!"

"So what are they up to?" Dang made the remark sound as casual as he could.

"I think they were pawing over the site records last night. They just sod off after dinner and leave me on my own."

At that point Chang arrived with Wildman's breakfast and a bowl for Keith. "I hope dog like." Chang averted his eyes and quickly moved away.

"Keith says thank you," called out Wildman at the retreating back of Chang and then surveyed his plate. "The man's done us proud!" He picked up the knife and fork and attacked his breakfast with relish. Keith gave the contents of her bowl a good sniff and then started to bolt the food down.

"That dog's got a bloody good appetite!" commented Dang as he watched the dog demolish its breakfast in double quick time. "So what do your colleagues plan to do today?"

Wildman finished his mouthful before replying. "Haven't the faintest idea, not that well up on police procedure. If you wanted me to hazard a guess..." Rather than finish the sentence he continued eating.

"Okay!' said Dang, beginning to get a feel for Wildman's character. "We want you to guess."

Wildman paused to emit a loud burp. "Sorry about that. I told you Keith was the one with impeccable table manners." He paused again as if trying to remember what he was going to say. "Ah yes, my guess! We'll I should imagine they'll question everyone next to work out where everyone was when Ginthem went walk-about. If they find out where he was they might work out where he went. They need to find a body."

"You think he's dead then?"

"Oh they know he's dead. No chip signal!" Wildman continued to eat his breakfast. LeBon nudged Dang which made the man check the time.

"Well we need to start our shift. Perhaps we'll catch up later."

"I'm not going anywhere, so more than likely." Wildman gave them a quick smile and farewell nod before returning his attention to his breakfast.

Dang strode towards the door with LeBon trailing in his wake. "Bit of a weird one!" remarked LeBon.

"Might be worthwhile cultivating a friendship though, could be useful!" LeBon nodded but did not really understand what Dang meant. He would just do what he always did and follow the senior driller's lead. Not wise to contradict your lead driller if you wanted to progress in the job and many lead drillers took full advantage of that fact.

Wildman finished his breakfast, removed his hat and extracted a dog biscuit from the inside head band. He held out his hand and Keith shook it with her paw. Wildman stroked the dog's head and tossed the biscuit into the air. Keith expertly caught it in mid air and crunched away at it. "Good girl," whispered Wildman and gave her a pat on the head before rising from his chair and casually strolling across towards where Rolm sat. Keith padded along behind him.

"Mind if I join you?"

Sara looked up in surprise and flashed a nervous glance towards where Gurd sat before replying. "I'm busy with something."

"I promise not to disturb you but it's either you or the ugly looking bastard over there." He gave a sideways nod towards Gurd.

Rolm gave another nervous glance towards Gurd before she just shrugged her shoulders and carried on working on her CommsLink. Wildman sat down next to her but not too closely and made a fuss of Keith. They sat in silence while Wildman ignored the unfriendly stares from Gurd. This continued until Gantz and Delgardo entered the block.

While Gantz perused the food dispenser menu Delgardo cast her eye around the room. She spotted Gurd first but he ignored her. Then she saw Wildman sitting next to Rolm. "Wildman's here boss, shall I call him over?"

"No leave him alone, he's not part of this investigation." Gantz made her selection of a cereal and a fruit juice and waited for it to be served up.

"But he's one of us boss." Delgardo was surprised by Gantz's attitude.

"He's a pilot who happens to work for the police. Goodridge picked you for this case so you I trust. Wildman just happened to be available so he's not part of this investigation." Gantz turned to look at Delgardo. "We don't discuss the case with him, understood?" Delgardo nodded and made her selection from the menu just as Chang emerged from the kitchen. When he saw they had used the food dispenser he retreated to the kitchen with a worried expression on his face.

"Boy is that guy weird or what!"

"You should have got Chang to make you breakfast, it was even better than the meal he prepared last night." The cheerful advice was called out by Wildman.

"Ignore him," whispered Gantz. Reluctantly Delgardo obeyed, picked up her plate and followed Gantz to a table.

"Stuck up cows," murmured Wildman under his breath. Rolm sneaked a look at him and then returned to her CommsLink.

Delgardo pushed the pieces of meat and cheese around the plate with her fork. "Should have listened to Wildman!' Gantz ignored the remark and took a spoonful of cereal. After her second spoonful she dropped the spoon into the bowl and pushed it away.

"Perhaps we should have." Delgardo stifled a giggle and Gantz smiled. "Alright we take menu recommendations from him but we still keep him out of the case." Delgardo nodded her agreement.

The door slide open and Petre Ull walked in. He ignored the food dispenser and called out for Chang. The man popped his head out of the kitchen and nodded to Ull. The site manager gave a quick look round the room and headed towards Gantz and Delgardo.

"Can I join you?" He hesitated until Gantz nodded and then sat down opposite her and next to Delgardo. He had no intention of having his breakfast spoilt by having to look at her. "I've taken the liberty of putting a schedule together for interviewing the crew." He waved on his CommsLink and opened up a file containing a list of names each with a time against them. Delgardo shifted to the side of the table so she could also read the image as it floated in front of Gantz. "If it meets your approval I'll download it to you and the crew."

Gantz ran her eyes down the list. "You're not on it."

"I thought you already did me yesterday but if you need to speak to me again I can make myself available at any time today."

"Thank you, this will do nicely. If we need to speak again I'll let you know.""

Ull hesitated. He expected more. He was not quite sure what else but certainly some negative comment. To fill the void he continued talking to explain his list selection. "Milton and Will have only just started their shift and Mol and Sara will have dinner soon and then probably sleep and Sligo and Dirk are sleeping at the moment so I put Zon and Boni down first. I thought by the time you finish with Zon, Boni will have finished cooking for Mol and Sara. I should warn you that Boni... Well he doesn't cope with people very well."

"We read up the crew profiles Petre."

"Yes, of course you did. You should be able to catch Milton and Will when they come off shift and Sligo and Dirk are always up early so they would be available before their shift starts if you're ready for them."

"Thank you Petre, you've obviously taken care over the arrangements. Please download it to me when you're ready. I assume we can use your office for the interviews?"

"Sure, no problem. I can work just as well in here. Only pressing job today is taking an inventory of the stores and constructing an order for new supplies." He paused again. "So I'll be right here if you do need to speak to me."

"Thanks again."

Ull was saved from more stilted conversation by the arrival of Chang with his breakfast.

***

It was again stuffy in the office. The day was hotting up already and it promised to reach temperatures more like they were used to in the South. Delgardo fiddled with the air conditioning unit but could not manage to get more than a trickle of cool air. She resorted to kicking the unit but it did not improve the situation. 'Typical shit Corporation maintenance' she thought. 'Say what you like about the New Brethren but their companies provide good customer service.' She gave the unit one last frustrated kick before abandoning her efforts. Ull had cleared his desk and so she set out her CommsLink ready to record all the interviews. She had brought a spare chair from the accommodation block not wishing to spend the rest of the day propping up the wall.

"How do you want to handle this boss?"

"You can take the lead but tone down the aggression. There's a time and place for that and we need to get these people talking."

"You think I went over the top with Ull?"

"You must have noticed he's avoided eye contact with you since our first meeting." Delgardo nodded. "Try a different approach. This time we want information from them so we need their cooperation. I'll interrupt as necessary and signal to you if I want you to stop. At the moment we want to find out what happened to Ginthem and find his body. Only then will we be sure if we're dealing with an accident, a suicide or a murder."

"You haven't ruled out the suicide option then?"

"I think it most unlikely considering the report from Goodridge but until one of the other options firm up I'm loathe to discount it."

"Ready to start then?"

Gantz nodded. "Call in the first one."

Zon Willard took his time responding to Delgardo's call. He mumbled something which might have been an apology for his lateness and then took his seat across the desk from them. Delgardo waved the CommsLink on and recorded the date, time and the full names of those present.

"We just need you to run through your routine for the day Laslo Ginthem disappeared."

Willard glanced from Delgardo to Gantz and then back again. "Is that it?" He obviously expected a series of questions and looked a little confused.

"We need to ascertain where everybody was during the course of the day and who saw Ginthem and when. Armed with that information we might be able to determine where he went or at least in what direction. We need your movements in the camp, the times and who and what you saw. Give as much detail as you can remember, no matter how trivial you might think it."

"Right!" Willard paused to collect his thoughts. "I got up about 6.00, washed and dressed and sorted out my washing cabinet. I CommsLinked my parents and then went to have breakfast. I must have got there just before 08.00. I passed Mol in the corridor as he was heading for his room. Sara was still in the recreational area. Boni was in the kitchen and I ordered breakfast. I must have stayed there until just before 10.00 talking to Sara. She went off to her room and I went to the office for a routine maintenance check on the purification plant. I don't think that took me more than an hour so I must have left at 11.00, perhaps a little before and went back to the Rec. As I was going in I glanced back and saw Ginthem standing by the storage bins."

"What was he doing?"

"Nothing! He was just standing there staring at them."

"How long was he there for?"

"I don't know. He wasn't there when I came out of the office, at least I didn't notice him, and I just glanced back and saw him before I entered the accommodation block."

"There was nobody else around?"

"No."

"Okay, please continue."

"Well I stayed in the Rec watching a holo-tab. I got up to get a cup of coffee and happened to see Ginthem walking past. He was heading towards the path down to the jungle. I'm not sure of the time but the tab I was watching had just ended so I guess it must have been about 14.00. It could have been a little earlier but it could have been later. Sorry I can't be more precise but," he paused, "time keeping isn't really my thing. I took the coffee back to my room and stayed there until Ull called a meeting. That was about 16.30. Everyone was already there by the time I turned up."

"Despite the fact you were one of the nearest to the meeting point?"

"Lousy time keeping! If you check my record you'll see I've had numerous fines for being late. I get easy distracted on trivial things and before I know it I'm late. Petre Ull keeps lecturing me about it."

"And after the meeting?"

"Ull split us up into search groups. I paired up with Ull, Sligo and Dirk were together and we all searched the mine. Kept calling out but there was no reply. We did all the tunnels but no trace of him. Mol and Sara helped Boni search the camp and then the jungle from the path East until they got to the Gap. Milton and Will from the path West until the river. There was no sign of him so we informed central sometime after 20.00 or it might have been a bit earlier. As I said, time keeping isn't my thing! I stayed in the Rec chatting to Ull until Sligo and Dirk finished their shift and then did a routine maintenance check on the drill head before the night shift started. I then went to bed."

"You didn't speak to Ginthem at all?"

"Might have said hi when he arrived but the interview with him for yesterday morning was cancelled and so I never got the chance."

"How did he seem to you?"

Willard shrugged his shoulders. "Alright I guess."

"Nothing about his attitude?"

Willard scratched behind the ear which hid his implant. "Only seen a few inspectors but this one wasn't as chatty as some. Other than that, well I don't know, as I said I never spoke to him."

"Was anybody else in the recreational area when you were speaking to Ull?"

"Just us, oh and Milton and Will but they didn't stay for long before heading back to their rooms. Mol and Sara went back to bed as soon as the search finished. Sligo and Dirk left to do what was left of their shift and didn't come into the Rec again until their shift ended which was my cue to go to the drill head."

"Well thanks Zon I think that will be all." Delgardo glanced at Gantz and she nodded to confirm. "Perhaps if you could send in Chang?"

"Sure!" Willard looked relieved and got up and left the office immediately.

"Get anything from that?" Delgardo twisted round in her chair to face Gantz.

"Unfortunately it doesn't exclude anyone if this turns out to be murder. Gurd and Rolm could have been asleep but either one could have slipped out after Willard left the recreation area. If of course he left to go to his room rather than follow Ginthem. We have no idea where Edmurson and Albright were and if

Dang and LeBon had finished their shift why didn't Willard see them enter the block? Still, only the first interview, the picture should become clearer."

"No," Delgardo paused to select the right phrase. "No feelings?"

"I get the feeling he wasn't telling us everything but no more than that. I told you I can't read minds!"

"It's just enhanced intuition!" There was a hint of sarcasm in Delgardo's remark, which Gantz chose to ignore.

"Just intuition Sonia."

There was a timid knock on the office door and then it slid open to reveal a nervous looking Boniface Chang. He appeared to have physically shrunk since breakfast. Hovering in the open doorway until Delgardo gestured for him to enter, he did so with obvious reluctance. He sat down and continuously rubbed his hands together as they lay in his lap as he waited for them to start. His eyes continuously darted from side to side as if he expected some hidden assailant to suddenly spring forth and attack him. Delgardo waved on the CommsLink and recorded the date, time and participants.

"We just need you to run through your routine for the day Laslo Ginthem disappeared."

"I didn't do anything!" Chang vigorously shook his head.

"We're not accusing you of anything Boniface. We just need to know what you did, where you were and who you saw. It will help us find out what happened." Delgardo made every effort to soften the tone of her voice but Chang just looked more alarmed. Chang's eyes displayed a desperation as he glanced from Delgardo to Gantz and then back again. "There's no need to worry Boniface we just need some information." Unfortunately even Delgardo could hear the urgency slip into her attempt to reassure him. She felt Gantz touch her leg and she sat back in her chair.

"Hello Boni. Do you know who we are?" Gantz's voice was soft and smoothing. Chang nodded. "We're the two people who were silly enough to have breakfast from the food dispenser this morning." Chang nodded again. "We'll not make that mistake again." The remark appeared to calm Chang a little. "Do you remember yesterday morning?" Gantz paused but Chang just stared at her with a vacant expression on his face. "What time did you get up yesterday?"

"Early."

Delgardo bit her lip. If Gantz had not been there she would have slapped Chang by now. Nobody was this dumb, it surely had to be an act.

"Do you remember the exact time?" Gantz leaned forward and rested her arms on the edge of the desk.

"03.00. Meal for night shift and breakfast for early."

"And who did you see?"

"Gurd and Sara first then the man and then Dang and Will."

"By the man, do mean the inspector Laslo Ginthem?" Chang nodded. "What time did you see Gurd and Rolm?"

"Early." Gantz leaned forward a little more and Chang looked up and they made eye contact. Delgardo noticed that Chang's eyes now remained fixed on Gantz. "Straight from shift. They ate and then went to room. Then man come." Then an unusual thing happened; Chang almost smiled. "He used food dispenser like you."

"Silly man!" remarked Gantz.

Chang nodded. "Then Dang and Will come in for breakfast. They eat and go on shift."

"What did you do then?"

"Clear kitchen and go to room."

"When did you come out again?"

Chang struggled with that question for a moment. "End of early shift meal and breakfast for late shift."

"You're doing very well Boni. Now try to remember what happened then."

"Dang and Will eat then go. Sligo and Albright then eat and then they go."

"Did you see Zon Willard?" Chang shook his head. "What happened next?"

"Petre call me and say meeting for everyone. He says the man is missing and we must find him. I help Gurd and Sara look here and then go to room."

"What did you do next?"

"Late shift meal and night shift breakfast."

"Did you do anything else?" Gantz wanted to confirm that Chang appeared to either cook, clear up or sit in his room.

"I did nothing!"

Gantz decided that they had come full circle. Any attempt to find out what Change did with his time would seen as an accusation that he had something to do with Ginthem's disappearance. Gantz also felt a little guilty of taking advantage of the poor man.

"Thank you Boni. You have been very helpful. You can go now." Chang did not need to be told twice and he scurried from the office. Gantz sat back in her chair.

Delgardo looked at Gantz. "I take it you got more out of that than I did?"

Gantz ignored the inference. "Not a particularly reliable witness but we found out a little about the relationships between crew members."

"We did?"

"Petre, Sligo, Will, Sara and Dang, Gurd and Albright! Not sure about Willard because he didn't mention him by name."

"He doesn't like Dang, Gurd or Albright! What do you make of the fact that Laslo Ginthem was 'the man'?"

"About as much as you do at the moment!"

***

The next two names on their list were Milton Dang and Will LeBon but the first two interviews were over quicker than anticipated so they decided to get Mol Gurd and Sara Rolm in before they retired to their rooms to sleep. They called in Mol Gurd first. Although he had time to change he arrived at the office with his work clothes on. He made a point of patting himself down before he took his seat. Clouds of dust billowed from his body and he looked rather pleased with himself when Delgardo started to cough as she inhaled some of the particles. He folded his arms across his chest and sat facing them with his legs wide open. A smirk played across his mouth. Gantz ordered a water for Delgardo and one for herself. She stared at Gurd but did not offer him a drink. Delgardo thanked Gantz and took a sip from her drink. She then went through the formalities with the CommsLink recorder.

"We just need you to run through your routine for the day Laslo Ginthem disappeared."

"Am I under arrest for something?"

"No, you're helping us with our enquiries."

"I don't have to answer your questions then." The smirk on his face got bigger. For the second time that day Delgardo had to restrain herself from slapping someone.

"And I don't have to keep this mine open!" It was Gantz who spoke but her tone was calm and matter of fact. "So if you're not going to answer Officer Delgardo's questions nicely you can go and tell Ull you just got the mine closed." Gantz moved forward towards the CommsLink. "Interview with Mol Gurd ends." She looked up at Gurd. "You still here?"

The smirk slowly dissolved on Gurd's face. "You can't do that!" He sounded far from convinced by his own words.

"Watch me!" She called Ull on her CommsLink. "Ah Petre, bad news I'm afraid..."

"Hold on, hold on. I didn't say I wouldn't answer your questions."

"It's alright Petre Mol Gurd has decided to be cooperative but you can tell the rest of your crew this arsehole came bloody close to having your operation closed down." She paused. "Yes I'll tell him that. Bye." She waved off her CommsLink. "He said you were a dick! I found it difficult to disagree. Now you'll say sorry to Officer Delgardo for being disrespectful and answer her questions." Delgardo struggled to keep a straight face. She was surprised at the language Gantz had used but even more amazed at the deadpan delivery. She watched the vain on the side of Gurd's head pulsate. He was obviously struggling to control his temper.

Gurd's top lip curled up. He blew his nose into his fingers, wiped them on his jacket sleeve and waited for Delgardo to start to questioning. There was a long silence as Delgardo hesitated, unsure of whether she should restart the questing. That hesitation unsettled Gurd, it suddenly occurred to him that these women actually expected him to apologise. 'Fuck that!' he thought. He would stare them out.

Delgardo decided she would play Gurd the same way as Gantz had. "Don't make the mistake of thinking you can intimidate me as easily as you do Rolm." Delgardo sat back in her chair, folded her arms across her chest and sat with her legs wide open. "And don't make the mistake of thinking my boss makes idle threats."

Gurd glanced at Gantz. For some reason he knew the bitch wasn't bluffing, she would close them down. He also knew if he lost the crew a bonus on Zelman crystals some of them would not think twice about exacting punishment. None of the others would attempt to stop them. In fact they would cheer them on. He licked his lips. "I'm sorry." He almost choked on the words and promised he would get the bitch back for this.

Delgardo went through the motions of starting the interview again. "We just need you to run through your routine for the day Laslo Ginthem disappeared." She got immense pleasure from the discomfort etched in Gurd's face. Whatever Gantz had it was a lot more than intuition.

"We finished the shift just before 3.00. We went and had breakfast and then went straight to our rooms. Never left until Ull woke us up and said this Ginthem had gone missing. Me and Rolm with that idiot Chang searched the camp and then we had to go and search the jungle up to the Gap. Couldn't find him and so went back to bed. Stayed in my room until our shift came round again."

"Did you see anybody else at breakfast that day?"

"No. Well, of course the idiot was there."

Delgardo thought about pulling him up about the offending comments regarding Chang but decided not to sink to his level and try to be professional. "When did you turn up for the meeting?"

"When Ull called us."

"What time and who was already there? And try and answer without trying to be smart. You're not suited for it." Her professionalism lost out to her dislike for the man sitting in front of her.

Gurd flashed her a nasty look. "About 15.30, 16.00? Could have been later. Ull was already there with Edmurson and Albright. Dang came out of his room the same time as us and LeBon followed us in. That lazy sod Willard was the last one to arrive as usual."

"Did Willard come from his room?"

Gurd scratched his head. "Might have done. I didn't notice, I was half asleep."

"What about Chang?"

"He was there. I remember him staring at Ull with his mouth open when Ull asked him if he'd seen Ginthem. I guess he was in the kitchen."

"You never saw or spoke to Ginthem that day?"

"No."

"What about the day he arrived?"

"Saw him in the Rec room on the night he arrived but never spoke to him. Is that it?"

Delgardo glanced at Gantz. "For now Gurd but I have a feeling we'll chat again." Gurd snorted in response to Gantz's comment, got up and left the office knocking his chair over on the way out. It was obvious he did it intentionally.

"Nasty piece of work. If Ginthem was murdered I really hope he did it and he resists arrest."

"Try not to let him get under your skin, it'll cloud your judgement." Delgardo nodded her understanding. Gantz tapped her on the arm to get her attention. "What was the bit about intimidating Rolm?"

"Oh yes! Sorry, I forgot to mention it. As I was going to my room last night I bumped into Gurd and Rolm outside one of the rooms. He was gripping her arm. Let go as soon as he saw me but something was going on there."

"How did Rolm look?"

"Frightened. Got away from him as soon as he let go of her arm." Gantz nodded. "Any ideas boss?"

Gantz played back part of the interview recording. 'Dang came out of his room the same time as us and LeBon followed us in.'

"Could be I read too much into it but 'the same time as us' could suggest they either both came out of their respective rooms at the same time or were coming out of the same room."

"Rolm! With Gurd!" Delgardo pulled a face. "Surely not!"

Gantz checked the site records. "Gurd has the room directly opposite Rolm's." Gantz pulled up the schematics for the accommodation block. "Which room were they outside?" Delgardo pointed out the room position. "Sara Rolm's!"

"Gurd claimed he was waking her up." Delgardo felt unease with the idea of Gurd and Rolm together. "But..." Delgardo shook her head. "I can't believe it."

"I might be wrong but one thing I'm a hundred percent sure of; Gurd is nervous about something. If the relationship isn't based on mutual consent that could explain it. Either way we need to keep an eye on him. I doubt if Mol Gurd is the type of man to be bullied by two women."

There was a knock on the office door. Delgardo waved it open to reveal Sara Rolm. She hovered outside until Delgardo gestured for her to enter. Despite her muscular build she appeared as timid as Chang had been. Delgardo hoped this wasn't another interview she would have to hand over to Gantz. She got up and went round the desk to pick up the chair and then offered Rolm a seat. Returning to her side of the desk she waved on the CommsLink and repeated the standard ritual.

"We just need you to run through your routine for the day Laslo Ginthem disappeared."

"I came back from the night shift with Mol and after having a drink, ate a meal. I then went to my room."

"With Mol?" Gantz glanced at Delgardo for she thought the question, although it could haven been taken either way, was far from being subtle.

There was a hint of panic behind Rolm's eyes for a second and then she recovered. "I think he went back to his room a few minutes later, at least I heard somebody in the corridor and assumed it was Mol. I didn't leave until Petre's call woke me up to tell me to attend the meeting. He said that Laslo was missing and we split up in teams to search for him. I was with Mol and Boni and we searched the camp. Then Mol and I went down to the end of the path to the mine and searched the jungle from there across to the Perrin Gap."

"Was there any trace of Laslo?"

Rolm shook her head. "But Dang said they found what looked like a trail which led to the river."

Delgardo glanced at Gantz but her face showed no indication of what she thought about that statement. "You saw nobody else between your shifts?" Rolm shook her head again. "Can you remember the order in which the crew arrived at the meeting?"

"Erm..." Rolm's brow knotted in concentration. "Petre, Sligo and Albright were already there. As I came out of my room I saw Dang come out of his. When I got to the end of the corridor Will had caught me up and we entered the Rec at the same time. Zon was last as usual."

"And Gurd?"

"He came out with me, at the same time." Delgardo thought the last part of that sentence was hastily added.

"You never saw or spoke to Ginthem that day?"

"No."

"What about the day he arrived?"

Rolm hesitated. "I saw him in the Rec room on the night he arrived but never spoke to him."

Delgardo turned towards Gantz to see if she wanted to ask any questions. Her reply was a slight shake of the head. Delgardo turned back to Rolm and thanked her for her cooperation. She then quickly added. "If you need to talk to us about anything which concerns you please don't hesitate to contact us. And I do mean anything." Rolm looked taken aback at the remark and in her confusion both nodded and shook her head before she got up and walked out of the office giving a silent sigh of relief.

Delgardo had left the door open and watched the back of the retreating Rolm. Even at this distance she could see the hunched shoulders drop as her body relaxed.

"She's not telling us everything either!" Delgardo spoke without ever taking her eyes off Rolm.

"And you didn't need to be a Gnostic to know that!"

Delgardo smiled. "Are you trying to tell me that's the secret of your ability? You just observe body language?"

"And I listen. Petre, Mol, Boni, Sligo, Zon and Will. Then we have Dang and Albright."

"You think she's lying about Mol being a friend?"

'More like she is used to calling him by his first name, he is her work partner after all."

"I think it strange anyone could regard Gurd as a friend."

"I think it stranger that although she never talked to Ginthem she referred to him as Laslo!"

***

They had some time to wait until Dang and LeBon came off shift so Gantz set up the time-line holograph on her CommsLink. They started with a three dimensional model of the camp, overlaid that with the time-line and then fed in the approximate timings and positions within the camp of the people they had so far interviewed. At the moment it was very limited but they played it through and watched the images representing the various characters move through the model of the camp. It failed to tell them anything they did not already know. They then decided to stretch their legs and take a stroll around the site. Their first port of call, being the closest, were the storage bins. There were six of them by the landing pad, three metre square with only one visible access point. The nearest one to the office was the one connected to the pipe which contained the ore sledge. It emitted a low hum and when Delgardo touched it she could feel a slight vibration. As an experiment she attempted to uncouple the pipe from the storage bin but was unsuccessful.

"I didn't think it was going to be that easy!" Delgardo walked round the bin to inspect it further. The bin looked incredibly heavy and Delgardo reasoned that to get it onto any ship which was not an ore transporter would require specialised equipment. "They would have to have outside help if any of the crew wanted to run off with this."

"Perhaps they have but that wouldn't explain Laslo Ginthem's disappearance."

"Perhaps he somehow discovered their plans?" Delgardo sounded far from convinced by her own suggestion.

"I think we should concentrate on finding out what happened to him first before we start to speculate on why it happened."

Delgardo nodded her agreement and they wandered off towards the path at the far end of the camp. They paused and looked down it towards the mine entrance on the right and the start of the jungle to the left. Gantz continued walking down the path and Delgardo followed. At the bottom they stopped and looked around. To their right the ore sledge pipe ran down the path by the hillside and disappeared into the mine entrance. The dim floor lights made little impression on the darkness and the silent blackness was far from inviting. To the left a tangled mass of vegetation filled the gap between them and the rising side of the next hill. It was dotted with the odd thin-trunked tree which bent over as if the effort of standing upright was too much for it. At places the vegetation had been cut back forming little pathways. Most stopped after a few metres but two carried on, one to the West and one to the East.

"You take the East and I'll take the West. Time yourself and when you reach the end, time yourself on the way back as well. Then time the walk up the path back to the accommodation unit. I'll do the same. We can then feed the information into the time-line model."

"Do you want me to do the mine as well?"

Gantz shook her head. "We'll do that with Ull after we finish the interviews. The Corporation won't like us going in there unaccompanied and I won't like us going in there without a map. No idea how extensive the tunnel system is!"

"Okay boss." Delgardo set off on the Eastern path.

Gantz called after her. "We'll meet back in the office." Delgardo did not look back but raised a hand in acknowledgement. The path meandered a little which suggested that whoever made it was making some effort to cover more ground. At places the path widened where the searchers had apparently paused and trodden down more undergrowth. Delgardo scanned the area but concluded that Laslo Ginthem could have been lying a few metres away and she would have stood no chance of spotting him. As the valley began to widen she noticed the path took a more direct route. She reasoned the searchers must have come to the same conclusion about finding Ginthem as she had and given up. They were told to search as far as the Perrin Gap and it appeared that less than half way there they had decided reaching the Gap was good enough. A limited search like that had little chance of succeeding but at least they could report back they had tried. Delgardo was hot and sweaty by the time she finally reached the Gap. She stopped her timer and stared out at a vast sea of snake grass which writhed in the breeze. Coming in on the patrol ship they had been too high and traveling too fast to recognise the grass. She had seen the ingenious plant in small cultivated patches grown in New Brethren settlements but never such a vast amount of wild plants. The New Brethren ate it but it had been banned from commercial production by the Federation due to unfortunate side affects in people on some medication. She could not remember exactly what those side effects were but they must have been quite serious for it to be banned. A shame really, for she had tried it once and it had been fairly tasty. It was also very nutritious and incredibly hardy, it could resist the encroachment of the jungle so needed very little attention. It made the New Brethren, rare medication users, almost self sufficient for food in snake grass alone. After one last look across the Gap she restarted her timer and set off back towards the camp site.

Gantz had set off and kept a keen eye on the pathway. The vegetation had been well cut back so the going was relatively easy. The path went in a straight line, deviating only go round the odd outcrop of rock or patch of razor wood, so-called for the vicious thorns it bore. The undergrowth was now shoulder high and trees were becoming a more regular feature. She paused more than once to crouch down and inspect the path and it only confirmed her first thoughts.

She heard the river before she actually saw it, and even then she only saw it at the last minute. The path and the vegetation abruptly stopped and Gantz found herself standing on the edge of a small ravine. Almost ten metres below where she stood, in a ravine cut through the soil by its swirling waters, was the river. Not wide but fast flowing. If somebody had fallen or been thrown down there the current would have whisked them away down river. Gantz paused the timer she had running and stood gazing down at the white foaming water for some time, thinking. Despite her doubts she had to admit it was possible for Laslo Ginthem to have fallen into the river. She had been studying the path but if her mind had been on something else she could easily have stumbled over the edge. But why would Ginthem have walked this way? Just to think over something which was troubling him? Gantz would take a walk to aid her thinking process so perhaps he did the same. It was no good speculating, what she needed was more information. She restarted her timer and headed back to the office for the next interview.

Milton Dang entered the office with a swagger and greeted them with a 'Good morning Officers' before taking his place in the chair provided. Unlike Mol Gurd, Dang had showered and changed for the meeting. Gantz could detect the fragrance of his after shave from where she was sitting. Delgardo went through the usual procedure and opened with her standard question.

Dang shifted in this chair to find a more comfortable position, half closed his eyes and stared into the distance to indicate he was attempting to recall every detail. "I was late getting up, had rather too many Parado pills the night before. Will was already in the dinning area and Laslo Ginthem was at another table eating something from the food dispenser. I asked Boni to whip me up one of his specials. Ginthem left just as I was getting my breakfast. He never said anything, just got up and left. Will and me then went on shift." Dang paused and then said. "I don't know if this is significant, probably not, but I had to power down the drill at one stage and I thought I heard a noise from one of the tunnels. Bit difficult to judge exactly which tunnel because you get a lot of echo down there. I asked Will if he had heard it but he said no. He said he thought I was hearing things but I swear I did hear something."

"Could you describe the sound?"

Dang's expression was one of feigned anguish. "I only caught it as the drill-head powered down." He sighed as if he was struggling to find the right words to describe the sound. "It could have been a voice shouting out or something hitting the walls or floor of the tunnel." He shrugged his shoulders. "To be honest it could even have been the noise of the drill head powering down echoing back from the tunnels. Sorry I couldn't be of more help."

"Don't worry. Even the smallest thing, no matter how trivial, could be of help. What time did you her this sound?"

"It must have been near the end of shift. I doubt if we continued to work for more than ten, twenty minutes before we decided to call it a day. We came off shift early. We were having trouble with the power coupling and I planned to report it to Zon for him to look at. We came back to the dinning area but there was no sign of Boni, perhaps we were too early for him, so we grabbed a tray meal from the food dispenser and took it back to our rooms. I was still tired from the previous night so dropped off to sleep straight away. Petre Ull's call woke me up and he said a crew meeting had been called. He told us that Ginthem had gone missing and organised search parties. Me and Will searched along the edge of the jungle for signs that anybody had gone that way and thought we found a path. We cut back the undergrowth as we went to speed up our progress, didn't know if the poor man was hurt out there and unable to communicate! We called out at regular intervals but never got a reply. We went as far as the river's edge. It's a bit of a drop and not very easy to spot. We reckoned if Laslo had gone that way he could have wandered over the edge if he wasn't paying enough attention. Of course the path we were following wasn't all that clear and it might have been made by an animal. However, if I were asked to hazard a guess I would say that's what happened to him. The river flows fairly strongly and he could have been taken down river. Likely to have been washed up at the Van Doren Flats about twenty kilometres down river.

It's a wide bend and the river is quite shallow there so the chances are a body could get washed up in the shallows."

"No attempt was made to widen the search to incorporate this area?"

Dang allowed himself a small smile in response to that question. "No easy way for us to get there. Hacking through twenty Ks of jungle on a hunch isn't going to go down well with the Corporation and being a mining camp they don't supply us with boats!"

"Of course! When you went to the meeting can you remember who was there and when they arrived?"

"Petre, Sligo and Dirk were already there. They were the ones who reported Laslo missing. As I came out of my room I almost bumped into Mol and Sara. I saw Will come out of his room so he followed us in. Zon brought up the rear as usual."

"And Chang?"

"He was there because Petre talked to him first but I didn't notice him before that. Boni has the ability to merge into the background I'm afraid.

"Please carry on."

"Well that's it really! After the search we came back to camp, Petre contacted control and me and Will went to bed."

"You never saw or spoke to Ginthem that day?"

"Except for seeing him at breakfast, no!"

"What about the day he arrived?"

"I saw him briefly as we came off shift and had a quick chat. Seemed friendly enough, which is why I was a little surprised when he ignored us the following morning." Dang shrugged. "Perhaps he had things on his mind, who knows with people eh?"

"What did you talk about?"

"General stuff. You know when you first meet somebody. How was his trip up here, what the latest news was from New Eden, any juicy gossip from control?"

"Did you see or speak to him again later?" Delgardo, having found somebody who had actually spoken to Ginthem, was eager to to see if his attitude had changed.

"I saw him later when I came into the Rec but he was chatting to Sara before she went on shift. When she left with Mol Laslo went to his room. Last I saw of him." Dang gave a questioning look at the two police officers. "Anything else you need to know?"

Delgardo glanced at Gantz for confirmation before thanking Dang for his cooperation. The man gave them a smile before leaving.

"Helpful! Complete opposite of Gurd. Interesting that he claims Rolm was chatting to Ginthem."

"Yes." For a positive comment Gantz's reply sounded very noncommittal. Delgardo had the urge to question Gantz but the arrival of LeBon in the office doorway forced her to put the idea on hold. She offered LeBon a seat, went through the usual routine and opened with her standard question.

"I got up about 03.00, got ready and went for breakfast. Boni was there and Ginthem was just getting his breakfast. Milton was late getting up, had rather too many Parado pills the night before apparently. Ginthem left just as Milton was getting his breakfast. He never said anything, just got up and left. We then went on shift." LeBon appeared remarkably shy for a miner. He half mumbled his sentences and avoided eye contact. He was in stark contrast to Milton Dang and the comparison was also true for looks. His eyes were slightly bulbous in appearance, his nose a little on the large size, with thin lips and virtually no chin. The poor youngster was also suffering from a severe case of acne.

"Anything happen while you were on shift?"

LeBon thought about that for some time before answering. "Only that Milton thought he heard somebody in one of the tunnels. I never heard anything."

"I'm surprised you could hear anything with a drill-head running." It was Gantz who interrupted.

LeBon seemed to be confused over the question and he frowned. Then his face lit up. "Milton powered down the drill-head, he said there was trouble with the power coupling." He nodded to himself, gave a small smile and returned his attention to the office floor.

"What happened when you came off shift?" Delgardo gave him a prompt to put an end to the embarrassingly long silence.

"We came off shift early. We came back to the dining area but there was no sign of Boni, perhaps we were too early for him, so we grabbed a tray meal from the food dispenser and took it back to our rooms. Petre Ull's call woke me up and he said a crew meeting had been called. He told us Ginthem had gone missing and organised search parties. Milton and me searched along the edge of the jungle. We went as far as the river's edge. It's a bit of a drop and not easy to spot. We reckoned if he had gone that way he could have wandered over the edge if he wasn't paying enough attention."

"When you went to the meeting can you remember who was there and when they arrived?"

"Petre, Sligo and Dirk were already there. I came out of my room and was behind Milton, Mol and Sara. Zon arrived after everybody else."

"And Chang?"

LeBon looked confused again. "He was there."

"When did he arrive?"

"I think he was there all the time."

" Please carry on."

"After the search we came back to camp, Petre Ull contacted control and Milton and me went back to our rooms."

"You never saw or spoke to Ginthem that day other than at breakfast?"

"No."

"What about the day he arrived?"

"He was in the Rec room when we came off shift and Milton talked to him. Milton talks to everybody. I was playing a holo-game."

"What about later that day?"

"I saw him later but he was chatting to Sara before she went on shift. When she left with Mol he went to his room."

"Any idea what Sara was talking about?"

"Couldn't hear. I was watching Mol."

"Why was that?"

"He was playing a holo-game as well, the one where you're an interceptor pilot and are blasting the aliens. You know the one?" Suddenly LeBon was animated. Delgardo had stumbled upon something he was interested in.

"Beltas III!"

"Yeah, awesome game!"

"I prefer Battlestar; Ground Zero! All that flying makes me airsick."

LeBon laughed and he was transformed as his features softened, even the acne did not look so bad. "Perhaps that was the problem with Mol! I never thought of that. Thought him being distracted by Sara was what put him off. Kept crashing or getting well blasted by the aliens. Never seen him play so bad!"

"Why was Sara distracting him?" The question wiped the smile off LeBon's face and he became sullen and stared at the floor again. Delgardo repeated the question. "Why do you think Sara was distracting Mol?"

LeBon rubbed his nose and shifted uncomfortably in his chair. "It was near shift time. Perhaps he was worried they'd be late."

"But he was playing Beltas III! Don't see how he could be that worried about time. How was she distracting him?"

"He kept looking over so wasn't paying enough attention to the game. It's a hard game, you have to concentrate." He glanced up in the hope he had turned the conversation back to the game. The look on Delgardo's face disabused him of the idea.

"Why would Mol keep looking at Sara?" LeBon shrugged his shoulders and stared even harder at the floor. "Are you afraid of Mol Will?"

"No!" An awkward silence filled the room. Delgardo resisted the temptation to break it and was finally rewarded. "He's alright but sometimes..." LeBon fidgeted again. "He's alright if you keep your nose out of his business."

"And what business is that?" LeBon reverted to shrugging his shoulders. The awkward silence returned. Delgardo glanced at Gantz who gave a small shake of her head. Delgardo assumed it was a sign for her to drop the subject but could not resist one more question.

"Is Sara afraid of Mol?"

"No!" The look in his eyes gave that lie away.

***

They realised they had now been awake for nine hours and had not eaten since breakfast. The air conditioning unit in the office was still limping along like an old man taking his last breath so they took the opportunity to return to the relative coolness of the dining area to grab a bite to eat before they interviewed Edmurson and Albright. This time they waited patiently by the food dispenser until Chang appeared. When he did and saw who was waiting a look which could only be described as sheer horror gripped him. He visibly shrunk in front of them.

"You want me?" There was desperation in his voice. It was obvious he wanted the answer to be no.

"Only to cook lunch." Delgardo smiled in the hope this would reassure him. Instead he looked suspicious.

"It's lunch time, we're hungry and we're not making the same mistake as this morning." Gantz's comment appeared to settle his nerves a little and he nodded. They ordered from his specials screen, a fresh fish dish for Delgardo and stuffed vine leaves for Gantz. Then, much to Chang's surprise and relief, they went and sat a a table without any further interrogation.

"It wouldn't take much to get a confession out of him." Delgardo nodded in the direction of Chang as he retreated into the kitchen.

"A confession to what though?"

"Anything we cared to suggest!"

Gantz smiled. "Has it ever occurred to you he has carefully constructed a persona which makes you disregard him as a suspect? He's more like a shadow than a real person. How many people actually noticed when he arrived at the search meeting? Could remember seeing him anywhere else but here? If you don't see him he must be in the kitchen. I bet if you asked them which room he occupies they would struggle to answer."

Delgardo eyed Gantz warily, unsure whether to take her seriously. "You don't really think..." The sentence faded on her lips as she detected a smile return to Gantz's face.

"Made you think though! I wouldn't discount anybody at the moment. A lot of lies and misdirection during those interviews."

"You mean Rolm denying she spoke to Ginthem?"

"Among other things. Boni claiming he fed Dang and LeBon but both of them saying they picked up a tray meal. Their answers being so alike it would be easy to come to the conclusion they worked on their story before we got to see them. Let's just eat. When we've finished the interviews we'll have a debrief. I don't really want to speak here." Delgardo looked around her. Dang and LeBon were sitting at another table with Willard and Wildman. Ull was in the recreational area working on his CommsLink. She nodded her understanding and got up to help herself to a drink from the water cooler.

Milton Dang watched Delgardo as she walked to the water cooler. "You know she's not that bad looking! A bit flat chested for my taste but would do for you Zon." Willard gave Dang a cold stare but said nothing. "Perhaps Wildman here could arrange an introduction for you."

"I wouldn't waste your time Zon, you're not her type. Apparently, according to the locker room gossip that is, she has a regular girlfriend back in the city." Wildman flashed a smile at Dang.

"Definitely your type then Zon." Wildman noted the sullen look Willard gave Dang.

"I've got some checks to do." Willard shoved his plate away and got up. He nodded at Wildman and LeBon before leaving but deliberately ignored Dang.

"Mind you..." mused Dang turning his attention to Gantz, "the other one is a bit of a looker. Much more my type!"

"I'd steer clear of Gantz."

"Why's that old man, more locker room gossip?"

"She's New Brethren but, more than that, the rumours are she's a Gnostic."

"What the fuck's that?"

"An actual real life prophet!"

Dang laughed out loud. "A prophet? Corp, these Brethren weirdos are something else. What does she do? See the future? We could ask her how big our bonus is going to be. We could start ordering stuff on account. Fancy your own private space ship Will?" Dang found this very amusing and LeBon nodded his head and forced out a half-hearted smile. Dang's laughter died down and turned to Wildman. "You believe this shit Wildman?"

"I'm just telling you the rumours. One thing for sure is, don't underestimate her. She might not look much but she was involved in that terrorist incident a while back. She was on the investigating team for that series of grizzly murders and, despite being shot up herself, took out the leader of the terrorists. Those who have worked with her say once you get to know her she's alright but she scares the shit out of some of the officers."

"Religious mumbo jumbo Wildman! You might be scared of her but I'm not!"

"Just trying to tell it to you straight Milton. You do what you want but don't blame me if she rips your balls off!"

Dang laughed again. "Might be fun watching her try!"

"It certainly would, let me know if you plan to give her the opportunity." Wildman gave Dang a wink. "I'll have the ship powered up and an ice bucket on hand to keep your balls fresh until we reach a hospital."

Dang laughed again and slapped Wildman on the back. "I'm beginning to like you." Dang returned his attention to his meal.

***

Sligo Edmurson was huge. Delgardo studied him as the giant of a man towered over her. Dang had been well built and Mol was a beast of a man but Edmursom dwarfed them both. Even when he sat down she had to stare up at him. She had dealt with violent people before, some drunk, others half crazed by over medication and she had handled them with ease. Faced with Edmurson she had doubts about her ability to control him in a violent situation. His mere presence undermined her confidence

119

and ego. As she went through the opening interview preamble she kept a very close eye on him.

Edmurson sat stroking his beard as he considered Delgardo's opening question. "I woke about 09.30, dressed and went for breakfast. I always have fruit for breakfast so Boni didn't bother to come out of the kitchen. Dirk never eats breakfast so only comes out of his room in time to go on shift. After breakfast I went down to the machine store. We have a small gym set up down there. I worked out for a couple of hours and then came back and showered. Came back in here about 15.00 got myself a cup of coffee and waited for Dirk and Ginthem to turn up. He was supposed to come to the drill-head with us. Dirk joined me just before 16.00. We waited half hour but no sign of Ginthem. I then reported his no show to Petre. He called a crew meeting and organised a search. Me, Dirk, Petre and Zon searched the mine tunnels without any luck and then we all met up back in the Rec. Petre reported Ginthem had gone missing to control and me and Dirk went on shift. I never saw Ginthem at all that day."

"Can you remember the order that the crew arrived at the meeting and where they came from?"

Edmurson stroked his beard again and then slowly nodded his head. "Sure. We were already there with Petre. Milton I think was first or it might have been Mol, then Sara followed by Will. They sort of all arrived at the same time so it's hard to remember the exact order but Will was definitely the last one. Oh, except of course for Zon who arrived a couple of minutes after everyone else. No sense of urgency that one!"

"What about Chang?" As Delgardo asked the question she remembered Gantz's comment on the man.

A look of concentration furrowed Edmurson's brow. "He was there!" Edmurson hesitated. "But I don't remember him coming out of the corridor. He must have come from behind us, from the kitchen."

"Could he have come from outside?"

Edmurson gave the question some consideration. "He could have. I just assumed it was the kitchen because Boni is either in his room or in the kitchen."

"He doesn't mix with the rest of the crew?"

Edmurson gave this question even longer consideration. He seemed reluctant to answer for some reason. "You've interviewed Boni." It was a statement, not a question, and although Delgardo picked up on the inference she only nodded her head in confirmation. She wanted Edmurson to elaborate. There was another long silence before he finally replied. "Boni's not right in the head. You must have seen this." He hesitated again. Sligo Edmurson was not a man who would speak ill of others. "Most of the crew avoid him, socially. Milton torments him and Mol is a bully. Boni stays in his room or the kitchen if there's any chance of either of them being in the Rec."

"The rest of the crew allows this to happen?"

Edmurson averted his eyes. "When it started some of us defended Boni but it only seemed to encourage them. They were then warned by Petre but it just continued behind his back. I then warned Milton to cut it out but I think he just then avoided doing it in front of me. I also warned Mol who told me to mind my own business. We had a," Edmurson paused, "we had a frank exchange of views but I think, again, it only deterred Mol from doing it in front of me. I tried to explain to Boni but he still rarely took the chance of coming into the Rec."

Delgardo wondered if the term 'a frank exchange of views' was a euphemism for something a lot less convivial. If so Gurd was either a lot braver or a lot more stupid than she gave him credit for if he took on Edmurson. She also warmed to this, apparently, gentle giant who had attempted to protect Chang.

Picking up Gantz's observation about Boni's use of names. Edmurson called everyone by their first names, even the ones he obviously did not like. She pushed such thoughts to the back of her mind. Just because she liked Edmurson and disliked Gurd it made very little difference, both should be considered suspects. She used her follow up question. "You said you never saw Ginthem that day. "What about the day he arrived?"

"I saw him just before we went on shift but never spoke to him. He was in the Rec that night but he was talking to Sara. He went to his room shortly after. He never came back out again."

"How did Gurd react to Sara talking to Ginthem?" Delgardo saw the opportunity to confirm LeBon's story.

Edmurson reverted to stroking his beard. He was either deep in thought attempting to remember the scene or was reluctant to speak ill of another member of his crew. "Mol gets protective of Sara." He stopped stroking his beard but averted his eyes again.

Delgardo glanced at Gantz for guidance. There was a slight pause before she shook her head. Delgardo thanked Edmurson for his cooperation and asked him to send in Dirk Albright. Edmurson rose from his chair and ducked his head to enable him to get through the doorway. His shoulders almost rubbed the sides of the door.

Delgardo turned her head to look at Gantz. "Another one being economical with the truth?"

Gantz nodded. "He's avoiding telling us something, but whether it's got anything to do with Ginthem or just unsavoury crew secrets I'm not sure! I get the impression our Mr Edmurson is very protective of the other crew members. Of course how far that protection would stretch to we have no way of knowing."

"Would save a lot of time if you could just peek inside their heads and find out what's been going on."

"I would if I could, but I can't."

"You can't or you won't?"

"Both! I've already told you I have limited abilities and messing with somebody else's mind comes with risks I'm not willing to take." The look on Gantz's face and the tone of her voice, and the sudden appearance of Albright, discouraged Delgardo from pushing the point any further.

Albright marched into the room and when offered a seat he moved the chair back half a metre before he sat down. He folded his arms across his chest and glared at the two police officers. 'Not another Mol Gurd!' thought Delgardo, but Albright looked more angry than insolent. Delgardo prepared the recorder and opened with her standard question.

"I didn't do anything!" The vehement tone in his voice was surprising as Delgardo had not made any accusation.

"I'm not suggesting you have. We just need to establish where everyone was during the day."

"I was with Sligo all the time you can ask him." Delgardo could now detect indignation in his voice.

"Not all the time. Edmurson had breakfast alone and then had a workout in the gym, alone."

"Just because I've got a record you bastards are trying to blame me. I'm an easy target aren't I?"

"Well you're certainly acting like a suspect!" Delgardo was getting annoyed with this idiot.

"Fuck you!" yelled Albright and he jumped up from the chair, knocking it over and took a step towards the desk. Delgardo was quick to respond. She jumped up drawing her side arm and pointed it straight at Albright.

"Back off and calm down." There was a moment of silent tension before Albright suddenly swung round and punched the

123

side wall of the office. He actually left a dent in the wall along with a smear of his own blood. The shock seemed to surprise him and he stood staring at the bloody mess which were his knuckles. Light from the doorway was suddenly blocked out. Delgardo spun to her left a little and found herself pointing her weapon at Edmurson. The giant held out a hand and stopped in his tracks. Delgardo noticed there was a tremble in her hands and she gripped the gun more firmly.

"It's okay Officer Delgardo, the situation is under control." From behind her came the smoothing tones of Gantz;s voice.

"Under control!" Delgardo could not believe her ears. "The lunatic has lost it. Look what he's done to the wall. He's a bloody maniac!" She suddenly realised she was shouting and sounded a little hysterical. She fought to control herself, this was not the image she wanted to present to Gantz.

"She's right." It was Edmurson who was now speaking. "He worked himself up waiting for the interview. He gets nervous and then gets agitated. Once his temper goes he blows his top. He's alright now." Edmurson still held one hand out towards Delgardo, as if it would offer some protection from her weapon. He now slowly reached out his other hand towards Albright. "You're alright now aren't you Dirk?" Edmurson's huge hand engulfed Albright's shoulder and gave it a gentle squeeze. Albright was still staring at his bloody fist. His whole body was shaking and he was now taking deep breaths. "Good Dirk, deep slow breaths like we practised." With each breath he became calmer and the shaking finally stopped.

"Put the weapon away Delgardo." Gantz's voice was no more than a whisper in her ear. She hesitated for a second but then slowly lowered her arms. Letting out the breath she had been holding, she reluctantly returned the weapon to her holster. At the same time Edmurson lowered his defensive hand.

He groped around for the chair and pulled it upright, keeping his other hand on Albright's shoulder.

"Sit down Dirk, it's alright. I'll stay with you." Edmurson glanced up at Gantz and she nodded her agreement. He guided Albright towards the chair and pressed down on his shoulders to lower him into it. "I'm sorry Officers I should have warned you but he appeared calm when I sent him in here."

"Does this a lot does he?" The sarcasm and anger still coloured Delgardo's words.

"He gets anxious. It builds up and he has panic attacks. Sometimes his temper gets the better of him and the attacks turn violent. Since we started working together we've been working on controlling the temper. I swear to you he hasn't had one as bad as this for a long time. It's the stress of this business that's all!"

"How, in Corps name does he get through psyche evaluation?" Edmurson appeared to ignore the question and crouched down to be level with Albright.

"You coach him through it don't you Edmurson?"

Delgardo glanced at Gantz. "Coach him! He needs help not a coaching session."

"But he'd be taken off operations." Gantz smiled at Delgardo. She did not return the smile, she could not understand how Gantz could take this so calmly.

"Dirk got into trouble when he was younger because of his temper but the medication they put him on helped keep it under control." They both turned at the sound of Edmurson's voice. "He was fine but then halfway through the last tour he started to have trouble again. We thought he must have built up an immunity to the medication. We were going to report it at the end of the tour so they could prescribe new medication."

"And then you discovered the Zelman crystals!"

If Edmurson was surprised that Ull had told them about the crystals he gave no indication of being so. "Control would pull him out of operations until the medication brought the problem back under control. He'd get the bonus from the last tour but not this one."

"And this one would be the big pay off!" Edmurson nodded.

"You made him stay in his room as much as possible to avoid Ginthem?"

"And Ull had arranged for Ginthem to visit the drill-head with you and Albright!" Delgardo nodded her head in understanding. "That must have worried the pair of you!"

"No, that's not right. Dirk would have been fine with me there." He looked in desperation from Delgardo to Gantz and then back again. "It would have been fine. I know what you're thinking but Dirk wouldn't hurt anybody." Delgardo made a point of looking at the dent in the wall. Edmurson turned to Gantz. "He wouldn't, I swear to you."

"Take him back to his room and calm him down." Gantz leaned forward to press home her next point. "I suggest you get him to provide a written statement Sligo and make him understand we might have to speak to him again." Edmurson nodded his understanding but looked downcast so she added. "You can be present at any such interview."

"Thank you Deputy Gantz."

"Now go, I want that statement downloaded to my CommsLink within the hour. I'll send you the necessary link and the details we are interested in." Gantz waved him away. Edmurson helped Albright to his feet and guided him out of the office.

Delgardo turned towards Gantz to speak but stopped as Gantz raised a finger. "I know what you're going to say but let's not get ahead of ourselves. There's no evidence yet that Laslo Ginthem was murdered!"

CHAPTER SIX

Gantz suggested taking another stroll around the camp before they started work on the time-line model again. She said it would give Edmurson and Albright time to complete the latter's statement. Delgardo thought it was good idea for it would allow her to compose herself after the incident with Albright. She was somewhat embarrassed by her behaviour and expected Gantz to warn her about her future reactions or at least give her a severe talking to. However Gantz proved to be sympathetic. Even when Delgardo pointed out that she had remained calm throughout the incident Gantz just smiled and remarked how she felt they were never in any danger. Albright's anger was never really directed at them, they had merely been the trigger for it.

They walked on in silence from the office, across the camp and down the path towards the mine entrance and the jungle; there was a limited choice when it came to stretching your legs in this particular location. They came to a halt at the edge of the undergrowth and took in the view down the valley towards the river and the mountains beyond. It was some minutes before Delgardo ventured to speak.

"Why were you so sure Albright wasn't going to attack us?"

"You were pointing a gun at him. He's not that bright but he's not that stupid either!"

Delgardo smiled. "It was more than that. I came that close to shooting him." She indicated a small gap between her thumb and forefinger to illustrate her point. "You were calm right through the whole thing."

"Intuition Sonia. I just had a feeling!"

"You felt it or knew it?"

"I felt it. No matter how many times you ask the same question the answer will always be be same. I can't read anybody's mind. It's empathy not telepathy." Delgardo nodded. "Does that disappoint you?"

"No, well perhaps a little! You just seem so confident it's hard to believe it's just empathy."

"You don't have faith in your own abilities?"

"I'm not sure I have to the same extent as you!"

"Then that's a lack of faith, not a lack of ability. Try to relax more."

"Then I'll not keep losing it when interviewing?"

"You're doing fine." Gantz gave a rare smile. "Sometimes unsettling the interviewee is just what you want. Take them out of their comfort zone and they can slip up."

"I'll try and remain calm. Just give me the nod when you want me to turn into the attack dog."

"Come on let's get back and feed the new data into the model." Delgardo nodded and followed Gantz back up the path towards the office. She still thought there was more to the locker room rumours about the Gnostics than Gantz was willing to admit.

Just as they were passing the the accommodation block Petre Ull stepped out of the doorway. He paused until they came level with him and then fell into step alongside them.

"How are the interviews going?"

"I assume you've heard about Dirk Albright's outburst then!"

"Was I that obvious?" Ull gave a sigh. "I should have warned you about Dirk but he really has been in control of himself. That was totally out of character for him. He has had a few panic attacks over the last couple of days but we put it down to the stress of the inspection but they were mild, nothing like what you witnessed. Unfortunately the disappearance of Ginthem and your arrival has only upped the stress levels." He rubbed his chin thoughtfully. "And Milton hasn't helped. He does have a tendency to wind people up. I'm sure there's no malice in it but the sarcasm can be a touch on the brutal side." He glanced at the two officers and caught the expression on their faces. "Look these are miners! These tours can be rough, both physically and mentally but these lads are tough. They can handle the banter. They can dish it out as well as Milton can."

They had arrived at the office. "I'm sure they can Petre. Do you need to use the office?"

"Just some bits from the store if it's convenient?"

"You go right ahead." Something caught her eye and she half turned. Wildman was standing by the ship. He raised a hand to gain her attention. "It looks as if our pilot needs a word. Sonia, start feeding the data into the model." She handed Delgardo her CommsLink. "I better see what this sad excuse for a police officer wants." With that she marched off towards Wildman. Delgardo and Ull watched her for a few seconds and then entered the office.

"What's the problem Wildman?"

"The ship." Wildman knelt down and pointed to the underside of the hull. Gantz knelt down and peered under the ship.

"It's muddy!"

Wildman nodded. "Thought you'd like to know I've been talking to people."

"And I bet you've been a right little gossip."

"Need to break the ice boss and you two are the talk of the camp. Can't be all one way so I give a little information and get a little back." He flashed her a trademark smile.

"Okay so what did you get back?"

"Milton fancies himself as a cut above the rest. All cocksure and friendly but he's a nasty little shit. I have a feeling he either knows some of the crews little secrets or enjoys inventing them to give him an opportunity to needle them."

"Anything specific?"

Wildman shook his head and then pointed at the underside of the hull again for effect. "Any Corporation rules about crews on operational tours as far as sexual orientation is concerned?"

Gantz was surprised at the question. "None at all. Sexual relationships within a crew are banned, for obvious reasons, especially in a remote site like this. Celibacy is hard enough for six months without having two of your crew grunting away in the room next door. I'm sure it goes on but..."

"If an inspector got wind of it!"

"Why the sexual orientation question?"

"Something Milton Dang said about Zon Willard. It might have been nothing. Also there's something about Mol Gurd and Sara Rolm. Again nothing solid, just a feeling."

"Sonia thought the same thing but had trouble pairing up Sara with Mol, another nasty piece of work. Keep up the gossip." Gantz pulled herself to her feet. "I take it the gossip does revolve around us?"

Wildman stood up. "Well you're stuck up cows as far as I'm concerned but you're both hot as far as Milton's concerned. I think they're more interested in keeping tabs on how the investigation is going."

"Okay but try and keep my character assassination down to a minimum please." Gantz turned to head back to the office.

"By the way boss, Milton reckoned you were hotter than Sonia."

Gantz did not reply but allowed herself a small smile.

***

By the time Gantz got back to the office Ull had picked up what he was looking for and Delgardo had finished the data transfer, including the details from Albright's statement. It had arrived just as she had started to download the details from the other statements. "That man's impossible! We're in the middle of an investigation and he's worried about scratches on the hull of the ship. Wants me to put in an official report so he doesn't get blamed for the damage. I never realised we were so short of pilots we had to hire people like him." She paused as if she had just noticed Ull. "Oh hi there Petre."

Ull smiled back at her. "You should try managing a drilling crew sometime!"

"No thanks Petre."

"Wise decision Deputy Gantz." He half-heartedly nodded a farewell to Delgardo and squeezed past Gantz to leave the office. Gantz took her seat next to Delgardo.

"Well let's see if this provides any useful information." Delgardo muttered under her breath as she entered the last download from Albright. "I've also put in the timings for the walk to the river and the Perrin Gap. Let's run the river scenario first as that was the quickest route."

Delgardo waved the model on and they watched as the colour coded figures moved through the holographic depiction of the camp. They paid most attention to the white figure which represented Laslo Ginthem. It appeared in the dining area of the accommodation block. Other figures joined him and then his figure moved to the door and disappeared.

"I wonder where he went to?" Delgardo mused. Two more figures left the block and walked to the mine entrance. "Well there goes Dang and LeBon!" The two figures disappeared to indicate their entry to the mine. The seconds ticked by and the hour moved on to 11.00. A yellow figure representing Zon Willard appeared from the purification plant and walked to the accommodation block. The white figure suddenly appeared at the storage bins. "The purification plant has a separate entrance so Laslo could have been in the office." Gantz nodded. Nothing more happened until Dang and LeBon appeared from the mine and walked to the accommodation block. "They didn't say anything about seeing Laslo and they would have had a clear view of him!"

"If he was still at the bins. Just because the figure is still there it doesn't mean the real Laslo was! Of course Willard didn't say anything about seeing Dang and LeBon and they didn't mention seeing Willard."

The seconds ticked by again and suddenly the white figure started to walk back towards the accommodation block. "That's where Willard spotted him." The figure continued until it reached the mine and then started to flash to indicate the walk to the river. Both Delgardo and Gantz's attention was now on the flashing figure. The seconds ticked by and Delgardo found she was breathing in time with the flashes. Her heart skipped a beat as the figure changed its colour to red. Laslo Ginthem was now dead but his model figure was still walking towards the river. The flashing continued for some time before it finally stopped. At that point Gantz paused the model.

"Almost twenty extra minutes to reach the river."

"If Willard got the time right."

"But that timing was me walking down a path cleared by Dang and LeBon, supposedly. I think that's too tight a timescale. Willard needs to be at least half an hour out and

134

possibly three-quarters. Any earlier than that and he might have run into Dang and LeBon."

" Or missed them completely. Still possible though boss!"

Gantz shook her head. "Dang was too eager to guide me to the river. That path might have been cut back by him but I don't buy the idea Laslo created it in the first place." She paused as she saw the doubt in Delgardo's face. "It went almost straight to the river. Even when it slightly diverted for some obstacle it immediately returned on course. How did Laslo, who had never been here before, manage to go straight to the river? Also the path looked too well trodden and at the end of the path the area on the edge of the drop to the river even more so."

"So you think what?"

"What did you have for lunch?"

Delgardo looked puzzled. "I had the fresh fish, why?"

"And where do you think Chang got fresh fish from now the daily transport has ceased?"

"Ah!" Delgardo had finally caught up with Gantz's thinking. "Chang's regular fishing spot!"

"If Dang hadn't been so lazy and had cut a meandering path to the river I might have swallowed it."

"But why try to misdirect us? Do you think he murdered Laslo and was leading us away from where the body actually is?"

"I think it might be a lot simpler than that! What has been the great concern of the crew from the moment we arrived?"

"Keeping the drill-head going."

"And if we start searching the river from here down to the flats which Milton Dang so helpfully pointed out?"

"It could take us weeks if not longer before we gave up and looked elsewhere, and drilling could continue!" Delgardo sighed and her brow furrowed. "They don't care what happened to

Laslo and don't want him found if it means closing down the drilling."

"Quite possibly."

"So what do we do now?"

"Well I suggest we do the opposite to what Milton Dang wants and start our search in the mine."

"Are you going to close them down?"

"Not unless I have to! At the moment they'll cooperate if they think it will keep the mine open."

"We could still be wasting time. He also went on about this mysterious noise near the end of the shift. Perhaps he threw that one in as a backup plan. Laslo could be lying out there somewhere in the undergrowth. Out towards the Perrin Gap. That lazy pig Gurd wouldn't have made a thorough search!"

"Unlikely. During our walks did anything catch your eye out there?" Delgardo thought about it for a while before shaking her head. "Me neither. After almost three days in this heat I would have expected to see carrion circling overhead if he was out there. If we doubt he could have made it to the river there is no way he could have made it to the Gap. He's either in the river or in the mine."

"How do we find him if the search party failed?" Delgardo then answered her own question. "If they bothered to look for him!"

"If our assumption is correct and they want to keep the mine open then if they found the body they would have told us but moved it out of the mine first."

"Unless they or at least one of them killed him."

"Which without a body will be hard to prove. Another stumbling block is motive. So far, no body and no motive. The only thing we're not short of are suspects. Our model didn't actually rule anyone out. All the timings are suspect as we got

136

them all from suspects. The only time we can rely on is the one from Laslo's chip."

"The motive's got to be the crystals. What did you say earlier? The most common reasons for murder are sex and credits!"

"If it is murder. But why would the crystal find cause anybody to murder Laslo? You heard what Petre Ull said; the bonus for this tour would be the biggest payday any of them have ever had and are ever likely to have. Where's the benefit of killing him? All that has done is bring us in and threatened to close the mine!"

Delgardo scratched her head. "Unless somebody thought the bonus wasn't enough!"

"But they have to get round the Corporation security measures."

"No matter what system is in place there's always somebody who thinks they can get round it." Delgardo paused and smiled. "Otherwise we would be out of a job!"

Gantz returned the smile. "Okay, credits are still on the motive list but I prefer the other one, sex!"

"Sex?" Delgardo looked far from convinced. "How could sex be a motive?"

"The Corporation bans any sexual relationship between members of a crew. That doesn't mean it never goes on but if Laslo was a stickler for the rules he could pull the crew out if he found out it was going on. Wildman thinks, like you, there could be something going on between Rolm and Gurd. He also hinted there might be something going on with Willard and one of the crew."

"Wildman says?"

"Yes, sorry but a slight deception on my part. I thought Wildman might be of more use gathering information so I've made a point of cutting him out of the investigation. I wasn't sure they would trust him any more than I do but he at least is picking up on the current gossip. Anyway, anything caught your eye there?"

"Nothing obvious. If Willard is having a relationship with one of the crew they're being very careful about hiding it."

"If it's Rolm I should imagine they would! However, the suggestion is it's a homosexual relationship."

"Makes sense! Gurd keeps a close watch on Rolm so I doubt if it's her. The obvious reason for keeping it quiet is that it's a homosexual relationship. I doubt if that would go down well with some of the Neanderthal types on the crew." Delgardo noticed the expression on Gantz's face and smiled. "Yes I know we live in a liberal Federation but that doesn't mean all the citizens hold the same liberal views." She paused to reflect on her own statement. "Believe me I know!"

Gantz fought the urge to offer sympathy for Delgardo's situation. However well-meaning it would sound patronising so Gantz consoled herself with the fact that her disciplined upbringing restricted probing too deeply into the human mind. "Well either way if Laslo was talking to Rolm he could have found out."

Delgardo nodded, thinking Gantz certainly played her cards close to her chest. The sidelining of Wildman was obviously for the benefit of the crew. "That puts Gurd to the top of our suspect list then!"

"Not necessarily. If Laslo did intend to pull out the crew any of them could have killed him. Back to the credits motive, but in this case it would be a misguided attempt to protect their bonus."

"I still fancy Gurd for it! If it's not consensual sex then he could lose a lot more than just his bonus."

"You really don't like him do you?"

"I've met men like him before!" Delgardo paused as if she was considering elaborating on that comment. "He's a bully and a misogynist. He's the sort of man who would kill Laslo for just looking at Rolm. Wouldn't want anyone messing with his property."

"Don't let it get personal Sonia. That will only cloud the issue."

"Impartial all the way with the investigation boss, but I can still hope he did it."

Gantz nodded. "Yes you can still hope."

"So what next boss? We have multiple possible suspects and motives if we ever find a body."

Gantz checked the time. "To early to take a look at the mine, we'll wait until the break between shifts. So let's reconstruct Laslo's movements and consider what his motives were."

"Do you want a drink first?"

Gantz realised that she had not had a drink since lunch, not a good idea in this heat. "Yes please. I'll have one now and a Koolbot to go. I think Ull keeps a case of them in the store back there. While you do that I'll contact Goodridge and get him to find out how much leeway Laslo allowed with the sexual rules for operation staff."

***

Goodridge answered her call almost immediately. It was good to see a familiar, friendly face.

"How are you doing Kanah?"

She could recognise the concern in his tone of voice. Theirs had always been an unusual relationship. He was her direct superior but he was also a member of the New Brethren which meant he respected her standing as a Gnostic; a prophet, in so much as she was the first step on the New Brethren's journey towards their God. Not a human-like supernatural being but more a representation of ultimate knowledge. To the New Brethren knowledge was not a sin which man had to pay a price for but a gift from God. The journey would take them from the individual to a state of oneness with humanity and on to a state of oneness with God. Kanah Gantz, like all the Gnostics, was the bridge between man and the angels. No wonder Goodridge showed such concern for her well-being.

"I'm fine thank you sir. I'd be even better if I thought we were making progress here."

"You have my full confidence!"

Again Gantz detected a hint of doubt in his voice. "I need some more information on Laslo Ginthem. I need to know if he followed the rules rigidly or if he allowed some latitude? Specifically in the area of sexual relationships between crew members."

"I can help you out on that Kanah. I've put in more time on researching Ginthem's background. First, in answer to your earlier question, he apparently has had previous contact with a couple of crew members. Some time back but he has made inspections on crews which contained Zon Willard and Sara Rolm. Different crews, both larger than the one you're dealing with so the level of contact, if any, would have been limited. Both inspections were before they both joined the current crew.

For once I got a low level Corporation employee who was helpful and they gave me a lot more detail about Ginthem which probably answers the question you just asked. The official version was he would report any non-compliance with Corporation rules and guidelines. When pressed, it was conceded all inspectors are allowed some latitude in their interpretation of the rules and guidelines within...blah, blah, blah. It seems he was thorough but a practical man who understood the pressures remote drilling crews would be under.

140

I got the impression he was rather more liberal minded than you would expect from a Corporation employee. I could check on the specifics for you but would guess from what I've learnt so far, unless it was causing problems, he would overlook what the crew got up to in their off duty time."

"If you could double check sir it would be appreciated."

"Will do! While I was having such success I decided I'd push my luck and mentioned the Zelman crystals." Goodridge paused to smile. "That certainly had an affect! I was referred upwards several grades. They were not happy with the fact I knew about the crystals. I asked if the find had anything to do with why they were monitoring Ginthem's chip and they came out with the usual corporation line about commercial confidence, which is their way of avoiding any awkward questions. I then remembered we are in the midst of renegotiating all corporation licenses so got in touch with Danal Odewaya who is helping to set up the New Brethren Corporation. He's been heavily involved in all the negotiations, including those with the mining corporation. The fact that we are setting up our own corporation has been an open secret for the last six months. The corporations aren't happy about it but don't see us as a threat to their profits; we're small fry! However, Danal said a find of Zelman crystals would send alarms bells ringing. They would have sent Ginthem out to confirm the extent of the deposit and ensure none of this got out of the camp."

"So monitoring Ginthem's chip was some sort of security measure against any action by the drilling crew?" There was a hint of disbelief in Gantz's voice.

"Oh Kanah, the corporations are more paranoid than that! It was also security against any action we took. Danal said a find of Zelman crystals is just the sort of thing which would encourage the idea of a break away from the Federation. Of course we'd never contemplate that course of action and we wouldn't even have attempted to ditch the Mining Corporation, we're not geared up for that type of industry. Of course the corporations don't know that! From the information he has obtained from his contacts Danal thinks the corporation may believe the New Brethren have killed Ginthem to close the mine as the first step in taking it over. It appears unofficial approaches have already been made to the Federation for assurances that they would send in Colonial troops in the event of that happening."

Gantz was shocked at this news. "I had no idea! The crew have talked about huge bonuses but I never imagined any of this."

"It frightened the Council so much that Lisbeth Smith has ordered Danal to give assurances to the Mining Corporation and to sign the new licenses immediately. Assurances are also being given to the Federation. It appears there's unrest on Solar 2 again so if they think another planet is causing trouble the Colonial Corps would be stretched. Add that to the fact they might now worry about the loyalty of the Colonial troopers Morgan had recruited and trained. The whole situation becomes very delicate."

Gantz sighed on hearing this news, an action inherited from her human side. "I've been using the threat of closing down the drilling as a way of ensuring cooperation from the crew." She sounded crest fallen.,

"Kanah you're in charge up there and you must do what you think is best. However keeping the drilling going would go some way to appeasing the corporation, at least until Danal can wrap up the license negotiations. Once that's in place the whole situation will calm down." Goodridge could see the expression on Gantz's face. "I'm sorry to put this added pressure on you." He left it at that, not wanting to undermine her confidence any further by suggesting he was still worried if she was fully recovered from her last ordeal.

"Have the crew been made aware of all this?"

"Once I'd spoken to Danal I got back to the corporation and agreed we would keep the drilling going if we got full cooperation from the crew. I get the impression the crew will be kept in the dark about all this. I doubt if they trust them enough to keep them fully informed."

Gantz pretended that the last piece of information had cheered her up. "Thank you sir. I'll keep the threat of closure over their heads and hope they don't call my bluff!"

"You have my full confidence Kanah."

"Thank you sir." Gantz ended the link. She did not believe the last remark any more than Goodridge did.

***

Despite the heat, stepping out of the office was a relief. The ineffective air conditioning had slowly turned it into an oven. You could almost taste the heat in the very air they breathed. Out in the open the Sun's rays were countered by a breeze which came in off the Perrin Gap and was funnelled down the valley.

"So Laslo wasn't uptight about sexual rules?" Delgardo pressed a cooling pad round the back of her neck which she had found while searching for the Koolbots. She pocketed a couple each for her and Gantz and then filled the Koolbots with fresh water and set the bottle on 'ice cold'. It would only take a few moments before the water was at the required temperature.

"Well, that's reading between the lines. The official version was he would report any non-compliance with Corporation rules and guidelines. When pressed by Goodridge it was conceded all inspectors are allowed some latitude in their interpretation of the rules and guidelines within...blah, blah, blah. Goodridge was

good enough to give me a précis of the actual conversation."
Gantz decided there was no point in giving the other bad news
to Delgardo.

"Sex slips down the motive list." Delgardo wanted to say
that sexual jealousy would still be a motive for Gurd but did not
want Gantz to warn her again about letting personal feelings
cloud her objectivity.

"Don't worry Sonia it still doesn't let Gurd off the hook!"

'Damn it!' thought Delgardo,'Was that a lucky guess?' She
decided Gantz had either turned intuition into an art form or she
was still playing down her abilities. "So what now? We've
already had a look at these things. I can't see a way in."

Gantz walked around the storage bin, carefully stepping
over the ore sledge pipe. She squatted down on her haunches
and put a hand on the pipe. She could feel through her finger
tips the pipe vibrating. How could they bypass the security
measures? Her thoughts were interrupted as she felt something
wet touch her hand. She looked down and saw Wildman's dog,
Keith, licking her hand.

"Sorry boss but she must like you. As soon as she saw you
she made straight for you. Usually only this enthusiastic for
sausages!" Wildman sauntered up to the storage bins. "If you're
thinking of supplementing your pension by making off with a
storage bin full of crystals I'm afraid to tell you I couldn't get
the ship off the ground with that strapped to the hull."

"Ever fly ore transporters Wildman?"

Wildman removed his beaded pill-box hat and moped the
sweat from his brow. "Met some people who did when I was
flying inter-planetary for one of the Corporations. Miserable
bunch of sods. Mind you, so would I be if all I did was short
hops from places like this to the city and then back again.
Bloody things fly themselves. The pilots are just baby sitters for
the ore. Not my idea of a proper job!" He whistled and Keith

144

abandoned Gantz's hand to return to her master. Wildman squatted down on his haunches and rubbed the back of Keith's ears.

"Ever met one who got rich quick?" Delgardo asked.

"No, but I've heard of a few who tried to get rich quick. Trouble is not many of them got very far. Any valuable cargo and the transporter is monitored. If they overrode the automatic pilot to set a new course the Corporation would know about it and the chances are their security teams would be waiting for the transporter when it arrived at its new destination. One pilot jettisoned the bin on route and then later bailed out and crashed the transporter. Had an accomplice pick up the bin. Only one I know who managed to get away with it. Of course now the bins are tagged as well as the transporter."

Gantz stood up and leaned against the bin. "So it can't be done!"

"I didn't say that. The Corporation is hardly likely to publicise the ones who got away." Wildman gave his dog one last rub behind the ear and then stood up as well. "If there's a market, and there is, then there's always somebody who will be tempted. And the temptation doesn't come any bigger than Zelman crystals."

"Any ideas?"

"I hope you're not suggesting I'm the type who would give something like that any serious consideration?"

"Not serious consideration, no!"

Wildman smiled at Gantz's comment. "Well, if credits were no object and with a bin full of Zelman crystals credit's wouldn't be a problem, I'd look to maximise the delay between me ripping off the Corporation and them realising it."

"And how would you do that?" It was Delgardo who jumped in and posed the question.

"Well, just off the top of my head." Wildman paused but hardly long enough to have only just come up with a workable idea. "I'd send the crystal bin back but not necessarily with the crystals in it. Then arrange for an off-world transport to pick up the real bin and the crew. By the time the Corporation checked the bin I'd be in hyper-drive to who knows where." He thrust his hands deep into his pockets and rocked back and forward on the balls of his feet. "Not sure if I'd get away with it though! Still, there might be some who would consider it a risk worth taking."

"You think that scenario is possible?"

"If you fancy spending the rest of your life in hiding avoiding any scanners. Fairly comfortable hiding mind you!" He pulled a face, indicating the idea did not appeal to him. "Not for me though. I need to be free to go where I please."

"Nor me." Gantz stared around at the other storage bins. "But it might appeal to some. I wonder how many of the crew would have to be involved for a plan like that to work?"

"I wouldn't like to say." Wildman turned on his heel and sauntered away. "Remember I'm supposed to be on their side." He whistled a nameless tune as he headed towards the accommodation block, Keith trotting by his side.

"Ull would be the one to confirm the crystal find." Gantz nodded to acknowledge Delgardo's comment. She tried to imagine what she would do with a scenario like the one Wildman had suggested. It would take time to organise any off-world transport. The nearest possibility would be the asteroid mining sites about two months away by hyper-drive. She wondered if that was the true reason for the crew's willingness to sign up for an extra tour?

"What if they delayed registering the find? Those weeks of poor production levels could have hidden the fact they had switched to the crystals. I thought it was a bit of a coincidence they found the crystals just before Ginthem turned up. It would also give them time to organise the off-world transport."

"It's a good scenario Sonia. Makes the crystal motive a lot stronger, if Ginthem was killed!" There were now so many questions going round in her head Gantz needed to give this more thought. She checked the time.

"Well I'm not wasting any more time theorising on a motive until we're certain we have a crime!" Gantz turned to face Delgardo. "Find Ull and tell him I want to inspect the mine now. If he argues, and I'm sure he will, tell him he can keep the drill-head working but I want to see the rest of the mine. If he still argues point out I'm quite willing to close the drilling down straight away."

"Can you actually do that boss?"

"Not without good cause, but the bluff has worked before so let's give it another try." Delgardo gave a wry smile, nodded, turned and jogged back towards the accommodation block. Gantz uncrossed her fingers.

***

"It's not safe to allow you into the mine while the drill-head is in operation. It's against Corporation policy and would invalidate our liability insurance." Petre Ull was far from happy with Gantz's request. He stood with his legs spread apart and his arms folded to illustrate he would not be moved on this point.

"I'm sure Officer Delgardo explained I don't want to stop the drill-head so I'll keep well away from it. However, I intend to search the rest of the mine for any clues to the disappearance of Laslo Ginthem and I have no intention of delaying that search until the end of the current shift. I can do this with your cooperation, which I would prefer, or without it. I'll not ask you to work your shifts around my investigation so please don't expect me to work my investigation around your shift pattern. Do I need to point out this is a possible murder case?"

Ull gave a snort of disbelief. "You have no evidence of that. The man wandered off into the jungle. Milton found a path which had been made and it went right up to the river's edge. That might be evidence of an accident or suicide but you can't call it murder based on that."

"Except that the path was well worn. It's more likely to be a path made on Boniface Chang's fishing visits. We've timed the journey from here to the river and there's no way Ginthem could have got there between the time he was last spotted and the time his chip ceased to function. Add that to the fact your alternative scenario has been suggested by several of the crew and I grow suspicious and start to lean towards the murder option!"

Ull dropped his arms down by his side and his expression of grim determination dissolved into one of abject misery. 'That bloody idiot Milton had to push his luck!' thought Ull. 'He couldn't leave it alone, despite what I told him.' Ull pushed his hands through his hair and sighed. "Look Deputy Gantz you need to understand the pressure this crew is under. They were looking at possibly the biggest payday of their life and then Ginthem goes missing and it's all under threat. A few of them..." Ull struggled to find the right form of words which would not make the situation worse than it already was. "When we couldn't find Ginthem we all guessed he must be dead." He paused again, reluctant to actually voice the thought which filled his head. "I know this will sound bad but a few of the crew thought if the poor man is dead would it matter that much to anyone exactly when the body was found?"

"To his family, yes!"

Ull hung his head. "We didn't consider that aspect." He almost mumbled the sentence. "I know this looks bad but I can assure you there's nothing sinister behind the..." Ull struggled again to find the right word. "The misdirection." He glanced at Gantz and then at Delgardo but found no consolation there. "If you sign a waiver I'll get you some safety helmets and guide you through the mine." The tone of his voice indicated he had conceded defeat.

They both signed the waiver, picked up their safety helmets and followed Ull down the path to the mine entrance. They stopped as they were about to enter.

"There's emergency lighting in all the tunnels but it is just that. You'll need to use these if you want a good look round." Ull handed them both a light-stick. "Twist the end to turn it on." They had both used light sticks before so nodded their understanding. "Ready?"

"Yes," confirmed Gantz who then glanced at Delgardo. She was staring into the dark recess of the mine and nervously licked her dry lips. "You okay?"

Delgardo did not take her eyes off the mine. "I get a bit claustrophobic." She swallowed the lump in her throat. "I'll be alright though."

Gantz gave Delgardo a reassuring pat on the shoulder. She turned to Ull in time to see a smug smile of satisfaction at Delgardo's discomfort. "We're ready!" The tone of Gantz's voice made the smile vanish and Ull led the way into the mine.

The main mine tunnel was almost circular in shape. It allowed all three of them to walk side by side but only because Gantz and Delgardo were less than two metres tall. Walking either side of Ull meant their heads did not hit the tunnel roof as it curved down to the walls. To their left the ore sledge pipe ran along the floor just behind the row of emergency lights. On the other side ran another row of lights. They gave out a dull yellowish light which only managed to illuminate the tunnel with the help of the natural daylight from the entrance. The tunnel slowly curved to the right with only a slight gradient. After no more than fifty metres the entrance and, therefore, its light source was lost from view. The visibility was now poor. The floor lighting provided no more than a guide to lead them into and out of the mine. They paused and twisted on their light sticks. Now the area immediately around them was illuminated as if they had suddenly been transported outside. Gantz studied her surroundings. The walls were remarkably smooth. The surface had a dimpled effect caused by the action of the drill-head. For some reason she had expected rough hewn walls as if the miners here had cut the tunnel by hand with picks and chisels. She put her ignorance down to her New Brethren farm upbringing. In that community an unnecessary level of manual labour was included along with the computer controlled machines. It was seen as good for the body and the soul.

"Shall we move on?" The sound of Petre Ull's voice shook her out of her reverie.

"Yes but a little slower now." Gantz nodded towards Delgardo who in response pulled out her CommsLink and inserted a small jack into the implant just behind her ear. She adjusted the CommsLink, removed a small device from her jacket pocket and began to scan the area.

"If Ginthem is dead you won't pick up his chip." Ull addressed Gantz but his eyes were fixed on Delgardo.

"Not that kind of scanner." Ull waited for further explanation but Gantz offered none and slowly followed Delgardo who was inspecting the walls and floor of the tunnel as she went. Ull brought up the rear.

After another fifty metres Gantz stopped and gestured for Delgardo to do so. She was peering down a secondary tunnel to the right.

"Where does this go?"

Ull thought about misleading her but then remembered the result of Milton attempting to do that. "That was our first offshoot tunnel. The ore seam petered out pretty quickly. It's too dangerous to go down there."

"Why's that?" There was a hint of suspicion in her voice and Ull realised his honesty had sounded like an attempt to stop her investigating the tunnel. Not for the first time Ull wished he had been honest with them from the start. He had underestimated them and now they were wary of anything he said.

"We discovered an underground cavern. There's a ravine in there. Nearly lost a drill-head when we broke through because the ground just fell away. It's deep, very deep so we steer well clear of the area."

"Don't you have scanners to detect things like that?" Gantz knew next to nothing about mining but it seemed strange to her to risk a machine worth so much.

Ull sighed. "Well yes but..." He sighed again. "Look, let me explain something about this job. The Corporation, well all Corporations not just this one, want to maximise their profit. The drill-heads might cost millions of credits to buy but basically they're poor quality. The drills themselves break or shatter at regular intervals, the site is littered with the remains of them, scanners break down or need constant recalibration. I could go on but hopefully you get the picture. The drilling crews spend most of their time on shift doing minor repairs and I need to help Zon with the computer maintenance because, despite having two hour windows between shifts there's usually more work than one tech can handle. The short range scanner needed a spare part which we didn't have in store. Another credit pinching idea from the Corporation to keep the bare minimum spares on site. It was only the diligence of the crew on shift which stopped the whole bloody thing tipping into the ravine.

151

They noticed a change in the tunnel walls as it entered the cavern." Ull paused to collect himself. The memory of the incident still made him angry. "Another example of the stress the crew has to cope with. I'll not bore you with the trouble and associated hazards of the roof supports."

"I didn't know that Petre, and I now do appreciate the stresses and strains both physical and mental your crew must cope with." Gantz paused to judge Ull's reaction. He appeared to relax a little so her comment must have been appreciated. "Could Ginthem have come this way?"

"As far as I know he never entered the mine. If he had wanted to come in here I would have escorted him the same way I have you! Corporation procedures don't allow people to wander about down here on their own. It's why we have two-man drilling crews. It doesn't take two people to operate a drill-head! Ginthem would know the rules."

"He was seen heading this way and we know he didn't walk to the river to throw himself in. Did he know about this ravine?"

"I didn't mention it." Ull then realised that perhaps Gantz was thinking Ginthem might have committed suicide by throwing himself into the ravine. "One of the crew might have mentioned it!"

"Perhaps it was Sara Rolm, she appeared to have spoken to him the most." Ull sensed that Gantz had intended there to be some significance in the remark but it was lost on him; he was not even aware Sara had spoken to Ginthem! He could do no more than shrug his shoulders. "Perhaps you could lead the way please Petre." Ull took the lead and they entered the offshoot passage.

This tunnel curved to the left and ran level for a few metres before it gradually began to slope upwards. The walls had the same dimpled effect but after about twenty or thirty metres the left side of the tunnel became rougher. Ull gave an explanation.

"This is where we broke through to the cavern." As if to illustrate his point the left-hand wall fell away and the tunnel widened. They ventured a few more metres before Ull stopped and held up his light stick. The others followed suit and most of the cavern was illuminated. The roof arched up and disappeared into the darkness where the light sticks could not reach. About two metres away they could see the edge of the ravine which ran across their path. It had to be at least twenty metres wide and ran from one end of the cavern to the other. It was an impressive sight but Gantz found her attention was taken from her surroundings down to her feet. She was standing in a puddle of water.

"I wouldn't go too close to the edge, I'm not sure how stable it is!" His warning was directed at Delgardo who had ventured forward to peer into the abyss.

"How deep is it?" She asked, taking a step back from the edge.

"No idea! None of our instruments could register the bottom, all short range. We need more sophisticated ones. But watch this." He took his light stick and hurled it towards the ravine. They watched as it somersaulted through the air before starting its descent. Delgardo, who was closest to the edge, followed its path, down and down, the light it shed slowly fading until it was finally swallowed up by the blackness. She gave an involuntary shiver and took another step back from the edge. "It's been reported. No doubt somebody would be interested in studying it when the Corporation closes the mine down."

"It's wet!" Both Ull and Delgardo turned at the sound of Gantz's voice.

"What?" Ull had heard what she said but did not understand what she meant by it.

"The floor's wet! There are some puddles of water." She indicated towards the cavern and the walls of the tunnel. "No running water here. No stalactites or stalagmites and yet the floor is wet. How did the water get here?"

Ull looked bewildered but Delgardo bent down and held a probe into the puddle at Gantz's feet. Ull pulled out another light stick and twisted it on to provide extra illumination. "Consistent with drinking water. This isn't a natural spring, it's more like what you would expect from a purification plant." They both turned towards Ull for an explanation.

"We have hoses down here to help damp down the dust. Perhaps one sprung a leak." In response to Ull's suggestion they all retraced their steps inspecting the ground as they went. The entrance to the side tunnel was dry, as was the main one.

"Water didn't run down here from the pipe, it was sprayed. There's an even spread right across the floor from wall to wall from this point on." Delgardo squatted down and pointed to small damp patches on the floor. Gantz looked at Ull again.

"I can't explain it! Sometimes the vacuum at the drill-head fails and dust escapes but it couldn't end up here." He shook his head and looked genuinely puzzled. "And why bother to damp down the dust when nobody comes down here!"

"Sweep the walls and floor Sonia." Delgardo obeyed the order. A pale blue light from the scanner played across the tunnel wall. Ull and Gantz could only watch and wait.

Progress was terribly slow as they moved forward centimetres at a time. They were almost back where they started at the edge of the ravine before Delgardo raising a hand brought them to a stop. Ull stretched his neck to get a better view. He could see a tiny mark on the tunnel wall now showed red amid the pale blue scanner light. "What's that?" he asked nobody in particular.

154

"Trace!" murmured Gantz vaguely. She too was staring intently at the red smear.

"Trace of what?"

Gantz glanced around at Ull as if she had only just noticed him. "Blood or skin or both."

"Both!" confirmed Delgardo.

"Enough for a DNA match?" asked Gantz eagerly.

"More than enough." Delgardo marked the position on the wall and checked her CommsLink. "Bloody link is poor this far underground." All three held their breath for the few seconds it took to test the trace. "Laslo Ginthem!" They released the breath they had been holding.

"Obviously he did venture down here." The remark was aimed at Ull.

"Bloody fool to come down here on his own. Must have wandered down here and over the edge."

"The lights aren't good but they're not that bad."

"Perhaps he was careless, not watching were he was going."

"Get that a lot do you? Mine Inspectors who get careless when walking around mines?"

"Perhaps he did it on purpose."

"Perhaps he did!" Gantz gave Ull a long hard stare. "Perhaps he then washed down the tunnel." Ull turned white in response to that remark. His hope in the idea of Laslo Ginthem's suicide was draining away faster than the blood from his cheeks. He felt a weight had been placed on his shoulders and they visibly sagged.

Delgardo was now working her way along the wall and marked several other places. Ull stepped forward to get a better look but Gantz put out a hand to stop him. "No need to contaminate the scene anymore than we already have. We'll stay here and let Delgardo do her job. Ull nodded his understanding and took a step back. They watched as Delgardo moved to the rough part of the wall where the tunnel had merged with the cavern. No more marks were made so she slowly worked her way back, this time checking the floor. When she got back to the point where the dimpled wall had changed to a rough surface she bent down and marked the floor, directly under the last mark on the wall. After a few moments she brought a small box out of her pocket and using a pair of tweezers placed something from the floor into it. She then connected the box to her CommsLink.

"Do you know what Ginthem was wearing the day he went missing?"

Ull dithered. "I never saw him that day. I'll call Zon and ask." Ull pulled out his CommsLink and contacted Willard. "Zon can you remember what Ginthem was wearing when you saw him heading for the mine?" Ull paused and by the expression on his face he did not like Willard's response. "Then think harder man, this is important." There was a longer pause this time. "Are you sure? Then double check with Chang and call me right back." Ull pocketed his CommsLink. "He's pretty sure he was wearing a regulation work suit. All the crew wear them when they go on shift..." His voice trailed away. Ginthem had dressed to visit the mine. It was so obvious they had all missed it. "He intended to come down here but why not wait for the arranged trip with Sligo and Dirk?"

"If we knew that we'd be closer to knowing what happened down here."

Ull sighed. "Of course, why bother with a protective suit if he planned to come down here and throw himself into the ravine?" He sighed again. "It's not suicide is it?"

"It seems unlikely but perhaps people who commit suicide aren't expected to act rationally. Let's wait and see what else Delgardo comes up with."

By this time Delgardo was systematically working her way across the floor. She had already made another mark on the floor of the tunnel. Ull propped his light stick up against the tunnel wall, walked across to Gantz and took her one and did the same on the other side of the tunnel. "We may be here for some time," he said by way of explanation. Delgardo had already propped hers against the wall where the last mark had been made. Gantz offered Ull her Koolbot and he gratefully accepted it and took a long draught from it. As they waited, Willard called back and confirmed that Chang had supported his view that Ginthem was dressed in a protective suit as one of the spares was missing. Gantz nodded and relayed the message to Delgardo. The two police officers said nothing more but Ull knew they must be thinking exactly what he was now thinking; one of his crew was a murderer!

CHAPTER SEVEN

Once they were back in the office Delgardo busied herself processing the data she had collected in the mine. Gantz used the time to report in to Goodridge. The priority was to attempt to recover the body of Laslo Ginthem. However, Goodridge was at a loss about how to go about it.

"Have you any idea how deep this ravine is?"

"None at all! There're no instruments here that can measure it. It could be at least a kilometre if the short range scanners are no use."

"It might take some time to organise a team to deal with this. That is if this planet has the required equipment and expertise. Can you hold on there for a couple of days while I try and arrange something?"

"I wouldn't dream of pulling out until I get to the bottom of this."

"All credit to you Kanah but you've only just got back from medical leave. I only intended for you to make a quick assessment. Are you sure this is murder?" Gantz glanced at Delgardo who nodded. Gantz gestured for her join in. Delgardo waved her CommsLink into conference mode and the holographic image of Goodridge floated in front of her.

"Good afternoon Officer Delgardo."

"Hello sir. I've completed the analysis of the murder scene."

"And so what makes you certain our Laslo Ginthem was murdered?"

"We found traces of his blood and skin along the walls of the tunnel. Taking into account his height it would appear that he was feeling his way along the wall and travelling at speed. The walls are rough but not rough enough to break the skin if it was a casual brush with the surface. If he was feeling his way along using the wall as a guide it means somebody had switched the emergency lights off. If he was travelling at speed it seems reasonable to assume he was being chased. We then found trace on the floor where the wall blood trail came to an end. I think he stopped to rest and perhaps listen for his pursuer. The trail was then lost but picked up again nearer the centre of the tunnel floor. Close by we found a fragment of finger nail. The most likely scenario was he was dragged from the side of the tunnel, clawing at the rough floor in an attempt to slow his progress, and then thrown into the ravine. If he walked over the edge accidentally or threw himself over the edge why would there be signs of a struggle?"

"Reasonable as far as it goes, but how would our killer find Ginthem in the dark? He might have run away from an attack or even just a threat! You might have a struggle but it could be the result of Ginthem flailing about in a blind panic."

"Somebody attempted to wash away the evidence by spraying the tunnel with water. Why do that if Ginthem just walked over the edge in the dark? I also checked what equipment comes as standard in a drill-head. As well as a first aid kit and emergency rations there's a night-sight visor just in case the emergency lights fail. I want to go back and check them for trace but the chances are if they thought about hosing the tunnel down they've wiped the visor clean or tossed it into the ravine."

The holographic image smiled. "Well done Delgardo. Any suspects Kanah?"

160

"One thing we're not short of! How some of them passed their psyche evaluations is beyond me. So far we can't exclude anybody. Laslo was murdered between shifts at a time when not one of the crew can voucher for another. It could be anyone of them or all of them. If we actually had a motive it might help. The obvious one is the find of Zelman crystals but why that would cause any of the crew to want or need to kill Ginthem is a mystery at the moment."

"What's your next move?"

"Give some more thought to a motive but our best chance is finding some evidence when we recover the body."

"Keep me informed if there are any developments. I'll contact you as soon as I have some news about a recovery team. Be careful Kanah."

"You know me, always err on the side of caution. I'll be fine." Gantz ended the link.

"What next boss?"

"I'm going for a walk. It sometimes clears my mind of clutter and helps me concentrate. I want you to find out as much about Zelman crystals as you can. What do they look like, how can you identify them. We'll met back here in an hour and tell Petre Ull to make himself available as I'll want to speak to him again."

***

Wildman was teaching Keith to balance a mug on her head, much to the amusement of Milton Dang and the amazement of Will LeBon when Petre Ull entered the accommodation block. He helped himself to a coffee and sat on the table next to where Dang and LeBon were seated. He did not look a happy man.

"So what are our lovely ladies of the law up to now?" Dang leant back in his chair and looked over his shoulder at Ull as he spoke, a smirk on his face.

"They've just finished designating the tunnel leading to the ravine as a crime scene."

The smirk was wiped from Dang's face. "What about the river trail?" Ull glanced towards Wildman and Dang, acknowledged the gesture, got up, moved to Ull's table and sat opposite him. "So what about the river trail?" Dang leaned forward and lowered his voice. LeBon gave Wildman a nervous glance and then got up to join the others.

"I told you not to elaborate, you bloody fool!" At that moment Ull would have liked no better than to punch the smug face of Dang.

"Hey! I just offered them an alternative."

"You made straight to the river using the path Boni uses when he goes fishing. How stupid do you think they are? They know exactly what time Ginthem's chip went off-line and using the time when Zon saw him heading that way worked out he didn't have enough time to get to the river. Your brilliant idea directed them right to the mine."

"Yeah, but who's to say he didn't fall into the ravine or jumped?" There was a hint of desperation attached to LeBon's question.

"Because whoever was responsible tried to hose the tunnel out to get rid of any evidence. They didn't do a very good job of it." Ull glanced at Dang. "Sounds like one of your brilliant ideas!"

"Don't you try and fucking pin this on me."

Ull waved Dang's objection away. "I'm not accusing you of anything Milton. I'm just wondering if hosing the tunnel was another one of your embellishments?"

"No it bloody well wasn't! I only pointed them towards the river to delay them. How was I to know one of these lunatics had killed him? Are they closing the drill down?"

162

"They haven't said anything and I didn't push the point. At the moment they've just scan-sealed the tunnel." Ull looked directly at Milton Dang. "And I don't want anyone attempting to sneak in there because the scanners will pick you up." Dang picked up the inference and glared back at Ull.

"What do we do about this?" LeBon sounded nervous.

"There's not a lot we can do. I'll call a crew meeting for the end of the late shift. By that time we might have a better idea of what Gantz plans to do."

"I say we throw Dirk to them." There was a matter of fact tone to Dang's suggestion.

"What exactly do you mean by that?"

"Come on Petre, we all know it was a risk keeping him on the crew! As soon as the panic attacks came back we should have reported it and got him replaced. It was only Sligo who wanted to keep him on. If anybody is likely to have lost it and attacked Ginthem then it's Dirk."

"I'm throwing none of my team to them! If one of us did do it I'll wait for Gantz to find the evidence."

"And if that causes them to close down the drill-head?" Ull hesitated replying so Dang pushed home his argument. "What's the point us all losing our bonus when we're just delaying the obvious? Do a deal with Gantz, we hand over Dirk and she lets us keep drilling."

"Hand him over? And what evidence do we have Dirk is responsible?"

"Come on, we could be inventive. Zon could say he saw Dirk following Ginthem and me and Will could say they passed us as we were coming off shift. We could be all contrite about it, you know, misguided desire to protect one of our own."

"I don't want to hear any more of this Milton. We're not setting up Dirk to be the fall guy. What if he's innocent?"

163

"For Corp's sake Petre, with his medical condition they'll go light on him. We could all donate a percentage of our bonus for when he gets out."

"If he gets out! He'd be up for murder Milton, not another bar fight."

"You're looking at worst scenario there. No way would it be that bad. We could say it was an accident. They got into a disagreement which turned into a bit of pushing and shoving and Ginthem lost his footing and fell into the ravine." Dang caught the expression on Ull's face and quickly turned to LeBon for support. "What do you reckon Will?"

LeBon hesitated and glanced at Dang. The look on his work partner's face forced him into a stammering reply. "Well...I can sort of see Milton's point. The chances are, well, Dirk could be responsible and, well... Perhaps it's something we should at least discuss at the team meeting?" LeBon averted his eyes when he saw the look of disgust on Ull's face.

"The boy's right Petre! We need to discuss our options at the very least."

"If you want to bring this up at the meeting then that's your prerogative but you'll get no support from me. In fact I'll fight you all the way on this."

"It'll be a democratic vote like always Petre."

"The vote won't be binding if it means us perverting the course of justice."

"You weren't so picky about the rules when you agreed to delay reporting the crystal find. In fact if memory serves me correctly, it was your idea!"

"That's completely different. We delayed it to allow us to sign on for another tour. You can't compare that to setting up an innocent man for murder."

"Moot point there! Unless you know Dirk is innocent?"

Ull jumped up from the table, knocking his chair over in the process. "I've had enough of this conversation. I'm warning you Milton, don't push this." Without waiting for a reply Ull turned his back and stormed off.

"Something you said?" The question came from Wildman who had paused in his dog training to get himself a mug of coffee. Dang glanced round and wondered if Wildman had been close enough to hear any of their conversation.

"Is that what passes as your interrogation technique?"

Wildman smiled. "It was a mildly amusing comment which fell on stoney ground." He finished filling his mug and returned to his seat.

Dang studied Wildman for a few moments. He couldn't work out if he was an oddball playing at being a policeman of a policeman playing at being an oddball. "How's the investigation going?" Wildman looked up but just shrugged his shoulders and continued sipping his coffee. "Ull says they reckon it's murder." Dang paused for Wildman to comment but just got a nod as acknowledgement. "Found signs of a struggle in one of the tunnels." He paused again but just got a bored nod of acknowledgement. "They think somebody threw Ginthem into a ravine."

"Well that would be murder then!" Wildman pulled his CommsLink from his pocket and opened it up. He showed no sign of wanting to join in with this conversation.

"What do you think they'll do next?" Dang moved round in his chair to face Wildman.

Wildman sighed as if irritated by the question. "Report back and get in a team to locate the body. With any luck that will be it and we can go home when the new team arrive." He returned his attention to his CommsLink.

"With any luck? What does that mean?" Dang leaned forward in his chair.

Wildman sighed again and snapped shut his CommsLink. "Well that's what I'd do but this Gantz doesn't strike me as the sort to just sit back and go with the flow. She'll more than likely want to spend the time looking for a motive and then a suspect. It's what these police types do."

"Don't regard yourself as much of a police type then!"

"As I've said before Milton, I'm a flyer who happens to do it for the police. I didn't know this Ginthem and so, let me be brutally frank here, I really don't care what happened to him. By the same rationale I don't care if none of you, one of you or all of you are involved."

"You seem to know about motive and stuff."

Wildman gave an exasperated sigh. "I spend a lot of time with police types so it rubs off. I used to spend a lot of time with miners so I know a find of Zelman crystals is worth killing for!"

Dang was taken back by that remark. "What you mean by that? Why would anyone want to kill Ginthem over the crystals?"

"A good question Milton and one Gantz and Delgardo have asked themselves too. It doesn't seem a very likely motive, unless..."

Dang leaned forward even more in anticipation of Wildman finishing the sentence but he showed no intention of doing so. "Unless what?"

"Unless somebody wasn't content with just a bonus!" Wildman gave Dang a look which said 'work it out for yourself', which he did.

"They think one of us is trying to cheat the others out of the bonus?" Wildman just cocked his head a little to one side. "They think one of us is trying to make off with a whole storage bin of crystals?" Dang shook his head. "They think one of us would try and cheat their own crew?" He sat there open mouthed.

"Any more unlikely than one of you killed Ginthem for no apparent reason?" Wildman gave Dang a little smile and opened up his CommsLink again.

*****

By the time Gantz had finished her walk she had formulated her course of action. She arrived back at the storage bins later than she had intended, for her walk had taken her back to the river. She now stopped by the ore sledge pipe and stared at it, taking a large swig of ice cold water from her Koolbot. Delgardo, who had been sitting in the doorway of the office waiting for her to return, got up and walked across to join her.

"Ull's in the office waiting. He wanted to know what all this is about. I said I didn't know!" There was a faint trace of admonishment to her last sentence.

"Sorry, but I needed to sort things out in my own mind. I've been thinking about what Wildman said. If a swap like that was planned it would make more sense if, when the transport arrived, they picked up the one currently coupled up to the ore sledge pipe. Also, unless the whole crew are in on the plan, it wouldn't raise any suspicions. So, like you, I was thinking, what if they found the crystals earlier than they said? What if the low production figures had been caused by them switching to mining the crystals? They could have been mining them for the last three weeks! How long would it take to fill a storage bin? Also they would need time to arrange an off-world transporter. Fill a bin with the crystals, switch back to ore or just waste rubble. When that's full call control and ask them to pick up their first delivery of crystal."

"Ah!" Delgardo picked up on the idea. "Uncouple the bin and load it onto the Corporation transport and then call in the transport that's waiting in orbit. Just carry on as normal until the off-world transport arrives. The delay in reporting the find

167

would buy you the required time. The Corporation wouldn't expect the bin to be ready any earlier. The ore transporter leaves with the phoney crystal bin and the off-world transporter comes in to pick up the real crystal bin." Delgardo paused to give the idea further consideration. "It would give them, what, possibly five hours head start before the Corporation found out? Any hyper-drive trail would have dissipated by then so tracking them would be almost impossible. I suppose it could work and if you're right then the bin should be almost full of crystals. They'd have trouble explaining that away, how you fill a storage bin in a couple of days!"

"Did you find out the information I asked for?"

"I've identified the instruments they use and the expected results on testing."

"Good! I'm going to ask Ull to stop the drilling and uncouple the pipe so that he can make a test. I need you to keep a close eye on him to ensure he follows the right procedure and uses the correct instruments. Is that understood?" Delgardo nodded her agreement. "Do you know what these crystals look like?"

"In their processed form they're quite distinctive but in their raw state they look like," Delgardo struggled for an example. "Well they look like rock!"

"Even better! The Corporation wouldn't notice anything untoward until they tested the contents of the bin."

"Giving them more time after the switch. I guess we owe Wildman on this one."

"I suppose so but it goes against my better judgement to give the man credit for having a devious mind."

"No more devious than you boss for putting it all together!"

Gantz gave a rare smile. "Or you for making the suggestion in the first place. Okay, let's get Ull out here. Tell him what we want him to do." Delgardo quickly trotted back to the office.

When Ull stepped from the dark confines of the office the expression on his face indicated he was not a happy man. He strode up to Gantz and faced her with his hands on his hips. "What in Corps name do you want to check the storage bin for?"

"To check its contents and to ascertain how full it is."

Ull shook his head, not understanding her request as if she had spoken some long forgotten language. "It's got crystals in it and with any luck it'll be almost a quarter full. What's the bloody point?"

"Humour me. And before you ask, as soon as the tests are complete you can continue drilling."

Ull shook his head again but pulled out his CommsLink and contacted Edmurson at the drill-head. "Sligo I need you to power down." He paused to listen to the reply. He checked the time. "No stay there. Hopefully this won't take long. I just need to uncouple the pipe and do some tests. I'll let you know when you can power up again." He paused again and nodded his head in response to what was being said at the other end. "Okay power down now." He shut the CommsLink and walked over to the pipe. He put out a hand, rested it on the pipe and waited until the vibrations stopped. Then, giving Gantz another disparaging look he started to uncouple the pipe. Once the pipe was off Gantz could see the inlet had automatically reduced in size to become a very small inspection gap. Ull fed a fine cable through the access point and into the storage bin. He then opened up his CommsLink and connected the other end of the cable to it. Delgardo kept close and raised herself on tiptoes to observe over his shoulder exactly what response the machine was giving. She reacted quicker than Ull and dropped back on her heels, a look of confusion on her face. Ull just continued to stare at the device. He then disconnected the cable, reconnected it and repeated the test. There was a look of disbelief on his face as he slowly turned to face Gantz. He motioned to speak but no words came out. He licked his lips and cleared his throat before trying again. "It's empty!"

***

Either Petre Ull was a very good actor or his disbelief and confusion were real. He just stood and stared at Gantz as if he hoped she would explain what was happening. Unfortunately Gantz was just as confused but hid the fact better.

"Perhaps you could now inspect the other bins please."

Ull did not seem to hear her. "It's empty!" He looked from side to side as if the answer was laying around on the ground somewhere. "It can't be empty! Where are the crystals?"

"Petre, I think we need to inspect the other bins." Gantz was using her calm, reassuring voice again.

Ull stared at her again and then slowly nodded his head. "Yes, check the other bins." It did not sound like he actually understood why he should but he withdrew the cable from the bin and moved to the next one. He again fed the cable through the inspection hatch. Delgardo followed him and kept a watchful eye on his every move.

"Fifty-seven percent ore." His tone was flat. No surprise this time. He looked up at Gantz for guidance, as if not sure what to do next.

"Check the others please Petre." Gantz was now getting suspicious of Ull's reaction. The bins were too big and heavy just to swap around and she doubted Ull was so unobservant he had failed to notice if the pipe was coupled to a different bin. Her hand slowly moved to hover just above the holster where her side arm rested. She watched him intently, alert for any sudden move. Delgardo was close enough for him to grab her. Attempting to take Delgardo hostage would have been a very stupid thing to do but desperate men were prone to make

170

irrational decisions. Ull moved to the back two storage bins. He was partially hidden from view behind the bin he had just checked. Gantz moved forward and to one side so she could keep him in full view and watched him as he repeated the inspection test.

"Empty!" Again no surprise from Ull but he had expected them to be empty. Gantz glanced at Delgardo who nodded to confirm the read out. Ull stood and stared at the original bin and shook his head.

"Last one please Petre." She moved with him to keep him in her line of sight. If he was going to do anything foolish this would be the time. She unclipped the top of her holster and moved it out of the way so her finger tips rested on the handle of the weapon. Delgardo had been stealing quick glances at Gantz and had picked up on her nervousness. This time she positioned herself a little bit further away from Ull but close enough to keep an eye on the read out. Her hand also moved slowly towards her holster. As Ull fed the cable into the last of the bins she unclipped the top of her holster and slipped her hand around the butt of the weapon.

This time it was Delgardo's reaction which caught Gantz's eye. Her eyes widened in amazement and her mouth dropped open a little. Ull just sighed at the inevitability of it. "Empty."

Delgardo looked at Gantz and echoed Ull's response. "Empty!"

'Shit!' thought Gantz.

***

Gantz sat in the office and stared out of the window at the storage bins. She had been like that for several minutes and Delgardo was getting restless. The idea of the switched bins had seemed such a good one she had convinced herself they would crack the case as soon as the original bin was discovered to be empty. It had appeared the motive for Githem's murder was confirmed but they now had the additional problems of where the crystals were and how they had been spirited away. Delgardo couldn't stand the silence any longer. "Do you think Ull was faking his surprise?" It was the only thing she could think of saying to get Gantz talking again.

Gantz continued to stare at the bins and Delgardo wondered if she had actually heard the question. The silence went on for so long that Delgardo was about to repeat the question when Gantz finally managed to drag her eyes away from the bins. "What do you think?"

"I think..." Delgardo hesitated. 'Why ask me?' she thought, 'You're the Gnostic, surely you can tell!' "I think he was just as surprised as we were!"

"I agree, yet I was so sure there was a bin switch I doubted my own intuition. Like you, I expected him to react when we caught him out. I was ready to shoot him!"

Delgardo sensed that Gantz's last sentence had worried her boss considerably. It was not the sort of reaction she expected from the heroine of the Midwich case; the woman who had killed the terrorist leader single-handedly and saved her lover's life. Perhaps Gantz had got it right and the reality of the situation lacked the romantic gloss of the published story. When she had also reached for her weapon the consequences of taking another life had not occurred to her. The adrenalin rush had blocked out the thought. Gantz's remark now made her think about it. She had never even fired her weapon in anger let alone come close to killing anyone. Her bravado in front of her colleagues back in the locker room suddenly seemed rather foolish and immature. For the first time she realised the situation she found herself in could be dangerous. Even confirming that Ginthem had been murdered hadn't seemed real before now. He was just a faceless name you could not see or touch. There was nothing to relate him to a real person, not even a bloody mangled body.

"Are we missing something?" The sound of Gantz's voice thankfully brought Delgardo back from her unwelcome private thoughts.

"Other than a body, a suspect, a motive and a bin full of crystals?" Delgardo regretted the remark as soon as she made it but it did help a little to relieve the stress she was experiencing. However, Gantz smiled and nodded her head.

"You sounded like my colleague Vitch Tolman. Always can be relied upon to come up with the inappropriate comment at just the right time."

"I didn't mean..."

"I know Sonia, Vitch refers to it as a release valve. Perhaps we should bring Wildman on board to inject a little humour into this case. He certainly strikes me as a bit of a joke!"

"So what do we do now?"

"A good question! As far as the crystals are concerned I think we sit back and see what happens with the crew. Now Ull knows they're missing it won't be long before all the others do. Any solidarity they may have had over the Ginthem case could disappear pretty quickly judging from Ull's response. He appeared to take the idea that of one of his crew was a murderer in his stride but could barely control himself when he realised one or more of them had somehow made off with the crystals. He said something about a meeting at the end of the current shift. I should imagine that will be lively, to say the least."

"Should we turn up at that?"

Gantz shook her head. "I'd like to but I think our presence might cramp their style. I'll let Wildman know and he can keep an eye on them. He seems to have wormed his way in, at least to the extent they probably ignore him. For somebody with such outlandish dress sense and attitude he merges into the background quite well!"

"You're hoping the missing crystals will shake them up?"

"Oh yes! If, as seems likely, Ginthem discovered the crystals were missing and if that was the motive for getting rid of him then, now it's out in the open, we'll have members of the crew suddenly very interested in identifying the killer or killers! So far they've been desperate to keep the drill-head working but now they'll be desperate to find the crystals."

"And the killers will start to get desperate too." Delgardo paused. "Which means things could turn nasty!"

"That had occurred to me already. I'm going to report back to Inspector Goodridge and ask for backup. In the meantime we keep together and cover each other's back. At the first sign of trouble we'll lock them in their rooms and sit it out."

"Why not do that now?"

"Because leaving them to stew over this could work to our advantage. I'd still like to solve this case by the time the backup arrives." Gantz thought it best not to mention the delicate political situation which had also coloured her decision.

"So we keep up the pressure on them?"

"Yes, we get them all back in for questioning." Gantz paused and drifted into thinking mode. After a few moments she continued. "I don't want to run the risk of making too many assumptions so let's start with Sara Rolm. I had almost forgotten about her. I'm still interested in why she lied to us about speaking to Ginthem. We'll get Zon Willard in as well. I'd like to know why neither of them admitted to having met Ginthem before. He might have discovered the crystals were missing the same way we did or he could have been informed."

Delgardo nodded. "I'll arrange to get them both back in here. What about Dang and the misdirection, as Ull called it?"

"I would guess our Milton Dang thinks he's a lot cleverer than he really is but I don't see the harm in applying a little more pressure on him. We'll get him back in after we speak to Sara and Zon and after the crew meeting. He might not be so cocksure then."

CHAPTER EIGHT

Gantz had been so wrapped up in the case she had not checked for messages. It was only when she was about to contact Goodridge that she noticed two messages from Nemi. She played them both back and smiled on hearing his voice and seeing the holographic image of him. The first message was in reply to the message she had left after packing her bag in her apartment. He had asked her to call back at a specific time when he would be available to speak. The second message contained a gentle chide for not calling him back, remarking that he understood a case was far too important to interrupt just to call a friend. She wished she could call him now but he would be busy at this time. For some reason she wanted to tell him he was more than just a friend but something like that should be said face to face and not left as a hologram message. She sighed realising that by the time she did get to speak to him she would have lost her nerve and would say nothing of the sort. She recorded a short message. It had all the warmth of an official debrief report but at least she did have the courage to blow him a kiss at the end. She even regretted doing that but had already sent the message. It was foolish to even consider a relationship between a human and a half breed Gnostic. Neither side would be happy with the idea. Even Nemi's boss, Morgan, called her 'monkey girl'. She knew the reason he did it and there was no malice in the words but she also knew there would be plenty of malice in the remarks made by other humans if her secret became common knowledge. She pushed such thoughts to the back of her mind and called Goodridge to update him on the situation.

Goodridge looked pensive after hearing her report. "I don't like the sound of this one bit Kanah. I don't like the idea of putting my people at risk."

Gantz realised Goodridge was contemplating pulling her out. It was the intuition of her human side as her non-human abilities were useless with a holographic image. "Sir, there's only nine crew members here and three police officers. We're armed and they're not! We can keep the situation under control."

"Kanah, it's a mining camp so there are plenty of things which can be fashioned into a weapon. I'm unwilling to take risks with only the three of you on site."

"Sir, if you pull us out wouldn't you be putting some innocent civilians at risk? We can't assume the whole crew are involved. What's the point of us being here at all if it isn't to protect civilians?"

Goodridge tried to suppress a smile. It was both annoying and gratifying when one of his officers used his own principles against him. He knew Gantz was perfectly right. His fondness for her and the fact he was a New Brethren made him over protective of her. On the other hand, how could he live with himself if he was partly responsible for the death of a New Brethren prophet? "Alright Kanah but be careful. I'll try and find a couple more officers to send out with the recovery team. Hopefully the delay will be minimal. At the moment I've got people at the university converting a planet survey scanner so that we can probe your ravine. That seems to be the easiest problem to solve. Getting a recovery vehicle small enough to fit into a mine tunnel is proving to be more difficult. A scaled down patrol ship like the one which took you out there seems to be the best idea but of course such a thing doesn't exist on New Eden. At the moment we're cutting up a full size one with the intention of scaling it down ourselves. I've been promised everything will be ready by tomorrow so, with luck, if I can get the Corporation to provide the transporter, it should take off tomorrow night and will be with you early the day after."

"Good! I'm sure we can keep the lid on our disgruntled miners until then and once we recover the body hopefully some forensic evidence will pinpoint the killer."

"That reminds me, how are you getting on with Officer Delgardo?"

"She's good sir but I expect that's why you picked her!"

"I've heard good things about her and thought this would be a good opportunity for you to have a close look at her. Had a bit of a troubled background, abusive father I believe, so I'm glad she's proving to be an asset."

Gantz wondered if her past explained her reaction to Albright's violent outburst and her loathing for the bully Gurd. 'Well if she has problems in that area she's keeping them under control' she thought. "She's proving to be an asset sir."

"Good, good. Well I'll let you get on and I'll make myself unpopular by attempting to hurry up those conversions. Take care Kanah."

"I will sir." Gantz watched the image fade as the link closed down. She was alone again and the walls of the room started to close in again. She wasted no time in packing up her CommsLink and leaving in search of Delgardo.

***

While they waited for Rolm to arrive Gantz and Delgardo reviewed the current situation. They decided there were some things to do while they waited for the recovery team to turn up. The crew meeting was scheduled for the end of the current shift and Gantz wanted to speak to Wildman as soon as possible afterwards. Delgardo also needed to make forensic tests on the night-sight visor stored at the drill-head. Gantz was not hopeful as far as the forensics were concerned. The night-sight was checked to be in working order at the start of each shift as part of the safety routine so the chances were several of the crews DNA would be found. If it had been wiped clean then it would only have DNA from the subsequent shifts so would tell them nothing. The only hope they had was a long shot that it had not been wiped and contained the DNA of somebody other than members of the drill teams. Considering the way the investigation had gone so far Gantz did not believe they would be that lucky.

"Did anything interesting come up during your research into Zelman crystals?"

"Well, other than the technical details, tests and results you wanted there wasn't much we didn't already know. One interesting fact did come up and it might explain something which has been worrying me. We were told the Corporation sent Laslo out here because of the falling production figures but Ull had already reported the discovery of the crystal find. I guess I never appreciated how big a deal this was. So far the crystals have only been found in asteroid belts and pretty low yield finds at that. It's costly to mine asteroids, as the profit margins are so low. It's only the fact the crystals are so important which makes the effort worthwhile. The extra mining and transport costs aren't the only problem. Because of their value they are obviously a prime target for piracy so security adds even more to the cost. If the Corporation have found a source for the crystals on a planet the sky's the limit for the profits to be made. They can mine, refine and assemble hyper-drive engines here and drastically slash all those costs. Perhaps Laslo was sent out to confirm the find. It could explain why they kept very quiet about this. It could also explain why they were monitoring his ID chip. If it got out, there would be a chance the New Brethren administration would want to renegotiate the contract for the mining concession." Delgardo paused and smiled. She anticipated Gantz's next question. "So I checked. The contract is currently up for renewal."

"And as the rumours are the New Brethren are already thinking about moving into the manufacturing side for the patents they hold which are currently licensed to the Corporations, they wouldn't want to run the risk of the New Brethren moving into the mining business if they got wind of crystal deposits on the planet."

"Not only that, but they could refine and start producing hyper-drive engines. I doubt if the Corporations would welcome a move like that! In fact something like that would be worth killing for."

"You're not attempting to suggest a New Brethren conspiracy?"

Delgardo thought about it. "It never occurred to me but now you mention it." Delgardo shook her head. "No. I could see the New Brethren having members working within the Corporations but not in a mining crew. Anyway all the New Brethren had to do was leak the discovery before the renegotiations started. Killing Ginthem to bring us in to find out about the crystals is ridiculous."

"I'm glad you think the idea of the New Brethren killing people for financial gain is ridiculous."

Delgardo suddenly realised her own insensitivity in suggesting such a thing to a New Brethren prophet. "Sorry boss that was my mouth running way ahead of my brain. No offence intended."

"None taken Sonia."

Delgardo gave a little inward sigh of relief before she continued. "If Laslo was really here to check the quality and production levels then he probably did the same tests we've just done."

"And being an experienced mining inspector he might have also worked out how they were syphoning off the crystals!"

"It provides a very plausible motive for getting rid of Laslo."

"Hold the fort here. Delay Rolm if she turns up. I'm going to report in to Goodridge. I want him to arrange for the monitoring of any transporters which move into orbit anywhere near this camp. They have to get the crystals off this planet somehow. I might also request some Colonial trooper backup. We've got enough problems down here without an armed crew of a rogue transporter turning up!" Gantz got up and left the office to make the call in the privacy of her own room.

Delgardo hoped Gantz was just being over cautious. A few dishonest, unarmed, miners she could deal with but the idea of facing the equivalent of space pirates made her decidedly uneasy. They were a rare occurrence but such were the profits to be made by hijacking transporters there were always people willing take the risk. And those willing to take the risk were determined to get away with it. They tended to be brutal and ruthless. Delgardo's experience was limited to dealing with 'Medheads' and domestic disturbances. She remembered her fear with the Albright incident and had no wish to repeat the feeling.

Sara Rolm suddenly appeared in the office door way. "Petre told me you wanted to see me again?" Her voice betrayed a mixture of confusion and suspicion.

Delgardo jumped at the sound of Rolm's voice. She could feel her pulse racing and she waved Rolm into the office and gestured for her to take a seat. She smiled at Rolm and busied herself with setting up the CommsLink to give herself time to calm down. It was embarrassing having this irrational bout of nerves. She was a professional and needed to control her emotions.

"Thank you for coming back for another chat." Her own voice sounded strained and she paused to cough as if to clear her throat. "Deputy Gantz has just been called away but should be back in a few minutes. We just wanted to go over your earlier statement." She glanced up and saw the look on Rolm's face. "Nothing to worry about, just need to clear up a few details." Rolm nodded but looked far from being reassured.

A few minutes of nervous silence followed before Gantz finally entered the office. She apologised to Rolm for keeping her waiting and then settled down behind the desk.

"I hope Officer Delgardo explained we're just clearing up a few details from your first interview?"

Rolm nodded. "I can't think of anything else to add to what I've already told you."

"Well it's more clearing up some confusion your statement caused." Gantz paused to allow Rolm time to worry about what the next question was. It appeared to work as Rolm licked her lips nervously. "How do you get on with Milton Dang and Dirk Albright?" From her reaction Rolm was certainly not expecting that question.

"Alright." She glanced from Gantz to Delgardo and back again. They appeared to be waiting for more, which unsettled her. "I get on with them alright. They're on different shifts so I don't get to see them that often."

"Any less often than Sligo Edmurson or Will LeBon?"

"No, they're on another shift as well." There was a wariness underpinning her reply.

"It's just that Dang and Albright were the only ones you didn't refer to by their first names. As I said it's only a minor detail but we concern ourselves with detail. Being on first name terms tends to suggest a more familiar and friendly relationship. Last names suggests a more formal or uneasy relationship."

Rolm hesitated before answering. "I didn't realise I did that!" She stared at them in the hope it was enough to satisfy them. They just stared back and she felt under pressure to say more. "Well they're alright but I guess I get on with the others better." She hesitated again. "I tend to talk to them more so have got to know them more. Dang can be a bit superior and Albright can be a bit intimidating."

"That's understandable Sara. We know Albright has trouble with his temper. Nerves got the better of him when we interviewed him." Delgardo glanced at Gantz in surprise after that remark. A bad case of nerves appeared to be a bit of an understatement when she had been forced to draw her weapon on him.

"It has a lot to do with his medical problems," Rolm pointed out in Albright's defence. "Is that it?" she asked more in hope than expectation.

"Just one more little detail. You said that although you saw Ginthem on the day he arrived you didn't talk to him. Is that right?" Rolm stared back at Gantz and nervously began picking at some loose skin around her fingernails. She was beginning to understand where this line of questioning was leading but was reluctant to say anything so she just nodded her head. "And yet some of the crew claim they saw you talking to him and in your original statement you referred to him as Laslo. A term you use for people you talk to and get to know. And apparently you have met Laslo Ginthem before; he was an inspector on your previous crew."

There was a long silence before Rolm finally answered. "I couldn't remember him but he must have recognised me and

184

came over the evening he arrived. I didn't want to get involved. We just chatted, that was all."

"Chatted about what?"

"Just chat! I can't even remember what we said."

"Did you chat about Mol Gurd?"

Rolm averted her eyes and concentrated on picking more skin from her fingers. "He's my lead driller so I guess he got mentioned."

Gantz waited in the hope a protracted silence would again pressurise her into saying more. Unfortunately Delgardo got impatient and jumped in. "If you're afraid of Mol Gurd you don't have to be. We can help and we can protect you."

Rolm snorted at the remark. "Yeah, sure! The last person who promised that ended up dead!"

"Are you talking about Laslo Ginthem?" Gantz put her hand on Delgardo's arm to stop any more interruptions.

"I've finished talking. Are you going to arrest me or can I go?" Without waiting for an answer Rolm stood up and avoided any further eye contact with the two police officers.

"You can go Sara but if I find out Mol Gurd had anything to do with Laslo Ginthem's death I will arrest you for withholding information." Gantz paused. "But you can come and talk to us any time you like. We've dealt with people like Mol Gurd before." Rolm shrugged her shoulders, turned and walked out of the office.

"You want me to get her back in here?" Delgardo was already half out of her seat.

"Let her go. Give her time to think it over. Gurd isn't going anywhere."

Delgardo reluctantly slipped back into her seat. "Have we just got another motive added to the list?"

***

Zon Willard turned up late and mumbled his usual apology. He looked relaxed and displayed no sign of agitation over being called back.

"Just a couple of follow up questions Zon."

"Sure, what do you need to know?"

"Why didn't you tell us you had met Laslo Ginthem before?"

Willard looked confused but not thrown by the question. "But I haven't!"

"He inspected your previous crew; the one you were on with Sara Rolm."

"Ah, Sara said he went over to talk to her because he recognised her but she didn't mention where from."

"But he didn't remember you?"

Willard smiled. "Sara was the only woman on that crew as well so it would have been hard not to remember her. I was a junior tech. It was a large desert complex and I was one of several low levels working under a senior tech. If Ginthem was the inspector he would have spent time with the senior tech." Willard grimaced. "To be honest if an inspector had asked to talk to a junior tech I wouldn't have been chosen. Senior tech like to demonstrate they run a tight unit to inspectors so they would be unlikely to select a junior who would turn up late for an interview." He shrugged his shoulder to emphasise his inability to cope with timekeeping.

"Did Sara tell you what she and Ginthem talked about?" There was a change in Willard's demeanour which Gantz noticed. "I'll remind you that we are now running a murder investigation."

Willard shifted uneasily in his chair. "Look, I honestly don't know but she was fairly upbeat after talking to him but was then very depressed when he went missing the next day."

"And you put that down to what?"

186

"I don't know and I'm not going to speculate."

Gantz studied him for a few minutes. The silence had an affect and Willard did not look as relaxed as he done when he first arrived. Gantz finally broke the silence, much to the relief of Delgardo who was willing her to ask the next question. "Anything to do with Mol Gurd and his relationship with Sara?"

Willard now looked very uncomfortable and delayed his answer until he had thought through the consequences. "Their shift partners! As far as I know that's the limit of their relationship."

"Never even wondered about it?"

"No!" The reply was instant. "You don't speculate about Mol Gurd's business.' Willard paused and rolled his tongue around the inside of his mouth. "Mol Gurd's not a man to cross. Now if we've finished here I've got a crew meeting to go to and Petre won't be happy if I'm late again."

Willard rose. He hesitated but as Gantz did not protest he proceeded to leave the office. Neither officer spoke until the door slid shut and it was Delgardo who jumped in first. "Did you read anything into that last remark or have I lost my objectivity again?"

Gantz said nothing but she did have a fleeting thought that Gurd might have ruined somebody's elaborate plan to steal the crystals. Perhaps that was the solution to the problem. They had always assumed the murder was linked to the crystals but what if the two incidents had nothing to do with each other? Should they be looking for a murderer and separate thief?

***

The entire crew assembled in the recreation area. Edmurson and Albright were still in their protective suits, having just come off shift. Ull took his place at the head of the table. He looked at those around the table and studied them one by one. A week ago he would have classified this crew as his extended family. Not angels by any stretch of the imagination but he had believed they shared a bond which went beyond just a cooperative work team. Now that delusion was well and truly shattered. Sitting at the table was a murderer and a thief. In fact those terms could apply to all of them. The only thing he was sure of was that he didn't kill Laslo Ginthem and he hadn't stolen the crystals. His eyes came to rest on Milton Dang. The man had a smirk on his face. He was ready to throw Dirk Albright to Gantz and Delgardo and would enjoy undermining Ull's authority by attempting to talk the rest of the crew into supporting the idea. 'I wonder if he'll look so pleased with himself when he finds out the crystals have gone missing?' thought Ull. 'Unless the little turd already knows!'

He saw some of the others were getting impatient with the delay to the start of the meeting and were chatting amongst themselves. No doubt anticipating what all this was about. He took a deep breath and started. "Thanks for being here." He paused to allow them to settle down and give him their full attention. "I thought I better keep you up to date with what's been happening." He paused again. "Despite some foolish attempts to divert their investigation," he glared at Milton Dang, "Officers Gantz and Delgardo confirmed, earlier today, that the mine inspector, Laslo Ginthem, was murdered." He paused, not for dramatic effect but for his eyes to sweep the group looking for any telltale signs which would give him some indication as to who was responsible. Dang still had that smirk on his face but he had been expecting the first revelation. Will LeBon was watching Dang from the corner of his eye, no doubt waiting for his crew partner to make his move. Mol Gurd sat picking his nose and his expression had not changed. Sara Rolm was staring at the floor so had her face hidden from sight. Sligo Edmurson had a slightly sad expression on his face and he glanced around the group, no doubt wondering which of his work colleagues was responsible. At least Ull hoped this was the case. His judgement of character would take another blow, possibly a terminal one, if Edmurson was responsible. Albright frowned, clutched his fists tightly and gave the appearance that he was working his way up to another violent panic attack. Zon Willard looked unconcerned and Boni Chang, as usual, just looked confused. Ull still could not really believe any of them were capable of murder or theft but the evidence said otherwise. He continued with his briefing. "They found evidence of a struggle in the tunnel leading to the ravine and believe he was thrown into it. No doubt more police will be turning up in an attempt to recover the body." He glanced around the table but was met only by subdued acceptance of the inevitable rather than any shock.

"Are they going to close the drill-head down?" It was Dang who asked the question which was on everybody else's lips. All eyes were suddenly fixed on Ull. He gave a cold hard stare back at Dang. He knew the question was just a way to introduce the idea of sacrificing Dirk Albright. 'Let the little shit carry on and make a fool of himself' thought Ull, 'I've got a little bit of information which will kick the legs from under that plan.'

"They haven't said." Ull left it at that and watched the reaction of the others, especially Dang.

"Of course they will! They'll close us down until they recover the body and examine it. If we're lucky they'll have enough evidence to find out which of you dick-heads did it. Then they might let us start up again. Of course if we're unlucky they wont find the body or it won't hold any clues and they'll ship us all back for interrogation. You can all kiss goodbye to your bonus, that's for sure!" The crew nodded in agreement with Dang's statement.

The depression was almost visible as, to a man, the crew slumped in their chairs. Chang, who had really only followed suit and had not really fully understood what was going on, raised his hand as if he was asking permission to speak. "No bonus?" The question had the effect of turning the knife into the wound and caused one or two audible groans from around the table. Ull's eyes flicked from one crew member to another but saw no clue as to who was faking their reaction.

"My fucking ticket out of this shit-hole went down the fucking ravine with that bastard Ginthem!" Albright thumped the table and rocked to and fro in his chair until Edmurson placed a hand on his arm to calm him down.

Dang gave a little smile as all eyes were now on Albright. "We all lose out, unless..." He rubbed his chin and looked deep in thought.

"Unless what?" Mol Gurd leant forward.

"No, it's a mad idea." Dang shook his head. They would have to drag the idea from him.

"Come on Milton if you've got an idea let us into it." It was Willard who had now joined in.

Dang looked reluctant to speak. Ull had the urge to speak out but kept silent. 'Let him show the others what a little shit he really is' he thought.

"Come on Milton, if there's any chance of keeping the drill-head working we need to know what it is." The deep tones of Edmurson, the crew's voice of reason, was music to Dang's ears.

"It just occurred to me..." He paused again and glanced around the table. They were all hanging on his every word, with the exception of Ull who looked as if he had just eaten something very unpleasant. "Well, it occurred to me that if they had the murderer in custody they might have a more relaxed attitude to keeping the operation up and running. At the

190

moment all of us are under suspicion so all of us will be escorted back for further questioning."

"Brilliant idea Milton!" Willard's comment was heavy with sarcasm. "I can't wait to hear the rest of it. What do we do? Ask the killer to give themselves up? Solve the crime ourselves?" Willard shook his head. "You're a bloody idiot!"

"Well my plan is a tiny bit cleverer than that Zon." There was real venom laced in the pronunciation of Willard's name. Nobody calls Milton Dang an idiot. "What I suggest is we all agree to put a percentage of our bonus into a pot for the person who volunteers to confess. They get their share of the bonus when they get out of the cubes."

"It's fucking murder Milton, how long do you think you get in the isolation cubes for that?" Willard looked around at the other faces for support but was amazed to see that some of them were giving the idea serious consideration.

"What if nobody wants to volunteer? Do we draw lots?" Much to Dang's surprise it was Edmurson who asked the question.

"Well we could do!" Dang hesitated. "But, as Zon has already pointed out, you're looking at serious iso-time. We need an edge to reduce that time. Who wants to be a rich centenarian?"

"Give 'em Boni!" Gurd found his own suggestion so amusing he laughed until he almost choked in a coughing fit.

"You arse Mol! Who's going to believe Boni is smart enough and big enough to over-power Ginthem?" The rest of the crew laughed at Edmurson's comment, even Chang who hadn't worked out the implications of the conversation.

"You don't have to be smart or big to push somebody into a ravine Edmurson, and the New Brethren are soft! A moron like Boni would get off with a slap on the wrist compared to what one of us would get. We all point the finger at him who are they going to believe? Him or us?"

"He's got a point there!" Albright had relaxed and threw his weight behind the idea, not realising he was Dang's intended sacrificial lamb.

"No" said Edmurson. "If we do this it must be a volunteer. I'm not prepared to lie to the police and blame anyone."

"I can't believe you're actually considering this!" Ull had finally had enough. He never thought any of his crew would give Dang's idea serious consideration.

"Oh come on Petre, we've already bent the rules to stay on here for the bonus. It's a lot of credits we're talking about! I can't see the harm in just talking about it!"

"Sligo's right. I don't see any harm in just talking about it." Ull wondered if Albright would have been as quick to add his support to the idea had he known Dang intended for him to be the volunteer. The others were all now looking at Ull, expecting him to take the lead.

"Do what you damn well like." Ull sat down and slumped back in his chair at a complete loss as to what had happened to his crew. He wanted no part in this and averted his eyes to stare at the floor. One by one the crew turned away from Ull and gave their full attention to Dang. Willard was the last but even he turned his back on Ull.

"So what do you reckon is the edge Milton?" It was a smiling Albright leading the way this time.

"You!"

"What?" The smile vanished from Albright's face.

"You're the one with the medical condition Dirk! You just lost it and before you knew what had happened poor Laslo had gone over the edge. It was an accident and who's to say it wasn't?"

"Fuck off!" Albright jumped to his feet, knocking his chair over. Edmurson had to restrain him to prevent him from clambering over the table to get at Dang.

"Hey Dirk, you were keen a minute ago!" Gurd's laughter again turned into a coughing fit.

"This isn't funny!" shouted Edmurson over his shoulder. He struggled to get Albright back onto his seat.

"You've got to admit with a performance like that it wouldn't take much to convince the police. He's already lost it in front of them. Probably already top of their suspect list. He'd more than likely get off with a secure hospital stint and a medication order." LeBon had timed his comment to perfection. Albright stopped struggling and sat breathing heavily. Edmurson slowly released his grip.

"I don't hear any of you volunteering." Edmurson glanced round the table.

"Because we would all get life in the iso cubes, or as long as it took to turn our brains to mush. You know once Dirk is back on his medication he'll be fine. The authorities, especially the New Brethren, aren't going to give him life for an incident based on a mental aberration. Dirk is the obvious choice. Calm him down and talk to him Sligo. We'll all donate a percentage of our bonus." Dang paused to glance around at the circle of faces. They all nodded, with the noticeable exception of Ull who still sat staring at the floor. "See, we'll all back him up. We'll say we warned Ginthem about his condition but he kept pushing Dirk about his temper. An accident waiting to happen!"

"How do we explain suddenly changing our stories?" It was a surprising question, coming as it did from Gurd.

"Misguided loyalty to a member of the crew. We all thought it must have been an accident and it's only now it's been confirmed Ginthem was tossed over the edge, that we realise it must have been Dirk. The only missing piece is Dirk's confession."

"It's worth a try surely?" asked LeBon. "We were all keen when it was a matter of drawing lots, or was it only a good idea if somebody else drew the short straw?"

"Dirk is the obvious choice." Gurd managed to keep a straight face making that comment.

"But only if Dirk agrees." Dang added the comment for the benefit of Edmurson. If the big man could be won round then he could convince Albright. Edmurson stroked his beard, deep in thought. "You know it makes sense Sligo. Everyone would benefit if we keep hold of the bonus."

"What bonus? You stupid bastard!" All heads turned towards Ull who had returned to his feet.

"The crystal bonus Petre, the crystal bonus!" Milton looked confused at having to remind Ull of that.

"There is no bonus Milton because there are no crystals. Gantz had me test the storage bins. They're all empty! One of you shits has already robbed us of any bonus." There was a stunned silence around the table.

Nobody had taken any notice of the apparently dozing Wildman and Keith who were laid out on one of the sofas at the other side of the recreational area. Wildman opened one eye to observe the scene. He took in every expression on every face and wondered how, in a group of such stupid people, one of them could be clever enough to be able to steal a storage bin full of crystals. It defied logic.

***

"How can the bins be empty? We've drilled for days now since finding the seam, there should be something in the bin!" Edmurson directed his question at Ull. Dang's supremacy had not lasted long.

194

"Somebody has worked out a way of syphoning off the crystals." Ull looked at each face in turn. "Anybody care to own up and tell me how they did it?" The faces remained blank. "I didn't think so!"

"Perhaps we hit a break in the seam today." Dang sounded as if the remark was made more in hope than expectation.

"So where are the crystals from the other days? Which of you bastards are trying to cheat us?" Gurd gave each of the crew a threatening stare.

"Could the drill sensors be malfunctioning and not filtering the crystals?" Even Dang was now looking to Ull to provide reassurance.

"When was the last time you checked them Zon?"

Willard thought hard. 'Not since we reset them for the crystals."

"Fat lot of use you are as a maintenance engineer!" sneered Dang.

"They shouldn't need checking that often." Willard sounded defensive. They were all staring at him now and he was not keen on how unfriendly those stares were.

"Might have guessed a lazy sod like him would be lax on the maintenance checks. Always bloody late! Anybody other than Ull would have got rid of him long before now." One or two of the crew murmured their agreement with Dang's comment.

"Are you telling me we could have millions of credits worth of crystals dumped with the waste?' Albright had recovered from the shock of being the crew sacrificial lamb. "For Corp sake! Have we been digging crystals out of one tunnel and dumping it in another as back fill?"

"Calm down Dirk. We don't know anything yet. The malfunction idea is just that! An idea."

"Unless it's not a malfunction."

"What are suggesting Mol?" Willard was now alert to any criticism.

"How do we know Willard didn't cause the malfunction? He could have set the sensor up wrong. Between shifts he's the only one who goes to the mine for maintenance checks, or so he says! He could be spending the time sifting through the waste and pocketing the crystals."

"By hand?" Edmurson made a sound which could have been a laugh. "You're a knob Mol!"

"You watch your mouth Sligo. You aren't so big that somebody won't shut it for you." Gurd made the threat but gave no indication that he intended to follow it up with action. "Who knows what he gets up to during the shift breaks, and who's to say he doesn't slip into the waste tunnel at other times?"

"And get buried in rock that's spat out by the waste pipe?" Edmurson had turned now to face up to Gurd.

"Might be worth the risk, depending on how easy it was to pick up the crystals." Dang was now siding with Gurd's idea. "Even the time between shifts would give him enough to make his share of the bonus look like chicken feed." Dang paused and looked straight at Ull. "Let's face it Petre he's the one with the technical skills to pull it off."

"This is just ridiculous speculation." Ull sensed the mob mentality had shifted its focus from Dirk to Zon and was eager to inject the calming influence of reason into the situation.

"Wouldn't be so protective just because he warms your bed Petre?"

The silence that remark brought on the group was deafening. Uneasy looks were exchanged. What members of the crew did in their private lives were always kept out of the public domain. Dang had overstepped the mark and he suddenly realised it from the looks given to him by the rest of the crew. He was on the verge of apologising but swallowed the words before they could leave his lips. Milton Dang was not that sort of man. Instead he just gave a smirk and looked away.

All eyes reverted to Ull. "We'll check the calibration on the sensors and test the waste." There was a general mumble of approval. "But we do it under the supervision of Deputy Gantz. If the crystals have been stolen it's a police matter now," he paused and then added, "and then nobody can accuse Zon of fiddling the results. If we can salvage the situation we might save a little of the bonus." He glanced round but could see the crew were far from happy with his last remark.

"Ull's right." All heads turned towards the sound of the voice. Wildman was now sitting up scratching Keith behind the ear. "You've fucked this up big time. Your only hope now is to fully cooperate with Gantz and Delgardo.." He paused and gave a little mischievous smile. "Unless you plan to toss them into the same ravine."

CHAPTER NINE

Delgardo was having trouble with the stifling heat of the cramped office. The temperature had gradually risen during the day and had been retained in the office despite the fact the sun had sunk below the horizon long since. She excused herself and told Gantz she planned to take a walk to cool off. Gantz reluctantly let her go. She did not like the idea of them separating now the news of the missing crystals would soon be common knowledge. However, the crew meeting was just about to start so she limited herself to warning Delgardo to keep her break to a minimum. When Delgardo left, Gantz relaxed for the first time that day. She had the feeling the lull in their activities would not last much longer than the end of the crew meeting. Her relaxation period did not last long. Without the distractions of the case she suddenly noticed how oppressive the heat was in the office. She pulled herself to her feet and walked to the doorway. A cool breeze enveloped her body and refreshed her. She sat down by the doorway and rested her back against the outside wall of the office. Another gust of cool air swept in from the Perrin gap and she closed her eyes. A second long day was beginning to take its toll and she almost drifted off to sleep. The vibration of the metal coil in her ear woke her; a call was coming in on her CommsLink. She glanced down at the display on her wrist band and saw it was Nemi calling. Her spirits lifted and she returned to the office, quickly opening up her

CommsLink. The familiar face and grin of Nemi appeared, floating just above the device.

"Finally got the time to talk to me then!"

She smiled and then suddenly remembered the kiss she had blown to him at the end of her last message. Embarrassment sent a rush of blood to her cheeks so she replied rather formally. "I've been busy. This case is turning out to be more complex than I had imagined."

"Well as long as you're enjoying yourself!"

She hesitated and then realised Nemi was teasing her. In the past couple of years she had got used to his odd sense of humour. She did not always understand it but was getting used to it. Humour was something she had always struggled with but she was beginning to appreciate it with the help of Nemi. It was probably one of the things which attracted her to him. "I'm surprised you found the time to call me with Vitch having been posted there."

"Believe it or not, we haven't met up yet. We were both too busy yesterday when he first arrived but we plan to make up for it tonight. I've found a few really awful Federal bars, all in the line of work of course! I need to find out which ones should be off limits to the troops."

"Wasn't that the excuse your boss Morgan used when he first arrived on New Eden?"

"Shouldn't try and fool a Gnostic, should I?"

She shook her head at the remark and what it inferred. He was teasing her again. "And exactly how many bad Federation bars are there?"

"Two actually. The Federation quarter is tiny and the Corporation quarter is non-existent. Nearest thing to a totally New Brethren city so far. By all accounts Vitch is bored silly already, hardly the centre of criminal activity! I'll tell him your case is turning into a major one and sit back and watch his reaction."

'You're a wicked man Ja Nemi! You," she was interrupted by a knock on the office door. "Give me a minute please," she called out over her shoulder before turning back to holographic image "I'm sorry I've got to go." Her hand hovered over the terminate control. "I miss you." The words were blurted out before she cut the link. As the image faded she saw Nemi blow her a farewell kiss. She caught her breath and felt a rush of blood to her checks again. She felt elated and excited by Nemi's gesture and took a few moments to compose herself before letting the waiting visitor know they could enter the office. By the time Ull entered she had recovered and greeted him with a rather stern countenance.

"I'm sorry to disturb you Officer Gantz but I wonder if I could talk to you about the," he paused and then added, "crystal situation." His usual air of natural authority had been replaced by a more subservient tone. It did not go unnoticed by Gantz.

"You want me to do you a favour Petre?"

Ull shifted his weight from one foot to the other. The question made him feel embarrassed and uncomfortable even though it was a mild reproach. He was glad the Delgardo woman was absent, he was sure her comments would have been a lot more barbed. "I know I could have been more helpful and supportive but I've always been defensive where my crews are concerned. Until you confirmed Laslo Ginthem had been murdered I couldn't believe any of my crew were capable of that." He hesitated and took a quick glance at Gantz. "I also wouldn't have believed any of my crew were capable of cheating the others." He hesitated again. He had to ask this woman for help or watch his crew tear themselves to pieces. "They're turning on each other and there's nothing I can do about it."

"And what do you think I can do about it?"

201

"They think Zon Willard tampered with the calibration of the scanner on the drill-head."

"Could he have, and to what end?"

"He's responsible for maintenance so calibrating the scanner is part of his duties. It's set to identify what we're currently drilling for and diverts it down the sledge pipe, any waste product is pushed down a secondary pipe to backfill abandoned tunnels. They think he's diverted the crystals with the waste. Zon wouldn't do that!" The last sentence was said with conviction.

"You were equally confident none of your crew could toss Laslo Ginthem into the ravine or cheat the others out of their bonus! Could he have done it?" Ull hesitated so Gantz added. "And by that I mean has he got the technical skills?" Reluctantly Ull nodded his head. "Have any of the others got the required skill set?"

"I very much doubt it, with the exception of me."

"So the crew have two suspects!" Gantz wondered if this concern over the reaction of the crew lay a little closer to home than Zon Willard but she did not allow him the time to respond to her remark. "So what exactly do you want me to do?"

"They want to check the waste tunnel. I told them the missing crystals were now a police matter so you needed to make that decision and make all the tests." His voice trailed off and he averted his eyes.

"And to protect Willard if the crew's suspicions turn out to be true!"

"Even if you find nothing they'll just think he's moved the crystals elsewhere." He looked up at Gantz. "Either way they'll want to beat the truth out of him."

"Then the first thing we do is check the calibration on the scanner. Delgardo needs to examine the drill-head anyway."

Gantz was careful not to specifically mention the night-sight visor. "Where are they all now?"

"They're all waiting in the Rec. I passed Officer Delgardo on the way here and asked her to babysit them. They're not going to let anyone out of their sight but I thought she would stop any arguments getting out of hand." Gantz got up from her seat and gestured for Ull to lead the way. As he turned away she could not resist a little smile. Asking Delgardo for help must have really stuck in his throat.

An expectant hush fell on the recreational area when they entered. All eyes turned towards them. Delgardo nodded to Gantz in recognition. "They've all been good little miners." The remark drew a few sour looks from the assembled crew.

Gantz stepped forward and cast her eyes along the row of expectant faces. She certainly had their full attention. "Let me make this clear to you all. The missing crystals are now a police matter and I will not tolerate interference from any of you. Petre Ull has requested our help in checking the calibration of the drill-head scanner and inspecting the waste tunnel. I have no intention of undertaking these tasks with an audience so all of you will stay here." There were a few disgruntled faces and mumbled comments but no objections were made out loud. Ull had prepped them well, no doubt with promises of recovery of the crystals and a continuation of drilling. Gantz turned her back on them and gestured for Wildman to approach. He did so with some degree of reluctance.

"You want me to come with you?" There was a hint of desperation in his voice, hoping the answer would be no!

"Sonia will be doing the technical tests. I want you to keep an eye on this lot and make sure none of them leave the building." She paused to glance down at his hip. "I suggest you go and get your sidearm." Wildman appeared to be about to question her request but then thought better of it and quickly walked off to his room. He returned a few minutes later, patted the holster now attached to his belt and gave Gantz an unconvincing nod of reassurance. She leaned forward to whisper in his ear. "Don't worry Wildman, you only need to pretend to be a police officer for a short while." Wildman glanced from side to side and then slightly raised the flap on his holster. Gantz peered down and somehow managed to conceal her reaction. "We'll talk later Wildman."

"Yes boss." He made an embarrassed retreat to the doorway and made an attempt to look like a guard, his hand resting on his gun holster.

"Right, let's get on with this." She marched out of the door closely followed by Delgardo and Ull.

"Anything up boss?" Delgardo kept her voice low to avoid Ull overhearing.

"I'll tell you later."

They continued along the path to the mine entrance. Delgardo took a deep breath as they entered to steady herself but she still felt the walls closing in on her. Ull was in the middle of the three again with Gantz to his left and Delgardo to his right. The gloom enveloped them and Delgardo glanced over her shoulder for one last look at daylight as they followed the main tunnel round a bend. The steady rhythmic beat of the ore sledge which she had hardly noticed before was now prominent by its absence. The silence was only broken by the echo of their own footsteps. She could feel the palms of her hands were becoming sweaty. They passed the entrance to the ravine tunnel with its 'Do Not Enter' holographic sign flashing its warning, and several other abandoned side tunnels. Most were full or partially full with waste from later excavations. Peering through the gloom ahead Delgardo could just make out what appeared to be the end of the tunnel. As they drew closer she realised in fact that the tunnel split into two. One turned right

204

off the main tunnel and she guessed that it headed for the centre of the mountain; the other veered slightly to the left and continued with a downward gradient. At the junction Ull stopped.

"This is the tunnel which followed the original ore seam." He gestured to the right. "It has various off-shoot drillings which were used as backfills once the ore seams were exhausted. This one leads to the drill-head and the crystal seam." He pointed down the left hand tunnel. Delgardo noticed two sledge pipes ran out of the tunnel, one ran back to the entrance while the other curved around and disappeared down the older tunnel. She then caught sight of Gantz.

"Are you alright boss?" She could see that Gantz was holding onto the side of the tunnel to steady herself. Her mouth was open as if she was having trouble breathing and her frame was stooped.

"I'm alright." Gantz tried to give Delgardo a reassuring smile but it came out more like a grimace.

"You don't look that good!' volunteered Ull. "Are you ill?"

Gantz waved away their concerns. "Perhaps I've got a touch of your claustrophobia Sonia." She took a deep breath. "Come on, let's get on with this. I'll be fine." She wiped the sweat from her brow and led the way forward. Ull and Delgardo exchanged worried looks and then followed Gantz into the tunnel.

***

Delgardo began to appreciate how Gantz felt. As they moved down the tunnel she had to wipe the sweat from her palms on her uniform to dry them. Logic told her the tunnel was exactly the same size and yet the ceiling and walls seemed to close in on her. Even the emergency lighting appeared to shed a duller light. It came as a relief when she saw the drill-head take shape in the gloom indicating the they were near the end of their journey. She gave a quick glance at Gantz but her superior appeared to have regained her composure.

"Let's get on with this Sonia. Start on checking the calibration."

Delgardo pulled out her CommsLink and attached a thin probe to one end. She then inserted a small jack-plug into the implant behind her ear. Ull stood behind her and looked over her shoulder. He had a vested interest in observing the results. Once the probe was inserted into the control panel on the drill-head the calibration reading was displayed.

Ull gave a sigh of relief. "It's calibrated correctly." He smiled as his faith in Zon Willard was rewarded.

"Now it does!" Delgardo could not bring herself to confirm Ull's statement without adding a qualification. She glanced over her shoulder and Ull took an involuntary step backwards under the force of her disapproving stare. She returned her attention to the drill-head and opened the panel marked 'For Emergency Use Only'. Placing her CommsLink to one side she sprayed on forensic gloves before carefully removing the night-site visor. She scanned its surface, both inside and outside, and waited for the results. If she had expected a helpful result she hid her disappointment well.

"Plenty of trace boss but not much help. It's been handled by Edmurson, Dang, Gurd and Willard."

"Zon would handle all the equipment as part of his maintenance schedule." Ull was quick to explain away the presence of trace from Willard.

Delagardo gave Ull another disapproving glance. Ull sensed he was irritating her, took another step back and stared at his feet.

"Can you analyse the rock strata to confirm the presence of Zelman crystals?"

"Sure boss, I downloaded the test parameters when I did the research." Delgardo paused to dry her sweaty palms again. "Still a bit claustrophobic," she said by way of explanation, "How are you feeling?"

"I'm okay, but I'm developing one mother of all headaches." The grimace on her face indicated she wasn't as okay as she claimed.

Delgardo nodded, gave Gantz a quick reassuring smile and busied herself with setting up the test. Both Gantz and Ull stretched their necks to watch the results of the scan. A pale blue light played across the darker area of rock. "Well that confirms the presence of Zelman crystals."

"How can you tell?" asked Gantz who expected to see some kind of response to the scan.

"The light turned red boss."

Gantz glanced at the scan light again. It was blue but then almost instantly turned red as the pain from her headache intensified. Almost too late she realised what was happening. She fought against the pain and from the corner of her eye she saw the scan light flicker between red and blue before finally returning to blue. A surge of pain hit her brain and she physically staggered back several paces. The pain intensified but she fought back drawing upon all her childhood training. The effort was too much and she sunk to her knees. Delgardo rushed to support her, a worried look on her face.

"Boss, are you alright? What can I do? What's the matter?"

Gantz waved her away as images filled her head. She was suddenly back in the new build of the Midwich settlement being hunted by a shapeless figure. The pain of her wounds returned and she desperately struggled to get away as the figure relentlessly came closer and closer. She looked up and suddenly the figure came into sharp focus. It was Ja Nemi and he pointed his gun at her. His smile was cruel and distorted his face. She cried to call out but the words would not form. Her view zoomed in on the hand which held the gun and she could clearly see his finger start to squeeze the trigger. She clawed at the ground and found her own weapon. The shots exploded in her head and she screamed as Nemi's head disintegrated and wiped the cruel smile away.

"No, no!" The words came out as a half defiant shout, half painful scream. Delgardo wrapped an arm around the shoulders of the crouching, shaking figure of Gantz in an attempt to comfort her. The shaking intensified and Delgardo worried that Gantz was having some kind of fit. Ull was torn between offering to help or retreating in fear and revulsion. His indecision resulted in an inability to do anything and he just stood and stared at the scene.

Gantz was now bent double, her head almost touching the tunnel floor. She was mumbling and Delgardo strained her ears in an attempt to understand what she was saying. Now she was back in her home commune standing with the others in a circle watching their parents say their last goodbyes. She saw the flames engulf the meeting house and the image of her father stretching out his arms, pleading with her to help him. The pain in her head intensified and she saw herself push him back into the flames where his flesh bubbled and melted in the heat. Her screams reverberated inside her head. The shaking was now on the verge of violent flailing and Delgardo tightened her grip, fearful that Gantz would do herself physical damage. Then, as suddenly as it started, the shaking stopped and Gantz was on all fours her breath coming in short gasps.

"Are you alright boss?" The response from Gantz was a nod of the head followed by a shake of the head. Her breathing became more regular but from the expression on her face she was still struggling with the pain. She pushed Delgardo away and dragged herself to her knees. "Boss you're scaring the shit out of me!"

"We've got to get out of here." Gantz struggled to her feet but then wobbled. Delgardo moved to support her but Gantz held out a hand to keep her at arms length. "We need to leave here now!"

"But boss," Delgardo never got to finish the sentence. Gantz flipped up the flap on her holster and drew her sidearm. She pointed it straight at Delgardo.

"I said we need to leave NOW!" She almost screamed the last word. Delgardo's initial confusion and concern rapidly turned to unease verging on fear as she stared down the barrel of a firearm held in a hand which displayed a worrying tremble. She held out her hands hoping to demonstrate she was no threat to Gantz and took a tentative step backwards. Ull stared wide-eyed at the latest development and took two steps back. "I want your weapon Sonia." Gantz gestured with her spare hand. The idea of arguing the point briefly crossed Delgardo's mind, but only briefly. She nodded her agreement and slowly withdrew her sidearm and held it out towards Gantz. "On the ground please Sonia and then turn around and start heading back to the surface, same applies to you Petre." Delgardo obeyed, placing the gun carefully on the ground before turning and heading back up the tunnel with Ull who did not need to be told twice.

When they reached the start of the tunnel Delgardo ventured to speak as Gantz appeared to have calmed down. She obviously recognised them as she had referred to them by their first names. Other than her incomprehensible actions she appeared to have returned to her normal rational self.

"If you tell me what the problem is boss, perhaps I can help!"

"I'm sorry Sonia but I can't take the risk."

"Boss?" Delgardo was confused.

"The light stayed blue Sonia!"

Delgardo was even more confused. "No boss, it turned red."

"She's right!" Ull risked adding his opinion to back up
Delgardo.

"Which is why I can't rely on you anymore. It's why I can't
rely on anybody any more. You'll stay with the others until the
recovery team arrive. You will send them straight to me, is that
understood?"

Delgardo decided the best course of action would be to
humour Gantz. Perhaps she had come back to work too soon
after the trauma of her last case! "Understood boss. I'll keep
everybody in the accommodation block until the recovery team
arrive. Nobody leaves and nobody enters the mine. I send the
recovery team directly to you as soon as they arrive."

"Good! I can't stress enough the importance of not entering
the mine again."

"Understood boss. What do I report to Inspector
Goodridge? I need to fill him in with what you've discovered."

"Keep moving, I'll report to Goodridge."

"Okay boss, whatever you say."

They trudged on in silence until they exited the mine. "Up
the path, we need to go to the storage bins." Neither Delgardo
nor Ull questioned her further and they made their way to the
bins as requested. "Right Petre, I want you to uncouple the ore
sledge please." Ull risked a backward glance but saw the
strained look on Gantz's face. He did as he was asked. "Right,
back to the accommodation block." Gantz waved her gun hand
to encourage their compliance. "I'll be keeping an eye on the
sledge and if there is any attempt to recouple it I'll shoot the
person responsible. Is that clear?" Delgardo and Ull turned,
nodded their understanding of the order, if not the reason
behind it, and then entered the accommodation block.

Wildman was the first to notice that Gantz held the other two at gunpoint. The rest of the crew followed his eye-line and joined him in his surprise. Gantz did not give any of them time to react. "Right Sonia, explain the rules." With that she backed across the floor and down the corridor which led to the sleeping quarters.

When she heard the bedroom door slide shut Delgardo shouted at the assembled crew. "Shut up and sit down. Ull, explain the rules to them." Without waiting for a reply she turned to Wildman. "I need your firearm." She gestured with her hand to indicate the urgency of her request. A pained expression crossed Wildman's face. He opened the flap on his holster and waited. Delgardo reached across into the holster and retrieved a dog biscuit. She gave him a venomous stare. "Where for Corp's sake is your weapon?"

"In my locker, back at base. I don't like guns." His timid reply trailed off to an embarrassed silence.

"You arse!"

***

As soon as the door slid shut her self-control weakened. The moment she relaxed she collapsed onto the floor. The effort of maintaining her composure had taken its toll and she sobbed uncontrollably. Her human emotions were running riot and now, for the first time since arriving, it came home to her just how frighteningly alone she was. She never gave a thought about the constant link with her fellow Gnostics and via them to the Collective, it was part of her natural state. Even coming out to this remote location had been tolerable. She had Delgardo, Wildman, then the other humans to interact with and the case to occupy her mind. Being alone in her room had given her a taste of isolation but now she was really on her own and the incident in the mine had shattered her years of training. Where

211

before her emotions had been half hidden, a safe hazy image, they were now raw and frightening. She stared down at her hands and watched as they trembled. For the first time in her life she was truly alone with no hope of that changing in the short term and it scared her, more than she could ever have imagined.

'Keep occupied' that's what she told herself. That ploy had worked during the other evening until sleep engulfed her but could she afford the luxury of sleep now? The door was secure and she had the only weapons. True, if they put their minds to it, they could break the door down but she had two guns and two spare magazines, more than enough to shoot all of them if she had to. She dragged herself to her feet and crossed to the other side of the room. It was an effort as she felt exhausted. Pulling herself up onto the bed she stood on tiptoes and looked out of the window. It gave a clear view of the storage bins and she could see the uncoupled sledge pipe was still where they had left it. She opened the window so she could hear any movement outside. It took her last reserves of energy and she slumped down onto the bed, propped up in the corner. She attempted to pull her CommsLink out of her pocket and then suddenly remembered she had left it in the office. Her spirits sunk. The idea of taking a risk and leaving the relative safety of her room to retrieve it briefly crossed her mind but fatigue finally overtook her and, thankfully, she drifted into a fitful sleep.

The nightmares she suffered after the Midwich incident returned but now they were fragmented and interspersed with other images from her childhood. Again she was in pain and scrabbling in the dirt attempting to get to her gun. Again it was tantalisingly out of reach and again a shadow fell across her. She looked up but this time it was Nemi pointing the gun at her. Her body gave a jerk as if it was trying to reject the image conjured up by her mind. Suddenly she was standing in a circle with the other Gnostics and watching her father burn. She wanted to help him but couldn't. He put out his hand, imploring her for help and she pushed him back into the flames. She thrashed about on the bed. It didn't happen like that, or did it? Suddenly it was dark and she could feel her mother but couldn't reach her. Her body jerked again at the sound of the gunshots. Nemi's bloody, lifeless body fell forward and landed on top of her. She cried out in her sleep but exhaustion still gripped her and the cycle repeated itself. Again she was in pain and scrabbling in the dirt attempting to get to her gun. This was not the kind of deep sleep she required to mend her shattered mind and body.

Delgardo had been standing with her ear pressed against the door of Gantz's room. At one point she thought she could hear weeping but couldn't be sure. It was all quiet now so she returned to the recreational area. Most of the sullen-faced crew were still sitting in exactly the same positions they had been when she left. The notable exception was Mol Gurd who appeared to be confronting Wildman. Whatever had been going on between the two of them had been ended by Keith the dog. She stood in front of Willdman, obviously protecting him. Her mouth was curled back in a snarl to reveal a set of vicious looking teeth and her body was tensed, ready to pounce. She let out a low growl and took a step towards Gurd. The miner growled back, spat at the dog and returned to his seat. Delgardo joined Wildman by the door.

"Trouble?" She kept her voice low so the others wouldn't hear.

"Mister Gurd voiced the opinion that armed with only a dog biscuit I wasn't in a position to stop him leaving if he so wished." Wildman's reply was intentionally loud enough so everyone could hear. "Keith disabused him of the idea."

Delgardo turned to face the crew. "Nobody goes anywhere until the recovery team arrives." She glanced back at Wildman. "I'm going to report the current situation to Goodridge, will you be okay here?"

Wildman forced a smile. "Unless they all decide to leave!"

"Do you have your stun stick, or is that in your locker as well?"

"It's in my room."

"Go and get it now, I'll keep an eye on this lot. But make it quick, I want to contact Goodridge sooner rather than later."

Wildman nodded and rushed off to his room. He paused outside Gantz's door but all was silent so he entered his room and pulled out his bag from under his bunk. He rummaged through it until he found the stun stick and a bundle of cloth. The former he clipped into his belt and the latter he unwrapped. Emptying the dog biscuits from his holster he slipped the unwrapped gun back in its place and fastened down the flap. Tossing the bag back under the bed he hurried back to the recreational area to relieve Delgardo. He smiled and patted the stun stick as he took up his position by the door. Delgardo gave him a nod and a smile in return and hurried off to her room to make the call to Goodridge.

***

Delgardo composed herself before making the call. She wondered if Gantz had already contacted Goodridge and, if so, what had been said. If Gantz had been coherent then her own version of events would not sound very convincing. She needed Goodridge to take her seriously and speed up the recovery team's arrival. One dog and two stun sticks were not much of a deterrent if the crew took it into their heads to follow Gurd's example. She took deep breaths to calm herself as she waited for Goodridge's holographic image to appear. When it did he

214

appeared dishevelled and greeted her with a yawn. Delgardo realised what the time was and that she had woken him up.

"I'm sorry to disturb you sir."

The image glanced sideways as if checking the time on some unseen clock. Goodridge gave another yawn. "This better be good Delgardo. Where's Kanah?"

"She hasn't been in contact?" Delgardo gave a sigh of relief, her story would sound plausible at least.

The question suddenly made Goodridge alert. "What's happened?"

"I don't really know sir but I think Officer Gantz has had something like a panic attack." Delgardo really thought it was more like a complete mental breakdown but panic attack sounded a more diplomatic term for starters.

"Kanah Gantz doesn't do panic Delgardo, now tell me exactly what's happened and where in God's name she is!"

"I know it doesn't make sense sir but please bare with me. She disarmed me at gunpoint and has now locked herself in her room. She ordered everyone to remain in the accommodation block until the recovery team turn up and has threatened to shoot anyone who attempts to recouple the ore sledge pipe." She paused as she realised the last part of that sentence made no sense at all.

"Are you telling me she has closed down the mining operation and is now holding you and the civilians hostage?"

It sounded insane coming from somebody else but..."Yes sir!"

"Tell me exactly what happened to trigger this behaviour."

Delgardo was relieved Goodridge appeared not to have dismissed her story out of hand. "We checked the storage bins today but they were empty. We had a theory the crew had been mining the crystals for some time and were planning to steal the bin so we checked to confirm how much Zelman crystals had been mined. If there was more than could possibly have been recovered in two days then it would have supported our theory."

"But you say the storage bins were empty?" Goodridge's tone of voice was a mixture of confusion and disbelief.

"Yes sir!"

"All of them?"

"Yes sir. The Zelman crystals had disappeared. The site manager had already arranged a crew meeting to report the fact that we considered Ginthem to have been murdered and he also broke the news about the empty bins. The crew had started arguing amongst themselves and were blaming the technician, Zon Willard, for interfering with the calibration of the drill scanner to divert the crystals along with the drill waste so he could recover it at a later date. Petre Ull, the site manager, asked us to investigate. All three of us went into the mine. When we reached the current drill tunnel Officer Gantz seemed to feel unwell, I thought she might be feeling a bit claustrophobic. She said she was fine so we carried on to the drill-head. I tested the scanner and the calibration was spot on. Officer Gantz complained of having a headache but other than that she appeared to have recovered. It was just after I did the test on the rock strata that she had what appeared to be some sort of fit. She screamed, shouted out and then collapsed with what I can only describe as convulsions. After a few minutes she calmed down and said we had to leave straight away. I attempted to ask her to explain and that was when she drew her weapon, disarmed me and marched both me and Ull out of the mine. She then forced Ull to uncouple the ore sledge pipe and threatened to shoot anyone who tried to reconnect it. She left orders that everybody should stay in the accommodation block until the recovery team arrived. When they arrive they should report directly to her and not enter the mine. She then locked herself in her room to report to you. I haven't heard from her since and obviously neither have you sir."

"Indeed!" Goodridge looked deep in thought. He stayed that way for some time. "She give no reason for her sudden change and bizarre actions?"

"Well, she said that the light stayed blue. When I tested the rock strata the positive result turned the scanner light red. It quite clearly turned red sir, Ull saw it as well. She said she couldn't trust me any more."

"You both had entered the mine before. Did Kanah display any symptoms then?"

"Not that I could detect sir. I do get a bit claustrophobic and I did the first time but I must admit I did feel worse at the drill head."

"Could that have affected your judgement over the test results?"

"No sir and as I said Ull confirmed the test was positive."

"Did Ull complain of any symptoms?"

"He never said sir," She hesitated before continuing. "I must confess I didn't ask him though."

"Check with him Delgardo and check the others for any symptoms, no matter how mild or temporary they might have been, especially near the drill-head."

"You think there might be something toxic down there?"

"If I was confident we knew about every plant, gas, mineral or micro-organism native to this planet I would say no but we're nowhere near identifying everything which might be on this planet. Just because we haven't come across anything doesn't mean it doesn't exist. We've only surveyed a small percentage of this planet to that level of detail." Goodridge fell silent again. It was a long shot because if there was anything toxic on this planet the Collective would surely have informed the New Brethren, unless there was something on this planet which was toxic to humans but harmless to the Collective. He thought it doubtful but he could hardly explain his reasoning to Delgardo. "What's the situation there at the moment?"

"The crew seem calm at the moment. One trouble-maker by the name of Mol Gurd attempted to leave the block but Officer Singh, or rather his dog, dealt with the situation. Gurd is the sort who likes to push against authority so I think it was just a case of sheer bloody mindedness."

"Is this Officer Singh armed?"

"No sir, we only have two stun sticks and the dog. Do you want me to run some tests in the mine?"

"No, keep everyone out of the mine. We'll reassess the situation once we have more bodies up there. Don't put yourself in danger Delgardo. If it looks like the situation is turning nasty lock the crew in their bedrooms and wait it out. I'll get to work on sending help there as soon as possible. Good luck." Goodridge moved out of shot before the image faded as the link was cut. Delgardo was reassured by the urgency demonstrated and gave a sigh of relief.

***

Delgardo was preoccupied with what she should do with the crew until the recovery team arrived so never noticed the figure hiding in the shadows at the end of the corridor until it was too late. The swinging fist caught her on the side of the head and the force of the blow caused her hit the other side of her head against her bedroom door. Momentarily dazed she had no time to react as her right arm was jerked up behind her back and her right shoulder jammed against the corridor wall. She was held in a vice-like grip, her left arm pinned to her side by her attacker's body. His right arm held her secure while his left hand closed around her throat and stifled any sound she attempted to make. The rough stubble of a beard scratched her neck and she could smell his stale breath and sweat. There was an faint odour that she recognised, the distinctive sickly sweet smell associated with a certain sexual stimulant. She knew it was Mol Gurd even before he whispered into her ear.

"Not so tough now are we? Lost your little girlfriend haven't you? So who's going to protect you now?" Delgardo swore at him but it just came out as a rasping gurgle. Gurd gave a nasty little laugh. "I know what somebody like you needs." He gave her cheek a long slow lick and her body shuddered with revulsion. "You need a proper man!" He released the grip on her throat and slid his hand down to her chest and gave her breast a squeeze. "Make a sound and I'll break your neck." The threat was whispered into her ear and she believed him. The fingers of her trapped left hand wiggled about trying to find the handle of the stun stick which hung from her belt. "Not much tit, perhaps you're bigger down there." His hand slid slowly from her breast towards her crutch. In desperation she stretched her fingers and could feel the edge of the stun stick but couldn't get a grip on it. His fingers now fumbled with the fastenings on her uniform . She attempted to head butt him but he was too close for it to have any affect and it just earned her a brief respite as he temporarily removed his hand to punch her in the throat. She gasped as the blow had the affect of choking her. He pressed his body closer to hers and she suddenly felt his tongue slip into her ear. She closed her eyes tight; perhaps having her neck broken was a better option than this. His hand was now inside her uniform and his fingers probed her pubic hair. He shifted slightly to thrust his hand forward to reach inside her and she managed to get a grip on the handle of the stun stick. A slight finger pressure on the handle made the stick sprung out to its full length with a loud snap and hit Gurd in the right testicle. He gave a half-scream half-groan and released his grip as his hands instinctively recoiled to protect his groin. He was bent double, eyes bulging with his mouth wide open yet he made no sound. There was enough of a target for Delgardo to thrust the stun stick back into his groin and give him an electrical shock. The sound he made now was all scream as he crumpled onto his knees before rolling onto his side and curling up into a protective foetal position. His whole body was trembling.

"You fucking shit!" Delgardo spat the words out and pushed the end of the stun stick onto his temple. Another charge now might not kill him but it would fry at least part of his brain. She smiled at the thought of it and her finger hovered as she looked into Gurd's eyes. He knew the consequences should she attack him again and there was fear reflected in those eyes now. Her smile widened and her finger twitched. Gurd's body convulsed in expectation.

The smile suddenly vanished from Delgardo's face. She had recoiled from the idea of taking pleasure from inflicting pain as quickly as the stun stick had snapped back into its handle. That was her father and she wasn't her father's daughter, she was better than that. She gave the trembling body of Gurd a prod with her toe. "Get up and get back into the Rec." Gurd looked up at her, fearful this was just a cruel trick. "Shift your sorry arse now or I'll shrivel your other ball."

The threat was taken seriously and Gurd pulled himself to his feet. The pain was still etched on his face but he gingerly took a few wobbly steps. "It hurts," he whimpered.

"Good, now speed up or that fat arse of yours will get the same treatment." Delgardo adjusted her dress as she followed the limping, bandy legged Gurd down the corridor. She wiped the remains of his saliva from her cheek and ear and vowed to take a shower at the first opportunity.

***

Milton Dang had an idea of what Mol Gurd was up to when he requested permission from Wildman to go to the toilet. Gurd never asked anyone's permission to do anything. He kept one eye on the corridor entrance and was somewhat surprised when he heard the cries which drew the attention of the rest of the crew, but only because he recognised the sound came from Gurd. Wildman had taken some hesitant steps towards the corridor at the first cry but Dang had reassured him that it didn't sound as if Delgardo needed any help. Wildman, with some reluctance, returned to his position at the doorway but kept a wary eye on the crew. He was rather surprised none of them gave any indication of being worried about what was happening to Gurd.

All eyes were fixed on the corridor and the sight of Gurd finally hobbling out raised a couple of smiles but mostly indifference. Milton Dang's smile was the broadest. "Bite it off did she?" He laughed at his own suggestion and Gurd flashed him a hateful stare before collapsing into the nearest chair. The impact caused him to cry out in pain again and he suddenly vomited onto the floor. "Boni, it looks like Mol has sent your breakfast back! Clear it up, there's a good chap." Dang gave a little giggle. Chang got up out of his seat but was pushed back down by Ull.

"You stay where you are Boni. Gurd can clear his own bloody mess up!" Gurd gave Ull an equally hateful look but the site manager ignored it. He'd had enough of Mol Gurd. The idiot deserved all he got. The man kept what little brains he had in his dick. However, the sight of the look on Delgardo's face as she followed Gurd out of the corridor sent a shiver through his body. It was an accusing stare which she directed at each member of the crew in turn. At that moment Ull regretted he had turned a blind eye to what had been going on between Gurd and Sara Rolm for he now saw that same accusing look reflected in Sara's face.

Delgardo let her look of revulsion linger over the crew until every last one of them reverted their eyes. Even Dang looked away but a smirk remained on his lips. She then rejoined Wildman at the door.

"You alright?" he whispered under his breath.

"I could do with a shower." Her voice was flat and Wildman shuffled on his feet in embarrassment.

"You want me to handcuff him?" Wildman was surprised that Delgardo had not already down so.

Delgardo glanced back at the prone figure of Gurd hanging off the edge of the sofa above the pool of vomit and remembered how close she had come to frying his brains. "No, leave him." She noticed the look Wildman gave her and added, "He's not going to cause any more trouble."

Wildman shrugged his shoulders in resignation for he was far from convinced that a man like Gurd would ever learn self control, but Delgardo was now in charge in the absence of Gantz. He thought it was time he made some sympathetic comment. "Look, I can do the first watch. You have a shower and get some sleep in." He hesitated. "I assume help is on its way?"

"Goodridge said he'd try and speed things up. I'll take you up on the offer but if this lot turn nasty call me and we'll lock them in their rooms. We'll sit it out until help arrives."

"I'll be alright." He tapped the stun stick at his side. "They've had a demonstration of what this can do so that should keep them quiet for a while. I've got Keith as well!" He smiled. "Thanks also to Mol Gurd they've had a demonstration of what she can do too." Delgardo, at that moment, didn't really appreciate Wildman's attempt at humour over Gurd. She just nodded and made her way back to her room. Wildman noticed that all the others watched her intently. The confidence in his earlier statement slowly dissolved.

CHAPTER TEN

Vitch Tolman was perched on a bar stool staring intently at the drink in front of him. He looked far from enthusiastic at the prospect of consuming it. The main body of the drink was a redish-brown colour and it was topped by a cream coloured foam. He waved a hand at it but the liquid did not react.

"Is it supposed to look like that?" His tone suggested he secretly hoped the answer to that question was in the negative.

"Yes," confirmed Nemi, "it's perfect, trust me!"

Tolman reluctantly picked up the glass, staring at it at arms length. "It doesn't look very attractive!"

"Well, no! It's not highly coloured, doesn't change colour, foam up in your mouth or sparkle as it warms up. The point isn't to look at it but to drink it Vitch!"

With a top lip already curled up in disgust Tolman brought the glass up to his mouth. He hesitated but caught the look on Nemi's face so took a sip of the drink. He swilled the liquid around in his mouth before finally building up enough courage to swallow it. Nemi looked on in expectation. "Well?"

The pained expression on Tolman's face faded a little and he took another sip. "Not as bad as it looks!" Tolman licked his lips and took another larger mouthful. "What did you say it was?"

"Beer, New Brethren beer."

"Beer?" Tolman inspected the contents of the glass again. "Isn't that a fizzy drink?" He had a vague recollection from his youth of some asteroid miners drinking beer once. "Not the right colour either!"

"You can have different types of beer Vitch. You probably remember the Corporation version of it." Nemi pulled a sour face. "New Brethren beer is to beer what Altarian spirit is to synthetic spirit." Nemi saw, from the look on Tolman's face, that that particular comparison had fallen on stoney ground. "Have you never tried alcohol before?"

"Always been a Parado man myself. Pop a couple in the evening to relax. How did you get into this beer stuff?"

"My boss, Morgan, is into alcohol. He and Mel Hann were drinking partners. Morgan likes his Altarian spirits, but then he can afford them, then he and Mel discovered New Brethren beer at a commune social. Morgan has tried to adopt me as his new drinking partner but I can't really take spirits so I've acquired a taste for this stuff." He held up his own beer and took a long draught.

"If you don't mind me saying, I wouldn't really put you and Morgan together."

"You're not the first person to pass that comment Vitch but, then again, Morgan and Mel Hann appeared to be complete opposites. I think I remind Morgan of Hann so he's adopted me."

"What was so special about Hann? I wasn't on Goodridge's team when he had that case, I joined after. The Hann case was his only unsolved one and it dented his reputation so at the time officers weren't exactly rushing to join his team."

"There wasn't anything special about him, in fact as the oldest junior officer in the fleet he was regarded as a bit of a failure. Had an enquiring mind though and wouldn't let the investigation into the mass suicide rest, even when Carter closed it down. A nice man but with low self esteem. I could never understand that! I always looked up to him."

"Whereas I get the impression Morgan always looks down on people." Tolman took another sip of his drink and this time without pulling a face.

"Just a front Vitch. A complex character is our Commander Morgan! I thought, later, that he envied Hann a bit."

"Are we talking about the same person here? The man can be rude to the point of being offensive and has never struck me as the sort who cared a solar fart about anything or anybody."

Nemi smiled and took another gulp of beer. "As I said, all front. He envied Hann for embracing emotions about things and people where he was frightened of them so suppressed them. The strange thing was I think Hann envied Morgan. He wanted to have a devil-may-care approach to life but it just wasn't in him."

"Then you must be the result of a combination of both of them. You get shot at, blown up and then mindlessly run at some lunatic to draw their fire and save Kanah but then pussyfoot around over your relationship with her!" Nemi's usual response to comments about his relationship with Gantz was to roll his eyes and sigh but this time he just gave a wry smile. It was a change which Tolman picked up on. "Do I detect a touch of acceptance there?"

"She finished her last message to me by blowing me a kiss!"

Tolman gave Nemi a look which suggested he thought his friend was joking with him. "Are we talking about the same Kanah Gantz?"

"She's probably just finding the isolation a strain."

"I know it's a bit remote, but isolation? There's a crew of nine stationed there and she went with two other Officers!"

"You forget she's a Gnostic Vitch! All her life she's had the others in her head, not to mention the blue monkeys!"

Tolman raised his eyebrows at the last comment. "Blue monkeys?" He gave Nemi a disapproving look.

"A bad habit I've picked up from Morgan." Nemi paused to take another long drought from his beer. "And 'The Collective' is such a crap name, makes them sound like some chorale group or artsy commune! I would have thought Kanah could have come up with a better name to describe them."

"And what was Kanah's response to that?"

"Told me to come up with a name for something I could never comprehend while describing it with something as primitive as human language."

"Now that sounds more like the Kanah I know. Have you used the blue monkey term in front of her?"

"She's okay with that. Morgan even refers to her as the monkey girl but she takes that in her stride too!"

"I can see why Goodridge and Morgan don't get on!" Tolman took another swig of his beer. "Still, good to hear you and Kanah are sorting yourselves out, even if you have to keep her isolated to do it."

"One blown kiss doesn't make an argument for some great love affair Vitch."

"Perhaps not, for ordinary people! However I should imagine for Kanah, emotions are more naturally felt rather than displayed. Don't take this the wrong way but blowing that kiss must have required real effort on her part."

"Thanks for that vote of confidence!" Nemi pulled a face of mock sadness.

"You know what I mean."

Nemi smiled. "I know what you mean!" He drained the last of his beer. "Fancy another?"

Tolman glanced down at his glass and was surprised to see it was almost empty. He too drained his glass. "I'll risk another, it's not as bad as it looks." He put out a hand to stop Nemi using the bar menu to order more drinks. "But this is my round. Is that the correct term?"

"A bit of an antiquated term, have you been watching old holo-films?"

Tolman ordered two more beers. "In fact I have! After the Midwich incident I looked up 'The Village of the Damned' which you mentioned and found an old holo-film of the same name. That led me on to find some ancient two dimensional film and I've been watching those. Pretty weird on the eye but some of them were quite enjoyable. There were even some without product placement. How did those ever get made?" The two beers rose up from the serving hatch in the bar and Tolman handed one to Nemi.

"Thanks." Nemi took a sip from his new drink. "People used to pay to go and see them in big public spaces. There were huge screens, bigger than the wall ones we have now."

"People used to mingle with complete strangers?" There was a hint of disbelief in his voice.

"Mass entertainment used to be very popular, not only films but sports events and plays!"

"Weird!" Tolman took a large gulp of his beer.

"Better get used to the idea Vitch if you've moved into the New Brethren quarter. Very keen on their social events are the New Brethren! Amateur team games, music concerts and dances are very popular."

"Dances?" Tolman sounded slightly horrified at the suggestion.

"Dances which include physical contact with complete strangers." Nemi smiled when he saw the reaction that statement brought. "Of course you don't stay strangers for very long!"

"And nobody sues for invasion of body space?"

"They're all brothers and sisters Vitch! How long have you lived there now?"

"Just a couple of weeks and I've spent most of that time here, only getting home for the odd day or so."

"Not experienced the hand shake yet?"

"The what?"

"Somebody holding out their hand like this?" Nemi demonstrated with his own hand.

"Yeah, on the day we moved in with our new neighbour. I guessed it was some New Brethren thing." Tolman shrugged his shoulders. "Showing me they weren't armed?" Nemi had a fit of the giggles. "What's so funny?"

"I think that was how it originally came into being. It's a general welcome. Usually reserved for friends. You're supposed to put out your hand and shake theirs." Nemi again demonstrated using his own hands. "Although you both should be using the same hand, it works better!"

"That's just plain stupid!"

"It's the friendly thing to do. Do you want to practise?" Nemi held out his hand again.

"Piss off Nemi, I'm not holding hands with you!" Tolman was convinced Nemi was winding him up.

"You'll get used to it Vitch. You're a friend now!"

"Yeesss..." Tolman did not sound very enthusiastic.

"And you've experienced the link which very few friends have. You're in a very select club."

"Not all friends have experienced that?" That comment took Tolman by surprise. Nemi shook his head. "What about Morgan?"

"Not even Morgan. In fact especially not Morgan!"

"But he took on the Commander job. He's basically the military advisor for the New Brethren, surely they made the link with him."

Nemi shook his head again. "They won him over with the job offer. He couldn't resist the chance of moulding Colonial units into what he considered to be real soldiers. He got tired of baby sitting piss poor recruits on planets which nobody else wanted to be stationed on." Nemi paused to take a sip from his drink. "You didn't think the New Brethren saw him as a potential member did you?"

Tolman fell silent and thought long and hard about how to phrase his next remark. "I thought they might have got into his head to plant the idea, after all he has chosen to defend the New Brethren when they have, technically, broken Federation law."

It was Nemi's turn to look surprised. "Do you think that's what they did to you?"

Tolman hesitated again. "It has crossed my mind." He saw the reaction that remark got from Nemi. "I'm a police officer! I've sworn to uphold Federation Law and yet I know the New Brethren are running a program to genetically alter their children and I've kept quiet about it. I've compromised myself."

"If you're right then they didn't do a very good job did they?"

"What do you mean?"

"Why leave you with doubts? If they got you to accept the breaking of the law why not remove your doubts while they were about it?"

Tolman gave that argument consideration while he sipped his drink. "That might have been to hide the fact they planted the idea." He did not sound convinced by his own explanation.

"A devious idea Vitch which requires a devious mind to implement it." Nemi paused for affect. "Does that strike you as an accurate description of Kanah Gantz?"

"No." The reply was emphatic. It was still fresh in his mind how he doubted Gantz during their last case and he was loathe to give any suggestion that those doubts still lingered. "But I experienced the link via Simon, not Kanah."

"And you think Kanah wouldn't have known if Simon had messed with your head?"

"They can't lie, can they!"

"Not to each other."

"What do you mean by that?"

Nemi took a large swig of his drink before answering. "You think I've not had doubts do you? Just because the Collective and the Gnostics can't lie to each other doesn't mean they can't lie to us! Bloody difficult to get away with a lie when you share your thoughts like they do but we can't do that. I've always had that niggling thought at the back of my mind. It might even explain my reluctance to develop any kind of relationship with Kanah. I'll never have the kind of relationship she could have with another Gnostic. It's a little frightening to be an open book to your partner while never really knowing them."

"So how do you cope with the doubt?" Tolman had never considered the emotion side, only the legal position.

Nemi smiled. "The same way we limited humans deal with each other, trust and faith! That's what Morgan hates. It's the reason he calls Kanah monkey girl, he hopes to goad her into dipping into his head and taking away his doubts. The idea of faith is an anathema to him. He wants what you're afraid of. He wants them to take away his responsibility for the decision he made. The fact that they'll not do it is what sustains my faith in the decisions I've made."

"But we are still conspiring to break Federation Law."

"Technically, as you said yourself." Nemi took another mouthful of his drink. "The genetic engineering law was born out of fear. Society are quite happy to scan for disease and genetically correct any defects, who could argue against that? And what's wrong with selecting the sex or hair colour or eye colour of your children? All very innocent and perfectly acceptable now, but frowned upon at one time. However, suggest enhancing human abilities and the fear kicks in. The spectre of the super-human looms large over humanity. It's on a par with robots and why limits are imposed on artificial intelligence and capabilities. We're capable of producing replicants and don't think it hasn't been suggested by the military! But what if the super-humans or robots developed to such a stage where ordinary humans were surplus to requirements, a drain on resources?" Tolman made no reply, just took a large gulp of his drink. "The New Brethren believe in the oneness of the human race and see the Collective's mental ability as a way of achieving that next step in human development." Nemi paused to smile at the idea which still amused him. "Which is why they consider the Collective as Angels!"

"Are you saying what they're doing is little more than picking the colour of their children's eyes?" Tolman did not sound convinced.

"I'm not even saying it's little more than removing a defect, although I should imagine the New Brethren would see it that way. The ability to mentally influence or even control somebody scares the shit out of me. I could make quite an extensive list of people and Corporations who would misuse an ability like that."

"And you don't think the Collective or the Gnostics would misuse the ability?"

"Well you're the detective Vitch. Any evidence they have misused the ability, like humans would?"

Tolman took a sip of his drink as he gave that some consideration. "No, I admit I haven't any evidence but why did you add that little proviso at the end?"

Nemi bit his lip. Morgan had always said he was too honest and his reluctance to tell even a half truth was the reason he had slipped in the last part of his question. "Is that the detective in you coming out?" Tolman did not reply, he just gave Nemi a long hard stare. "You're almost as bad as Kanah, can't get anything by her either." If Nemi had hoped to bypass the awkward question with a lighthearted throw away comment he was sadly mistaken. Tolman's stare just became more intense as he waited for an explanation. Nemi's resistance crumbled. "The Collective had to influence those first settlers. Mating with what they thought where a species of monkey would have been unthinkable to devout New Brethren. A lot of mental anguish and downright damage was caused by that. And did the children's transformation from abomination to prophet occur without a little help?"

"I never gave any thought to how it all started." Tolman took another sip from his drink. "Even when I found out what was going on I never really queried the premise. I guess I thought if somebody like Kanah Gantz was a Gnostic then how bad could they be?" Tolman paused to glance at Nemi. "She was..." His voice trailed off.

"Those doubts again?"

"You have as well? Despite how well you know her!"

"How well do you know anyone?"

"But she could tell you had doubts." Tolman was struggling with the concept.

"I would think so and she could influence, manipulate me to remove those doubts but that would remove my faith in her. Perhaps that may be the point!" Tolman nodded but whether it was to signify his understanding or just to acknowledge Nemi's point, even he was not sure of. Nemi continued. "When we first landed on the planet Lisbeth Smith quickly attached herself to the investigation via a relationship with Able Carter, the lead investigator. Of course it might have been natural attraction rather than manipulation but the first meeting was obviously engineered."

"And her rise up the New Brethren hierarchy has been phenomenal! Natural talent or manipulation?" Nemi shrugged his shoulders and Tolman did not want to labour the point. "For a social night out this has got suddenly very deep!"

Nemi smiled. "It's a side affect of the alcohol Vitch. I believe the term used to be called 'talking bollocks'."

Tolman returned the smile. "Is that the same as 'Corpspeak'?"

"Very similar I should imagine."

Tolman was about to comment when the vibrating coil in his ear alerted him to a call. The following call sign told him it was from Goodridge. "Sorry Nemi but I've got a call I need to take." He slipped his hand into his jacket and pulled out his CommsLink and set it to audio.

"Probably Carla checking up on you!"

"I wish! It's the boss, Goodridge."

"Tell him you're off duty."

"As if!" Tolman whispered. "Evening boss, what's up?" He screwed up his face in concentration, attempting to hear over the background noise of the bar. "What!" His face took on a serious complexion. "Hold on boss it's too noisy here." He indicated to Nemi the booths around the edge of the bar and Nemi nodded his understanding, picking up the two drinks and heading for the nearest booth. They were private sound booths and the background noise of the bar was dramatically reduced as they took their seats at the table. "That's better, can you repeat boss?" Tolman fell silent as he listened intently. "Is she safe?" At that remark Nemi started to become concerned. His immediate thought was something had happened to Tolman's partner, Carla. Tolman glanced up at Nemi. "Look boss at the moment I'm with Ja Nemi." Nemi mouthed the words 'Anything I can do?' and Tolman nodded. "Look boss, I doubt if it's a case of him being willing to help, rather more like could we stop him."

Nemi suddenly felt a knot of tension form in his stomach. The conversation now sounded as if it concerned Kanah Gantz. It was difficult for Nemi to refrain from interrupting now as he desperately wanted know what had happened to Kanah. The tension knot in his stomach grew the longer the conversation continued. Finally Tolman told Goodridge that he would call him back as soon as possible and Nemi jumped in straight away. "Is it Kanah? Is she okay?"

"As far as we know she's okay but things have got a bit weird at the mining camp."

"What do you mean, fucking weird!" Nemi checked himself, gripped the edge of the table and let out a long deep breath. "Sorry Vitch, please carry on." He took a large mouthful of his drink.

"It seems Kanah, the mine manager called Petre Ull and Officer Delgardo visited the drill-head. Kanah appeared to be unwell but insisted on continuing. They were doing some checks on the equipment when Kanah had some kind of fit. She then ordered everyone out of the mine and when they queried the reason she drew her weapon, disarmed Officer Delgardo and marched them at gunpoint out of the mine. She forced them to disconnect some pipe thing to prevent any further drilling and then locked herself in her bedroom and threatened to shoot anybody who attempted to start up the drilling again. At the moment she's refusing to let Delgardo into her room, in fact just refusing to even speak to her." Tolman paused to let that sink in. "Goodridge is worried he sent her off too soon after the trauma of her last case." He paused again as he remembered the earlier conversation with Nemi. "Could the isolation have pushed her over the edge?"

"Kanah's stronger than she looks." Nemi sounded far from convinced by his own statement.

"I thought that about the Gnostic Simon but I saw what happened to him when he had the run-in with your Benson!"

"Kanah's more used to dealing with humans than Simon was, and Benson used to frighten me."

"Have you heard of Gnostics being susceptible to fits?"

"No but I haven't met that many of them." Nemi realised that comment was far from being helpful. "Kanah had never mentioned any side affects of being a Gnostic, certainly not fits. I can't believe the isolation is responsible either. She's trained to keep her mind isolated, at least from humans." Nemi suddenly realised that most of what he knew about Gnostics was either assumption or based on one example.

"From what Goodridge has told me some of the mine crew sound like unsavoury characters." Nemi shrugged his shoulders. The truth was he now had doubts and really had no idea just how much her last case affected her and he had even less idea what the last few days of isolation had done to her. He suddenly realised his relationship with Kanah was based on very little. As Tolman had observed, her emotions were felt and that was how she shared them with others. Of course that method did not apply to him and she always had trouble expressing her feelings in words. It was a sobering thought that his relationship with her was based on perhaps no more than hope on his part.

"Lisbeth Smith would know about her mental state, or at least a better idea than me."

"Then we might be able to find out, Goodridge said he was going to call her next."

"What do you plan to do next?"

"Goodridge is getting a recovery team together. We think the murder victim is at the bottom of some underground ravine. He's got techs dismantling one of our patrol ships. The idea is to scale it down and then reassemble it in the cavern where this ravine is. The trouble is that takes time but it's the only way of getting the thing through the narrow tunnels. Our next problem is getting the team and the equipment to the camp. We've only got patrol ships so Goodridge approached the Corporation for one of their transporters. Unfortunately they're being far from helpful. The site manager has reported the situation to them and, well let's just say they're far from happy about Kanah closing down a site which is producing Zelman crystals. You know how much they're worth?" Nemi nodded. "The Corporation won't supply a transporter until we have reopened the mine. The only way to do that is to break in and arrest Kanah when she is armed and our two officers in situ aren't. The stupid bastards can't see that's a course of action which can only lead to a bloodbath!"

"Tell them to go fuck themselves, I'll supply the transport!" Nemi pulled out his CommsLink from his jacket pocket.

"You can arrange that?"

There was a slight hesitation before Nemi replied. Despite his bravado statement he was far from sure he had the ability to deliver on such a promise. However, he faked his confidence for the benefit of Tolman. "Courtesy of the New Brethren Government the new garrison here has just taken delivery of a brand new Colonial Class patrol ship. We've just finished diagnostic tests and the next thing is a series of flight tests. The sort of trip you're talking about would tick all the test check boxes in one go." Nemi paused to make a call. "As one of those boxes is a planet orbit trial we can also cut down the journey time." He winked at Tolman who smiled seeing a little of the old Nemi had returned. The call was a holographic link and the head of Stenna Morgan suddenly appeared, hovering above the table top. "Hi boss!" Nemi indicated that Tolman should move round next to him.

"An unexpected pleasure Nemi, as I didn't call you you must be after something." The disembodied head turned slightly as Tolman moved within scan distance. "Bloody Vitch Tolman!" Morgan returned his attention to Nemi. "He hasn't arrested you has he?"

Nemi ignored the remark. "Kanah Gantz is in trouble boss. We need to get some bodies and equipment to the Arkin mountains asap."

"What's the monkey girl got herself into this time?"

"It's a bit complicated to go into now but the short version is she's closed down a Corporation mine and threatening to shoot anybody who attempts to reopen it."

"I told you they were unstable Nemi, this is the sort of shit you get if you date a Gnostic!" Nemi smiled, Morgan had dropped the monkey reference. "So what do you want from me?"

"Permission to use the new patrol ship to get bodies and equipment out there. The Corporation are being fuckwits about providing a transporter."

"And you expect me to give you official authorisation to use a multi-million credit vehicle still under test to fly Tolman out there? If they have already pissed off the corporation by closing one of their mines sending a Colonial force up there will send them running to the Federation. Apart from that you do realise Goodridge will get him to arrest her?" Morgan's head shook from side to side. "Permission denied and you're witness to that Tolman, understood?"

"Understood," replied a dejected Tolman.

"Now stop wasting my time." Morgan paused. "And if you damage it I'll take the cost out of your wages which will mean I'll own your sorry arse for eternity." The image flickered and then disappeared. Tolman gave Nemi a quizzical look, not understanding the last remark.

"He's going to let me steal it!" said Nemi with a smile.

Tolman now realised why Morgan and Nemi infuriated Goodridge so.

***

Once Delgardo had left the Rec and they all heard the swish of her bedroom door as it closed, the crew gathered round one table and lowered their voices. Wildman risked moving away from the main door and closer to the group. He wanted to get close enough to overhear their conversation but not too close as he feared they could turn on him. However, they appeared to ignore his stealthy approach so he sat on the edge of a table within earshot of their conversation. They obviously did not consider him a threat to whatever their plans were or, and this was an offence to his ego, an insignificant obstacle to their plans. He strained his ears and could make out most of the conversation or at least enough to fill in the blanks.

"She's gone the same way as bloody Ginthem!" Milton Dang's remark was met with nods of agreement from some of the crew.

"We don't know what happened to Ginthem." As always Ull was the voice of reason but at the moment logic would only be accepted if it backed the crew's prejudices.

"We know he chucked himself down the ravine and you don't do something like that unless you've lost your wits!" said Albright to nobody in particular.

"One of us threw him down the ravine Dirk. You heard what they said, somebody attempted to clear up afterwards. Ginthem couldn't have done that if he'd thrown himself!" Edmurson was quick to correct Albright.

"Only got their word for it and the Gantz woman has gone mad. Wouldn't surprise me if this whole thing is a New

Brethren plot to close the mine and grab the crystals for themselves."

"I saw them find the evidence Dirk and the last thing we need now is some mad conspiracy theory."

"And you said she had some kind of fit down there." Dang's remark triggered more nods of agreement, as if it validated Albright's wild assumption.

"You said even the Delgardo woman reacted badly to entering the mine." Edmurson looked around the table for confirmation from the others.

"A mild case of claustrophobia, no more than that." Ull made another futile attempt at reason.

"Does strange things to people! It's the dark and the feeling of the walls closing in on you. All that rock above you which could give way at any moment."

"Don't be an idiot Mol, the mine is perfectly safe!"

"You know that Petre and we know that, but do they?" Dang paused for dramatic effect. "And Wildman told us that the Gantz woman is regarded as some kind of prophet." He looked over his shoulder and addressed Wildman. "Isn't that right?" All eyes turned towards him and Wildman reluctantly nodded. "Some mutation which affected her brain?"

"That's what the rumours say." Wildman realised those words could be taken either way and he saw the look Ull gave him.

"An abnormal brain! Who can say what could trigger a fit or even a complete mental breakdown!"

Before Ull could respond Albright offered his opinion. "The woman's locked in her room threatening to shoot anybody who doesn't do exactly what she says. She's even turned against Delgardo!"

"What does Control make of this situation?" Edmurson addressed his question to Ull.

"They are in contact with Gantz's superior, an Inspector Goodridge. I get the impression that particular relationship isn't going too well. They're not happy she's closed down the operation. They consider it an unlawful action which far exceeds her authority." Ull paused as he realised his next statement would only feed their irrational attitudes. "They claim it's an act of irresponsibility verging on madness."

"I told you!" Albright slammed his fist onto the table to emphasise his point. "A bloody mad woman."

"The question is, what are we going to do about it?"

"We can't do anything about it Milton, this is a police matter."

Milton laughed. "It's a fucking police matter alright! The mad woman's the police officer in charge!" The others joined in the amusement. "And what do you expect the police to do? Delgardo handed over her gun to a mad woman and Wildman is armed with dog biscuits!"

Again Wildman became the centre of attention. The way things were going with the crew he had no intention of sharing the fact he had now recovered his weapon. That was a card he would play when he needed to. He just hung his head in fake shame.

"Fat lot of use the police are to us!" Gurd highlighted his remark by spitting on the floor in the direction of Wildman.

"So the question remains, what are we going to do about it?" Ull noticed that the crew did not turn to him for an answer. Their attention remained fixed on Dang, waiting for him to answer his own question. With a self satisfying smile he obliged them. "Look, the way I see it is this. We can't restrain Gantz. We'd have to break in, which would alert her and she's armed. Even our inept police friends aren't stupid enough to have tried that!"

"So what do we do?"

"Well correct me if I'm wrong but there are two things which need to be done. One," Dang held up a finger to illustrate, "make sure she doesn't decide to come out of that room shooting and with a mad woman and a gun that is a real risk." That revelation came as a surprise by the look on some of the attentive faces. "And two," a second finger was raised, "get the mine re-opened. Control will regard that as our responsibility and every minute that drill-head is silent means lost bonus for us."

"With the crystals missing there's no bloody bonus anyway!" There was no hiding the misery in Albright's voice.

"They're not missing bonehead, they're somewhere in the mine. Even if Willard doesn't tell us where they are it's only a matter of time before we find them."

"I didn't steal the crystals!" Willard sounded quite adamant about that but the others gave him looks of contempt. "You all heard Ull, the sledge filter was working correctly."

"Now it is!" sneered Gurd. Willard thought about protesting again but decided it would be a waste of time. As long as they were concerned about getting the drill-head restarted it stopped them questioning him further about the missing crystals. They would eventually get around to it and he was convinced it would be an unpleasant experience, especially for him. Best to keep quiet and delay that moment for as long as possible.

"How do we deal with Gantz? She's threatened to shoot anyone who attempts to recouple the pipe."

"And I should point out that her bedroom window overlooks the storage bins." Wildman folded his arms across his chest and gave Dang a look which defied him to deal with that problem.

"How long has she been awake for?" He paused to look around at the others to push his point home rather than get an answer to his question. "We wait for a few more hours and then sneak out and recouple the pipe. While we're waiting Willard works on the door lock of her room. You can lock it from the outside and stop her from opening it?" He glanced over at Willard and the technician nodded his head. "Once we get the pipe reconnected we can power up the drill-head and search the mine for the crystals. If she can't get out of her room there's nothing she can do about it."

"What about Delgardo?" asked Edmurson.

"What about her? She's asleep as well. By the time she wakes up it'll be too late. How's she going to power down the drill-head and uncouple the pipe without our help?"

"That bloody stun stick can be persuasive, ask Mol" Gurd gave Edmurson a nasty look over the remark but held his tongue.

"If you all stand up to her she won't give you any trouble." Wildman had moved closer to the group huddled around the table. He was now almost part of it.

"What makes you so sure? I get the impression she's not the sort to back down in an argument."

"I think you're right Sligo but she's under orders from Goodridge. She's told me if you lot turn nasty we lock you in your rooms until the recovery team arrive. Gantz going off her head is bad enough, I doubt if Goodridge wants to make it any worse by getting us to lay into you lot. As your boss says, Gantz is on shaky ground closing the mine down so Goodridge will want to avoid any complaints of police brutality."

"So you're saying if we refuse to let you lock us up you won't lay into us with the stun sticks?"

"Locking you up would be unlawful. Even if one of you is a suspect we can't lock you up for the time it'll take to get a recovery team out here."

"How long do you figure that would take?" Dang was enjoying getting support from this unexpected source.

"Wildman scratched his head. "Will the Corporation give them a transporter?" He directed the question at Ull.

"At the moment, no, not until the mine is reopened."

"Which isn't going to happen unless you do it or until the recovery team arrive. That leaves them with two choices, get the Colonials to lend them the only Colonial class patrol ship this planet has or transport everything in ships like my one. No way are they going to get permission to use the Colonial ship for a police investigation like this! To get the men and equipment out here in ship like mine is impossible. You'd need several and that would leave very few ships, if any, left for normal operational duties. I doubt if Goodridge has got that much influence with his bosses. Even if he did they haven't got the right equipment and are having to improvise. The quickest I can see help arriving is three to four days. This Gantz incident has caused enough problems so they'll be very careful not to do anything which would lead to more complaints. Negotiations could drag on for ever!"

"I thought you were too smart to be a police officer!" Dang gave Wildman a wink.

"They'll get a complaint about that bitch Delgardo from me." Gurd snarled.

"Unprovoked attack was it Mol?" asked an amused Dang.

"That's right! Her word against mine. Any of you lot see me touch her?" None of the others contradicted him but their looks spoke volumes.

"You think the law would be on our side?" There was a fair amount of cautious doubt in Ull's voice as he was still reluctant to support Milton Dang's plan.

"Gantz hasn't given a valid reason for her actions, in fact she hasn't given any reason at all! If the decisions she made are a result of her unstable mental state then they were made when she was obviously unfit for duty. Delgardo has made no attempt to relieve Gantz of duty so I would imagine any of her decisions are also now suspect."

Ull scratched his head. "I guess when you look at it like that."

"I say we go with Milton's plan. Locking the Gantz woman in her room is just a way of safely restraining her." It was the first time LeBon had spoken.

"Good point Wiil!"

"We should do the same with that Delgardo, she threatened me! Held a gun to my head." Albright's voice was full of indignation.

"You did lose it Dirk. You were pretty scary." Edmurson adopted his usual smoothing tone with Albright.

"She was still going to shoot me! It took the mad woman to calm her down. We're not safe while either of them are free."

"Then we get Willard to lock them both in!" Dang spread his arms out to indicate the simplicity and all encompassing nature of his plan.

"It makes sense" remarked LeBon.

"And Wildman will back us up that we had no other choice" added Edmurson. Ull turned to Wildman to see what his reply would be.

Wildman nervously glanced around at the expectant faces. Prompting from the sidelines was one thing but he wasn't completely sure about throwing his hand in with these people. He decided upon a cautious approach. "I don't think we need to lock Delgardo in. With Gantz you can claim it was a justified precaution considering how she's behaving but that's not the case with Delgardo." He paused to study their faces again in an attempt to gauge their mood. "As I said, she'll avoid any confrontation."

"Can we be sure about that?" asked LeBon.

"Look, are we going to talk about this endlessly or fucking do something?" Albright again thumped the table with his fist.

"I suggest we take a vote on my original plan." Dang wanted the decision made. He could see Albright was beginning to get agitated and the last thing he wanted was the group to be further distracted by one of his panic attacks. "I propose we lock Gantz in her room, recouple the sledge pipe and power up the drill-head." He immediately raised his arm. Albright and LeBon quickly raised their arms followed by Gurd. Edmurson heisted but finally raised his arm. Chang looked around, somewhat confused but raised his arm when he saw Edmurson raise his. Gurd stared at Rolm in an intimidating way and she slowly joined the others. "You going to be last as usual Zon?" Willard responded to Dang's sarcasm by giving a half-hearted gesture of raising his hand. "Are you with us Petre?" Ull glared at Dang but raised his arm nonetheless. "Unanimous!" declared Dang.

"What about the other bitch?" snarled Gurd.

"I propose we leave Delgardo alone." Dang had raised his hand before he had finished speaking. He was followed by Ull and Edmurson. Chang mirrored Edmuson and he was quickly followed by LeBon and Rolm, the latter despite Gurd's look of disapproval. Willard was the last to respond. "Carried by a majority. I suggest we have something to eat to pass the time until we're sure Gantz is asleep. Make yourself useful Boni." Chang jumped at the mention of his name and scurried off to the kitchen. "You better get started Zon. The sooner she's locked in the better, a mad woman armed with a gun rushing in half way through my meal would give me indigestion." Dang smiled at his witty remark. None of the others joined in and Willard groaned as he reluctantly pulled himself to his feet. The thought had occurred to him that if Gantz happened to leave her room and find him tampering with the door mechanism, indigestion would be the least of his problems.

Wildman, unnoticed by the others, had discretely withdrawn to his original position by the door, thus distancing himself from them. Experience had taught him the benefits of sitting on the fence.

***

There were moments when Nemi felt his life was a little surreal. He was having one of those moments now. Less than three years ago he had been a junior NCO in a second rate Colonial Unit and now, recently turned twenty-three years of age, he had just commandeered a multi-million credit patrol craft and nobody turned a hair. He realised, of course, it was Morgan's authority backing him up which made it possible, or rather in this case the assumed authority given to Morgan's aide, but even that seemed a little unreal. Less than three years ago Morgan had been an officer in charge of a second rate Colonial unit and an officer with a black mark on his record at that! If these people, who were now rushing about eager to fulfil his orders, knew the truth he wondered what their reaction would be. The patrol craft had a three man crew and they were all New Brethren. Therefore, when Nemi explained that the test schedule would run alongside a rescue mission involving Kanah Gantz, any lingering doubts about Nemi's authority were quickly dispelled. Not only did they recognise her as one of the prophets but the co-pilot was also a volunteer for the New Brethren special program. He had a daughter who was part of the program in the Midwich settlement. With no formal authorisation and without checking back to Morgan, Nemi had effectively stolen a powerful Colonial space craft.

There were also two civilian technicians on board who were responsible for running continuous diagnostic programs to

248

monitor the performance of the new ship. The fact that they were also New Brethren was further reassurance for Nemi. Tolman, who was nominally in charge of the recovery team, could not spare any extra officers so Nemi had hand picked two trusted troopers to provide additional security. All of this had been accomplished within an hour of receiving Goodridge's call. Tolman and Nemi were now watching the take off, via a small monitor, from the relative comfort of the troop carrying section of the ship. They had both arrived in Port Nilmon by ground transport, Nemi in a troop carrier being delivered for the new garrison and Tolman by river on a supply ship, so this was their first aerial view of New Eden's second city. Unluckily, or perhaps luckily as the space port was situated in the industrial quarter, it was now dark so the vista was limited to a vast swathe of twinkling lights. They just caught sight of the moonlight reflected off the surface of the river as they crossed it before the monitor changed to a mixture of dark shadows as they flew across the jungle on the north bank. In a few minutes they caught sight of the river again as they recrossed it and flew over a landscape of fields, germinating sheds and growth barns which stretched from Port Nilmon along the south bank and down to the capital city, New Eden.

Both men had seen New Eden from the air enough times to recognise where they were flying over, even in the dark, so knew what their arrival time would be. Tolman had called ahead to ensure the cargo of the deconstructed police patrol craft and the two technical crew responsible for putting it together were waiting with the three man recovery team at the space port. The ship was on the ground for only a few minutes before the cargo and extra personal were aboard and they were taking off again. This time they all waved on their seat harnesses and adjusted the oxygen nose tubes as they prepared for the ship to leave the planet atmosphere and go into orbit. The only people busy now were the two civilian technicians who were monitoring every movement and reaction of the ship. Nemi smiled to himself as he thought of the number of boxes which would be ticked on the testing schedule, take off, landing, cargo, personal, achieving orbit and distance trials. The smile got bigger when he thought of the time saved getting to Kanah Gantz.

The only negative news was a report from Goodridge on his conversation with Lisbeth Smith. She confirmed that Gantz was still suffering the effects of her last case. Nemi was a little hurt that he had to learn she was suffering from reoccurring nightmares from another Gnostic rather than from Gantz herself. True she always had trouble converting her emotions into words but surely she could have made the effort for him. Perhaps their friendship was just that and he had been foolish to read any more into it. Such thoughts only added to the stress he felt for her well-being. Nemi was now a confused and worried man.

***

The nearer they got to the descent towards the Arkin mountains the more agitated Nemi became. As soon as they re-entered the planet's atmosphere and dispensed with the oxygen masks and safety belts Tolman moved to sit next to Nemi. He felt he needed to distract the young man and had been thinking of a way to achieve this for the last half hour. An update on his young son had been the first idea but that would involve him talking and the aim was really to get Nemi talking to divert attention from his current troubles. He had finally come up an idea which would involve Nemi taking the lead while at the same time satisfying Tolman's curiosity.

"Nemi, ever since my..." he paused to select the right word or phrase. Talk or communication sounded ridiculous. "Ever

250

since my link-up with the Collective I've been coming up with questions I should have asked. At the time..." He struggled again.

"They didn't seem necessary?" Nemi gave a weak smile as he guessed Tolman's intention.

"Yeah it was all perfectly clear at the time. Same with you?"

Nemi nodded. "So what do you need to know? Mind you I can't promise I will know, Kanah never really talks about them and changes the subject whenever I do."

Tolman nodded his understanding. "If they are really sentient beings how have they keep themselves a secret for so long? I attempted to find some information on the first contact but there was remarkably little about it."

"Big embarrassment at the time Vitch. They looked so much like us they had to be intelligent. Man's first contact with intelligent aliens was all over the media. The trouble was, well you've seen them, dumb monkeys. All attempts to interact with them failed. Not entirely down to the fact they did not have the ability to make sounds. They quickly worked out man was a potential danger to them."

"Yeah I get all that and the eventual cross-breeding to provide a safe conduit between them and us. But why didn't the initial planet survey pick up any signs of an advanced society? Why didn't they find evidence of their power sources, their cities, their communication networks!"

"Because there wasn't any evidence! As far as we know they have no power generators, at least none which we can detect. No artificial structures have been found, despite the fact that we have scanned every square metre of the planet. There's evidence of extensive tunnels beneath the surface but they don't appear to be artificial either. And for a species able to mentally communicate with any other member anywhere on the planet via a neural network what use would roads be?"

"How can a civilisation leave no evidence of an intelligent civilisation?"

"You mean round houses, pyramids, castles, railways, roads and hideous black monoliths which pass for Federation homes or Corporation offices and factories?"

"And energy generators. Even hyper-drives leave particle trace!"

"Lots of natural energy sources in the universe Vitch, suns, wind, even volcanoes demonstrate the energy within planets. Man has harnessed them so why not the Collective? Just because we don't know how they do it, doesn't mean they don't! Just because they look a bit like us doesn't mean they've developed like us."

"In other words you don't know!"

Nemi smiled, the first time he had since leaving the bar in Port Nilmon. "The Collective like their privacy Vitch."

"So why go to the effort of making contact at all and why with the New Brethren?"

"Why link with me and you and not Goodridge or Morgan? They saw something in us and they must have seen something in the New Brethren. As to why? Well they needed an ally to help protect them from the encroachment of the colonists!"

"And the breeding program?"

Nemi hesitated before attempting to answer that particular question. "They're a dying race! Perhaps the thing they have in common with the New Brethren is the belief, or more likely the urge to attain immortality or a version of it. The Gnostics, and especially the next genetically engineered generation, are the New Brethren's next step towards their God. The next step in man's evolution. For the Collective it's a way of salvaging their culture. The new Gnostics will have the same abilities as the

Collective so can share their culture, history, values and whatever else the Collective see as their unique identity. A better option than being forgotten?"

Tolman looked thoughtful. "I don't know if that's sad or uplifting! Did you get this from Kanah?"

"Kanah tells me nothing. The dying race thing I picked up during the link but whether it's true or not..." Nemi shrugged his shoulders. "I made the rest up, at least the Collective bit. Like you I've made decisions which compromise my position as a member of the Colonial Corps. My version of events helps me live with those decisions."

"Thanks Nemi, I think this might help me too."

"Oh, thank you Vitch for taking my mind off Kanah."

"Was I that obvious?"

"Don't need to be a Gnostic to see through you Vitch!"

***

By the time Chang had cooked them a meal and they had eaten it another two hours has passed. Now they had decided upon a course of action their spirits were lifted and there was much light-hearted chat during the meal, mostly revolving around how each of them were going to spend their share of the bonus. It was rare to have the opportunity to all eat together so they made the most of it, pushing several tables together and indulging in various medication to enhance their mood or perhaps to give them some artificial courage for the task ahead. Wildman sat at one end of the table observing their behaviour. All the rifts, altercations and accusations of the past couple of days appeared to have been forgotten, swept away by the promise of the elusive bonus. They now looked the close knit crew which Petre Ull always considered them to be. It was, therefore, surprising to Wildman that Ull's bonhomie appeared a trifle strained. After listening to them for several more minutes he realised the reason for this. A sea-change had taken place and now it was Milton Dang whom the crew looked to for leadership. Petre Ull 's position had been usurped. It was Milton Dang who took centre stage.

Wildman found this a strange turn of affairs. He considered Dang to be one of the more odious members of the crew. The man could be charming or spiteful as the mood took him but above all he was a manipulator. That air of superiority which Edmurson had captured so well in his wood carving was now plain to see. Wildman was surprised none of the crew had noticed it, not even Edmurson. Perhaps he had captured the essence of Dang without realising what he had done! The other strange thing was this apparent celebration of a bonus when the crystals which would earn it were missing. His bin switch idea had been proved wrong so the logical place for the missing crystals was somewhere in the mine. True, it would only be a matter of time before they were found but would the crew get that time? Ull had said Control were refusing at the moment to provide a transporter but that situation could change at any time. This obsession with getting the drill-head powered up again to boost the bonus seemed to Wildman to be the crew getting their priorities wrong. Locating the missing crystals should be the first thing on their agenda. He had the urge to point this out but although he had won some element of trust with them he did not believe it went as far as taking advice from him. He would bide his time and make the suggestion once they had achieved their main objective. He turned his attention to Zon Willard. The young man was joining in with the conversation but did not appear to have his heart in it. No doubt being the prime suspect responsible for diverting the crystals had dampened his spirits. Wildman wondered if he was indeed the culprit. Diverting the crystals seemed, to Wildman at least,

254

a ridiculous thing to do. Willard had the technical knowhow to pull it off but what then? The man was basically lazy and it was hard to visualise him toiling away for hours on end to retrieve the crystals. Then again he was a plug-head which would suggest he was not that bright so perhaps he did not think it through. Wildman toyed with various ideas. Perhaps he was brighter than he appeared, the insert might have been, like a lot of youngsters, an alternative to putting in any effort. Now that fitted Willard's character.

Wildman turned his attention to Ull. An unlikely suspect but the reasonable, hard working persona could be just a front or perhaps he had tired of baby sitting this bunch of dysfunctional wasters. Why share the bonus with them? It seemed out of character but substantial amounts of credits had corrupted better men than Petre Ull. He also had the technical capability to divert the crystals and he was bright enough to come up with a plan to get away with it. The hard work of recovery would not have been a problem for him and his plans for the bonus had been modest compared to the others. Wildman wondered how much of the crystal ore he would need to steal to outstrip the value of his share of he bonus. Now that would be clever. When the crystals are found who could tell if any of them are still missing? Wildman nodded to himself in satisfaction at working out that particular angle. Ull looked a better bet than Willard.

Wildman cast an eye over the rest of the crew in an attempt to assess any other suspects. He dismissed Boni Chang straight away, the man lacked the intelligence but more importantly the nerve to pull something like this off. Milton Dang was nowhere near as clever as he thought he was but he would certainly have the nerve and arrogance to think he could get away with it. He also, more than any of the others, appeared to be obsessed about getting the drill-head back up and running. Searching for the missing crystals seemed to be of little concern. Was that because he already knew where they were hidden? Wildman mentally added him onto the suspect list along with Ull and Willard. Edmurson was placed on the same list as Chang. Wildman doubted if the huge man had the technical knowledge but more than that he doubted if the man was capable of cheating the other members of the crew. His dream was to buy a farm with his bonus. A modest desire considering the size of the possible bonus! It somehow fitted with the simple and straightforward nature of the man. Albright was considered to be too unstable to have carried off such a deception and if his concern over the missing crystals was fake he was undoubtedly a better actor than he was a miner. Also being Edmurson's shift partner would have made it difficult to tamper with the drill-head scanner, even if he had the ability to. Mol Gurd was placed firmly on the suspect list but Wildman did wonder if his dislike for the man had influenced his decision. A more unpleasant individual it would be hard to find and he would be quite capable of cheating the other members of the crew. His offensive character did not necessarily mean he was stupid but did he have the wit to devise such a plan? Wildman doubted it but Gurd remained on the list. LeBon and Rolm were more of a problem for Wildman. Both were dominated by their respective shift partners and neither appeared to have the nerve or skills required. However, enforced subservience could build up resentment to a point where the idea of cheating their persecutors out of a huge bonus could become very appealing. Perhaps that would be the only motive they required. Not to enrich themselves, just to deny it to Dang or Gurd. Outside bets, but he would add them to the list as a precaution. Of course Wildman's list contained suspects for the crystal theft not Laslo Ginthem's murder. That was of little concern to Wildman.

Eventually they had run out of ways to spend their bonuses, from the meagre plot of land up to the palatial estate on Altar, and Dang rose from his chair. "Right, the mad woman is locked in her room and both her and Delgardo should be sound asleep by now. Who's going to help me recouple the pipe?"

Gurd pulled himself to his feet. "If you think I'm letting you out of my sight you're as crazy as the Gantz woman!" Wildman noted that Gurd's bonhomie had not lasted long.

"Well that's added some muscle to the brains! All we need now is somebody to act as lookout." Dang looked straight at LeBon and the youngster reluctantly stood up. "Excellent! Let's get started."

"What about the compound security lights? We can't switch those off from here." It was Ull who was the voice of caution.

"If she's asleep they don't matter and if she's not turning them off would alert her. She can't spend every minute standing on her bunk looking out of the window. Now let's get going, we've farted about for far too long all ready."

Gurd and LeBon followed Dang to the doorway. The rest of the crew immediately moved to the windows so as to watch their progress. The three men kept close to the wall of the accommodation block until the last minute. Dang pushed LeBon out into the open. The youngster looked up at Gantz's window and when he was sure he could not see Gantz, waved the other two forward. LeBon walked slowly backwards towards the storage bins, keeping a close eye on the window and the other two men scurried across the open ground to where the ore sledge pipe lay. Gurd curled his arms around the huge pipe and with a grunt raised it up and pushed it against the access hatch of the storage bin. It produced a loud metallic clang which earned Gurd a withering look from Dang who quickly bent down on the other side of the pipe to deal with the fastenings. LeBon stood half way between the block and the storage bins nervously glancing between the window and the activity behind him. He failed to see the ore pipe behind him and fell over it. He scrambled to his feet but failed to check the window for any movement until it was too late. He was looking to check on the progress being made on the pipe when the shot rang out.

Gurd screamed out in pain and clutched the back of his knee. He stumbled and dropped the pipe onto Dang who also screamed out as it landed on his foot. It had also knocked his hand into the half assembled fastenings and gouged a strip of skin off. It was a minor injury but produced a lot of blood. That, coupled with the shock of the gun shot, meant he did not hear the shout from the accommodation block. He just stood staring first at his bloody hands and then at the writhing body of Gurd who was still yelling and clutching the back of his knee with a bloody hand. Suddenly Ull and Edmurson were next to him. Ull put an arm around his shoulder and guided him back towards the block while Edmurson grabbed Gurd under the arm pits and dragged him away.

"Come on man" urged Ull, "before she takes another shot at us!" It was enough to snap Dang out of shock and he quickened his pace.

They reached the safety of the Rec and Edmurson gently placed the still howling Gurd onto one of the couches. Willard had already run for the first aid kit and was ready and waiting to deal with the injury. He gave Gurd a pain killer and quickly cleaned and sealed the wound to stop any further bleeding. "Best I can do for now! The bullet will have to come out but I'm not taking the risk." He moved away from the now sedated Gurd and turned his attention to Dang's damaged hand.

"Well, that went well!"

There was no time for anyone to respond to Wildman's remark as Delgardo appeared from the bedroom corridor. From the look of her dishevelled clothing she had been sleeping but she was wide awake now. "What the fuck is going on?"

Wildman quickly moved to place himself between her and the crew. "They've locked Gantz in her room and tried to recouple the ore pipe."

"And you let them?" There was real anger in her voice.

"I wasn't in a position to stop them! I warned them against it but they weren't in the mood to listen. You said if they turned hasty to lock them in their rooms but as I was on my own I thought keeping an eye on them was a better idea."

Delgardo's anger began to dissipate. She had given him those instructions and armed with only a stun stick he had little chance of stopping a determined crew. "Sorry Wildman, you're right. Whose stupid idea was it?"

"Milton Dang's. Couldn't miss the opportunity to undermine Ull's authority, I doubt if they'll listen to any more of his bright ideas. He's got a minor hand injury but Mol Gurd got shot in the back of the knee. Still, I doubt any tears will be shed on account of that."

"Why have they locked Gantz in her room?"

"To stop her coming out when she found out what they'd done. They'll claim it was for their own protection and hers. If you look at it from their point of view it's hard to argue against it. The fact she shot one of them rather proves their point. I'm not sure anything she's done makes sense and I doubt if any of it is legal either!"

"You should have woken me."

"I should have, I'm sorry, my mistake but I'm not used to situations like this."

"You and me both! Okay, look you go and get some sleep. I'll keep an eye on this lot." She patted Wildman on the shoulder.

"Thanks." He paused. "By the way, Ull has been in contact with his bosses and he knows they're reluctant to provide any transport for the recovery team."

"Shit! Well I suppose that was to be expected. I just hope I hear from Goodridge soon." Wildman nodded and made his way to his bedroom cursing his bad luck. They wouldn't try to recouple the pipe again and any chance of searching the mine for the missing crystals had been lost. He needed to think out his next move.

***

Delgardo sat at the table nearest the doorway tapping her stun stick idly on the edge of it. She maintained a steady beat and glared at each member of the crew in turn. It was a deliberate ploy to irritate them. Her abrupt awakening had ruined her intention of reporting in to Goodridge and now with Gantz's shooting of Mol Gurd she needed to update him. She had no intention of making the call in front of them and she did not trust them enough to leave them on their own while she returned to the privacy of her room. The ploy eventually worked or the crew just got bored, but either way one by one they retired to their rooms. She was now alone except for the heavily sedated Gurd. The call to Goodridge immediately lifted her spirits.

"Ah, Officer Delgardo, this is a well timed call, I was about to update you on the situation. Good news! Deputy Vitch Tolman is on his way with the recovery team." He could see the relief on her face. "Even better than that, the Colonial troops have supplied one of their vehicles for the trip so they should be with you by dawn. They have also supplied an NCO and two troopers so once they arrive at least your safety is secure. What's the situation there?"

"That's what I was calling about sir. I'm afraid to report that Deputy Gantz has shot one of the civilians." She saw the shock on his face so quickly added "It's not fatal sir but she hit him in the back of the knee and shattered the knee cap. He needs better medical attention than we can provide here."

"What happened and how's Kanah now?" Goodridge suddenly realised the last remark was a little unprofessional and so he added, "The troopers should be able to supply the necessary medical assistance for the civilian."

"I'm afraid we lost control sir. The miners took things into their own hands and attempted to recouple the ore sledge pipe. They attempted to reopen the mine." She added the last bit unsure of how much Goodridge knew about the detailed workings of a mine operation. "They hoped exhaustion would have taken its toll and she would be sleeping. They also interfered with her room lock mechanism to ensure she couldn't get out. There's been no contact with her since then."

Goodridge looked worried. "I'm sorry Sonia. I must take some responsibility for this situation. I thought Kanah was fit for duty but obviously that wasn't the case. Her..." He stopped himself from mentioning the mental strain Gantz must be having due to the isolation. His ignorance of the mental makeup of a Gnostic had contributed to this situation. "What's the position at the moment? Are you and Officer Singh safe?"

"At the moment things have calmed down sir. The shock of the shooting has done that. All the crew have retired to their rooms now so I don't expect any more trouble in the short term. Officer Singh and I are unharmed."

"Good! Not much longer now and Deputy Tolman will be there. Well done Sonia!"

"Thank you sir." Delgardo ended the call. She glanced over at the sleeping figure of Mol Gurd. She wondered if she should have mentioned the earlier incident with him but decided it would only make Goodridge feel even worse about sending her out here with the unstable Gantz. It was a problem which would have to be left for later. She had been so relieved at the time that she had not killed Gurd, she had failed to arrest him for assault. Knowing Gurd, her oversight would no doubt lead him to lodge an assault charge against her. Remembering the moment her stun stick made contact with Gurd's testicle brought a smile to her lips. Any black mark on her record was worth that moment.

CHAPTER ELEVEN

Delgardo was dozing when the call came in. It was still dark outside so she was surprised when informed the Colonial ship had arrived. The craft was too big to land at the camp site, even if Wildman's ship had not been there, so they had landed in the Perrin Gap. The co-pilot, Officer al-Rashid, explained that the recovery team had just set off in a ground vehicle and their estimated time of arrival was within the next half hour. He then downloaded a personnel list and cargo manifesto. Delgardo thanked him, remarking to herself what a polite, efficient and smart officer he was. The difference when compared to Wildman was startling. She opened the downloaded files and browsed the contents. The cargo manifesto contained a list of technical sounding items, a few of which she recognised as parts of a patrol ship but the more interesting file was the personnel list. The first name she recognised, Deputy Vitch Tolman, another hero of Midwich whom she had met briefly but never worked with before. Next were members of the recovery team, one of whom she had worked with before, and then came a list of the three Colonial troopers. It was the first one of the names which grabbed her attention; NCO Ja Nemi. She was actually going to meet the lover of Kanah Gantz. The man who risked his life for her and the man whose life she had saved. Deep down Delgardo was a romantic at heart and, although she had never experienced it herself with any of her girlfriends, a love which involved such self-sacrifice was the stuff of her dreams.

264

Now he was again coming to the rescue of his true love. Delgardo found her heart racing at the thought of meeting him in the flesh.

Her dreamy-eyed expression rapidly reverted to her business-like one when Petre Ull entered the Rec. He was closely followed by Boniface Chang who, with eyes averted, hurried past towards the kitchen area. Ull nodded a subdued acknowledgement to Delgardo and sat at a table far enough away to discourage any conversation. Delgardo wondered if this was a continuation of the bad karma from their initial meeting or whether he was embarrassed about last night's incident. Well she was bigger than any petty argument so she got up and strolled over to him. He reluctantly looked up when she stopped by the table and offered a weak smile.

"I thought you should know Deputy Tolman and the recovery team will be here within shortly."

"Oh! I didn't expect them to get here so quickly."

"They got a lift from a Colonial patrol craft. It landed in the Perrin Gap."

There was an awkward silence which Ull eventually broke. "I did advise them not to try that stupid stunt last night."

"I guessed you would. I take it Milton Dang was the ringleader?"

Ull nodded. "They wanted to lock you in as well. The crew voted against the idea."

"I don't for a moment think that was a unanimous vote."

Ull ventured a smile. "Mol and Dirk were the only ones who voted for it."

"I didn't know I was that popular with the crew!"

"Look," Ull hesitated, "I think we got off on the wrong foot that first day." He hesitated again. "I got over protective of my crew and..." His voice trailed away.

"Well you said they were no angels but I guess you didn't expect them to have fallen so far from grace?"

"What?" Ull looked confused.

"Sorry that might have made more sense to Gantz. You didn't expect much but you did expect more than that."

"I thought adversity would make their bonds stronger not make them fall apart."

"You're not the only person to have expected too much from people. " She pulled back a chair but paused to see if Ull would make any objection. He gestured with his hand that she should take a seat. Delgardo sat down and pushed a hand through her close cropped hair. "I was so excited when I was told I was getting an opportunity to work with the famous Kanah Gantz. I'd built up this image of her." Delgardo paused. "I guess people never live up to your expectations."

"Have you any idea what happened to her? Is there a history of fits or mental problems?"

"Our boss Goodridge thinks he put her back on duty far too soon. She was badly wounded during her last case and I've heard something like that can screw your head up."

"Shame! I mean I quite liked her." Ull grunted and flashed Delgardo a smile. "When compared to you that is! No offence Officer Delgardo."

"None taken Ull. I admit I can get in your face a bit." She gave a rare smile. "Fancy a cup of that awful synthetic coffee?"

"Thanks. Then perhaps we can start over again?"

"Deputy Tolman will be in charge now, I'll be back to supplying moody stares and a barely concealed threat of violence."

Ull smiled in appreciation of her self-mocking comment. "What's this Tolman like?"

Delgardo sauntered off towards the drinks machine but glanced over her shoulder to reply. "By all accounts he's a lot more laid back than Gantz. However, he's Gantz's partner and he's bringing along her boyfriend."

'Oh!' thought Ull. It didn't sound as if things were going to get any easier.

***

All of there crew were up, with the exception of Willard, and were finishing their breakfast by the time Deputy Tolman arrived at the Rec. Delgardo had been keeping a watchful eye out of one of the Rec windows so spotted his arrival as he led the group up the path and into the main compound. She quickly moved to the doorway and watched their approach. Tolman looked even taller than she remembered, the result of being born and grown up on the low gravity asteroid belt around Solar 2. The next figure she picked out was the one in the grey Colonial uniform with the red flashes which denoted that he was an NCO. Delgardo's romanticised image of Gantz and Nemi took another severe battering. Far from the tall, square-jawed adonis which she had been expecting Nemi was remarkable for his ordinariness. Short and with features which reminded her of pictures of an elf in stories from her childhood he lacked anything which would have made him stand out in a crowd. He just didn't look like the hero from the stories she had heard. She then recalled the words of Gantz when they had first met 'that makes it sound rather more dramatic than it actually was. I was scared most of the time and reacted instinctively. In the end I was just very lucky'. Delgardo pondered the fact that real life was a great disappointment when compared how real life was depicted by those not directly involved. After the experiences of her childhood she had always hoped the rest of her life would be different. She decided that had been a forlorn hope, fairy tale endings were reserved for fairy tales.

"Morning Officer Delgardo, Sonia isn't it?" Delgardo nodded and smiled, although she wasn't sure if Tolman actually remembered her from their brief meeting or had just done his homework on her.

"Didn't we meet at that awful seminar a couple of years back? You beat that fuck-wit O'Shea in an arm wrestling contest."

"Yes boss." She immediately warmed to the man, the arm wrestling incident wasn't on her service record and O'Shea certainly was a fuck-wit.

"Right, well we've left our vehicle down near the mine entrance with the equipment and the recovery team. This is NCO Ja Nemi by the way. The man to thank for us getting here in double quick time." Tolman paused to give a nod in the direction of the Colonial NCO. "The two troopers with him are just to provide a little extra security as we hear the locals are a bit pissed off. However, one of them is a specialist medic so I suggest we have a word with the manager while he takes a look at the injured man."

"Yes boss." Delgardo led the four newcomers into the accommodation block. The medic made his way directly to where Mol Gurd lay. He had come out of the sedation and was cursing and complaining. The medic ignored his protestations, immediately sedated him again and proceeded to work on the damaged knee.

Petre Ull got up from his chair and came to meet them. He obviously wanted the rest of the crew to be out of earshot. Delgardo made the introductions and then gave them a brief update, although Tolman appeared to have been kept up-to-date by Goodridge.

"Anything current on Kanah Gantz?"

"I attempted to check on her this morning but if she's awake she's not answering."

268

"Did she say anything when she shot Gurd?"

"Officer Delgardo was asleep at the time but I heard what she said." Ull stepped in to fill the gap in Delgardo's knowledge. "She repeated her warning that nobody should enter the mine."

"How did she sound?"

Ull thought about it for the first time. When the shooting occurred he had been preoccupied with getting his crew members back to safety. "She sounded exhausted but considering what had happened to her before, she sounded calm and lucid."

"Right the first priority is to get the recovery team set up. I hope I can rely on you to direct us to the location?" Tolman was eager to get the mine manager on side. If he was to salvage Gantz's career he needed this man's support."

"I'll provide any assistance you require but could I possibly have a word with you first," Ull paused, "in private?" Tolman nodded and Ull lead him out of the accommodation block, no doubt back to the site office.

"I bet he's going to ask to power up the bloody drill-head!" There was an air of inevitability in Delgardo's statement.

Nemi spoke for the first time. "They seem a bit obsessive about opening the mine."

"They're obsessive about the bonus the Zelman crystals will earn!"

"Bloody big bonus if they're willing to have their arse shot off by Gantz!" He fell silent and looked off into the distance. "And yet they kill the mine inspector, an act guaranteed to bring you people in with the inevitable conclusion of shutting the mine."

"None of it makes any sense! The murder, the missing crystals, the obsession, even at this late stage, of getting the drill-head working again! We, I mean Deputy Gantz and myself, thought the murder and the missing crystals might not be connected."

"Who do you fancy for the murder?" Nemi gave a little smile when he saw the reluctance displayed by Delgardo to say more. "Don't worry Delgardo I'm a nosey bastard. You police types like to be cautious, Kanah Gantz never talks to me about her cases either."

"It's just Deputy Tolman is now in charge..."

Nemi did not give her time to finish. "I'll prise it out of Tolman later. Relax." Delgardo did not really know how to react to that remark. "When Kanah had this, so-called, fit did she say anything? I'm asking this as a friend of Kanah who knows a bit about her background."

"Most of it was unintelligible and what parts I could hear were just garbled sentences and odd words."

"Try and remember exactly what she said. Even if it sounds rubbish we could use it to engage her when we approach her." Delgardo nodded. "Did she ever say who she thought was responsible for the murder? I'm not asking for names."

"No."

"Very unlike Kanah Gantz! No indications at all?"

Delgardo assumed Nemi was making an oblique reference to Gantz's supposed abilities. "She was very vague. I joked she should just pop into their heads and find out." Nemi showed little surprise at her suggestion or the implication she knew about Gantz's abilities. "All she said was that she was certain a lot or all of them were lying about something but couldn't tell what they were lying about." Nemi nodded but made no further comment. He thanked Delgardo and asked her to let him know if she remembered anything else which Gantz had said. He then wandered off deep in thought.

Delgardo watched him slowly stroll around the Rec, hands thrust into his pockets. She decided he was a very strange young man. He didn't look or behave like a man who had risked his life to save his lover, he had even referred to her as Gantz! If this was the man of Gantz's dreams then perhaps she had been mentally unstable all the time and the events of the last few days had just tipped her over the edge. Delgardo decided she would put her faith in Tolman. She suddenly noticed that Wildman had sidled up to her.

"That one makes me look hyper-active!" He nodded towards Nemi who was now inspecting Edmurson's carvings. "I expected him to rush in to get Gantz."

"How do you know who he is?"

"I know you don't think I'm much of a police officer but I am on the payroll so I got the same download from the rescue ship. I recognised his name and, like you, I've heard all the stories about the Midwich incident. I thought they sounded a bit fanciful at the time and having seen Gantz and now him I don't think my first assessment was too far off!" Wildman sniffed and scratched his ear. "Seems to be an art critic though by the amount of time he's spending studying Edmurson's carvings. Without waiting for Delgardo to respond he wandered off to join Nemi.

"Rather good aren't they?" Wildman nodded a welcome at Nemi and then added, "Officer Singh but you can call me Wildman."

Nemi looked the rather unlikely looking police officer up and down. He was back in his civilian clothing. "Police pilot I presume!"

Wildman smiled, so Nemi knew of the reputation of police pilots. "I've got the flying bug and they provide the most interesting opportunities."

"Well in answer to your first question, yes they are rather good. Not only can you recognise the crew members but the artist appears to have captured their characters. From the information we've had about what's been going on here I'd say that one is Milton Dang and that one is Mol Gurd." Nemi pointed to the right images.

"You noticed that as well! I'm impressed! I spotted it but I've had the benefit of studying them in action."

"Tell me about the others."

Wildman went through the images, starting with Petre Ull, pointing at each one in turn as he spoke. "The mine manager, a basically good man but too trusting. Thinks his team are his extended family. Zon Willard the techie. A lazy bugger who would have been sacked long before now if he wasn't the friend of Ull." Wildman put a lot of emphasis on the word friend. Nemi ignored the inference. "Took me a time to work out those two. Edmurson, the artist and yet the crudest image. Make what you will about that!"

"Modest and more concerned with the other members of the crew," suggested Nemi.

Wildman considered the remark for awhile. "You might be better at this than me." Nemi ignored the deliberate attempt at flattery so Wildman continued his tour through the crew. "Mol Gurd and Milton Dang you've already spotted. Dirk Albright, as you can see is the confused and angry one. Not sure if the man is confused about his anger or is angry about being confused! The sad Sara Rolm, but if I had to spend my working day with Mol Gurd I'd be miserable. Will LeBon." Wildman paused. "My first thought was shyness but there's something else there which I just can't get."He shrugged his shoulders and moved on. "Last but not least Boniface Chang. It depicts bugger all which with Boni is spot on." Wildman gave a little smile. "Find me a murderer and a thief clever enough to beat the Corporation security measures out of that lot!"

"You think it's the same person?"

"Only thing which makes any sense. The trouble is I could pick a couple I think capable of murder but they aren't clever enough to mastermind the theft."

"Why not an alliance of a couple of the crew or even the whole crew? Ull might be right about the crew being an extended family!"

"I hadn't really given any thought about a couple of them in it together. You might have something there but I doubt if they're all in it, you haven't seen them bickering! I'm surprised there hasn't been more violence, and I mean between the crew."

"By violence I assume you're talking about Gantz shooting Gurd?"

"Delgardo also used her stun stick on him."

"Popular guy! Any idea why?"

"Whatever happened, happened in the bedroom corridor so none of us saw what started it. All we saw was Gurd stagger out holding his balls." Nemi nodded. The look on Wildman's face told him it was a suspected sexual assault. Nemi wondered why Delgardo hadn't reported it, there was nothing about it mentioned in the download from Goodridge. He decided to change the subject and returned his attention to Edmurson's artwork. He wasn't at all sure if he trusted Wildman.

"Are these based on places around here?" Nemi pointed to one in particular. "That looks like the Perrin Gap where we landed."

Wildman nodded. "It's the view from this side. You were probably walking away from it. I know that one," he pointed to a carving just above the one they had been studying, "is of the Jinn mountains. Edmurson worked on a drilling rig in the desert south of the capital before he moved here. The others Edmurson said were just scenes he dreamt up. He must have got bored with views of mountains."

"Oh! I thought I recognised the village scene, just can't remember where. No good asking Edmurson then."

There was a long silence before Wildman ventured to speak again. "So what do you plan to do about Gantz?" He tried to make the enquiry sound as casual as he could.

"Get her out and take her home." Nemi gave Wildman a fleeting smile before he moved away. Wildman thought about following him but decided against it. He wasn't at all sure if he trusted Nemi.

***

Tolman had been gone for some considerable time. Nemi had passed the time by checking with the medic that Gurd was okay. In truth, after all he had heard about the man, he was far from caring about him but he always liked to show his appreciation of the jobs his troopers did. The medic's reply of 'he'll live' was delivered in a tone which suggested the trooper did not appreciate being verbally abused by somebody whom he was attempting to help. He had sedated Gurd again and Nemi didn't bother to ask if this was through necessity or choice. He told the medic to standby as he would no doubt be needed to help Kanah Gantz. As a practising New Brethren the medic reacted to this task with a lot more concern and enthusiasm. Nemi thanked him and moved on to the trooper who stood guard at the doorway. She had been one of the troopers who were part of the rescue force at Midwich and had helped evacuate Nemi to the hospital. He had been impressed by her calm efficiency that day so had picked her as one of the troopers to form the nucleus of the new garrison for Port Nilmon. She had been an obvious choice to accompany him on this trip.

"Sir." The formal greeting was accompanied by a small smile.

"Ruth, I'm keeping Mike the medic here to tend to Kanah Gantz when we get her out. He can then babysit this lot if need be. I want you in the mine to keep an eye on the recovery team. Don't let anybody else down that tunnel unless you clear it with either me or Deputy Tolman. Is that clear?"

Trooper Ruth Dulac gave another little smile. Nemi always referred to Trooper Dan Mikelson as 'Mike the medic' because, in his words, it scanned better than Dan the medic. "Yes sir. Do you expect any trouble?"

Nemi thought about that. "No, but I've got a bad feeling about this situation. It might be nothing more than indigestion from the awful food dispenser breakfast we had on the ship but..." She nodded her understanding. Nemi was renown for his laid-back attitude and this cautiousness was out of character. If he was worried then she would remain alert. He gave her a reassuring pat on the shoulder as he spotted Tolman and Ull return to the Rec and walked over to meet them.

"Problems?" Nemi eyed up the two men as he asked the question.

"Manager Ull here has requested to be allowed to reopen the mine. The drill-head is nowhere near where the recovery team will be working and he has questioned the legality of Deputy Gantz's action, in light of her mental condition."

"Which, at this point, we know nothing about." Nemi was calm and polite.

"She obviously had some mental breakdown and then disarmed one of your own people, held her and me at gunpoint, closed down the mine and shot one of my crew when he attempted to legally start up operations again. I think we can guess at her mental condition."

"Oh you're certainly free to guess at her mental condition but until we have somebody with a few more medical qualifications to assess her, then your guess is worth shit." Ull opened his mouth to protest and then thought better of it. He got off on the wrong foot with Delgardo and was reluctant to further antagonise Nemi and Tolman. "Once we can ascertain why Gantz thought it necessary to close down the mine or confirm she was in no fit state to make that decision we can revisit your request to reopen."

"This is what I told him but perhaps you were more succinct."

"I'm sorry gentlemen but you must understand I'm under pressure from the Corporation to get this mine working again. They see," he paused to carefully word the next part. "They see what they consider to be a rogue police officer illegally closing down this operation. An officer who appears to have had a complete breakdown. I have no choice but to formally lodge my protest with you. It's my responsibility to ensure the continued profitable running of this site." Ull spread out his arms, imploring them to see the situation from his point of view.

"Then I suggest we don't waste any more time. If you and Officer Delgardo can escort the recovery team to the ravine, NCO Nemi and I can go and deal with Deputy Gantz. We can then reassess the situation." Tolman's expression and stance mirrored Ull's. There was an awkward silence before Ull gave a deep sigh and nodded his agreement. Tolman called Delgardo over and explained what was happening. He watched Ull and Delgardo leave the block discreetly followed by Trooper Ruth Dulac. "I thought the miners back on Solar 2 were bloody-minded but this lot are verging on the obsessive when it comes to the profit margin. Come on Nemi, let's see if we can get any sense out of Kanah." Tolman strode off towards the accommodation corridor quickly followed by Nemi and the medic trooper.

***

Tolman knocked on the door and waited. There was no response so he tried again, a little louder. He pressed his ear against the door and tried for a third time but still no response. He called out her name and listened intently for any sound of movement from within. The last thing he wanted to do was attempt to enter before they had made contact with her. Although he found it hard to believe that she had suffered a breakdown the information from Delgardo on Gantz's behaviour did suggest otherwise. Fatigue could have finally overwhelmed her, she could be asleep which was the reason for this silence. He decided to try again and knocked even louder.

"Kanah it's Vitch, Vitch Tolman. Can you hear me?" He hammered on the door again. "Are you alright?" He licked his lips. Perhaps she needed reassurance. "It's alright Kanah. I've brought the recovery team. Nemi is here with some troopers. You're perfectly safe." He strained his ears and thought he could detect some indistinct sounds. "We want to come in and help you." His ears pricked up, there was definitely a sound then. He turned to Nemi and gestured him closer. "You try! She might respond better to your voice."

Nemi stepped forward, spread his hands against the door and rested his forehead on it. He wasn't sure how well she could sense him through the door, if at all. "Kanah, it's Ja. I'm here with Vitch and we need to talk to you." Nemi glanced at Tolman who still had his ear pressed against the door.

"I think I can hear her moving around." From the tone of his voice it was as if moving about equated with being perfectly fine. He waved on Nemi to try again.

Nemi hesitated. The words which Gantz had spoken on behalf of the Collective when he experienced the link came back to him. 'It is your psyche that we fear. The dark primeval recesses your species suppress are unknown to us. It would destroy us. We learnt that from our first contact with humans.

You humans only count your own kind when it comes to victims. Do you know how many of us were damaged before Kanah Gantz and the others were born? Do you know how many of us were damaged while she grew up?' Is that what had happened to Kanah? Had the isolation undermined her training? Had she delved too deep into the human minds here? Was she damaged and, if so, what would be the consequences of that damage? Would she be rejected by the other Gnostics and the Collective? Would that make her more human and, therefore, give their relationship a chance of working? For a brief moment that thought raised his spirits until the alternative hit him. He remembered that fraction of a second at the end of his link. Suddenly, and for only a fleeting moment, he had the most wonderful feeling of well-being. It was impossible to describe but if he had ever attempted it, then it would have been like all the best times of his life distilled into that one moment. Kanah's voice came back to him. 'If you suffered the worst of sharing your thoughts then it was only fair to let you sample the best. We saw in you what we saw in the New Brethren. We think you are a friend Ja Nemi.' If that was what her link with the other Gnostics was like, how could he wish to deny her something like that! He was fearful now but could not decide whether the fear was for Kahah Gantz or himself.

"Are you alright Nemi?" The sound of Tolman's voice dragged him back to the present.

"Not really," he whispered. He took a deep breath before continuing. "Kanah if you can hear me please let me know." The end of the sentence was lost as emotion got the better of him. He coughed as if clearing his throat would also clear the emotion. He glanced at Tolman again, more to delay speaking than anything else..

"Pretty sure I heard her voice. I think she said your name."

Nemi took another deep breath, he didn't want to falter over the next words. "I've come to collect that blown kiss."

"I think she's crying." An embarrassed Tolman whispered that remark.

'Shit!' thought Nemi. 'Last time I try anything as stupid as romance!' He took another deep breath. "Kanah I'm opening the door." He glanced round at the medic who hovered in the background and nodded. The trooper started working on the door mechanism. It was only a few moments before he nodded to Nemi that the task was completed. "I'm opening the door Kanah. I'll come in on my own. Vitch will stand in the doorway but won't enter unless you say so." Nemi stood back from the door and whispered instructions. "If she has lost it I'll distract her and you grab her. Mikelson, you then get in as quickly as you can and sedate her." He glanced at the trooper, knowing the idea of sedating a New Brethren prophet could well horrify him. "You okay with that?" The trooper swallowed the lump which had formed in his throat and nodded, although he looked far from enthusiastic about the idea. For his part Nemi suddenly realised that if Kanah could sense him through the door, he had just informed her of his plans. At that moment if Nemi had believed in her God he would have offered up a silent prayer. Instead he took a deep breath and then slowly expelled it. "Kanah the door is opening now." The door slid open and Nemi immediately stepped inside. Any hesitation would have displayed a lack of faith in her. He knew enough about Kanah to realise it was something she would have been acutely aware off.

When Nemi stepped inside and found a gun pointed in his face his faith took a severe dip. His earlier emotions returned when he looked beyond the muzzle of the weapon. Kanah Gantz was hardly recognisable. Her lank hair was matted and stuck to her sallow face. From the little he could see of her the most startling feature was those usually big bright eyes were now sunk into dark pits. If she hadn't been standing he would have thought she was dead. He said her name but it came out as a hoarse whisper. On hearing his voice she took a couple of steps back. Her arm trembled from the effort of holding the weapon out at arms length. Nemi could now see her dishevelled state of dress. Her uniform jacket was sweat stained and from the stains on her trousers it was apparent she had urinated in them. Nemi's heart sank. How did this happen to her? He wanted to wrap his arms around her and protect her and make her the Kanah Gantz of old but her weapon was still pointing directly at him. It wavered in her unsteady hand but with only just over a metre separating them even in this state she could hardly miss if she fired.

"Kanah, it's Ja, Ja Nemi." He was no longer sure she knew who he was. "I'm not going to hurt you. I've come to help you." He spoke slowly and deliberately despite the fact he could feel his heart hammering away inside his chest. "Please put the weapon down Kanah. We can talk this out." The last sentence was said more in hope than expectation. He was far from sure she was capable of talking at all!

"Nemi?" Her voice was frail but he drew hope from the fact she might have recognised him.

"Yes, it's Nemi." He smiled. She had always referred to him as Nemi and never used his first name. "Didn't think I'd leave you here did you?"

She brushed the hair from her face and Nemi got a good look at her eyes and he saw fear. The weapon was still trained on him. "Don't go into the mine?"

Nemi was confused by the question but then decided her mental state was probably mangling her words. "I won't go into the mine Kanah. Can you tell me why I mustn't go in?"

"I killed my father!" Her arm trembled even more and she used her spare hand to steady her aim.

280

Nemi was even more confused now. "No Kanah he committed suicide." As soon as the words left his lips he regretted them, they were hardly likely to comfort her. "You weren't responsible. They did it to try and protect their children."

"You want to kill me Nemi."

He started to panic now. Where did this idea come from. "No Kanah I could never hurt you." The idea of blurting out that he loved her briefly crossed his mind but making a declaration like that to a woman who was pointing a gun at him with Tolman and a trooper as an audience seemed ridiculous at that precise moment. He almost immediately regretted it as Kanah suddenly shifted her focus. Nemi didn't take the risk of taking his eyes off her as he knew she had spotted Tolman standing in the doorway.

"You went in the mine!" Her eyes flicked back to Nemi. "You went in the mine!" She stared accusingly at him. "You went in the mine!" She had raised her voice and anger underscored her words.

"No I..." The denial died on his lips as Nemi realised she knew Tolman had sent in the recovery team.

"They're infected. You've infected them!" She screamed the last words and the sound of the gunshot deafened them as it reverberated around the enclosed space of the bedroom.

Nemi never cried out. The force of the shot knocked him back against the wall. As he slid down onto the floor he left two bloody smears to mark his collapse to the floor.

***

Tolman was rooted to the spot. He could not believe what he had just seen. The urge to do something was countered by the feeling of being merely a spectator at an event he had no control over. His eyes were fixed on the weapon in Gantz's shaky hand.

Any second he knew it would point at him and he would never see Carla and Aaron again. A smile born out of hysteria formed on his lips; what a ridiculously stupid way to die! It disappeared just as quickly as he watched the weapon twist in her hand and slowly slip from her grasp and clatter to the floor. It was the sound of the gun hitting the floor which snapped him from his temporary paralysis. Nemi's earlier instructions hit him along with a surge of adrenalin and he spread his arms and launched himself at Gantz. His arms enveloped her and pinned her arms to her side. The force of his lunge, coupled with the instability of her stance caused them to topple over and hit the bunk bed. An intense pain shot up his arm as his elbow collided with the edge of the bunk. He cried out through gritted teeth but held on to her as if his life depended upon it. Ignoring the pain he hoisted her up onto the bunk.

The medic suddenly appeared by his side and he heard the hiss as Mikelson administered the sedative. Gantz grasped and then her whole body went into spasm before going limp in his arms. Tolman breathed a great sigh of relief, he was still alive!

"She's sedated sir."

Tolman turned his head towards the sound. "What?"

"She's sedated sir, you can let her go."

Tolman realised he still held Gantz in a vice like grip. "Yes" he stammered. "Yes." He reluctantly realised his grip and helped the medic place Gantz in a more comfortable position on the bunk. "See to Nemi" Tolman saw a fleeting hesitation in the medic's eyes. He was torn between loyalty to his religion and one its prophets and his commanding officer. "See to Nemi!" Tolman almost screamed the words and Mikelson scurried away to the body slumped in the opposite corner of the room.

Tolman pulled himself to his feet, rubbing his elbow in an effort to ease the throbbing pain in his arm. He then saw the doorway was crowded with miners craning their necks to get a better view. Delgardo stood in the front of them, mouth wide open as she stared at Mikelson cutting away Nemi's uniform to get at the wound.

"Clear the corridor Delgardo." Tolman took a step towards her but she continued to stare at the wounded Nemi. 'Do I have to repeat everything twice?' he wondered. "Clear the bloody corridor Delgardo." The order shouted at the top of his voice, finally had the desired effect. Delgardo turned towards him, mouth still gaping with eyes bulging from their sockets, and nodded her understanding. She turned on her heel, withdrawing her stun stick as she did so. The crowd by the door got the message and slowly retreated back down the corridor.

Tolman glanced back towards Nemi but quickly looked away. The medic, having sealed the wound to stop anymore blood loss, was now appearing to be desperately attempting to resuscitate Nemi. "Oh fuck!" whispered Tolman.

CHAPTER TWELVE

Tolman came face to face with Ull and Delgardo when he returned to the Rec. He didn't like the smug look of satisfaction on Ull's face but it was no more than he had expected. Tolman braced himself for the inevitable request to reopen the mine. To his credit Ull resisted the temptation to jump straight in.

"How's Officer Nemi?" The enquiry lacked any real concern, Ull's tone suggested a 'I told you so' attitude.

"Not as bad as it looked. At that range the bullet went straight through. Missed any organs, arteries or bone. The medic has cleaned the wound, sealed it and given him a painkiller shot. I thought he was attempting to resuscitate him. It brought Nemi round and he refused to be sedated. He'll be fine!"

"And Gantz?' there was more concern in Delgardo's question.

"She's been disarmed and sedated. We've got restraints on her so if she does come round she'll be in no fit state to cause any more trouble." Tolman hesitated before adding "She has been relieved of duty. I will assume control of the case." Ull glanced at Delgardo but said nothing. The thought did occur to him that was something Delgardo should have done right from the start but, having made his peace with her, he was loathe to recommence hostilities.

"What happens now boss?"

"Well we continue the recovery of Laslo Ginthem's body from the ravine. As you two are back I assume the team have started work?"

"They were unpacking the crates when we left them. The team leader said it would take two to three hours to unpack and assemble the vehicle. They haven't had a chance to test the reassembled vehicle so they also need to run through diagnostic checks and test lift-offs and manoeuvres before they risk a descent. The best guess they could make was they hope to recover the body by late afternoon. Of course, without knowing how deep the ravine is that's only a guess. Once they've set up the modified scanner and ascertained the depth they should be able to give you an accurate time."

Tolman nodded. "Good! I want to try and question Kanah again. Hopefully when she comes round from the sedatives she'll be calmer." Even as he said it Tolman thought it was a forlorn hope.

"Deputy Tolman." Ull hesitated, not really willing to ask his next question.

Tolman saved him the embarrassment. "You want to know if you can reopen the mine!"

"I think it would be best to get the crew back into a normal routine after all that's happened."

"You seem to have forgotten that one or more of your crew murdered Laslo Ginthem. Until we know who was responsible I find it hard to imagine getting back to a normal situation." Tolman took exception to the veiled suggestion that the crew were, somehow, now the innocent victims in this situation.

"The Corporation..."

"Fuck the Corporation! I'm more concerned with giving the victim's family closure and, hopefully, some justice. I'll review my position once I get more information from the recovery team."

"There's also the missing crystals to consider boss. After we checked the drill-head for any tampering we were going to search the rest of the mine to find them. If we send any of them back into the mine the rest will start to worry they are shifting the crystals to another hiding place. They're already suspicious of each other and the longer we leave them the more those suspicions will fester away. We have some volatile characters in here."

"Good point Delgardo!" Tolman eyed Ull. He could not understand this obsession with reopening the mine after everything that had happened. Surely the crew's first priority would be to find the missing crystals; after all it was those which would earn the crew a good bonus, not what they could extract before the body was recovered and arrests were made. "While we're waiting for the recovery team to report back we'll organise a search of the mine. Perhaps you'd like to accompany us or have the crew pick somebody?" Tolman directed the question at Ull. "Just in case they don't trust us to do a thorough job?" The implication was not lost on Ull but he refrained from comment and just nodded his agreement before rejoining the rest of the crew.

"I don't think he liked the last remark" observed Delgardo.

"Tough!"

"He's a decent man really. He's proud and doesn't like his integrity questioned."

"Bloody sensitive for a mine manager!" Tolman glanced at Delgardo. "Don't give me that look Delgardo, I've just seen my deranged work partner shoot her best friend and I've got some poor sod rotting away in some bottomless pit. I suggest you go into Gantz's room and find your service weapon. If Ull can't keep his crew in order you might need it."

"Yes boss." Delgardo turned and trudged off in the direction of the bedroom corridor.

"Any orders for me boss?" Wildman had sidled up to listen to the conversation between Ull and Delgardo. He stood giving his most disarming smile to Tolman. His dog, Keith had moved behind Tolman.

"And you are?"

"Officer Al Wildman Singh, police pilot boss."

Tolman looked him up and down. "Well for starters you can get back into uniform Singh."

"Everybody calls me Wildman boss." Wildman's smile got bigger.

"Everybody except me Singh and I'm getting mighty pissed off having to repeat myself around here. Get back into uniform!" The smile disappeared from Wildman's face. His usual charm appeared to have failed him for once. He averted his eyes and backed away. "One more thing Singh."

"Yes boss?"

"Get your dog to stop sniffing my arse." Wildman called Keith away and retreated to change into his uniform. Tolman was left to study the sullen group of miners listening to Ull explain what was happening. None of them looked pleased with the way the conversation was going. Tolman had grown up in a mining community on the asteroid belt around Solar 2 so he knew only too well what sort of people were attracted to the life but he couldn't understand this crew. Perhaps he had been away too long. Perhaps his life with Carla and the birth of his son had changed him more than he thought. No! He shook his head, there was definitely something very odd about this lot.

"Boss." Tolman turned round at the sound of Delgardo's voice. "Boss," she patted the holster strapped to her waist. "I retrieved my weapon. I thought you'd like to know NCO Nemi is back on his feet, well sort of! He's sitting on the edge of Gantz's bunk." She paused as a flicker of a smile crossed her lips. "He's holding her hand!"

288

Tolman stared at the corridor which led to the bedrooms. He never noticed that brief smile or the twinkle in Delgardo's eye. Even if he had noticed he would not have understood. He was bewildered at the news of Nemi's actions so how could he appreciate Delgardo's pleasure in rekindling her desire for a little romance in this sterile world?

**

Tolman stood in the doorway and watched Nemi. Sure enough Delgardo was right. He sat on the edge of the bunk and held her hand. A small dressing covered his wound and the only sign of his traumatic experience was his torn and blood-soaked uniform. The arrival of Tolman must have caught his eye because he turned and smiled at him.

"For Corp sake Nemi, she tried to kill you!"

"No!" Nemi attempted to wave the suggestion away but used the arm attached to his wounded shoulder and the pain which shot up his arm made him wince. "At that range even Kanah couldn't have missed. She tried to move at the last moment but was shaking too much. The crack at the back of the head when I hit the wall caused more damage. Good job I had those beers earlier or I could have really hurt myself!"

"Nemi, she was out of her head! You were just bloody lucky." Tolman wondered if Nemi was suffering from concussion. He stepped into the room and moved close enough to get a good look at Gantz. Other than her pale complexion and dark rimmed eyes she was now recognisable as the Kanah Gantz he knew. "You realise we have to keep her restrained?"

"Of course I do! The knock on the head made me lose a lot of blood but the brain is still intact Vitch. We need to get her back home to the Gnostics. Shame she couldn't tell us what happened."

"What happened? Nemi she had a breakdown! Does anything she's done remotely fit into her character? I don't want to believe it any more than you do but the poor girl has lost control of her mind. The only sensible thing you've said is that we need to get her back home out of this environment. Goodridge got it right, she came back too soon and you said yourself the isolation would have got to her."

Nemi shook his head. "Something happened Vitch. Kanah has the most disciplined mind I've ever come across." Nemi paused to correct himself. "With the exception of Lisbeth Smith but she's a freak even by Gnostic standards. From childhood Kanah's been trained to control her mind to protect her from us." Tolman remained tight-lipped. He had the urge to remind Nemi of the effect Elena Benson had upon the, so called, trained mind of a Gnostic called Simon. The consequences were nowhere as severe as with Gantz but it still required several weeks of therapy before he was back to normal. 'Whatever normal is for a Gnostic,' thought Tolman.

"You should get some rest before you make the trip back to the ship." Tolman gave Nemi a consoling pat on the back and turned to leave.

"I'm fine. I've sent Mikelson back to pick up a spare uniform for me. I'll rest until he gets back and then I'm ready to carry on."

"Don't be a bloody fool! Get back to the ship with Kanah. There's nothing to do here. While the recovery team are looking for Ginthem's body I'm going to search the mine with Delgardo for those missing crystals. Once we get the body back we'll hopefully find some forensic evidence to identify the killer and we can arrest them. If not we take the whole crew back. Should be out of here by tonight with any luck."

"I'll come with you on the search. If there's something in the mine which triggered Kanah's behaviour we could find out what."

Tolman thought of telling Nemi that there was nothing in the mine which could have triggered Gantz's behaviour and he was grasping at straws but he knew he would be wasting his time. "You're in no fit state to be wandering around a mine. Need I remind you that you said this was a police matter so I would be in charge?"

"I know I said that but I didn't know then you'd get awkward. I see it now as more a joint operation."

Tolman sighed. "You've been working with Morgan for far too long. I can see now why he irritates Goodridge so much. I suppose theree's no point appealing to your better nature and ask you to use some common sense?"

"None at all!"

Tolman gave another audible sigh. "I'll wait until you're dressed. But if your wound opens up again I'll get Mikelson to drag you back to the ship without the benefit of pain killers." Nemi smiled and Tolman gave a dismissive wave of his hand as he left the room. If the idiot wanted to do himself more damage in some vague attempt to justify Gantz's behaviour then Tolman refused to take any responsibility for it. He had warned Nemi and that was all he could do. Since Nemi met Gantz, while holding down a desk job under Morgan, he had almost been blown up and now shot twice, once by Gantz herself. In the two years he spent on active service with the Colonial Corps he had once bruised a finger dismantling a pulse rifle. Tolman decided that on the evidence so far if Nemi had a choice of returning to active duty or settling down with Gantz then the former looked like the safer option.

***

Tolman, Delgardo and Nemi set off for the mine accompanied by Ull. The start of the search had not been delayed due to the wait for Nemi's change of uniform as the crew had taken even longer to decide who would represent them on the search. Under normal circumstances Ull would have been the natural choice but his close links with Zon Willard had caused much debate. The site tech was still the crew's main suspect for misappropriating the missing crystals. The mere mention of this had diverted the meeting into another argument, Willard fiercely denying any involvement while some of the others, mainly Dang and Albright, continued to point the finger of suspicion at him. In the end it was Edmurson who broke the deadlock. He reasoned the people least likely to have managed to hide the crystals were the ones who spent the least time in the mine. When the crew grudgingly accepted the proposition it left them with a stark choice of Petre Ull or Boniface Chang. Edmurson quickly followed up his assertion by nominating Chang on the grounds that he had never been inside the mine, careful not to add the proviso 'as far as we know'. The ploy worked and Ull was quickly nominated and voted for before Dang had the chance to nominate himself.

Ull led the way to the mine entrance but stopped and turned to face them before they could enter. "Anybody else suffer from claustrophobia?" Tolman could not tell from Ull's tone of voice if this was a serious inquiry or just a sarcastic remark on his behalf. He, therefore, limited himself to a shake of the head. Nemi did likewise. "Right, I suggest we start with the backfill tunnel. If the drill scanners were tampered with it's where the crystals would have been diverted to." He paused to allow any objections. There were none so he gestured them to follow him.

Tolman glanced at Nemi just before they entered. Other than a pale complexion due to the loss of blood he appeared to be holding up. Mikelson had given Nemi a blood accelerator jab which would speed up cell reproduction and assured Tolman that within a few hours the colour would return to his cheeks. Tolman disliked the use of any form of medication, unless it was absolutely necessary. In his job he had seen far too much abuse of medication and also held the belief, strenuously denied by the Pharmaceutical Corporation, that all medication included an element which caused addiction. He knew for a fact the medication which was distributed to the masses was addictive, once on it citizens never came off it. The official term for it was 'assisted living', a way of making life tolerable for the jobless majority whose whole point of existence was to make it through to the next day. Tolman sighed. The dim, dank interior of the mine was obviously making him morose.

They passed the tunnel which led to the ravine and Trooper Dulac gave Nemi a nod of acknowledgement. She noticed his demeanour and had the urge to ask if he was alright but considered it an unprofessional thing to do in front of the others. Faint sounds of the recovery team assembling the rescue ship echoed from within the tunnel. Tolman hesitated but then decided to check on progress on the way back. He then increased his pace to catch up with the others. Soon the silence was noticeable. Delgardo looked uncomfortable but Tolman found it very relaxing. He had visited his father in the asteroid mines on numerous occasions as a boy but then it had all been noise and clutter. He had detested the mines back then but perhaps if he had experienced this kind of peace and tranquility he would not have been so eager to get away from them.

After passing several other off-shoot tunnels they at last turned off to the right as the main tunnel split into two. Tolman could see now there were two ore sledge pipes, one which they had followed through the mine and disappeared into the left hand split and one which curved round from that tunnel to the tunnel they were now in. They quickly reached the end of the sledge pipe and were faced with a mound of rubble which slowly rose up until it blocked the tunnel ahead. Delgardo set to work to test random rocks which had been spat out of the sledge pipe. Tolman and the other two men watched intently.

"I'm running the standard test for the presence of Zelman crystals." Delgardo talked them through the process. "If we find any trace of crystal the blue light will turn red." She tried the first sample of rock but with no positive result. The second and third sample were also negative. Clambering over the loose rubble she selected further samples from nearer the open end of the sledge pipe. Each tested negative.

"Perhaps the ore with the crystals have been buried under a top layer," suggested Ull. He helped her remove several lumps of rubble to uncover the ones below. This resulted in five more tests, all negative. Ull dug deeper and passed a succession of pieces of ore to Delgardo to test. All were negative.

"You sure that thing is working properly?" The question came from Tolman who also had a distrust of technology. From experience either shoddy production or poor maintenance meant almost everything was continually breaking down. His air conditioner at home being a fine example.

"There's nothing wrong with it." Delgardo tested another lump of ore and hurled it at the tunnel wall in frustration at getting yet another negative result. "I checked this morning and even calibrated it again to be on the safe side." Again and again she tested but the blue light stubbornly refused to turn red.

"So the crystals have been moved elsewhere!" Nemi was getting bored with this repetition.

"And whoever is responsible has picked up every last trace of crystal ore?" Tolman shook his head in response to his own question. "I find that hard to believe! I can't see who could work under that sort of pressure and be this thorough with the constant fear of being caught!"

"So this wasn't the method of stealing the crystals!" Nemi thought it was time somebody stated the obvious.

"Then how did they do it? There was crystal-bearing ore at the drill-head yesterday and the drill was working. Nobody came back into the mine after Gantz closed it down."

"Anybody check the storage bins?" asked Nemi.

"Not since we found they were empty" replied Delgardo.

"Then they must have pulled the plug on the scam after that. You should check the bins again." Nemi was eager to continue the search of the mine still clinging to the idea of exonerating Gantz by finding something, although he had no idea what that something could be.

"Still doesn't explain how they pulled off the scam." Ull sounded despondent.

"I suggest we worry about that after we've found the crystals." Nemi nodded his agreement to Tolman's statement although he could not have cared less about the fate of the missing crystals.

Reluctantly Ull led the way back to the main tunnel. Nemi pulled him back when they reached it and nodded towards the other offshoot. "Is that where Gantz..." He baulked at using the term 'had her breakdown'.

"She seemed unsteady on her feet just about here but it passed so we carried on to the drill-head. That was where she had the fit."

"Can we take a look?"

Ull shrugged his shoulders. He would have preferred to continue the search for the crystals but reasoned if he voiced any objection to wasting more time it would only result in them being even more determined to enter the tunnel. "After you gentlemen. It's only a short way to the drill-head and no side tunnels so you can't get lost." He had no wish to see the idle drill-head and be reminded of the lost production and consequently the lost bonus.

They had only journeyed a few metres into the tunnel when both Tolman and Nemi abruptly stopped. They glanced at each other.

"It's not just me then!" Nemi almost whispered the words.

"You feel it too?" asked Tolman.

"Oh yes, but I don't know what!" They stood still listening to their own breathing.

"Are you two alright?" There was a nervous edge to Ull's voice.

"You don't feel anything Ull?" It was Nemi who asked the question.

"No!" Ull actually lied for he was feeling far from comfortable but it had nothing to do with the tunnel, he had visions of Nemi and Tolman going the same way as Gantz. "Perhaps you two also suffer from claustrophobia." He didn't believe that for one moment but thought it might encourage them to withdraw from the mine.

"Tolman's father was a miner Ull."

"I can assure you I don't suffer from claustrophobia." Tolman wiped the back of his neck with his hand. He had started to sweat, which was another uncharacteristic thing for him to do.

"Gantz seemed to get worse the nearer the drill-head she got!" Delgardo was now reliving her last experience and getting as concerned as Ull.

"You don't feel anything Delgardo?"

"I suffer from mild claustrophobia so I've been uncomfortable from the moment we entered the mine."

"It hasn't got worse here?"

Delgardo thought about it. "Well now you come to mention it, yes but we're deeper and been in here longer."

"Did you feel the same yesterday?"

"I might have but I was paying more attention to Gantz." Delgardo was hesitant. She did feel worse now but it could just be imaginary, a reaction to Nemi's suggestion.

"I think it's time to back up." Nemi whispered the suggestion and took a step back to set an example.

"Shouldn't we continue to the drill-head?" Tolman felt this was the professional thing to do but his tone suggested he was willing to be talked out of the idea.

"Yes" said Nemi, "but I think that would be a very bad idea." He took another step back and this time Tolman followed suite.

"Could it be gas?" Tolman sniffed the air.

"Surely that would affect all of us!" Nemi glanced over his shoulder. "You two still feel alright?" Ull nodded but Delgardo reluctantly admitted she felt uncomfortable and that the walls were beginning to close in on her. "Let's go back to the tunnel entrance. Have you gas detectors set up down here Ull?"

"Of course! Standard safety procedures, but they can only detect known gasses. If we've discovered something new..." His voice trailed off. "Doesn't explain why I feel okay though." They were all now carefully backing away down the tunnel.

"Perhaps you only hit a gas pocket yesterday and it affected Gantz more for some reason or you've been exposed to small amounts for some time and have built up a tolerance." Tolman turned to Delgardo. "Can you scan the atmosphere in this tunnel and analyse its makeup?" Delgardo nodded and set to work adapting the scanner attached to her CommsLink. By now they were back at the tunnel entrance.

"How do you feel now?" Nemi directed the question at Tolman.

"Better, I've stopped sweating!" He showed Nemi the palms of his hands. "Can't get rid of the feeling or at least the memory of it. It sounds strange but the only way I can describe it is..." he hesitated using the word. "It's like a presence! Like when you feel somebody come into a room. You haven't seen them or heard them but you just know they're there!" He gave a nervous smile. "And I was critical of Kanah!"

"The air checks out okay. Nothing unusual or unidentified. At least it hasn't picked up anything unidentified but I guess it's possible there's something the scanner can't detect." Delgardo put away the scanner. Her last remark was a sign of desperation. They might be feeling better but she was rapidly developing a headache and she could feel damp patches of sweat under her arms and in the small of her back.

Nemi was standing apart from the others and stared back down the tunnel. "It's familiar!" The others turned towards him. "It's familiar and yet different."

"What?" Ull was now beginning to wonder if he was the only sane one in the group. Tolman and Nemi appeared to be having some sort of hallucination and Delgardo looked as if she was about to have a fit like Gantz.

"We get out of here now!" Nemi turned and ushered them back down the main tunnel towards the mine entrance. None of the others needed further encouragement.

***

Ull headed for the collection of tables which the crew had assembled around. He sat down in the space they had reserved for him and they all pulled in their chairs to get as close as possible to hear his update. Some couldn't wait that long.

"Did you find the crystals?" Albright asked the question before Ull's rear had actually made contact with the chair.

"Are they gonna let us reopen?" Dang raised his voice in the hope this would make Ull respond to his question first.

Ull glanced round the table and noticed Albright was showing all the signs of being agitated. Fearing the man would lose control again he decided to answer his question first. "We only got to search the waste tunnel and there was no trace of any crystals." He paused to let the bad news sink in. There was just a stunned silence accompanied by expressions of confusion and astonishment. "So the accusation against Zon that he diverted the crystals along with the waste were unfounded." He paused again but if he thought any of them were going to apologise to Zon Willard he thought wrong, although a few of them looked embarrassed by their earlier comments. "And in answer to your second question, no, I doubt very much if they're going to let us reopen." Ull's announcement was greeted with groans and swearing most of which was directed at joint targets of the police and Colonial troopers.

"Why didn't you search the rest of the tunnels?" Edmurson's low rumbling voice cut through the moans and complaints and suddenly quietened them.

"Yeah and why won't they let us reopen? It's not going to interfere with their recovery team!" Albright had shifted his interest away from the missing crystals.

"What happened Petre?" Edmurson had noticed the look on Ull's face which provoked his question.

"What are you holding back?" It was inevitable Dang would take the opportunity to undermine Ull.

"Come on Petre, we have a right to know what's going on!" The crew mumbled their support of LeBon's statement.

Ull would have preferred to have avoided recounting the incident in the tunnel but he saw no way of doing so now. "Something happened when they entered the drill tunnel." He was reluctant to expand any more and forlornly hoped he had said enough.

"Like what?" Dang narrowed his eyes in suspicion. "Not another one going off their head!' He smiled at his own joke but it dissolved on his lips as he saw Ull's reaction. "You've got to be joking! What happened?"

"Both Tolman and Nemi felt something when they entered the tunnel."

"Felt something! What the fuck's that supposed to mean?" asked Albright.

"Tolman described it as a presence!"

"A presence?" The smile slowly returned to Dang's lips. "A presence!" The smile grew broader as if repeating the word increased it comical effect. "Are they keeping the mine shut because they think it's haunted?" Dang started to chuckle. "Oh I want to be there when you report to Control that the mine's been closed because of a ghost!" He now threw back his head and roared with laughter. LeBon and Albright who had been smiling now joined in with the laughter. Willard giggled but tried to hide his mouth behind his hand, not wishing to let Ull see he was enjoying a joke at his expense. Even Rolm and Chang allowed themselves a smile. The only ones who did not seem amused were Ull and Edmurson.

"It could be the spirit of Ginthem!" The serious tone of Edmurson's remark stopped the laughter in it's tracks. They all turned towards him in stunned silence but Dang was the first to crack and burst out laughing again. The others joined in to varying degrees.

"Oh Sligo that's priceless!" Dang managed to get the words out between giggles. "And why would Laslo be haunting the rescue team and not one of us? If he was haunting anyone it would the person who tossed him into the ravine!"

"He could be trying to contact them to tell them who did it!" Edmurson was not the sort of man to be silenced by ridicule.

"For Corps sake Sligo, do you actually believe what you're saying?"

"All I'm saying is that some things can't be explained."

Dang retained his smile but could see some of the others lose theirs. Surely they weren't entertaining this ridiculous idea! It confirmed what he had always believed, he was far superior in intellect than any of the crew. "Sligo, tell me how a hyper-drive works."

"What?" Edmurson was confused by the strange request.

"Tell me how a hyper-drive works!"

Edmurson hesitated as he racked his brain for any information relating to hyper-drive engines. "I don't know!"

"Is that one of the things which you can't explain?" He paused to smirk at the others and give them time to appreciate his cleverness. "Does that mean the workings of a hyper-drive are supernatural?" He snorted his contempt.

"Are you telling me man is so clever we know everything there is to know?" Edmurson retained his composure.

"We know enough not to believe in ghosts and fairies. Next you'll be telling me you believe in God!" The look on Edmurson's face took Dang by surprise. "Well fuck me Sligo you're a closet brother!"

"I just don't think I know it all!" Edmurson retorted.

"It's them bastards!" Everyones head swivelled around at the sound of Mol Gurd's voice. He hobbled, with a pained expression on his face, from the couch where he had been sleeping off the sedative to the edge of the table. He shot an unpleasant look at Rolm who quickly got up and moved to let him have her seat. He eased himself down onto the chair. "Strange how an inspector arrives just after we find a crystal deposit and then disappears. In come those dyke bitches and tell us he's dead and one of us is responsible. We fall for all this and the next thing we know is more of them turn up in a ship capable of removing all of the storage bins."

"What are you suggesting?" Ull had preferred Gurd when he was unconscious.

"Who says Ginthem is dead? They do! Who said he was killed by one of us and tossed down the ravine? They do! Who says the crystals are missing? They do! Who keeps telling us we can't go back in the mine? They do!" Gurd paused to spit on the floor. "They come in here and flash their police badges and you all believe every word they say. The bonus split between nine of us would set us up for life. There's what, a dozen of them plus any still on the ship? How do we know this bloody recovery team is recovering Ginthem's body and not the crystals?"

There was another stunned silence around the table which was finally broken by Milton Dang. "Did Gantz shoot you in the back of the knee or the fucking head?"

"Watch your mouth Dang! You think you're a cut above us but you're as thick as shit!" Gurd waved a dismissive hand towards Dang.

"Coming from you Mol that's a fucking compliment! And how exactly did Ginthem get the crystals from the storage bin into the bottom of the ravine? Ull tested the bins not Gantz or Delgardo. Why would Gantz pretend to go off her head when she could have just closed down the mine? Sligo's ghost theory is more plausible than your ludicrous conspiracy theory. If you did a bit more thinking with your brains rather than your dick you'd be dangerous!"

"I've had enough of taking shit off of you!" Gurd pulled himself to his feet and then wobbled as he attempted to maintain his balance.

"Any time you want to try and stop me, feel free." Dang leaned across the table, emboldened by Gurd's incapacity.

"Shut the fuck up, both of you!" Edmurson snarled at them both and stood up stretching his massive frame to its full height. He glanced from one to the other until Gurd sat down and Dang sat back in his chair.

"This squabbling is getting us nowhere" declared Ull. "There's nothing we can do about this situation so I suggest we all calm down."

"There's no way I'm being cheated out of my share of the bonus by these religious fanatics!" Dang sounded defiant but his voice trailed off into silence.

"Don't be stupid!" Ull had no intention of letting that remark pass without comment. "Gantz might be a New Brethren prophet, whatever that is, but don't try and label the others like that just because you find it convenient." Dang looked away and adopted a pose which suggested he was sulking.

"Not so stupid!" All heads turned towards the other end of the table where Wildman had crept up unnoticed.

"You've got a nasty habit of sneaking up on other peoples' conversations!"

Wildman ignored Ull's comment. "The Colonial NCO, Nemi, is Gantz's boyfriend. Referred to by the New Brethren as 'Friend Nemi'. Our Tolman is the work partner of Gantz and is also referred to as 'Friend' by the New Brethren. The two troopers Nemi brought with him are also New Brethren. I don't know about the recovery team or any Colonials still on the ship but this is a New Brethren planet and, therefore, the chances are they could be New Brethren or more so called friends!"

"What about you and Delgardo?" Dang stopped sulking and eyed Wildman with suspicion.

"Delgardo's got this hero worship thing about Gantz which is why she ignored protocol when Gantz went off the rails."

"You forgot to mention yourself."

"Pilots are hard to come by and I've been sidelined by Gantz from the moment we arrived." He paused as he noticed he had the crew's full attention. "You've all jumped to the same conclusion, that greed has prompted one of you to steal the crystals but what if this has more to do with New Brethren ambitions?"

"What do you mean?" Even Ull was now being drawn in.

"Mining licenses are coming up for renewal, New Brethren want to move into manufacturing rather than license their patents and maybe mining as well, especially if this planet has a reserve of Zelman crystals."

"Are you suggesting this is all a New Brethren plot to close down the mine and stop the Corporation extracting the crystals until the license runs out?" Ull sounded incredulous at the suggestion.

"You said yourself the Corporation kept quiet about the crystals and haven't been falling over themselves to cooperate with the investigation. Don't tell me the Corporation haven't had the same thoughts."

Now Ull did not find the conspiracy theory quite as incredulous. "But if Githem hadn't been killed the police would never have been called in!"

"I refer back to our eloquent Mister Gurd's remark, who says Ginthem is dead? Who's to say that Ginthem isn't 'Friend' Ginthem?" Wildman could see some of the crew were giving this serious consideration. And he could not resist adding a further embellishment. "Or that one of you is a 'Friend' and informed the New Brethren and then disposed with Ginthem." A few glances were made in the direction of Edmurson.

"And who exactly are you?" asked Dang.

Wildman gave the briefest of smiles. "I'm just me! I'm a free spirit and I go where the wind takes me."

"You're an opportunist!" Wildman just smiled at Dang's suggestion.

***

As they settled down into their chairs Delgardo kept a discreet eye on the crew's reaction to Ull's update.

"They don't look too happy!"

"Well that's tough! There's no way anybody is going back anywhere near the drill tunnel until we find out what's down there."

Delgardo turned towards Tolman. "You think someone or something is down there?" From the tone of her voice suggested that Delgardo did not regard that as a serious question.

"If it was just me who felt it I would have put it down to something I ate but Nemi felt it as well!" Nemi absentmindedly nodded his head in agreement but his mind appeared to be elsewhere.

"But the tunnel was empty and there's nowhere to hide down there." Delgardo at that moment favoured the indigestion theory and only just resisted the temptation to ask if Tolman and Nemi had both eaten the same thing for breakfast.

"I wasn't suggesting we have somebody in a light-reflecting camouflage suit down there. I was thinking more of some kind of microorganism."

"Oh!" Delgardo felt a little foolish now. "Something in the air not the actual air itself?"

"If the air is fine, other than being a bit on the stale side, it's a possible option. It wouldn't be the first time we've found a harmful microorganism on a planet. There was one on Solar 2 whose spoors when inhaled caused violent stomach cramps and vomiting. We need to do a full bio-scan of the tunnel and..." He was cut short by a roar of laughter coming from the crew. "Well at least they've cheered up!"

"I think I heard the word ghost used." Nemi sounded very apologetic for mentioning it.

"Oh!" Tolman looked a little embarrassed. "I guess that's down to me for using the term presence. Bloody idiots! They have no idea what they're dealing with."

"Neither have we!" Nemi sounded rather deflated.

"Once we get the results from the bio-scan we should be able to come up with a way of countering its effect."

"Perhaps." Nemi did not sound convinced.

"It's got to be worth a try!" Tolman's enthusiasm was slowly being eroded by Nemi negativity.

"Of course it is Vitch, ignore me. It's just why would a microorganism affect you and I and reduce Kanah to a quivering wreck but leave all of that lot," Nemi nodded towards where the crew sat, "unaffected?"

"Delgardo was affected!" Tolman glanced towards Delgardo for support and she nodded in agreement.

"And what were your symptoms?" Nemi asked.

Delgardo thought about it for awhile. "I guess I got anxious! I felt the walls closing in on me, my head ached, I felt sick and sweaty."

Nemi turned to Tolman. "A match on your symptoms?" Tolman reluctantly shook his head. "Me neither but your description of a presence was how I felt."

"There might be something in our genetic makeup which reacted with the organism."

Nemi reluctantly conceded Tolman's point. "Or, as you suggested, the crew have been exposed to it over time and have built up an immunity to it. You have also pointed out this lot are a bit strange even for miners. Perhaps they have all been affected by it and it could explain why Albright's problems came back towards the tail end of the last tour. They don't exhibit the same symptoms as us but, again, perhaps they did at first and the continuing exposure has now just turned them in a bunch of bickering obsessives."

"You might have something there! It could explain their illogical obsession with continuing the drilling. Of course it would he helpful if we knew what Kanah was feeling."

"Agreed, but she's sedated and I'm reluctant to get Mikelson to give her a shot to bring her round considering what she was like. If we have to bring her round I'd prefer it to be done in the presence of another Gnostic."

Tolman rubbed his chin thoughtfully. "Then we'll have to rely on Delgardo."

"But I didn't have the same experience as Gantz!"

"No, but you were there at the time so you need to try and remember everything which happened and exactly what Gantz said, even if it made no sense to you." Tolman used his most professional voice. He was calm, reassuring but firm. Delgardo nodded her understanding. "Take it slowly, just think back to when you reached the tunnel opening."

Delgardo took a deep breath and tried to imagine herself back in the mine with Gantz and Ull. It was something she had avoided as she found the memory unpleasant, reliving her own claustrophobia. She closed her eyes as if that would help make the images more vivid. Her voice faltered as she attempted to remember the details. "We paused as we reached the mouth of the tunnel. She appeared unsteady on her feet. She had one arm on the tunnel wall to prop herself up. I asked her if she was alright and she said yes but she didn't look it. Ull said the same but she said she would be fine, said perhaps she was also a bit claustrophobic. We carried on to the drill head and she seemed to have recovered. I checked the calibration on the drill scanner and it was okay. We thought, or rather the crew thought, that Zon Willard had tampered with it to redirect the crystals along with the waste. Of course he could have corrected it but then of course we didn't find any trace of crystals in the waste tunnel." Tolman nodded to hurry her on to the things they didn't know. "Sorry! I then checked the night-site visor but all that proved was that Edmurson, Dang, Gurd and Willard had all touched it."

"Kanah was still alright at this point?"

"Delgardo nodded. "She appeared to be. She then asked me to analyse the rock strata to confirm it contained Zelman crystals. Oh, hold on! I asked her if she was alright as I was changing the scanner probe. She complained of a headache, I think she called it the mother of all headaches. I think she was attempting to hide the fact she didn't feel too good."

"But still in control of herself! No indication of what was about to happen?"

"No she looked how I felt so I didn't think anything of it!"

"No suggestion she was feeling nauseous? No comment on the walls closing in on her?"

"No just the headache."

"What happened next?"

"I did the test and confirmed a positive result." Delgardo hesitated. "I remember now! I thought it odd at the time but later events overtook it. She asked how I knew it was positive. All scanners have a standard response so I presumed she had missed it so I scanned again. Blue light to red. She went very quiet and I could see she appeared to be in pain. Then suddenly she staggered backwards and then sunk to her knees. I went to support her and asked what was wrong but she waved me away." Delgardo gave an involuntary shiver. "She then screamed 'No!' and bent double with her head almost touching the floor. I put my arm around her to comfort her. She was shaking and it just got worse. That's why we thought she was having some kind of fit. She was mumbling to herself as the shaking got worse and I held onto her for fear that she would do herself harm. Then, as suddenly as it started it stopped and she was gasping for breath. I asked her again if she was alright and she nodded and then shook her head so I don't know if it was in response to my question or something to do with what was going on in her head!" Delgardo paused to take another deep breath to help her get through the rest of her story. "She then pushed me away and staggered to her feet. This is when she said we had to get out of there. I tried to help her but she kept me at arms length. I was worried about her but when I tried to talk to her she drew her gun and threatened us. She took my weapon and marched us back here to uncouple the pipe. The rest you know."

"So this was a complete character change and was triggered by the test for the crystals?"

Delgardo gave the question some thought. "Well, yes and no! The fit happened at the same time as I did the test but whether that was the trigger or just a coincidence I can't say. At that moment I didn't recognise her and it scared the shit out of me when she pointed her gun at me but she seemed reluctant to disarm me and almost apologetic. It was weird!"

"You mentioned her mumbling at one point." It was the first time Nemi had spoken. "Did you hear anything of what she was saying?"

"Nothing that made any sense!"

"If you try and recall it anyway. Don't try and guess at what she meant, just repeat exactly what you thought you heard."

"Sure!" Delgardo tried to think of some way of presenting the ramblings in a coherent way but eventually gave up. She wasn't responsible for making sense of what Gantz said. "She said something about you trying to kill her." Delgardo paused to glance at Nemi but he remained deadpan. "You were trying so she had to stop you. Then, and this was almost incoherent, she either said that she had killed her father or she hadn't. She was repeating words over and over again and contradicting herself so it was very confusing." Tolman gave Nemi a questioning look but the younger man made no comment except to ask Delgardo to continue. "Most I couldn't understand but another word she kept repeating was mother, or at least it sounded like that!"

"That's it?" Tolman had hoped for more.

Delgardo shrugged her shoulders. "I'm sorry but that's all I can remember." Tolman nodded his understanding and thanked her.

"Are you sure she said mother?" They had fallen silent so Nemi's question took them by surprise.

"That's what it sounded like, but to be perfectly honest I couldn't say for sure!"

Nemi nodded but said no more. He appeared to be deep in thought for a few moments and then nodded again. "Remind me, who did the wood carvings?"

The irrelevant question took them both by surprise and Delgardo hesitated, almost unsure she had heard right. "The carvings on the wall over there?"

"Yes, which one of the crew did them?"

"Er, Edmurson."

"And that's the big one is it?" Nemi glanced round at the crew.

"The huge one."

"Oh!" Nemi took another look at him. "Approachable is he?" His tone of voice suggested that he hoped the reply was positive.

"He appears to be the best of the bunch."

Nemi nodded and got up from his chair. "I think I'll have a word." The mumbled remark was not directed at anyone in particular. He strolled off and took a meandering, slow walk around the tables until he finally approached the crew table.

Tolman watched him and sighed. It was obvious from Delgardo's account that poor Kanah was ill. Rather than admit it and come to terms with the harsh truth Nemi appeared to be blocking it out by diverting his attention towards trivia.

"The carvings?" Delgardo looked to Tolman for some explanation.

"The carvings, an inspection of the troopers, a check on the ship's testing schedule, anything really rather than think about Gantz. Despite what they might say the pair of them are very fond of each other. It must be hard for him, seeing her like this!"

Delgardo glanced across at where Nemi stood, pretending to study the carvings while he waited for the opportunity to talk to Edmurson. "I thought they were lovers! All the stories about them at Midwich gave that impression." She paused suddenly remembering that Tolman had also been there. She turned to face him. "You were there too! Was it like the stories?"

"Oh it's never like the stories Delgardo!" She looked disappointed. "It wasn't romantic in the sense you mean. I had very little to do with it I'm glad to say but I wouldn't do what they did to save each other unless I was protecting my partner or son." Tolman paused to reflect on his own statement. "Or does that qualify for your definition of romantic?"

"I've never felt like that for anyone! Perhaps I've never really been in love." There was a hint of sadness in her last remark.

"Or perhaps you're too sensible." Tolman saw that his last comment had not raised Delgardo's spirits. "Or perhaps you haven't been put in that situation." He hoped the additional comment had fared better but the look on Delgardo's face disabused him of that. Tolman looked away and decided dealing with women, as his partner Carla was always pointing out, was not one of his strengths.

Nemi waited until the crew meeting broke up before approaching Edmurson. He did so with some trepidation. The man was huge compared to the other miners and he dwarfed Nemi. It was intimidating standing in his shadow and having him look down at you with distrust in those eyes of his.

"I've been told you're responsible for the carvings!"

Edmurson gave Nemi a wary look. "What if I am?" His tone was defensive, as if Nemi had accused him of defecating on the floor.

"I was just admiring them and wondered if you could tell me more about them?"

Edmurson now looked confused but he edged forward, closer to where Nemi was standing. "What do you want to know?" His tone was still unfriendly but had lost it's threatening edge.

"Well the caricatures are obviously your fellow crew members."

"Cari-whats?"

"The portraits! They're very good at portraying the crew's characteristics."

"They all say they look like them." Edmurson's unfriendliness had now turned to pride in the results of his hobby. His confusion and mistrust of this apparently random conversation amid all of what was going on receded in the face of Nemi's interest.

"You've captured them remarkably well!" That comment from Nemi even produced half a smile from Edmurson. "It's the landscapes which interest me most. I can see that one is of the Gap, it's where we landed this morning, and that one I think is the desert south of New Eden, I recognise the mountain range in the background. I was stationed there when I first arrived on the planet." Nemi paused and glanced up at Edmurson who nodded.

"It's the view from the drilling platform on our last job. Most people say the Jinn mountains are a shit hole but there was something in the way the light hit them in the morning." Nemi looked up at Edmurson and noticed the twinkle in his eyes. The man had the appearance of a small out building but had the soul of an artist. Nemi was tempted to tell him he was wasting his talents being a miner but was loathe to be diverted from his questioning.

"It's the others which are tormenting me." He paused and pointed at a waterfall scene. "That reminds me of a place up river. A waterfall at the end of a lake on a tributary to the Jordan."

"No I made that one up." Edmurson tapped the side of his head. "Came from in here!"

"What about this one, the village scene?"

Edmurson shook his head. "Only ever been in a drilling camp or the city. I made that one up too!"

"You have a remarkable imagination my friend, the detail is amazing. I can imagine myself standing in that village."

"Thank you." Edmurson now had a broad grin on his face.

"When did you do these?" Nemi tried to make the question sound as casual as he could.

"While I was here. Not much to do when you're off duty stuck out here."

"So these are the last ones you carved!" Nemi pointed to the waterfall and village scenes.

"In the last couple of weeks."

"Thank you Edmurson. You have a rare talent, I should show these to an art dealer in New Eden. People would like these, especially New Brethren, they like wood carvings. Have you seen some of their buildings?"

313

Edmurson nodded. "You think they're that good?"

"I do!" Nemi risked a friendly pat on the back. "Thank you Edmurson, you've been very helpful." Nemi casually moved away, although it was hard to control his excitement. He needed to make a call and he knew it would be a difficult one to make.

CHAPTER THIRTEEN

Nemi sat on his own in one corner of the Rec. He needed to think things through before he took any action so he considered his options carefully. If he was right about what was going on here he was in dangerous territory. The problem he had was at the moment all he had was a wild theory but no solid evidence. Before he made the call he had to have something more convincing. He decided to play back all the information Gantz and Delgardo had gathered concerning Laslo Ginthem. Everything was normal when he first arrived but by the next morning he was acting strangely. Nemi replayed the comment from Ull about another mine inspector. 'He suddenly realised what would happen when he submitted his report. Production levels were not going to improve so his recommendation was to close the site. The crew would be split up and reassigned. The family would be broken up and dispersed and he would be partly responsible. He felt like shit and couldn't look them in the face. Wasn't his fault but he still felt bad about it.' So what happened on that first night? Something which made Ginthem think he was going to close down the mine? Why do that to a mine which had just found a Zelman crystal deposit? He had last been seen at the storage bins before walking past the accommodation block to the mine entrance. It seemed logical to Nemi that Ginthem would check the storage bins as part of his duties. Did he discover what Gantz and Delgardo had?

'That's it!' thought Nemi. 'The crystals aren't missing, they don't exist! But how did Ginthem come to that conclusion?' To Nemi it seemed obvious now, as it supported his theory, but Ginthem did not have his background knowledge. There was something he was missing. Ginthem did a standard record check on the first night and then talked to some of the crew. They all believed they had found a crystal deposit so it would not have been anything any of them had said, he had to have found something in the standard check. Nemi decided he would follow in Ginthem's footsteps but first there were other arrangements to be made. He got up and made his way to Kanah's room. She was still sedated but there seemed to be a frown on her brow. He wondered if her mind was still fighting those inner demons. Sitting on the edge of her bunk he gently brushed out of the way some strands of hair which had stuck to her face. She felt cold and clammy. Bending down he kissed her forehead and felt a knot of pain in his chest. He wondered if this would be the last time he would see her. They had never kissed except in the New Brethren greeting, holding both hands and kissing on each cheek. Not a proper kiss. They had hugged as friends, the same way he would hug Tolman or Morgan, if Morgan had been the hugging kind. Not a proper hug. He was racked with regret at the lost opportunity and fought back the tears. Morgan would rib him mercilessly if he could see him now. He wiped his eyes and got up. Reluctantly he left her, returned to the Rec and approached Trooper Mikelson who stood guard at the main door.

"Dan." Nemi avoided using the nickname 'Mike the Medic'. "I want you to evacuate Kanah Gantz. Get her back to the ship and keep her sedated."

"Yes sir. Do you want me to report back here?"

"No I want you to stay with Gantz, monitor her vital signs and under no circumstances let her come round." The trooper looked confused. "I know what you're thinking but believe me it's in her best interest to remain sedated until we can get her back. There's enough police officers here to keep an eye on the crew and Trooper Dulac is guarding the mine. Protecting Kanah Gantz is paramount!"

There was no real need to add the last remark. A New Brethren knew how important a prophet was. "Shall I evacuate the civilian as well?"

Nemi glanced over at Mol Gurd. The man sat with his leg up on one of the sofas, a miserable expression etched on his face. "No leave him where he is. He can't cause much trouble hopping about in here but the man's dumb enough to use the trip back to the ship as an opportunity to seek revenge on Gantz." Mikelson gave Gurd an unfriendly stare before heading off to get the ground vehicle which had been parked by the mine entrance.

Nemi's next task was to speak with Petre Ull. The man had now left the crew table and was sitting chatting with Tolman and Delgardo. He approached the table and noticed the concerned look on Vitch Tolman's face. Nemi gave him a reassuring smile. "I'm getting Mikelson to get Kanah back to the ship. I want him to stay with her and keep her sedated until we can get her back." Tolman nodded his understanding. "Can your people keep order here?"

"Now Delgardo is armed, that plus Singh and his dog should be enough. I doubt if any of them will cause any more trouble." Tolman glanced at Ull for confirmation.

"I think they've come to terms with the situation now. They're not happy about it but I think they've accepted the inevitable."

"Good! Well next I wonder if I could borrow you Ull?"

"What for?" Ull was surprised.

318

"I'd like to repeat the checks Ginthem made on his first night here. I assume you would know what the standard routine is?"

"Well yes but why would you want to do that? Gantz and Delgardo here checked the records."

Nemi turned to Delgardo. "Did you follow an inspection routine?"

"Well we made the obvious checks." Delgardo sounded defensive.

"I'm not suggesting you missed something." Nemi hesitated because that was exactly what he was suggesting. "I just think Ginthem may have found something which wasn't obvious. I don't know what it is which is why I want to repeat it step by step."

"You think you're on to something?" Tolman was now interested in this conversation.

"I've got a theory but need to find something to support it." Nemi saw the look on Tolman's face. "I'm not willing to look a complete idiot just yet so bear with me until I check this out." Tolman nodded his agreement. In general he trusted Nemi. The only proviso to that was where Kanah Gantz was concerned. If this was a desperate attempt to justify her behaviour he would let Nemi run with it for the time being. But not to the extent of sidelining the recovery of Ginthem's body and finding the missing crystals.

"Okay!" Ull pulled himself up from his chair. "I'll take you through the usual routine, not that I think it'll be much use."

"Thank you Petre, I hope I'm not wasting your time." Ull shrugged his shoulders. He had been wasting his time all day so far, exactly what he was wasting it on really didn't matter to him anymore.

"You want to come along?" Ull directed his question at Tolman who did not hear as his hand was cupping his ear as a message came through.

"They're almost ready to make the descent! I better get over there for this. Update me later if you find this mysterious thing you're looking for." Tolman got up and then glanced back to Delgardo. "You're in charge until I get back."

Delgardo watched the three of them leave the accommodation block. She thought that at least Tolman would return with some useful news. Although she was fascinated by her romantic back story of Nemi and Gantz she still regarded him as a little disappointing in the romantic lead part and he was now behaving like an idiot wasting time. Still, perhaps Tolman was right, the young man was desperate to find some distraction from Gantz's situation.

They separated as they left the block, Tolman heading for the mine and Nemi and Ull to the site office. Once there Nemi seated himself at the desk and waved on the computer. Ull had worked for the Mining Corporation for long enough to know inspection routines off by heart. Even so he called up the check lists on his CommsLink and displayed them. One by one Nemi slowly worked his way through each item. The trouble was Nemi had no idea if what he was observing was out of the ordinary. Everything appeared to be in order but if it hadn't then either Gantz or Delgardo would have noticed it. After an hour Nemi was bored and confused by the numerous charts and graphs which meant very little to him. His enthusiasm for the task was beginning to flag. Perhaps whatever he was looking for could only be spotted by a trained eye or, an even more depressing thought, his theory was based on a desperate need to convince himself Kanah Gantz had not lost her mind.

"Well that's it!" Ull sat back in his chair and folded his arms across his chest. His stance seemed to demonstrate to Nemi the task had turned out as Ull had expected.

"We've done every check which Ginthem could possibly have made?"

"All the compulsory ones."

"There are optional ones?"

"Nobody ever wastes their time with those."

"Can you confirm with absolute certainty that Githem didn't waste his time?"

Ull sighed. "Of course I can't! Ginthem was in here on his own."

"Then what sort of optional checks could he have made?"

Ull sighed again, this time loud enough so that Nemi would realise how pointless this was now becoming. "The sort of thing like checking the samples or..."

Nemi cut him sort. "But we've checked the samples!"

"We've checked the samples taken from the mine, that's standard procedure. The samples I'm talking about are the crew samples. It's an outdated thing which is why nobody bothers any more."

"I don't understand!"

"All crews used to have a reference sample case to test any finds against. Scanner technology has moved on since then but most crews held on to them for," Ull hesitated, not sure why crews had retained the sample cases. "I suppose it's a tradition thing. Like people collect old things from the past. Like why the emblem of the Mining Corporation incorporates an image of something called a pick which was a tool used by the first miners."

Nemi was struck by an idea or perhaps, like a drowning man, he grasped at a straw. "Can we check these samples?"

"If you insist." Ull didn't bother to wait for an answer and opened up the office safe. He extracted an object which looked like an old fashioned book. When it was opened it revealed a large number of soft plasi-glass wallets. Each one contained tiny trace elements of ore samples.

"You have Zelman crystals in here?"

"Trace elements. You'll find it towards the back, they're all in alphabetical order. You can't miss it because it's the smallest sample in the whole collection. Still worth more than all the others put together."

Nemi flicked through the folder until he found the right sample. "Can we test this?"

"Test it!" Ull almost laughed. "What for?"

"Humour me."

Ull breathed his biggest sigh of exasperation yet. He pulled out a fibre scanner and connected it to his CommsLink. "You know how this works?"

"Blue light turns red if it's positive."

Ull switched on and ran the scanner across the tiny trace of Zelman crystal. His mouth dropped open as the blue light stubbornly refused to turn red.

***

Dang and Albright had been plotting since Ull had left them. They waited for their opportunity to put their plans into operation and it looked like they would not have to wait long. First the trooper at the door left and then Tolman, Nemi and Ull followed him out. Dang and Albright glanced at each other and exchanged conspiratorial smiles. This only left Delgardo and Wildman on guard. Dang had already approached Wildman and confirmed that he would look the other way should they leave the Rec. The minutes had ticked by and Albright was beginning to lose patience and had suggested they jump Delgardo. Dang told him that was a stupid idea as Willdman could hardly turn a blind eye to that without incriminating himself. Albright's impatience was irritating but Dang could handle it and it did not prove to be a problem as the trooper returned and spoke to Delgardo. They both went to the bedroom corridor. After a few minutes they returned carrying Gantz on a stretcher. They left the Rec and Dang could see them through the window placing the stretcher on the vehicle which the trooper had obviously brought up from the mine entrance. Unfortunately Delgardo returned and took up her normal position by the door. Time dragged slowly by and Delgardo steadfastly refused to have a comfort break despite encouragement from Wildman who took one himself. Albright started to get agitated again and after another five minutes Dang was beginning to seriously consider the suggestion of jumping Delgardo and worrying about the consequences later. Then suddenly he spotted Delgardo get up and speak to Wildman, She then left the Rec heading towards the bedrooms. Wildman glanced across to them, gave a small nod of the head and turned his back on them.

The two miners wasted no time and headed towards the kitchen. They gathered up some Koolbots and an empty food container and clambered out of the window. Placing the bottles and container on the ground they bent double and ran past the door and windows of the accommodation block, keeping low enough to ensure nobody spotted them. Once hidden from view they raced over to the storage bins and recoupled the ore sledge pipe. They worked as quickly as they could while still keeping an eye on the accommodation block and the site office. Then they made the return journey, being careful to duck down as they passed the accommodation block windows. When they reached the end of the building they picked up the bottles and empty container and walked briskly down the path towards the mine. At the entrance they paused to take a look around and compose themselves. In the distance they could see the vehicle carrying Gantz back towards the ship. They both smiled, rather pleased with themselves for how well their plan had gone.

Trooper Dulac watched them come down the tunnel. The two men were chatting and strolling at a leisurely pace. Her hands instinctively raised the pulse rifle a little and turned towards the approaching figures.

"It's alright trooper your Officer sent us down here with some drinks and food for you." Dang gave her a broad smile. "He looks after you better than the deputy looks after his recovery team." He nodded towards Albright, ladened down with an armful of Koolbots. "Also got us to bring something for them." Albright attempted to give a friendly nod to the trooper.

"He never said you were coming." Dulac, wary due to Nemi's earlier instructions, kept the pulse rifle pointing at them.

"All got a bit busy up there. Your Officer has gone off with our boss to the site office, the other trooper has taken Deputy Gantz back to the ship and Deputy Tolman has come down here but you know that, you must have seen him!" Dang made the pretext of struggling with the Koolbot and food container. "Mind you I would have thought he would let you know we were coming. Perhaps he did but sometimes the signal gets disrupted down here." He gave her another friendly grin. "Dirk could drop the drinks off here if you would prefer to take them down to the recovery team yourself?" Albright bent down and started to stand the Koolbots in a line his side of the security laser. "Shall I put these down there as well?"

Dulac looked at the Koolbots and then back to the two miners. If she let them leave the drinks there she would have to leave her post to deliver them. "Alright you can take them down." Albright started to collect the drinks up again and Dulac tucked the pulse rifle under one arm and reached into her pocket for the laser control pad. As she turned to switch the laser off

Dang kept forward and gave her a vicious blow around the head with the Koolbot he was holding. Dulac staggered, dropped the control pad and attempted to swing the pulse rifle back into position. Dang was quicker and swung his makeshift weapon again and caught her on the other side of the head. This time he had the time to aim his blow and put more force behind it and Dulac toppled to the ground with a thud.

Albright dropped the drink containers and quickly helped Dang secure the trooper's hands and legs with wire. Dang gagged her and then they both dragged her off down the tunnel. At the first available side tunnel they dumped her and continued towards the drill-head. By the the time they reached the drill Albright was having second thoughts about their venture. As Dang prepared to power up the drill Albright laid a hand on his arm. "Is this such a good idea Milton?"

Dang could tell from the tone of his voice that Albright's anxiety was building up. "It's alright Dirk, nobody will get in any trouble for this. It's going to be alright! We have the legal right." Albright opened his mouth to object but said nothing. Milton was right, it would all be fine. He smiled and removed his hand. How foolish of him to think otherwise and get all worked up about it. Everything would be just fine!

***

Ull strode back into the accommodation block. The look on his face reflected the dark mood he was in. Wildman went to speak to him but Ull ignored him, brushing him to one side in his determination to reach the crew table. All the crew turned to watch him approach but not one of them expected what his next action would be. He went straight over to Zon Willard, grabbed him by the shirt front and hauled him to his feet. Willard's eyes widened in amazement but he never saw the punch coming which knocked him over the back of the chair he had been sitting in. The crew scattered from the table but then formed a ring around the two men as if they were school boys witnessing a playground brawl.

Willard staggered to his feet holding his face. Blood oozed through his fingers and trickled down the back of his hand. Ull took a step forward and Willard scurried around the other side of the table out of reach. "You back-stabbing bastard! Why did you do it?" Ull took another step forward and Willard backed off to keep himself out of reach.

"Do what?" Willard sprayed out blood and saliva as he attempted to speak. "I didn't do anything!" The denial came out accompanied by a strangled sob. He was now shaking from the shock of the assault.

"You lying little shit!" Ull bellowed the words and smashed his fist down onto the table. "How could you do this to me?" Ull's frame trembled with emotion. "After the way I've looked after you, after the things you said." Ull was now sobbing. If Dang had been there he would not have been able to resist a comment about a 'lovers tiff', but luckily Dang was not there. Even luckier still, for him, this incident proved a distraction to his absence.

Edmurson took a few steps towards Ull. "Petre, what's this all about?" His voice was calm and soothing, as always the conciliator. "This is Zon your friend, what could he have done to deserve this treatment my friend."

Ull raised his head and shot an accusing look at Willard, who turned away, unable to look Ull in the eye. "It was Dang, he made me do it. He said you'd never agree to open up another tunnel on a hunch unless it was your hunch. Dang said he had as much experience as you but you were jealous of him and would never listen to him. It always had to be about you and your standing with the crew. You wouldn't acknowledge Milton because it would diminish your own self-importance just the same way as you would never acknowledge our relationship." Willard's statement was interspersed with sobs. "They all knew about us but you could never admit it in front of them, never show any sign of affection for me outside of your bed. If he was right about that then perhaps his hunch about the crystals was right too!" He stumbled into a nearby seat as if he no longer had the strength to stand, let alone ran away from Ull.

"Made you do what?" Edmurson directed his question at Willard but, seeing that the tech had no intention of replying, he turned again to Ull. "What did he do Petre?"

"He stole the achieve sample of Zelman crystal, replaced it with what looks like toenail clippings and gave the original to Dang to pretend to find in the tunnel."

"But why?" Edmurson's question represented the confusion he shared with the rest of the crew.

Ull shrugged his shoulders. "If you believe him," the last word was loaded with venom, "so that we could all follow Milton fucking Dang's hunch!"

"Well he was proved right wasn't he? Might have taken longer than expected but we found the main deposit. Milton might have been like you, pretending to be something he wasn't, but he was right about his hunch." Willard was more defiant now the initial shock of the attack had worn off and Ull's temper had subsided.

"You stupid idiot, there are no crystals! The storage bins are empty and there's not even a trace sample in the backfill tunnel."

"There's no crystals?" Edmurson and LeBon asked the same unbelievable question at the same time.

"But we tested the ore seam!" Mol Gurd had now hobbled up.

"Well he did!" Ull pointed an accusing finger at Willard.

"But you did yesterday with Delgardo and it was positive!" Edmurson's remark silenced the crew.

Ull had struggled to make sense of it all but the fake archive sample convinced him of Nemi's explanation. "They think some microorganism in the tunnel has caused hallucinations. It explains Gantz's mental state, some inner demon came to the surface."

"Why haven't we been hallucinating?" Edmurson asked a reasonable question.

Ull smiled and shook his head. "For Corp sake Sligo what do all miners dream about?" Ull did not bother to wait for an answer. "The big find, the big payday! What else would we hallucinate about but a Zelman crystal find? We never questioned it did we? Because we all wanted to believe it but think about it! All the bickering and accusations," Ull paused to glance at Willard. " And betrayals. The obsession with keeping the drill-head going!" He looked around the faces which surrounded him but saw only confusion not realisation or even doubt.

It was Gurd who reacted with irrational denial. "That fucking Delgardo woman must be in league with Dang!" Gurd pushed his way into the centre of the group. "What are you up to Milton?" The crew looked around for a reply and it was then they finally noticed Dang and Albright were missing.

***

The projected holograph hovered above the desktop. It had been almost two years since he last saw Lisbeth Smith but she had not changed one bit, as far as Nemi could recall. She had never said anything but Nemi always got the impression she disapproved of his close relationship with Kanah Gantz. As Lisbeth herself had married a pure human this puzzled Nemi. It was also over two years since he last saw her husband Able

Carter who had headed up the Federal investigation into the mass suicide which Nemi became involved in. Rumours were rife, although these came mainly from Stenna Morgan, that all was not well with the marriage. Perhaps her own experience had influenced her opinion of Nemi and Gantz's relationship. It could also have been an attempt on her part to put some distance between herself and one of her mistakes. She had overlooked Nemi and he had been the one who finally uncovered the New Brethren breeding program. Lisbeth, the most talented of the Gnostics, was the sort of person who would fret over such an oversight like that.

"Ah, Nemi! I'm glad you've called. I've been struggling with the temptation to call you myself. How is Kanah? Goodridge's second hand accounts are far from satisfactory."

"We have her heavily sedated and I've just sent her back to the ship. She appears to have had a mental breakdown." Nemi could afford to be vague or misleading with what he said for Lisbeth's abilities were useless over a CommsLink conversation. Unfortunately facial expressions were limited where Gnostics were concerned so Nemi would have few clues on how reliable Lisbeth's words were.

"That's surprising to hear, Kanah has always been so mentally strong! Do you think the isolation, coupled with her recent experiences have weakened her to the point where she has let in a human mind? Goodridge fears he sent her back to duty too soon."

"I don't think that's the answer but at the moment I'm in a minority of one." It crossed Nemi's mind that the reference to letting in a human mind could have also have been an implied criticism of him or that she regarded any human mind as a source of infection. He disregarded the thought as he reasoned he was being illogical, mistrusting Lisbeth while trusting Kanah. In some ways they were one and the same person. That thought worried him more than his original one and he quickly moved on. "I need some information from you."

There was a pause as if Lisbeth was weighing up the consequences of her answer. "If I can help in any way I would only be too pleased. What do you think has happened to Kanah?"

"Who was Kanah's mother?" If Nemi's question had shocked or taken Lisbeth by surprise she gave no indication.

"Why is that important to you?"

"I'm sorry Lisbeth but I thought this conversation would be me asking the questions and you answering them, not the other way round!"

Again there was no indication as to whether his remark had irritated her or offended her. "You really have been around Morgan for far too long Nemi!" The hologram image smiled. Lisbeth could still turn on the charm when it was needed. "She was a member of the Collective, it was her father who was human. Is this really relevant?"

"Bear with me please. What happened to her mother?"

There was a longer pause now. "Like many of the Collective who came into contact with humans, she was damaged."

"Yes I remember my indirect conversation with the Collective. They were at pains to stress how many of them suffered when compared to the number of humans during that first contact period. What they didn't tell me was what became of them."

There was an even longer pause. "They had to be isolated for the protection of the Collective."

"Isolated, not disposed of?"

That remark brought the first visible reaction from Lisbeth. "We do not kill each other, unlike humans!"

"Are you talking about the Gnostics or the Collective?" It was a veiled reference to one particular Gnostic and Lisbeth picked up on the point.

"As far back as the collective memory goes no member of the Collective has ever taken the life of another." Lisbeth paused. "Although I have always considered the isolation of members of the Collective as almost as bad. I don't expect you to understand what isolation means to them."

"Are they isolated from each other or just the rest of the Collective?"

"What sort of species do you imagine the Collective to be?" Lisbeth's human side broke through as she sounded horrified at Nemi's suggestion. "They are held in an isolated commune. They are free to associate with each other but kept at a safe distance from the rest of the Collective."

"Because they're mad?"

"Because they have been infected by humanity!"

"I'm sorry, bad term to use." Nemi truly regretted his words despite the fact they probably summed up the condition of the damaged members of the Collective. "I'm just attempting to understand the situation!"

"I also apologise for the inference. I did not mean to suggest that all humans are dangerous and a threat."

"But you still keep them at arm's length, even the New Brethren versions!"

"All humans have the capability to become a threat. The New Brethren attempt to control their more base emotions but we appreciate how difficult it is to control a psyche moulded by millions of years of evolution." Nemi still took issue with the suggestion humanity was like some kind of disease which you could catch but resisted the temptation to argue the point. Now was not the time and when bringing up the subject with Kanah he had always struggled to defend, with any conviction, the worst excesses committed by humans on other humans.

"Kanah's mother and the others..." Nemi struggled to find an acceptable term.

Lisbeth saved him further embarrassment. "They have lost the natural balance in their part of the Collective mind. They would infect the Collective if they rejoined the neural network."

"So how do you know they are still isolated? Surely you can't make contact with them for that very reason."

"The commune is sealed. The cave network is extensive and they have comfortable living quarters. Are you suggesting Kanah has been in contact? That's impossible!"

"Comfortable or not if they are separated from the Collective they're still in a prison! They're still isolated from the rest of the Collective! Humans are lone animals but even with us the worst punishment we can impose on anybody are the isolation cubes. Three strikes and you're in isolation for life but they usually end up mad. Are the restrictions you've placed on them any better? Where is this commune?"

Lisbeth considered Nemi's statement. It revealed an appreciation of the Collective she found unusual for a pure human. Perhaps Gantz had seen this in him. "The commune is far to the East of here. We would never have agreed to the mining activity if there was any chance of it getting anywhere near them."

"If they are still where you put them! How long have they been there? Twenty odd years? Longer for some of them! Plenty of time to cover a considerable distance if they've escaped from your commune." Nemi was careful not to use the word prison again.

'They couldn't have escaped, the commune was sealed!"

"And it still is? When was the last time you checked?" The silence from Lisbeth answered his question. "You've never risked going back have you? Dumped them and forgot about them didn't you? Salve your conscience did it?" That was one remark which Nemi did not regret.

Lisbeth ignored the slight. "I need something more if I'm to risk sending anyone to check. There are three monthly supply drops and they are always picked up from the drop zone. Why do you think they've escaped and you've found them?"

"Kanah started acting strangely when she entered the tunnel where they are currently drilling. When they reached the drill head she had what was described as a fit. She then disarmed her colleague, disconnected the ore pipe so they couldn't power up the drill and threatened to shoot anyone who attempted to recouple the pipe. She made good that promise when a few of the miners tried. The crew are supposed to have found a deposit of Zelman crystals but they have mysteriously gone missing, in fact the only trace we have is from the archive sample which was switched so it appeared they had found it. " Nemi paused to draw breath. "Both Vitch Tolman and I are the only ones to have experienced anything like what Kanah had and of course we're the only ones here to have been in contact with the Collective, albeit via a Gnostic." Nemi paused again to study Lisbeth's expression in the hope of judging whether he was convincing her but the deadpan image told him nothing. "During Kanah's episode she kept mentioning her mother and she was rambling about killing her father." That comment did get a reaction from Lisbeth.

"Like me Kanah was present when our parents sacrificed themselves. We tried to ease their passing but don't think for one moment it was easy for us. We lost both parents within a short space of time and the circumstances of that loss weighs heavily on each of us." There was a slight hesitation before she added. "It's hard not to feel some responsibility for those sad

333

events. Kanah's isolation might have forced some unwelcome human emotions to the surface!"

Under normal conditions Nemi may have commented on the last remark but he was more concerned he might be losing Lisbeth to the idea of Kanah suffering a mental breakdown. "Also there's a miner here who does wood carvings as a hobby. He's produced two landscapes which were very familiar; a waterfall which we passed when taking Stern to his meeting and a village scene which I swear is the suicide village. He obviously has never been to either and thinks he just made them up. Sound familiar?"

"No it doesn't!"

"Well it relates to some of the human casualties so I guess you wouldn't remember it but I think he got those images from the Collective." He dried up at that point. It had sounded perfectly logical in his head but now he had said it all out loud doubts began to gnaw at him.

"I admit your story is feasible but I can think of alternative explanations which are much more likely."

Nemi sensed an uncertainty in her voice. "Look, these miners are desperate to continue drilling. A Zelman crystal deposit is every miners dream find and yet given the choice of searching for the missing crystals or carrying on drilling and they choose the latter. The crystals have never been found on a planet, only on asteroids. Doesn't that seem odd to you? Every time the crew have tested for crystals they've had a positive result but we haven't found one speck of crystal." Nemi paused as he realised it sounded like he was pleading. He decided to change tack. "I appreciate the risks involved for you in checking my theory but what are the risks if I'm right?" There was a long silence as Lisbeth evaluated the consequences. Nemi made one last effort. "We have a mining crew of nine here plus Tolman, Kanah and two police officers Delgardo and Sigh. Add to that a three man police recovery team, two civilian technicians, two troopers armed with pulse rifles and a three man Colonial patrol ship with two more technicians. I've got twenty four people out there, a police patrol craft and one of only two Colonial patrol ships on the planet. Enough man power, transport and fire power to go anywhere on this planet whether you want us there or not. What are these outcast members of the Collective capable of?"

Lisbeth did not need long to evaluate Nemi's last question. "I'll get confirmation of your theory." Lisbeth hesitated before continuing. "On no account must they be freed. You have the Council's full authority to take whatever steps are necessary to ensure they're contained."

"How do I do that without getting close to them?"

"They'll be wary of you and Tolman so you should have a little time on your side. It also depends how many of them there are. They'll be able to influence many for a short time but only control on a one to one basis. My advice would be not to get too close to them. I'll contact you as soon as I have any information." The holographic image flickered and died as Lisbeth broke the connection. Based on her last comments Nemi hoped his theory was incorrect.

***

The Rec was in turmoil when Nemi returned. Everybody appeared to be shouting at everybody else while Delgardo was attempting to talk to Tolman who had just returned to the accommodation block. Nemi stood for a few moments waiting for everybody to calm down. When it became apparent to him this was not going to happen he withdrew his weapon and fired a round into the ceiling. The silence was instant and every head turned towards him. "So what's happened now?" He waved his gun towards the crew. "And I'm only talking to Delgardo!"

"They didn't take the news about the crystals too well! Willard admitted getting the sample for Dang to plant but they refuse to believe there are no crystals. Apparently I'm in league with Milton Dang who has disappeared with Albright. They all think they have gone to get the crystals so we can fly them out of here. The more objections raised the more of us get dragged into the conspiracy."

Nemi sighed. He really couldn't be bothered with this petty squabbling right now. "Tell them to sit down and shut up or I'll have them all sedated." He turned towards Tolman and gestured to him to follow him where they were out of earshot of the crew. "I've got a theory about what's been happening here. I've been in contact with Lisbeth Smith and I'm waiting for her to confirm."

"What's she got to do with all this?"

"I think the crew have come across a group of feral blue monkeys who are trying to get out."

"What do mean by feral?"

"The first contact between the Collective and humans produced a lot of damage. Madness on both sides with the half breed Gnostics, the suicide village, the Brotherhood of the Jinn and the blue monkeys involved in all of that. It seems that rather than run the risk of them contaminating the rest of the Collective they isolated them, sealed them away in a cave complex well away from any other communes. I think they somehow broke out of their prison and managed to get to here. That ravine could be just a small part of an underground cave system." Nemi paused, realising he was now making up things to fit into his theory. He decided to restrict himself to what he thought he could prove. "Look no matter how they got here the point is I think they are here. Both you and I sensed something and we're the only ones other than Kanah to have had contact with the Collective. You said yourself the feeling was familiar.

Edmurson's carvings are of places which I recognise but he has never been to. The Brotherhood of the Jinn had collective memories of places they had also never been to."

"So you think they are controlling the crew?"

"I think they're influencing the crew. They probably sensed the drillers and planted the idea of the Zelman crystals because I should imagine all miners dream of finding a deposit. It seems Milton Dang might have been the one they latched onto. He was the one who pursued Willard to steal a trace sample so he could plant it in the mine."

"And it was his hunch as to where to start the next tunnel to find the crystals!"

"The tunnel is probably heading straight for them. We felt their presence as we entered the tunnel and it got worse for Kanah when she reached the drill-head."

"Even closer to them! When Delgardo did the tests for the crystals down there it was positive but negative everywhere else!"

"Obviously close enough for them to get Delgardo and Ull to see exactly what they were supposed to see. Perhaps it wasn't that easy for them to control Kanah."

"Shit!" Tolman had only ever considered the benefits of the Collective and the Gnostics. Kanah's intuition when dealing with suspects, the cooperation with the New Brethren and the apparently liberal attitude towards humans despite of their fear of them. The thought of feral blue monkeys frightened him and by implication the new generation of Gnostics now took on a new perspective. If human contact had contaminated those blue monkeys how would the genetically engineered Gnostics turn out? Had the New Brethren naivety and enthusiasm for producing the next step on their journey towards God only ended up creating a half breed species which would enslave mankind? "What happens if they manage to get out?"

"Without the Collective's restraint they can do exactly what they want, using us! Lisbeth said that on no account can we let them succeed."

"We keep the mine closed!"

"We seal the mine as soon as your team have recovered Ginthem's body. We blow the tunnel and seal them in for good."

Tolman said nothing. His first thought was that was an inhumane thing to do, even to feral blue monkeys, but then he realised his job sent humans to the isolation cubes. In some cases until they were broken mentally. Out of the corner of his eye he saw Delgardo hovering nearby, waiting for a chance to approach them.

"What's up Delgardo?"

"I wondered what you wanted to do about Dang and Albright. Should we search for them?"

"Bugger, I'd forgotten about those two idiots! I guess we better find them just in case they try and start up the drilling again."

"I shouldn't worry, Dulac won't let them get any where near the tunnel."

"But the trooper wasn't there when I left to come back here. I thought you'd sent her off somewhere else!"

"I didn't send her anywhere!" Nemi then had a thought. "Is the pipe re-coupled?"

"I didn't notice!" Without another word all three of them headed for the door. As soon as they were outside it was obvious the pipe had been reconnected.

"Can we disconnect it?"

"Not if they've powered up the drill!"

"Shit! I didn't want to go anywhere near that tunnel again but I guess now we don't have a choice." Nemi noticed the bewildered look on Delgardo's face. "We'll explain later but we have to stop those idiots drilling and seal up the tunnel."

"I'll go straight away."

Nemi had to physically restrain Delgardo. "No I'm afraid this is something only Tolman and I can do." Nemi pulled out his CommsLink to make some calls. The first was to trooper Mikelson back on the ship. "Ignore the previous instructions Mikelson. Make sure Gantz is comfortable and then get back here as quickly as you can. Stop off on the way and pick up a couple of magnetic grenades." He then attempted to contact trooper Dulac but there was no response.

"Magnetic grenades? Shouldn't we be down in the mine stopping those two?"

"They might not be in the mood to comply with any polite request and I want to keep as far away from the end of the tunnel as possible. If the worst comes to the worst we'll lob in the grenades. If we hit the drill head they'll clamp on and it'll be impossible to pull them off. A thirty second delay should be enough for us to get well clear."

"What if Dang and Albright think they can get the grenade off?"

"A ticking bomb should help to concentrate their minds."

"But if it isn't?"

"If they're that far gone there's nothing we can do to help them."

"And if your theory is wrong?"

Nemi shrugged his shoulders. Tolman was far from happy and turned to Delgardo. "Nothing you can do here Delgardo. Get back to the accommodation block. I need to have a word with Nemi in private." Delgardo was reluctant to go without further explanation but when she could see none was forthcoming she did as she was asked. Tolman waited until she was out of earshot before continuing. "I'm not happy to go down there and risk killing two people based on a theory!"

"Well let's hope we get confirmation from Lisbeth Smith before Mikelson gets back here with the grenades."

It was the matter of fact way Nemi framed his reply which concerned Tolman. His Colonial Corps background had come to the fore and Tolman found it difficult to recognise his friend. "This might be the way you go about things in the Corp but we do things differently in the police! Goodridge would never give me the authority to do something like this."

"Well my boss, Morgan, would! In fact he wouldn't even consider the option of attempting to talk them out. He'd call up the ship and use the pulse cannon to fire a couple of rounds into the mine." Tolman reflected on the fact that was probably true but it did nothing to ease his conscience. He stood and waited, hoping Nemi would get a call from Lisbeth Smith before the trooper got there with his deadly cargo. He hung his head, unable to look Nemi in the eye.

CHAPTER FOURTEEN

The ground vehicle roared up the path from the mine and stopped outside the accommodation block. Mikelson jumped out and presented Nemi with the two tiny magnetic grenades, small enough to conceal in the palm of your hand. Nemi held out one to Tolman who stared at it for a few moments before slowly shaking his head. Nemi slipped both objects into his pocket.

"Don't worry about it Vitch." The words were spoken with some warmth and affection which only made Tolman feel even worse about refusing to accept one of the grenades. Nemi turned to the trooper. "Right take us back to the mine and then wait. I need to check up on what's happened to trooper Dulac. You might have another casualty to take back to the ship." Nemi glanced at Tolman. "You ready? Or do you want to stay here?"

"I'll go with you Ja, I'm not letting you go down there on your own and I want to try and talk Dang and Albright out." He said it without much conviction having heard how Albright had reacted to Gantz and Delgardo's questioning.

"Let's get going then." Nemi sounded more eager than he actually was.

Mikelson drove them back to the mine entrance and then followed them into the mine. They paused at the ravine entrance to inspect the ground but only found the Koolbots and an empty food container. The security laser was still switched on so they had not entered that tunnel since Tolman had left.

"Looks as if they planned this." Nemi kicked one of the Koolbots with the toe of his boot.

"Delgardo said they waited until Wildman was on his own and then slipped into the kitchen, where they must have picked up those, and then climbed out of the window."

"Observant officer you've got there!"

"Bloody useless, which is probably why they slipped out while he was on his own. The police are the last choice of employment for pilots!"

"And Colonial troopers are the last career choice of anybody!" Nemi suddenly remembered Mikelson was with them. "No offence Mikelson."

"None taken sir, I'm New Brethren!"

"Yes I forgot, with you it's more of a calling than a career. Defending the faith and all that!"

"Something like that sir!"

"Well let's see if we can find our other New Brethren who was naive enough to think Dang and Albright were bringing her refreshment." Nemi joked about Dulac to hide the fear that the two miners might have killed her. He did not like losing troopers, a trait he shared with Morgan.

They continued down the main tunnel until they came to the first offshoot where they discovered Dulac's trussed up body. To Nemi's relief she had suffered nothing worse than a cracked head and dented pride. They untied her and Mikelson inspected her injuries.

"She seems fine but I'm just concerned about concussion."

"I'm fine sir! I'm sorry about this, they claimed they'd brought refreshments for the recovery team. I should have known."

"It's not your fault Ruth I should have brought more troopers. You might be fine but we'll get Mike the medic to check you out first." Nemi turned to Mickelson. "Get her back to the ship, patch her up and then get back here but wait at the mine entrance. Mikelson acknowledged he understood the instructions and helped the still dazed Dulac away. When they were on their own Nemi glanced at Tolman. "Are you ready?"

"As I'll ever be!"

Nemi suddenly turned and looked around the side tunnel. "Shit!"

"What is it?" Tolman could see that Nemi was concerned.

"They've taken her pulse rifle. Let's hope they haven't adjusted the setting. It would have been on stun but if they switch to full pulse and fire the bloody thing it'll bring the roof down." Nemi gave a macabre little grin. "Still that'll save us the bother!"

"Except we'll be there when it happens. This just gets better and better! Come on let's get on with this." They had just started to move off down the main tunnel when Nemi stopped.

"Call coming in from Lisbeth." He smiled at Tolman. "You're a lucky bastard!" Tolman returned the smile. It would be a huge relief to him to know either way. "Hi Lisbeth, excuse me for dispensing with the niceties but Tolman and I are in the mine. Two idiots have decided to start drilling again." Nemi switched to loud speaker so Tolman could hear what Lisbeth had to say.

"Stop them at all costs Nemi. You're right! We got close enough to the commune to realise they were all gone. We're opening up the complex to find out what happened. I should be able to give you more information in a few minutes."

"Considering the possible urgency to stop the drilling we'll continue rather than wait."

"Good luck Nemi, you know what the consequences could be if they escape!"

"Oh yes!" Nemi switched off the CommsLink. "You and the New Brethren's plans would come crashing down around your

344

ears." Nemi paused and looked at Tolman. "And every chance of a genocidal war between us and the Collective." He gave an ironic little laugh. "No pressure then!"

"Hey." Tolman nodded towards Nemi. "Toss me one of those grenades and tell me how to use it."

Nemi pulled one of the grenades from his pocket and tossed it towards Tolman, who caught it and stared at it warily. He had not really expected Nemi to actually throw the thing at him. "It's timer is preset. The impact of it hitting and sticking to metal will set it off. Throw it and run as fast as you can in the opposite direction. Simple!"

'Oh yes' thought Tolman 'Simple!' He gestured to Nemi that they should continue.

***

They hesitated when they came to the drill tunnel and exchanged looks.

"I don't feel the presence now!" Tolman looked confused. "What about you?"

"Me neither!" Nemi whispered although the sound of the drill would have covered their voices. "Perhaps they're too busy concentrating on Dang and Albright."

They warily took a first step, over the ore pipe and into the tunnel. Nemi slipped the grenade out of his pocket and held it in the palm of his hand. He could feel the sweat on his hands and now wished he had left Tolman behind. The idea of talking Dang and Albright into powering down the drill seemed a forlorn hope. They would be desperate to continue, driven on by the minds of the feral blue monkeys. The sensible option would have been for Nemi to creep up on them, toss in the grenade and then run for his life. The two miners would just be more collateral damage from the meeting of the Collective and humans. If he survived this Morgan would kill him for taking such a risk. His thoughts were interrupted by another call from Lisbeth. He held out a hand to stop Tolman and pointed to his ear to indicate he was taking a call. He did not want to risk putting the call on loud-speaker. Although he was sure the noise of the drill would mask the sound, if it was more bad news then there was no need for Tolman to share it.

"It's worse than we expected Nemi." There was a tremble in her voice which unnerved him. How could the situation be any worse than it already was and what could have shaken Lisbeth Smith so? "We think an underground earthquake caused a fissure to appear in the complex and they escaped through that." She paused again and Nemi grew more uneasy about what was coming next. "We found badly decomposed bodies in the complex and not all the deaths were caused by the earthquake." She paused again, no doubt for that piece of information to sink in. She obviously did not want to admit openly to the alternative; members of the Collective killing each other. Nemi remained silent as he did not know how to respond to this news. He knew from talking to Kanah that the Collective abhorred killing, to the point where they were vegetarians. He pondered the affect on the collective conscience of the knowledge that one of them had taken the life of another. One thing for sure was it would reinforce their fear of humans. Nemi needed to say something but could not find the words. It was Lisbeth who finally broke the awkward silence. "I don't expect you to understand what that means to us!"

That statement jolted Nemi's brain into action. "I can imagine what it must be like. Just because of our history it doesn't mean we're immune to the horrors of killing." The words sounded hollow to him; how would even a half human like Lisbeth understand humanity's continued history of violence towards itself? He did not understand it himself! Was he part of a naturally brutal species or just incapable of learning lessons from the seemingly endless series of conflicts humanity had stumbled into? If this had been caused by contact with humans perhaps the term 'infection' he heard associated with his species was not far from the truth.

"It wasn't meant as a criticism of you Nemi." He was sure it wasn't but he still felt sullied by association. He grunted in reply so Lisbeth continued. "We can only imagine a dispute over escaping their confinement escalated to the point where violence overtook reason. Although the bodies were badly decomposed we have identified most of them." She hesitated. "Kanah's mother is among the dead." Another pause to allow that fact to sink in. Nemi wondered if she had shared that particular piece of information to salve his conscience in preparation for any action he might have to take or to tap into the human emotion of revenge. It even occurred to him she might be lying for exactly the same reasons. Did she think he would baulk at causing the death of Kanah's mother? His silence prompted Lisbeth to continue. "It shows they have learned how to imitate as well as manipulate the emotions of humans."

'Well!' thought Nemi, 'Kanah is now human when it suits!' He was tempted to remind Lisbeth that she was also adapt at manipulating human emotions but resisted the temptation. He thought Kanah would have been proud of him for that. "I'm well aware of how dangerous they are. How many are we dealing with?" Another long silence followed.

"We estimate one hundred and eleven."

Nemi shut his eyes tight as if doing so would squeeze the reply out of his mind. He was not only appalled at the amount of damage caused by humans colonising this planet, but at the amount of damage which could be caused by that many blue monkeys who had lost their fear of contact with humans and any inhibitions imposed by the Collective. He glanced across at Tolman and was glad he had kept this conversation private.

However, from the look on Tolman's face he had been reading the worst into Nemi's reactions to the conversation anyway.

"I'll take whatever action is necessary Lisbeth if you can sort out dealing with whatever fallout there is from that action?" He paused. "And that is likely to be huge. Not only destroying a corporation mine and equipment but there's a chance of more casualties here, not to mention explaining away why we've done it!"

"Of course, but please remember Nemi, you must stop them from escaping!"

"Understood." Nemi switched off and pocketed his CommsLink before Lisbeth felt obliged to say something sincere and affectionate to him. He had no illusions about what Lisbeth really thought about him and he didn't want hypocrisy to be possibly the last memory he had. He was expendable and his heroic failure to survive this encounter would also dispense with the inconvenient liaison between a New Brethren prophet and a mere human. He took a deep breath and slowly let it out to dispel those negative thoughts and told himself he was over-reacting.

"Not good?" Tolman posed the question in such a way which implied that he did not really want an honest answer.

"Nothing we can't handle!" Tolman did not believe the bravado reply but found his continuing ignorance reassuring for some reason. He gave Nemi an encouraging thumbs up gesture and they slowly crept forward again.

They were thankful for the dull illumination given by the tunnel's emergency lighting. Keeping to the opposite side of the tunnel meant they were half hidden in shadow. Both men were bent double as if being smaller would offer extra protection from being spotted. It was not long before the two miners came into view. They were both concentrating on the drill head as it slowly bit into the rock face and sucked the waste rubble away.

Dang monitored the control panel and occasionally manually adjusted the drilling angle. Albright divided his time between glancing at Dang and then the drill-head. They were both so engrossed in watching the progress of the drill that neither bothered to check behind them.

Nemi transferred the tiny grenade from his right to his left hand so he could unfasten his holster cover and place his hand on the butt of his service weapon. Tolman, who had insisted on taking the lead so he could talk the miners into surrendering, did likewise. Nemi was surprised how little noise the drilling actually produced, he had expected it to be deafening. He wished now he had taken the time to be briefed better about the drilling process. It was another regret added to the pile which was building up for him. The one plus point he noted was the stolen pulse rifle which was leaning against the side of the tunnel just out of reach of Albright who stood to the right of Dang.

Tolman stood upright and took one pace towards the centre of the tunnel to allow him to stand without bending his neck. It blocked Nemi's view of Milton Dang but still gave him a clear firing line to Albright whose proximity to the pulse rifle made him the most dangerous one of the two. They were about five metres away and even Nemi's far from expert shooting ability was good enough to ensure he could take out Albright before he reached the pulse rifle. That at least would eliminate the possibility of them all dying by a pulse round accidentally bringing down the roof on top of them.

"Power down the drill and stand back." Tolman's voice came out a little too loudly even taking into account the noise from the drill. Nerves had got the better of him and Nemi hoped the miners had not noticed. The surprised look on their faces as they spun around at the sound of the command told Nemi they had not. Dang opened his mouth to speak but no words came out. "I said power down the drill and stand back." There was more authority in Tolman's voice now. Albright's eyes flashed to where the pulse rifle was propped. Nemi half pulled his weapon from its holster.

"Fuck off! You've got no authority down here." Dang had found his voice again although his logic appeared to have been lost at exactly the same time.

"I'm not going to ask again." Tolman made a great show of pulling his weapon half way out of its holster. Dang's eyes were drawn towards the action. His eyes narrowed and he glanced at Nemi and then at Albright. He was obviously assessing his options and calculating the risks involved.

"Before you make any decisions I suggest you tell me where you've hidden the crystals."

All eyes turned towards the sound of the new voice. Wildman stood in the centre of the tunnel with a gun pointed directly at Dang. The distraction was enough to encourage Albright to scramble for the pulse rifle. Within moments the scenario had changed. Albright now pointed the pulse rifle at Tolman and Nemi, dissuading them from drawing their weapons. Dang smiled, even though Wildman still had his weapon pointed at him. A low growling sound drew their attention to Wildman's dog who was bearing her teeth at Albright. Dang's smile quickly vanished as he noticed Albright's aim wavering between Tolman and Nemi and the dog.

"Look Wildman, I don't know where the crystals are!"

"Don't give me that shit Milton, I know you're behind all this! You made the original find and you've been the one most desperate to cover up what happened to Ginthem and get the drilling going again." Wildman gave Dang a hard eyed stare. "So I'll ask one more time, where have you hidden the crystals?"

Nemi watched this bizarre scenario play out in astonishment. His main concern had been to get the miners out

350

and seal the tunnel as quickly as possible before the blue monkeys had time to react. The strange thing was he still could not feel their presence. Were they no longer mentally probing the tunnel because the drilling had recommenced? The worry was what would happen if they suddenly decided to check up on progress. From the corner of his eye he caught sight of the unmistakable figure of Edmurson moving up alongside Wildman. This was getting ridiculous! How many more would join the party before Mikelson got back to the mine entrance.

Wildman gave a nervous glance at Edmurson as he drew level but the big man ignored him and moved past him towards Albright. "Dirk, put the rifle down my friend. This is foolish! Put it down and come back with me. You're only causing more trouble for yourself." Edmurson was using the calm reassuring tone which he reserved for dealing with one of Albright's episodes. His presence was giving Albright more options than he could handle. The pulse rifle still wavered between the two dangers and now his mind wavered between loyalty to Dang and Edmurson. This stand-off was also distracting Wildman as he seemed to have forgotten he'd still had no reply from Dang.

Tolman was still attempting to work out what he needed to do to resolve this situation peaceably and Nemi was calculating whether he could take Albright out without causing an indiscriminate gun battle when they both suddenly glanced at each other. The presence was back.

***

The drill-head suddenly powered down. It took everyone by surprise except for Milton Dang who smiled to himself.

"We've broken through to the crystal chamber!" His smile broadened. "Forget about the crystals which Willard stole Wildman, this find will make us rich."

Wildman glanced at the drill-head. Around the edge of the drill you could no longer see any rock. He returned his attention to Dang. "You've broken through into some kind of cave?"

"And it's full of crystals!" Dang was giggling now.

"How do you know that?" Tolman's question appeared to confuse Dang and the giggling stopped abruptly. "You can't see in there and you haven't tested for crystals so how can you be so sure?"

"I know!" Despite his statement there was less certainty in his voice now and he seemed to be struggling to come to terms with this contradictory situation.

"No trace of any crystals in the storage bins or the mine and yet you know they're here? Against all the evidence to the contrary!" Tolman pushed home his argument and Nemi realised what he was attempting to do. Tolman was challenging the control over Dang's mind and so occupying the blue monkey. If there was only one of them behind the drill-head they still stood a chance of blowing up the tunnel. This hope was strangled almost straight away by the thought that it was probably already contacting the others for help. He had to make the decision on whether to risk taking out Albright.

The silence was suddenly broken by the sound of Wildman's dog growling again. It had shifted its attention away from Albright and had taken a few steps towards the drill-head. It was crouched low to the ground as if preparing to launch an attack, lips curled back to revel its teeth. The hairs on its back stood up and the growls got louder. It took another two steps forward and then abruptly stopped, its tail dropping between its legs. It now appeared to be hovering between fight and flight. It was afraid but still wanted to protect its master.

All eyes now turned towards the drill-head and to the narrow gap between the tunnel wall and the drill. Thin, dirty white fingers suddenly appeared and curled around the edge of the drill. Wildman was the first to react and he shifted the aim of his gun away from Dang and, in sheer panic, fired four shots towards the hand. Dang and Albright screamed and clutched at their heads, causing the latter to fumble and drop the pulse rifle. The probing hand pulled back leaving half a finger on the tunnel floor and blood splattered up the wall. Nemi drew his weapon to take advantage of the confusion and take Albright out but Wildman now blocked his line of sight. The screaming stopped and Dang hurled himself at Tolman, the impact knocking him off balance and making them both crash to the ground. Albright snatched up the pulse rifle from where it had fallen but in his eagerness to retrieve it he had picked it up by the wrong end. Undeterred he used it like a club and swung it at Wildman, knocking his weapon arm up into the air. The follow-through back-swing caught him full in the face and he toppled backwards and hit the ground with a thump.

Albright had his blood up now and he advanced on Nemi with another swing of pulse rifle club. It hit Nemi dead square on his wounded chest and pain seared through his body as he felt the plasi-skin which was holding the wound together split. He staggered back and hit the side of the tunnel. He clutched at the re-opened wound with his left hand, dropping the grenade he had been holding. He looked up and saw Albright pull back the rifle to aim another blow, this time at his head. Nemi braced himself for the strike but it never came. Edmurson stepped in wrapping his arms around Albright, pinning his arms to his side. The big man pulled Albright away but the captive struggled madly. His flailing limbs and constant attempts to butt his head back into Edmurson's face caused them to topple to the ground. Edmurson wrapped his legs around Albright's and tightened his grip, shifting one arm to hold his head still. The constant head battering had left Edmurson's face a bruised and bloody mess.

Nemi scrambled along the tunnel floor desperately trying to retrieve the grenade which had rolled away down the slight tunnel incline. He had one eye on Wildman who had now got back to his feet and recovered his gun. The pilot looked around at the struggling figures as if now unsure of which side he was on. Nemi finally managed to grasp the grenade and he looked up. His eyes met those of Wildman and for an instant Nemi thought he read murder in those eyes. Suddenly Wildman made his decision and he turned and shot Dang in the buttocks. The miner released his grip on Tolman to clutch his backside. To complete the man's misery Keith the dog gave him a nasty bite on the arm and dragged him to the floor. Nemi pulled himself upright and staggered to the drill-head. He turned to face the others shouted out a warning and held up the grenade for them all to see. It was at that moment he noticed Delgardo had just arrived, no doubt looking for the missing Wildman and Edmurson. "Magnetic grenade! You've got thirty seconds to get out of here so move your arses!" He slammed the grenade against the drill and lurched forward. Tolman, now back on his feet, grabbed Nemi and pulled an arm around his neck to support him. They both half ran, half staggered down the tunnel. Wildman and Keith were already well on their way and Delgardo helped Edmurson drag an unconscious Albright away. After a few paces Tolman glanced over his shoulder and saw Milton Dang desperately trying to pry the grenade off the drill. "Leave it you fool," but his warning fell on deaf ears as Dang's efforts became more frantic.

Tolman had his head down as he half dragged Nemi along. All he could see were the boots of Albright as his toes bounced over the ground while he was being dragged along by Edmurson and Delgardo. Their progress seemed painfully slow as the seconds slipped by. Any moment Tolman expected to feel the blast from the grenade and could only hope they were far enough away to survive it. Despite the anticipation it still came as a shock when it finally arrived. The force knocked them over and a cloud of rubble and dust rolled along the tunnel until it finally engulfed them.

***

When Tolman came to it took him a while to work out where he was. The explosion had knocked out the emergency lighting and the tunnel was pitch black. He risked moving and found that, although every bone in his body ached, he appeared to be unhurt. Some rubble covered his feet and calves but this was soon shaken away. He felt his way back down the tunnel but only moved a metre or two before, from the incline of the rubble it was obvious the tunnel was completely blocked. He let out a sigh of relief when he realised how close he came to being buried alive. He shuffled around and carefully started to crawl back. He groped in the darkness, spreading out his hands, searching for the body of Nemi. He stopped when his hand touched what felt like a leg and he silently hoped it was still attached to his friend. There was a groan and he gave a sigh of relief. He slowly moved his hand up the leg until he heard a cough.

"Get your hand off my arse Vitch!" The voice was hoarse and it was followed by another cough and the sound of Nemi attempting to spit the dust from his mouth. "It's reserved for Gantz."

Tolman smiled at the fact Nemi could still joke at a time like this. "Are you alright?"

"Got one mother of all headaches, but I'm alive which has cheered me up no end! The gunshot wound is bleeding again and there's an awful pain in my right leg but other than that I'm fine!" Nemi spat again. "You ask some bloody stupid questions Vitch."

Suddenly the tunnel was illuminated again. It was at first so bright they both had to close their eyes for a few seconds from the glare. When they opened them again they saw Wildman standing over them with a light-stick in his hand.

"Got it off Edmurson." His opening remark was in response to the look of amazement on their faces that he had been efficient enough to have brought light-sticks with him. "He's back there cuddling Albright and sobbing his heart out." He handed Tolman and Nemi each a light-stick. They twisted them on and the extra light illuminated more of the tunnel. Sure enough Edmurson sat holding Albright in his arms. He was gently rocking backward and forwards. Delgardo knelt beside him, a comforting arm around the big man's shoulders. "Looks like he didn't realise his own strength. I don't think the explosion killed him, Edmurson crushed the life out of him." Wildman spoke in a hushed whisper to ensure he was not overheard.

"What happened to Dang?" Nemi looked at Wildman. "Didn't you shoot him?"

"Only in a fleshy bit! Keith gave him a bit of a nip but he was on his feet when we left,"

"Stupid sod stayed there trying to get the grenade off the drill. I looked back and saw him. Tried to warn him but..." Tolman's voice trailed off.

"And what were you doing back there?" Nemi gave Wildman an accusing look.

"For a while I got carried away with the crystal thing."

"Forget which side you were on?" Nemi wasn't going to let him off that easily.

Wildman avoided a direct answer. "Keith showed me the error of my ways. She's always been a better judge of character than me!" Wildman turned and moved off down the tunnel not wanting to continue this particular conversation.

356

Tolman and Nemi followed him and paused by Edmurson and Delgardo. One look at Albright's dead staring eyes made them move on without comment. They abruptly stopped again as they suddenly reached the start of the tunnel. Tolman glanced back and judged there to be over fifty metres of blocked tunnel behind them. He was amazed how much distance they had covered. It just showed the effect of fear and an adrenalin rush. "Should take them a time to dig themselves out of that!" He nodded in agreement with himself.

"I plan to do a better job than that! Once your recovery team has got Ginthem out I intend to seal the whole mine." Nemi saw the look on Tolman's face. "I don't care what the Mining Corporation thinks, Lisbeth Smith can sort that one out.' Tolman shrugged his shoulders. That was good enough for him. There was no way he would be involved in discussions between the Planetary Government Council and a major Corporation.

They walked on until they reached the security fence at the ravine tunnel. Tolman dug into his pocket and pulled out the device to switch off the laser scanner. "I'll check up on how they're doing. They were about to make the decent when I got called back to the camp. Let's try and wrap this up quickly so we can get out of this place." He had a thought and turned back to Nemi. "What happens about the trapped monkeys?"

"Again not my problem!" Nemi hesitated. "Well not at the moment. I expect Lisbeth will want somebody to clear up this mess and I can't see the Collective hunting down their own kind. If there's any legalised murder to be done they'll get the humans to do it. We're not squeamish about things like that!" Without another word Nemi limped off in the direction of the mine entrance.

Tolman watched him go and wondered if this cynical attitude was a temporary one brought on by the day's traumatic events or whether the NCO who was once considered too soft to be a Colonial trooper had changed forever. If it was the latter then how would this change affect his relationship with Kanah Gantz? Tolman knew he would also have to consider how his own attitude to the New Brethren, the Gnostics and the Collective had changed. However, that would have to wait for he had work to do so he set off down the tunnel which led to the ravine and the recovery team.

CHAPTER FIFTEEN

When Nemi reached the mine entrance he found members of the crew waiting, led by Ull. They had obviously followed Delgardo down and, remarkably, had obeyed her order to venture no further. Ull's eyes widened as he looked Nemi up and down. For the first time Nemi looked down at himself. His uniform was covered with dust and a large stain marked the place where his reopened wound had bled and soaked through. No doubt the rest of him looked a mess too. He nodded an acknowledgement to Ull, suddenly too weary to speak and sat down on the waste pipe. Ull approached and sat down next to him. They both sat in silence for a few moments.

"What happened? We heard what sounded like an explosion!"

Nemi sighed. He had no intention of giving any explanation, he would leave that particular job to Lisbeth Smith. What she would tell them he neither knew or cared. He doubted it would be the truth. Perhaps Ull would be the subject of a rare meeting with the Collective, but more likely some counselling and therapy sessions awaited him. After today's events the last option had taken on a rather more sinister interpretation to Nemi than it would have previously.

"The tunnel collapsed!" Nemi rubbed his weary eyes. He knew that story would never satisfy Ull. "I don't know what happened but Dang and Albright had powered up the drill. When Tolman ordered them to shut it down they attacked us."

"What!" Despite everything which had happened Ull was still genuinely shocked by Nemi's revelation.

"Look, there was something in the tunnel which affected everyone. What it was I don't know, some virus, fungi, gas leak! With the tunnel collapsed we'll never be sure."

"Was anybody hurt?"

It was the question Nemi had been dreading and he now wished he hadn't been the first one to leave the mine. Breaking bad news was more Tolman's area of expertise. "Dang refused to leave the drill head and Edmurson accidentally killed Albright in the struggle. The man was off his head and Edmurson was attempting to subdue him."

Ull glanced at the mine entrance, drew in a deep breath and slowly released it. "Anything we can do to help?" Ull asked the question to fill the silence rather than in the expectation there was anything they could do.

"The others appeared to be okay but you could help get Albright's body out." Nemi's suggestion was aimed at getting rid of these people and it worked. Ull nodded and waved at the others to follow him into the mine. Nemi gave a silent sigh of relief which turned out to be a little premature as Ull turned back towards him.

"I don't understand how the tunnel collapsed!"

Nemi could not tell if the expression on Ull's face was one of confusion or disbelief. "They attacked the trooper guarding the ravine tunnel and took her pulse rifle. It got confusing down there but I presume Albright fired it or it just went off in the struggle. A pulse round can cause a lot of damage and in a confined space..." He left it at that and Ull nodded his understanding. Nemi was getting rather good at lying, but the thought provided him with little consolation, in fact it made him feel worse. It was his openness and honesty which had attracted Kanah Gantz, although there was little point attempting to lie to a Gnostic anyway. If they wanted to know the truth they would find out. She would sense his uneasiness about the Collective. The fact those in the tunnel were tainted did not hide the fact they could, if they so wished, manipulate humans to do whatever they wanted. Nemi felt a fool. He had surely always known this but chose to ignore it. The New Brethren vision of the Collective as humanity's next step towards its God, as the Angels, had an hypnotic appeal which he had bought into.

The pain in his shoulder suddenly returned as if to remind him there was more for him to do. He looked up and saw Mikelson sitting in the ground vehicle a discreet distance away from the mine entrance. He waved him over.

"Get in touch with the ship and have another ground vehicle sent out, we're evacuating the camp." Nemi then remembered Trooper Dulac. "How's Ruth?"

"She's fine sir, eager to get back to duty. Looks a lot better than you!"

"Then get her to bring the other vehicle. Better to get back in the saddle rather than brood over the fact she was out-witted by two dumb miners."

"Yes sir, shall I attend to your wound?"

Nemi glanced down at the dark stain. "Wait and get the body they're bringing out onto the vehicle and then follow me up to the accommodation block. I'll have a shower first and then you can glue me back up. Also see if you can find another uniform." Nemi pulled himself up and trudged up the path to the main camp.

When he entered the Rec he saw the miserable features of Mol Gurd staring at him. Opposite him but at some distance, as if getting too close would infect them with his virulent personality, was Rolm and Chang. She looked, as usual, sad and he had a the usual blank expression on his face.

362

"What's happening?" Gurd managed to make the simple question sound intimidating.

Nemi was not in the mood to deal with this nasty piece of work. "Dang and Albright are dead! Two other people who couldn't do as they were told." Nemi surprised himself at the threatening tone of his voice. He accompanied it with a look filled with loathing. Gurd responded by spitting on the floor near Nemi's feet. Nemi looked at the spittle and then at Gurd. "I'll deal with you later!"

Gurd snorted and watched Nemi as he walked away. Mentally another name went on Gurd's list for retribution. As soon as his knee was fixed he would take his revenge on them, one by one. He would start with that bitch Delgardo and then this puny Colonial NCO. He turned away and caught Rolm staring at him. "What you looking at bitch?" Rolm averted her eyes. "You'll be on the receiving end of a good seeing to as well, when I'm back on my feet." Gurd then noticed Chang staring at him. "And what are you looking at retard? You want my fist in your face too?" Chang shook his head and looked away.

***

Nemi quickly showered. It revived him a little and if it had not been for his eagerness to get away from the camp he would have spent longer in there. Mikelson had turned up just after he had got out of the shower and the efficient trooper had managed to find yet another clean uniform, although this one was for an ordinary trooper and was a little on the large size for Nemi. It was, however, gratefully received and after Mikelson had resealed the gunshot wound and applied a support bandage to his leg, Nemi dressed. Another shot of pain relief raised his spirits so the sight that befell him when they returned to the Rec shocked him.

Delgardo was kneeling beside the body of Mol Gurd checking for vital signs. It was a pointless exercise as Nemi could plainly see. A large carving knife protruded from Gurd's chest and his clothing and the couch he sat upon was soaked in blood. Mikelson automatically ran to give assistance but merely confirmed that Gurd was dead. Delgardo stepped away from the body and walked across to Rolm who sat trembling, her bloody hands folded in her lap, her top splattered with blood. Delgardo knelt beside her and gently placed a hand on her shoulder.

"What happened Sara?" Her voice was soft and gentle and she never took her eyes off Rolm's, which were wide open and staring into the distance.

"You gave me the strength," whispered Rolm.

Delgardo tightly closed her eyes for a moment trying to shut out those words. She should have arrested Gurd when he assaulted her. Cuffed him and locked him in his room. The use of the stun stick on his genitals was an act of revenge and she remembered the temptation of applying another burst to his temple. She felt sick at the thought of it now. It was pride which had stopped her cuffing him then and there. The thought of having to admit what he had done, what she had allowed him to do! How many women had she talked out of doing exactly the same as she had done. Delgardo felt a failure.

"I did it!" She looked up at the sound of the voice. Chang stood just behind where Rolm was sitting. His hands were covered with blood and it was smeared over his top. "She didn't do it! Sara's kind, she couldn't hurt Gurd even if he hurt her. She tried to help him." Chang glanced over to Gurd's body and an expression formed on that usually expressionless face, it was one of disgust. "He was a bad man." The words were spoken in a matter of fact way without any trace of emotion.

Delgardo looked back at Rolm. She continued to stare into space. "Boni couldn't hurt anyone. I did it. I hated him!"

364

"Well nobody's going to miss this piece of shit!" Nemi tapped Gurd's leg with the toe of his boot. He turned his attention to Delgardo. "What do you do with this one?" He nodded in the direction of Rolm.

Delgardo didn't reply. She stood up, pulled Rolm to her feet, pulled her arms behind her back and cuffed her, gently pushing her back down into the couch. She then turned and did the same to Chang. Neither offered any resistance.

Nemi watched with interest. "Ah, let the courts sort it out! Not your problem hey?"

"More of my problem than you think!" mumbled Delgardo. She turned towards Wildman, who had returned with the rest of the crew. "Keep an eye on these two while I clean up." She did not wait for a reply and headed straight for the bedroom corridor.

"What was that all about?" Nemi directed the question at Wildman.

"Earlier spot of trouble with Mister Charisma over there." He nodded towards the body of Gurd. "Long story and if Delgardo wants to tell you about it she will. If not well, that's her business."

Nemi shrugged his shoulders, whatever had gone on it was none of his concern. He turned his attention to Mikelson. "Get somebody to help you bag up and shift this one." He turned to Ull who stood nearby looking dejected. "Tell your people to collect up their personal effects, we'll be evacuating everybody as soon as Tolman recovers Ginthem's body." Nemi waited for some objection but none came and the remaining crew shuffled off to do as he had requested. It then occurred to Nemi to check up on Tolman. He left the accommodation block and started to walk back down the path which led to the mine. He met Tolman half way down coming the other way.

'How's it going?"

"We found Ginthem! He was on an outcrop of rock about three quarters of the way down the ravine. Lucky really because there's an underground river at the bottom. If he'd fallen into that the body would have been swept away and we could never have recovered it. How are you?"

"I'm fine but you've got more trouble back there."

"What now?" Tolman sounded weary and more trouble was the last thing he needed.

"While everybody else was distracted somebody stuck a carving knife into Mol Gurd's chest."

Tolman groaned at the news. "Who's responsible for that?"

"Well you've got a choice, both Chang and Rolm claim they did it saying the other is innocent."

"A nice conundrum for the court if they both stick to their stories. Both providing reasonable doubt for each other. Could have cooked up the idea between them I suppose!"

"You think Chang is that bright?"

"No but Rolm might have talked him into it." Tolman sighed. "Oh sod it, I'll get Delgardo to sort it out!"

"Are your people pulling out now?"

Tolman shook his head. "They're going back down. If this mess isn't bad enough they reported they've found more bodies!"

***

Panic suddenly gripped Nemi. There had always been something in the back of his mind niggling away but events had happened so fast he had never had the opportunity to sit and think about it. That tiny niggle now came to the surface with a vengeance. Why kill Laslo Ginthem? If he was at the drill-head why get Dang to attack him? Why not just plant the thought that the crystals were there? Murdering the mine inspector was the one thing which would guarantee further investigation.

366

"Have they started back down yet?" There was an urgency in Nemi's voice which disturbed Tolman.

"They were starting off just as I left."

"Contact them right now, call them back and get your people out and clear of the mine." Tolman hesitated as if he was about to question the order. "Do it now!" Nemi almost screamed. "Killing Ginthem was the backup escape plan Vitch. There aren't bodies at the bottom of the ravine, there's over a hundred feral blue monkeys and you're about to help them get out of there!"

Tolman's face reflected the horror of the implications. He turned and raced back down the path pulling his CommsLink out of his pocket as he went. Nemi also reached for his to contact the ship. He spoke directly to the Captain and gave her detailed instructions. With that finished there was nothing he could do but wait. He was tempted to call Tolman but realised he would only just have got back. The seconds ticked by but they seemed like minutes. His ear coil vibrated and alerted him to a call, but it was from Lisbeth.

"We wanted an update on the situation. We think we know how they managed to cover such a distance in such a short space of time. We followed their escape route and found..."

"An underground river!"

"How did you know that?"

"We just found it as well. Look ,what's the range of," Nemi stopped himself referring to them as blue monkeys, "a member of the Collective?"

"What do you mean by range?"

"Could they control somebody from a distance of..." Nemi realised he had no idea how deep the ravine was so he went for the estimate. "Say a Kilometre or more.?"

"No control at that distance but a gifted member could possibly plant a suggestion."

"Can they make contact through rock?"

"No they need a direct line of contact. Why do you ask?"

Nemi suddenly had doubts about his theory. "I've got a mad idea but I need to check it out before I cause any more damage. The original tunnel is sealed but we think they took control of the pilot who picked up Ginthem's body. I think all along they planned to use the rescue team to get out."

"Nemi..."

"I know! They mustn't get out. There's already been collateral damage here, two dead, and there could be more."

"We'll deal with that! I'll have a team ready and waiting to care for the survivors."

Nemi gave a cynical smile at the term 'care' but let the remark pass. "I'll let you know how it turns out." He cut her off. He had no desire to continue a conversation with her and he needed to contact Tolman. He checked the time. Now minutes had passed and still no word from Tolman. Nemi called him and hoped he would be speaking to Tolman and not a blue monkey via him.

"Vitch get back here I need to check something out. Have you stopped any further descents?" Tolman confirmed the recovery team were preparing to evacuate. "Good, I need you back here to verify my theory before I make another move. This is a big enough mess as it is!"

An impatient Nemi waved at Tolman when he appeared from the mine. The urgency of the gesture must have been conveyed to Tolman for he sprinted up the path to join Nemi.

"What's the problem?"

"I planned to blow the mine to seal off the entrance to the ravine but after speaking to Lisbeth I have my doubts. I need to question Dang's partner."

"What did she say? You seemed so sure!" They hurried towards the Rec.

"They need a direct line of contact to influence so how could they do that from the bottom of the ravine and through more than a hundred metres of rock. I'm not using a Colonial ship to totally destroy a Corporation mine site unless I'm a hundred percent sure. The microorganism story and a stolen pulse rifle might explain away a tunnel but Lisbeth will have trouble selling that one if we have to destroy the whole mine complex."

They entered the Rec and Nemi headed directly towards LeBon who was piling his personal effects onto one of the tables.

"Did Dang ever go near the ravine?"

LeBon looked confused by the question. "We all did when we first found it!"

"I mean after that, especially recently."

"Ull banned everybody from the tunnel. It was too dangerous." LeBon's hesitant and evasive reply was picked up by Nemi.

"Don't piss me off or I'll get Deputy Tolman to arrest you for the murder of Laslo Ginthem."

"I didn't kill him! I didn't even know what happened." LeBon saw the look in Nemi's eyes. "Shit! Dang was talking to Ginthem and just lost it for some reason and attacked him. He ran off and Milton followed him. He said he wanted to apologise but Ginthem attacked him and in the struggle he fell into the ravine. It was an accident!"

"What were they talking about?"

"I don't know! You don't question Milton, you just do as he says. He told me to keep quiet otherwise they would close down the mine and we'd lose the bonus. I thought it was an accident I swear it!"

Nemi ignored the young man's pleas. "I'll give you one more chance. Did Dang ever go near the ravine?"

LeBon now looked very worried. He had just admitted to covering up the death. If it was proved to be murder he would be an accessory. Self preservation kicked in and he was now eager to be as helpful as he could be. "Ever since we found it he's been going back there."

"Why?" It was Tolman who was now confused.

"It's Milton! Ull banned us from going there so Milton had to go." LeBon licked his dry lips. "Milton was like that, if Ull said something Milton would take the opposite view. Being told not to go there compelled Milton to go there. It used to scare the shit out of me. He would stand right on the edge and look straight down. I stood well back, you didn't know how stable the edge was, it could have given way at any time. I think he got some kind of thrill out of it."

"How often did he do this?"

"At first once or twice a week but he must have got hooked on the adrenaline rush because at the end he would visit it before we started each shift."

"When did the regular visits start?"

LeBon shrugged his shoulders but then thought better of it and concentrated. "I guess a few weeks back."

"Before or after he found the crystal trace?"

LeBon gave that some more thought. "Before, just before!"

"Was there anything unusual about where he found the trace?"

"Like what? It was just part of the main tunnel wall."

Nemi was getting desperate now. There had to be more or could they have directed Dang from such a distance? "Was there some defect, some split in the tunnel wall?"

LeBon frowned. "There was a fissure in the wall. It was where Milton found the crystal trace. How did you know?"

"Wild guess Will. Was it large?"

"Big enough to get your hand into. It ran right through the tunnel. We followed it when we started to drill."

Nemi was prevented from any further probing by Tolman placing a hand on his shoulder. The Deputy nodded towards the Rec door and Nemi followed him outside.

"What's up Vitch?"

"The recovery team are on their way out but the pilot of the patrol ship hasn't returned yet. He's on his way back and hasn't picked up anybody."

Nemi bit his lip anxiously. "Vitch you can't trust what he says. If he's picked up any of the monkeys and gets back I won't be able to trust anything any of the recovery team say either. I'm calling in the ship now!"

"You can't do it Nemi! I have to go back and find out for sure. I can't sentence a man to death on a guess."

The sound of the Colonial patrol ship made Nemi turn around. It's shadow crept across the the camp site until it paused above him, hovering and sending dust swirling about him. The ship signalled they were ready and waiting for his command. He acknowledged and turned his attention back to Tolman who was already heading back towards the mine. Without thinking Nemi pulled his stun stick out from his belt and aimed it at Tolman's back. The Deputy's body went into spasm and he collapsed onto the ground. Although temporarily incapacitated Tolman managed to turn his head and give Nemi an accusing stare.

At that moment Nemi felt the loneliest man on the planet. He had the choice of never being forgiven for his action by Tolman or by his partner and baby son. Nemi, by instinct, had chosen Tolman. Nemi looked away not wanting to suffer the accusing gaze from his friend whom he had just robbed of his pride and sense of duty. The recovery team emerged from the mine and Nemi waved them forward. They stopped at the prone figure of Tolman and Nemi ordered them to take him back to the Rec. Tolman was now pleading with Nemi not to give the next command but he closed his ears to the sound. He opened a channel to the ship and after a moments hesitation he closed his eyes and gave the order.

A round from the ship's pulse cannon flashed by distorting the air as it passed and entered the mine. A thunderous roar could be heard from within the mine and before it had died away another round was fired. The noise was tremendous and the side of the mountain appeared to tremble as the maze of tunnels collapsed in on itself. A cloud of dust shot from the mouth of the mine and rolled up the path to engulf Nemi again. This time he did not care as it hid his shame.

***

Nemi had grabbed a chair from the Rec, positioned it against the accommodation block outside wall and made himself comfortable. He sat staring out at nothing in particular and brooded. His demeanour discouraged any of the others to approach, although in truth most of the others had no wish to engage him in conversation. The fact he had ordered the Colonial ship to seal the mine resulting in the death of one of the recovery crew was by now common knowledge. It seemed all the other death and mayhem which had occurred recently had suddenly paled into insignificance when compared to that. Even Delgardo avoided him, her romanticised view of him now shattered beyond repair. The crew would cast wary glances in his direction as they packed their personal belongings into the evacuation vehicles but none dared speak. It mattered little to Nemi that none of them attempted to console him for there was no way he could be consoled. The nameless crewman was the first and only person whose death Nemi was responsible for. In the five years he had been in the Colonial Corps he had only ever fired a weapon in anger once and he had missed. He wondered if he would have suffered the same nausea and guilt had he shot and killed Albright in the mine and at this exact moment in time he felt he would have. Both Mel Hann and Morgan had once said he was not really cut out to be a Colonial trooper and they were probably right.

"Sam Mendes. I thought you might like to know."

"What?" Nemi had recognised the voice but had not taken in the words. He shielded his eyes from the sun as he looked up at the figure of Tolman.

"The name of the recovery pilot. Sam Mendes. Had a social partner and two children. I thought you'd like to know."

"What are the names of the children?" Nemi gave Tolman a long hard stare. The deputy averted his eyes and walked back into the Rec. He had no idea what the children's names were and he felt a little ashamed he had attempted to make Nemi feel even worse than he already did.

Nemi just added the name to the long list going back more than twenty years. The unknown member of the Collective who had been chased off a cliff in an attempt to capture her, the survey scientist who was driven mad by the Collective entering his unprepared mind. The Brotherhood of the Jinn, a whole commune of New Brethren driven insane by the Collective's efforts to contact them and the feral Collective members damaged by that first attempt. Nemi had already lost count and he had not reached the suicide village where Kanah Gantz's father perished along with the others in a vain attempt to protect their children. They thought they had been given a gift but from where Nemi stood it now looked like a curse. Behind them he could see a long line of the dead and damaged, some he knew and others he had never even heard of. Somewhere at the back of the queue stood poor Sam Mendes. No doubt he would not have to wait for very long before somebody new joined him. Nemi felt physically sick.

His attention was diverted from his thoughts by something which caught his eye. In the distance, high in the sky, a faint black speck appeared. Nemi screwed up his eyes in an attempt to make it come into focus. It appeared to be getting bigger the longer he watched it. He guessed it was a ship long before he recognised the shape. He remembered Gantz's case notes and the idea of an off-world transporter coming to off-load the stolen crystals. His spirits sunk lower. The last thing he needed was a visit from space pirates. As he alerted the ship he wondered if Sam Mendes was going to have a very short wait indeed. He shielded his eyes from the sunlight as he followed approaching ship's progress. It was heading this way and by now there was no mistaking what it was. Rising from his seat he started to walk down the path towards the mine, keeping the ship in sight. There was no question it was the sister ship of the Colonial craft which stood in the Perrin Gap. Nemi was confused, why would the only other ship of that class which the planet possessed be coming here? He continued down the path until his own ship came into view. Sure enough the second ship descended and landed next to it. His curiosity was aroused and he watched intently as a ground vehicle appeared from the second ship's hold and headed towards him. It came to rest outside the collapsed mine entrance and when the occupants got out Nemi was in for another shock, the first two figures to emerge and walk towards him were Stenna Morgan and Lisbeth Smith.

Morgan, his trade-mark grin in place, approached Nemi. "That monkey girl will be the death of you Nemi!" Nemi's jaw dropped, he could not believe the insensitivity of the man.

"An innocent man..." His intended rebuke got no further than that as Morgan quickly interrupted.

"Who was bringing a cargo of trouble to the surface. It had to be done so get over it."

"What?" stammered Nemi.

The smile on Morgan's face lapsed momentarily as he glanced to one side. Nemi followed Morgan's eye-line to Lisbeth Smith. He stared at her for a few moments and then half mumbled, "Elder Smith!" The rather formal title indicated his subconscious had identified that her presence was not a social visit. He glanced back at Morgan and sensed the man's discomfort. "What's up?" The remark was directed at Morgan but it was Lisbeth Smith who replied.

"I have a proposition for you." She hesitated. "Commander Morgan was concerned your wound would prevent your involvement."

"This is Nemi you're talking to Lisbeth you can give it to him straight!" Morgan's remark clearly irritated Lisbeth, a remarkable feat considering her ability to control her emotions. "It's a search and destroy mission Nemi." Nemi had been so surprised by the sudden arrival of the new ship he had not considered the time factor. He did now, and understood Morgan's inference to the search and destroy remark.

"I prefer to see this as a change in focus." Lisbeth directed the remark to Morgan and then turned to face Nemi. "The prime objective is to locate any survivors and convince them to return to the commune. Mistakes were made and their isolation was, perhaps, too rigid. We need to contact them and negotiate a settlement which is agreeable to both parties"

Morgan gave an ironic little laugh. "You've taken to politics like a fish to water! She conveniently forgets to mention what the alternative is if the monkeys fail to listen to reason."

"Then I suggest you explain the situation to Nemi and let him decide which course of action to take. If he wants to volunteer I will of course be pleased but if he refuses, I for one will not think any less of him. He has already done more than anyone could reasonably expect."

"She's looking for volunteers for a search and destroy mission because she can't officially sanction one. There's no way she can explain away why she wants to hunt down a group of cave dwelling monkeys with Colonial troops. Even her own Council will ask awkward questions and the New Brethren aren't quite ready to go public with the truth about the origins of their own prophets. The consequences of that course of action would be almost as bad as the escape of our feral monkeys. Plans for dealing with the fallout of this little episode were started as soon as you reported it. We've brought two groups out with us. One is made up of Gnostics who will," Morgan paused to give another ironic smile, "process the crew and the recovery team. The second one is made up of Gnostic volunteers and hand picked New brethren troopers whose loyalty to their religion is obviously greater than their loyalty to the Corps."

"A little unfair Morgan" interjected Lisbeth.

Morgan ignored the remark and continued. "You're classed as a friend due to your old encounter with the Collective via Gantz, so are obviously more resistant or more frightening to the monkeys, or at least that's the theory based on your experience in the mine. Personally I wouldn't risk my life on that particular assumption!"

"We are taking volunteers from the Collective to negotiate. The troopers are only there as protection for the negotiators.""

Lisbeth's interruption appeared to exasperate Morgan. He turned towards her. "Can I have a private word with Nemi?" Morgan could not resist adding a mumbled, "Of course it won't be private for very long." If Lisbeth heard the last remark she chose to ignore it. She nodded and moved away back to the vehicle.

"Was that last remark really called for?"

"Have you forgotten about her and Able Carter? You really think they never pop inside your head to check you out or plant the subtle suggestion?"

"And have you forgotten that Kanah Gantz would know if she did anything like that?"

Morgan looked at Nemi and wondered if the boy was in love or just plain naive. He resisted the temptation to query Nemi's implied suggestion, now was neither the time nor place to dissect his relationship with Gantz. "She wants you because she thinks you'll go along with the idea of killing the rouge monkeys. Firstly for revenge because of your guilty feeling about the pilot. Not that I think you have anything to feel guilty about, you did what you had to do. The pilot was unfortunate collateral damage. You lose people in action!" Morgan paused to let his words sink in. "I just want you to think about what she's asking you to do. She says they're a danger but what have they actually done? They've escaped from the equivalent of one of our Isolation facilities. Being isolated from the rest of the Collective must be as bad for them as isolation from other humans is to us. And what was their crime? They got contaminated by humans! If they're willing to slaughter the infected what are they willing to do with the infectors?"

"You know they're not like that! If you think that why did you agree to become their protector?"

"I thought the New Brethren way of life was worth protecting. I believed the Gnostics might be worth protecting too if they combined the best of both species. I'm just not as sure as I was before. I'm certainly not sure enough to wipe out the equivalent of another village. I don't want you to have to live with that."

"You weren't responsible for that sir." Nemi was now embarrassed. Morgan had never spoken of the incident which haunted him. Nemi had only learnt of the story via Mel Hann.

"You don't have to actually shoot each one yourself Nemi just do nothing to stop it! Doing Lisbeth Smith's dirty work isn't going to bring back the pilot and isn't going to help Kanah Gantz. You don't know what, if any, damage has been done to Gantz and you'll not know until she comes round. As far as I can see Dang killed Laslo Ginthem and then died attempting to stop the mine being sealed. Albright was killed by Edmurson and you have people queuing up to take responsibility for the Gurd murder. The recovery pilot was collateral from sealing the mine. Was all that down to evil monkeys or just desperate ones?" Morgan paused. "Just think before you do anything you might regret."

"I'm not like you sir, I'm not going to kill anybody just for revenge." Nemi regretted the words as soon as they left his lips. The reference to the killing of Felix DeRoche for the murder of Mel Hann was guaranteed to open old wounds.

The angry look on Morgan's face confirmed that thought but the expression was merely a flash of emotion which dissipated as quickly as it had formed. "You're right Nemi, you're not like me! You're more like Mel Hann which is why this conversation should be the other way round."

The honesty in Morgan's reply hit home to Nemi. During the Federal Investigation of the suicide village Hann had always been the voice of reason, taking the cautious approach and wary of making assumptions. Although they had only spent a little time together Hann had become Morgan's firm friend and Nemi's role model. His death had profoundly affected both of them. "You're right boss." Nemi would at least concede that point. "Which is why I have no intention of volunteering for anything. In fact you'll be getting my resignation as soon as we get back to base. I want nothing more to do with the Corps, the New Brethren, the Gnostics or the Collective. This is all going to come tumbling down sooner or later. The Federation will find out about the genetic engineering or the existence of the Collective, or the New Brethren will implode when the truth about their prophets comes out or the Collective will tear itself apart because of the human infection. It doesn't matter which one, the only certainty is that it will end badly. You know that! You've always known that but you don't care because it'll give you a chance to defend some lost cause rather than destroy one. That's not for me Morgan. I don't want to be responsible for any more collateral damage."

Morgan did not reply. He knew there was no point talking to Nemi while he was in this mood but, more to the point, he knew Nemi was right.

Made in the USA
Charleston, SC
29 October 2015